A SURRENDER TO PASSION

"You shouldn't have returned," Bradley said as he walked toward her.

"I had to," Eleanor whispered.

He took her in his arms. She felt good against him, her softness molding to the length of his hard frame. His embrace tightened, and she did not fight him. Her lips welcomed his.

Eleanor's hands slipped up his back and twined together at his nape. Her eyes were closed, her lashes a black lace fan upon her elegant cheekbones. Her mouth was soft, her body pliant against his.

"Eleanor," he muttered thickly and trailed kisses along her arched neck to the base of her throat, "if we keep kissing like this, you know what is going to happen, don't you?"

"Yes," she whispered and pulled back to look at him with dark, passionate eyes.

"I won't let you go this time."

"I know. . . ."

HISTORICAL ROMANCES BY EMMA MERRITT

RESTLESS FLAMES (2203, $3.95)

Having lost her husband six months before, determined Brenna Allen couldn't afford to lose her freight company, too. Outfitted as wagon captain with revolver, knife and whip, the single-minded beauty relentlessly drove her caravan, desperate to reach Santa Fe. Then she crossed paths with insolent Logan Mac-Dougald. The taciturn Texas Ranger was as primitive as the surrounding Comanche Territory, and he didn't hesitate to let the tantalizing trail boss know what he wanted from her. Yet despite her outrage with his brazen ways, jet-haired Brenna couldn't suppress the scorching passions surging through her . . . and suddenly she never wanted this trip to end!

COMANCHE BRIDE (2549, $3.95)

When stunning Dr. Zoe Randolph headed to Mexico to halt a cholera epidemic, she didn't think twice about traversing Comanche territory . . . until a band of bloodthirsty savages attacked her caravan. The gorgeous physician was furious that her mission had been interrupted, but nothing compared to the rage she felt on meeting the barbaric warrior who made her his slave. Determined to return to civilization, the ivory-skinned blonde decided to make a woman's ultimate sacrifice to gain her freedom—and never admit that deep down inside she burned to be loved by the handsome brute!

SWEET, WILD LOVE (2834, $4.50)

It was hard enough for Eleanor Hunt to get men to take her seriously in sophisticated Chicago—it was going to be impossible in Blissful, Kansas! These cowboys couldn't believe she was a real attorney, here to try a cattle rustling case. They just looked her up and down and grinned. Especially that Bradley Smith. The man worked for her father and he still had the audacity to stare at her with those lust-filled green eyes. Every time she turned around, he was trying to trap her in his strong embrace.

EMMA MERRITT

SWEET, WILD LOVE

ZEBRA BOOKS
KENSINGTON PUBLISHING CORP.

ZEBRA BOOKS

are published by

Kensington Publishing Corp.
475 Park Avenue South
New York, NY 10016

First printing: December, 1989

Printed in the United States of America

Chapter 1

With no regard for man or beast, the sun bore down on the prairie. Its rays glinted on the miles of railroad track that lined the desolate ground. Heat waves undulated from the earth, long since dry and covered with dying grass. The only sign of life was the black locomotive that chugged tirelessly toward the frontier town of Blissful, Kansas. The lonesome echo of the whistle joined a thick spiral of gray smoke to herald the arrival of the Atchinson, Topeka, and Santa Fe.

Sitting in the passenger coach, staring out the window, Eleanor Hunt felt as if an eternity had passed since she'd embarked on her journey to Blissful; yet it had been just days ago. It seemed that Jeffrey was as far removed from her as he had been when she was in Chicago. With each passing mile her anxiety mounted. In his last letter he told her he was framed and jailed for a crime he did not commit. Now he was awaiting trial.

The rear door of the coach opened, and the conductor entered to walk up the aisle. "Not much longer, ma'am," he said when he reached her seat.

"Good," she murmured and returned his friendly smile.

Reaching up, he tugged the bill of his cap to settle it more squarely over his thick white hair. "I know you're ready to put your feet on solid ground."

Eleanor laughed softly. "Actually, I'm looking forward to taking a bath and getting into cooler clothes."

"Yep," he drawled and glanced out the window. "It's been mighty dry out here—and mighty hot."

Eleanor lifted a gloved hand to brush damp tendrils of black hair beneath the veil of her hat. Aware of her surroundings for the first time in several hours, she turned her head once again to stare out the window. "Is it always like this in the summer?"

"No, ma'am. This just happens to be one of the hot, dry ones. It's gonna be a rough year for the cattlemen."

"Just for the cattlemen?" she asked wryly.

The conductor grinned. "Well, mostly them. Blissful is a cattle town, you know?"

Opening her purse, she withdrew a dainty handkerchief with which she blotted perspiration from her upper lip and forehead. The train whistle sounded again, and he quickly straightened to grasp the gold chain and pull his watch from his coat pocket.

"Time for me to be moseying along," he announced a quick glance later. "I have work to do before we reach Blissful."

Long after he was gone, Eleanor continued to gaze out the window, but this time her thoughts did not return directly to Jeffrey or his dilemma. Ironically, the dry, cracked earth reminded her of her own life. In a sense, it too was barren. Having recently celebrated her twenty-fifth birthday, she had accepted that in society she was considered a spinster, and the thought never bothered her. Her concept of society and its values was different from most people's, and she delighted in being different— like the first time she wore bloomers in public. The gasps of shock and dismay delighted her; the shaking heads and whispered pity infuriated her.

Much to her family's chagrin, she did not equate

womanhood with marriage and raising children. She was not opposed to the idea, but she wanted more out of life. She wanted to have the right to a career, just as a man did. And for years she had fought for acceptance and equality, a chance to be recognized for her intellect and accomplishment . . . although she was a woman. But she had received little more than vilification and laughter for her labor.

While she readily admitted she was a crusader—more specifically, a *female* crusader, in a day when society did not recognize or want female crusaders—her decision to travel west by herself, defying family, friends and employer, was not her most daring escapade. Ever since her tenth birthday she had been defying the conventional strictures placed on women by men, and by some standards had more scars than accomplishments to show for it. If she were to believe her Aunt Edna, however, this trip to Kansas was by far her most disreputable. Only women of the night traveled without an escort, the grand dame of the Hunt family had loftily insisted as she disapprovingly looked down her crooked nose.

Eleanor smiled and twisted in the seat. As she brushed cinder dust off the skirt of her camel-colored traveling suit, she thought about Aunt Edna. How right she had been. Ever since Eleanor had left Chicago, she had traveled day and night, mostly at night. Was she now considered a woman of the night? Eleanor's eyes roamed the empty coach. If so, she was all alone and no one would know; thus her reputation was unsullied.

And for a woman, innocence or the loss of it was not the primary issue. Of greater significance was that her reputation remain unsullied. This was one of the inequities of society that angered Eleanor. Although she had challenged the strictures of society during her adult years, she had not broken this one. While she had had only one encounter with the carnal emotion known as

7

lust, her reputation was still intact, if not her heart.

Metal squealing against metal amidst a great gust of smoke and loud steam whistles, the locomotive chugged to a stop in front of the forlorn depot. Although the coach swayed from side to side, the conductor, entering the front door to walk down the aisle, ably kept his balance.

"Here we are, ma'am. Blissful, Kansas."

Cradling her black leather handbag in her lap, the shoulder strap looping down her arm, Eleanor continued to sit and stare out the window. She could not believe she had endured hundreds of miles of discomfort for this. Crude structures that looked as if they would fall at the least provocation lined a deeply rutted dirt street, now dry and dusty.

"End of the line," the conductor added softly.

"More like the end of the world," she muttered.

Although it was mid-morning, dozens of cowboys galloped their horses up and down the street, in and out of buildings. Barking dogs raced behind them. A revolver in one hand, a bottle of whiskey in the other, they whooped, hollered, and shot wildly.

A woman, scantily dressed, rushed out of a building into the street. Laughing and yelling obscenities, a cowboy swept her into his arms and settled her in front of him on his horse. While they galloped toward the train, the woman wrapped her arms around his neck and raised her face for his kiss—a long, indecent kiss! When they were only feet away from the train, the man lifted his head and leered through bloodshot eyes into the window at Eleanor. Dumbfounded, Eleanor could only stare at the spectacle.

The woman caught the cowboy's face and tried to pull his mouth to her lips again, but he shook free of her hands and kept staring at Eleanor. The woman turned to glare into the window. Obviously irritated, she said something. The man grinned . . . at Eleanor, exposing

8

rotten teeth. Then he winked. When Eleanor jumped back, he and the woman laughed.

This cannot be Blissful! Surely not! Dear God, she silently prayed, *please do not let Aunt Edna be right again. Let her be wrong one time in her life.*

Eleanor shuddered and wiped the delicate white handkerchief over her face as if to erase all traces of the man's indecency. This was like no other town she had ever seen during her twenty-five years, and until this minute she had not realized exactly how sheltered her life had been. For all her education and crusading, she was an innocent babe, totally unprepared for the likes of Blissful and its inhabitants.

And to think Jeffrey's life might depend entirely on her! For a moment she regretted her impulsive action in letting Allen Shea go to Springfield rather than her going, as Archer had ordered. But she had no time to dwell on past decisions.

She was unaware of the conductor's approach until he clamped a hand over the back of the seat. "Well, ma'am, this is Blissful. What do you think of her?"

Eleanor cleared her throat and lifted her head to smile into his kindly eyes. The vision of the man and woman still swam before her eyes. "Very little."

A quick grin eased across his wrinkled countenance. "Nothing quite prepares one for the reality of the West."

"I can see why," Eleanor answered, and almost as if she had no control over her eyes, they darted to the window again. But the offensive man and woman were gone.

"Don't mind traveling through it, myself, but I'm glad to return to civilization."

"Yes, I imagine so," Eleanor murmured, dimly aware of his words.

As brave and daring as she'd felt when she'd embarked on this journey into the wilds, a part of her wanted to

9

remain on the train and to return to Aunt Edna in safe and familiar Chicago. Still a greater part of her refused to give in to such cowardice. This was not a holiday trip. She had come to Blissful on business, and she would stay until she had accomplished it. Nobody, nothing, not even fate would deny her this chance to prove herself to Jeffrey and to her father. Yes, her opportunity had arrived, and although she admitted that she had nudged opportunity along, she would take advantage of it. She had overcome tougher foes than Blissful, Kansas.

Her resolution stronger, Eleanor reached up and tucked errant curls back into the elaborate chignon hidden beneath her hat. As if she had all the time in the world and were standing in Newland's Fashion Salon in New York City, having a gown fitted, she smoothed the red kid gloves over each hand. She stood and carefully hand-pressed the wrinkles from her suit jacket. That done, she reached for her parasol. When she stepped into the narrow aisle, the conductor picked up her valise and strode ahead of her. Straightening her shoulders, Eleanor followed him out of the coach.

As she descended the small metal steps onto the depot, she spied a tall, lanky cowboy leaning against the wall at the far end of the platform. With his back to her, he looked like the cowboy she'd seen through the train window. Gazing with horror at the man, she stopped. Then he turned, and she sighed her relief. It was a different man entirely. She stepped onto the platform to stand beside the conductor.

"Somebody is going to meet you?" His gaze swept from one end of the porch to the other.

"Oh, yes." Eleanor forced herself to smile and unfurled her parasol to position it over her right shoulder.

"Good." The man whisked the large gold watch from his vest. "We'll be taking off real soon. I'd hate to see you out here by yourself."

Silently agreeing with him, Eleanor tightened her grip on the handbag and looked around again. The man at the other end of the platform shifted positions, then resettled his shoulder against the wall. He nodded his head and grinned at Eleanor.

"By the time my luggage is unloaded—" she averted her face and tilted her chin in a deliberate snub to the stranger "—Mister Prescott will be here."

"Yes, ma'am." Almost as soon as he spoke the words, the conductor had disappeared into the train.

Soon three large trunks and four valises joined Eleanor on the platform, but not Harry Prescott. Lonely companions they were as the hour slowly whiled away, and she paced back and forth. Finally she lowered the parasol and walked inside the building to stand in front of the ticket counter. She spoke to the squat little man behind the desk. "I'm Eleanor Hunt. I'm expecting Harry Prescott to meet me."

He never looked up from the papers he was sorting. "Don't know 'im, ma'am. I'm new in town myself."

"Perhaps he left me a message?"

The clerk pushed his visor back and shuffled through the papers on his desk, all the time mumbling her name. "Nope." He finally looked up. "Nothing."

"How far is it to the sheriff's office?"

The man leaned back, his chair squeaking with the shifting weight. Through squinted eyes he peered at her as if seeing her for the first time.

"Too far, ma'am."

Eleanor looked over his shoulder and out the window. "It's hardly that far."

"Too far for a lady," he returned. "It's better you wait right here. Town's full of cowboys bent on having a good time at everybody's expense, ladies included."

Remembering the man who had ogled her through the

11

window, Eleanor sighed. Life in Blissful certainly was not as she had imagined. She took solace in the fact that she was only visiting, not here to stay permanently.

"Besides," he added, "even if it wasn't dangerous, you could lose all your luggage. I don't have nobody here to watch it for you."

He adjusted his visor, lowered his head, and returned to work, pointedly dismissing Eleanor without another word. She slowly returned to the outside platform, a gust of hot, dry wind assailing her nostrils with the noxious odor of the feeder pens. She was glad for her parasol. In Chicago she carried one because it was considered fashionable; out here she could see that it was absolutely necessary. Agitated, she paced, always careful to keep her distance from the cowboy.

She would give Harry Prescott another thirty minutes. If he did not appear, she would march straight to the jail, no matter what the depot master said. Her gaze inadvertently returned to the raucous activity on Main Street.

What are you doing here in Blissful? a small, inner voice asked. *You're an idiot if you think Jeffrey is going to appreciate your coming to help him. He doesn't want your help. He never has. Why should this time be any different? Besides, he's expecting Archer, not you.*

All during her journey Eleanor had felt twinges of guilt about her manipulation of duties, with Allen detouring to Springfield on his way to Blissful and with her arriving here at all. Now the twinge turned into full-fledged guilt. Only she had been at the office when Archer Cormack received her father's telegram asking him to take Jeffrey's case. Knowing he would be unable to do so because he was in New York on another case, Eleanor had forwarded the information to him. She also knew that Archer would wire back instructions for Allen Shea to depart immediately to Blissful to represent Jeffrey.

12

As usual, Allen would have his time in court, and she would spend hours doing research for a pending case in Springfield. Eleanor immediately forwarded the information to Archer in New York, but she also went to work on the home front. Her desire to help her childhood friend and to prove herself an attorney of repute motivated her to leave the notes she had already compiled on the Springfield case, together with a message asking Allen to complete them.

Although she regretted her action, Eleanor knew that if she had it to do over again, she would do the same thing. She quickly pushed her guilt aside; she had no time to dwell on the past. She consoled herself with the fact that Archer's telegram would reach Allen before he left Chicago, and he would be delayed a few days—a few days which would not matter to him, but which were highly significant to Eleanor. This would give her time to investigate the case and build a defense for Jeffrey. In other words, she thought, a small smile tugging the corners of her lips, time in which to prove herself a real attorney—Jeffrey's attorney.

The full force of her situation assaulted her. Jeffrey was not expecting her; *he was expecting a man, not a woman.* The words gained momentum as they echoed through her head. Always they returned to haunt her. Through the years the words had changed—"little girl" became "woman"—but the message remained the same: women, by virtue of their sex, were not allowed to do what men could do.

"All aboard." The conductor's voice rang across the platform to jerk Eleanor out of her troubled thoughts. As the train lurched to a start, he held on to a nickel-plated railing with one hand and waved with the other. "Enjoy your stay, Miss Hunt."

"Thank you. I . . . will." She forced the words through stiff lips.

13

"Unforgettable," he called out and grinned. At her quizzical look, he added, "Blissful."

Eleanor nodded her head and watched him disappear into the train. The engine gave one last belch, and a gray haze of smoke and cinder fell to engulf her as the train chugged slowly away. Coughing, she raised her handkerchief to her face and looked around.

She was alone—all alone—in this unforgettable, forlorn place. She had thought the name colorful and alluring when she had boarded the train in Chicago. Now she discarded any idea that its choice had been poetic. Someone with a perverted sense of humor had named this town, or it had changed dramatically since its founding. In her present state of mind she preferred to believe the former.

She had seen nothing blissful about Blissful. To stay alive in this place one had to know how to dodge—and dodge quickly: Bullets! Crazy cowboys! Cattle running wildly down the streets! Collapsing buildings!

Eleanor's gaze strayed to the far end of the platform. Still lounging against the wall, his sweat-stained hat pushed back on his head, was the wiry cowboy. Pretending to adjust one of the ribbons on her hat, she studied him out of the corner of her eye. His clothes were faded, the shirt mended so many times it reminded her of a patchwork quilt. The trousers were sprung at the knees. A silly grin plastered to his face, he never moved, only blatantly stared at her.

Eleanor shuddered, whether from fear or revulsion she did not know. The clerk had advised her to remain at the depot, but she felt no safer here. Irritated by her feeling of helplessness, she hastened to the far end of the platform, away from the man.

Slowly he angled away from the wall and followed her. Eleanor's heart felt as if it had stopped beating; she caught her breath. His grin widened to reveal stained,

14

uneven teeth. It was mid-morning, the sun shining brightly, not even a cloud to dot the sky, but she was frightened, not merely apprehensive. She had worried many times during her life. This time she was downright scared.

Inside her red kid gloves, her palms were clammy; her heart seemed to be beating at the base of her throat. As if it provided protection, and certainly it provided a foundation for her shaking hand, she clutched the shoulder strap of her handbag. She wanted to run. Dear Lord, she wanted to run! But where? Only one direction of escape was open to her: the main street of Blissful, Kansas. Paradoxically, the bowels of hell itself!

"Howdy, ma'am." His voice was scratchy. "You been waiting a mighty long time. Maybe I can help you." He stepped closer.

Eleanor's eyes narrowed perceptibly. She heard more raucous laughter and another flurry of gunfire down the street. Although she admitted she should not have traveled to this place unescorted, she refused to accept all the blame for her predicament. Had the superintendent of Hunt Cattle Station met her train on time, she would not be here alone now! Silently she cursed Harry Prescott.

"No, thank you." She marvled that she managed to keep the fear out of her voice.

"Don't like to see a lady all by herself." The man was not put off. Rather, he seemed more determined than ever to help her.

"Someone will be here shortly to meet me."

"I'll just stay here with you, ma'am, to make sure nobody harms you."

"I—can take care of myself." Unconsciously Eleanor stepped back, her expression registering distaste when she saw the revolvers that rested on each hip. Crude and disgusting. Totally uncivilized. Of course, people in

15

Chicago carried weapons . . . Eleanor would be the first to admit that. But the citizens of Chicago were more refined in their tastes. They carried them discreetly, women in their handbags, men in the inner pockets of their coats. Certainly not out where everyone could see them!

"Don't mean no harm, ma'am." He spoke again, repeating, "I'm just concerned when I see a lady alone without a man's protection."

"Thank you all the same. Someone is meeting me. I'll be quite all right until he arrives." Again Eleanor silently cursed Harry Prescott for not being at the depot when the train arrived. For well over an hour she'd been watching the juvenile performance of the cowboys as they raced their horses down Main Street and shot up the town. She had been forced to listen to their vile language and laughter. Why on earth did Harry Prescott think she had sent him a letter apprising him of her time of arrival, if not to meet her?

The stranger's grin widened. "Seems to me like you been waiting a mighty long time for this someone, ma'am. Now if it was me, and I knew you was arriving on the train, I'd make sure I was here when it rolled in from Chicago."

Eleanor straightened her back, drawing to her full five feet, seven inches. When she spoke, her voice was brisk. "Thank you for your concern, but as I've already pointed out, I'm quite capable of taking care of myself."

The man vigorously shook her words aside, the limp brim of his hat flopping in his face. "Maybe so, ma'am, but I don't reckon you want to spend the day at the depot. They're going to be loading cattle afore long. Gets dusty and dangerous." He winked. "And I'm not talking about the cows, ma'am. I'm talking about the cowboys. You might want to mosey on over to the hotel. I'll escort you." He bent, his hands snaking out to catch the handles of the valises nearest her feet.

Eleanor backed away from the man, her retreat cut short by the sound of a deep, masculine voice from behind.

"That's okay, Osborn." Although quietly spoken, the words were filled with authority. "I'll help the lady."

Startled, Eleanor spun around, the train of her camel's-hair traveling suit catching on the splintered floor. The man had moved so quietly she had not heard his approach. From behind she heard a thud which could have been her suitcases landing on the floor, but at the moment she was unconcerned about her luggage. She forgot her anger over Harry Prescott's not having met her on time. She forgot her apprehension about Osborn's overtures. Instead she concentrated on the stranger who walked toward her.

"Didn't mean no harm." Osborn held out his hands and slowly moved off the porch in the other direction. "Just giving the lady a helping hand. I was gonna take her to the hotel."

"No harm done," the man said dismissively and flipped a two-bit coin to Osborn, who grinned and caught it, then hurried away.

"If you'll just tell me who you're waiting for, ma'am—" The stranger turned toward Eleanor. His voice was naturally husky, his face rugged and handsome. A Stetson covered his hair, but dark lashes hooded sparkling green eyes. "I'll see if I can help you."

Totally mesmerized by his very presence, Eleanor never thought of answering him. The soft jingle of spurs brought her gaze down a lean, muscular physique, past the dark green shirt and gray trousers. Black boots, covered in a fine film of dust, clipped against the wooden floor as long, muscled legs brought him closer to Eleanor. Now her eyes leisurely traveled up past the nickel-plated revolvers—gleaming and dangerous and strangely exhila-

17

rating—to the open neck of his shirt.

Eleanor stared at the brown hair that swirled at the base of his broad neck . . . as dangerous and exciting as the weapons. Her eyes would not move past it. Her words completely obliterated by rampant emotions, she murmured, "I'm—Eleanor Hunt. Someone—"

"Eleanor Hunt. Alexander Hunt's daughter." A quality of disappointment, or perhaps dislike, changed the timbre of his voice and compelled Eleanor's face to rise until she gazed directly into piercing green eyes that were as sharp as his tone, almost angry in their assessment. They flicked over her in such an insolent way that she was acutely aware of her red felt hat, with its berries, plumes, and loops of silk. It matched her gloves and contrasted beautifully with her traveling suit and had been purchased with care and complete disregard for expense. Even more, his gaze made her aware of her disheveled appearance. Never had she seen such blatant hostility, nor had she ever felt so vulnerable. All of her shopping and expense had been for naught. With that one scrutiny, the man had completely undressed her and left her standing naked.

"Yes, I am. I trust you're from Hunt Cattle Station?" She spoke more sharply than normal, an overreaction to his hostility.

His expression never changing, the man simply nodded.

Irritation, frustration, disappointment . . . some elusive emotion made her retort, "You're late."

Again with an economy of motion, he shrugged. His gaze shifted to the assortment of trunks and valises that cluttered the depot, finally to return to her face.

He never uttered a word, but there was no need for him to do so. Eleanor knew quite well what he was thinking. She saw the contempt in the depths of those green eyes. She wrenched her gaze from his and studied her

18

luggage—three trunks and four valises, four large valises. She did feel a mite guilty. Still she refused to apologize to this man; she refused to look at him. Her chest heaved, and she inhaled deeply as if to draw in a large and needed amount of courage. "In case you're wondering, this is *all* mine."

"All yours?" he asked dryly.

"All—" Eleanor's head swung around and she saw his gaze fixed on her breasts "—mine. . . ." Her voice trailed into an embarrassed silence, and she felt herself swell and press against the constraining bodice.

The lazy green eyes rose, caught, and held hers. His lips slowly twitched into a mocking smile that Eleanor wanted to slap from his arrogant face.

"Well, ma'am, I'm glad it's all yours. It's something to be proud of."

"The luggage. That's what I'm talking about." Years of legal training instilled in her voice a dignity she was far from feeling. She only wished she could discipline her body as effectively; her breasts were throbbing, her heart pounding.

As if he somehow intuited her reaction to him, the man's smile widened, the green eyes holding her gaze firmly. "Oh, yes, ma'am, whatever you say, Miss Hunt."

Eleanor did not like the man one bit; in fact, she detested him. Her eyes flicked disdainfully over his work clothes, her dislike apparent in her expression. He was not the kind of person with whom she usually associated. She liked suave, sophisticated men.

Strangely she was more aware of this stranger than she had ever been of any man before. His very presence exuded raw masculinity. With his rugged features he was as wild and untamed as the land around her. Compelled by unfamiliar emotions, her eyes moved over his shoulders, his chest . . . his thighs. He was tough and sinewy. Her gaze ricocheted back and forth between the two revolvers. Hard. Gleaming. Lethal. This man was a maverick. But even the maverick had its appeal . . . especially to another maverick.

Like the guns he wore, this man was dangerous; he was deadly. Yet he excited her; every centimeter of her body quivered with awareness of him; every nerve ending was atingle. Blood coursed hotly through her body, causing her breath to shorten and her heart to pound furiously. That he affected her to such a degree angered and embarrassed her.

She cleared her throat and turned to walk briskly past him. "Load my luggage—" her voice was husky; she was losing control "—and we'll be on our way."

"Yes, ma'am, Miss Hunt."

Soft, masculine laughter followed her as she descended the steps and stood at the edge of the street. The parasol shielded her from the sun, but not from the man or his sensuality. Nervous perspiration trickled down the cleavage of her breasts and down the indentation of her back. Striving for nonchalance, inwardly running from the caressive sound of his voice, she moved around the huge flatbed work wagon loaded with hay and grain and searched for a carriage. Finding none, she looked in dismay at the dirty vehicle and panicked.

"Mister Prescott—"

The man dropped the trunk and stood contemplating her for a full second before his eyes darkened, and he hoisted the trunk over his shoulder. Moving down the steps, he said, "The name's Bradley. Harry couldn't make it into town today. That's why I'm here."

Eleanor's face blanched. Exhaustion, anger, and a small degree of guilt caused her to explode. How dare Harry Prescott dismiss her as if she were of no consequence! "Mister Bradley—"

"Not mister. Just Bradley. Bradley Smith."

Every word he uttered served only to make her that

20

much more angry. "Mister Bradley Smith-or-whatever-your-name-may-be, the trip from Chicago to this God-forsaken place has been arduous, to say the best. I have eaten smoke, soot, and cinders since the trip began. Two of my brand new traveling suits are ruined, stained from soot, burned from flying cinders."

Effortlessly, Bradley slung the heavy trunk into the bed of the wagon next to a bale of hay. "No one asked *you* to come."

The audacity of the man! "I happen to own Hunt Cattle Station, and I can damn well come out here if I want to!" Much to Eleanor's distress, her voice wavered . . . not a sign of tears, but a sure sign she was much too emotional and losing control. How many times had Archer warned her against personal involvement in any situation? And besides, what did it matter to her what this man thought? He was an employee, a lowly employee at that. Absolutely nothing more!

Bradley leaned back against the wagon, crossed his arms over his chest, and from beneath the brim of the hat surveyed her with interest. Softly he asked, "All of this anger and indignation simply because my name is Bradley and not Prescott?"

"No, because I'm a woman, not a man."

He hiked an eyebrow quizzically. Although Eleanor had never been one to respect temper tantrums as weapons of persuasion and certainly had never resorted to using them, she did not underestimate their value. She had seen women use them with great results. At the moment she felt like stomping her feet and screaming at the top of her voice. Still she managed to keep a shred of control in her voice. "All of this because meeting me is the least the cattle station superintendent can do. He knew when I was arriving. I sent word in plenty of time."

Bradley laughed mockingly and shook his head. "Just like a woman. Vanity! Vanity!"

21

"Certainly not. That's what I'm trying to explain. Had I been a man, Prescott would have made sure he was here to meet me on time."

"Well, ma'am," Bradley drawled, his gaze drifting down her body, "I beg to differ with you. I think any man alive would rather meet you on time than a man."

His blatant sensuality disturbed Eleanor. It seemed to dissipate her anger and to fill her with confusion. To hide her true feelings, she tilted her chin arrogantly. "Perhaps you don't realize the full significance of who I am, sir?"

Bradley touched a finger to the bridge of his nose and drawled sarcastically, "Oh, yes, ma'am, I'd have to be stupid not to know. You've told me several times over that you're Eleanor Hunt."

She fairly bristled. "*Miss* Hunt to you." After the words were out, she wondered why she was so indignant, why she allowed this man to infuriate her. Most of her twenty-five years had been spent fighting for equal rights for women in a male-dominated society, and now she was standing on the double standard afforded ladies in this selfsame society.

The green eyes twinkled, but the face was solemn. "All right. *Miss* Hunt it is. Where's the attorney Prescott asked for?"

Eleanor had known Bradley Smith for just a few minutes, yet he infuriated her. She was a mature woman, a trained attorney! She was the one who should have been ferreting for information, and guiding the conversation, not him. He had the ability to make her feel like a little girl, unsure of herself. For a second she questioned herself and wondered again if she had been wrong to come to Blissful. As soon as the thought flashed through her mind, she had her answer, Bradley Smith or not. She had made the right choice and could handle him.

Giving him a bright smile, she said, "Allen Shea is his

22

name, Mister Smith, and he's going to be here in a few days. Presently he's doing some work in Springfield."

"Is he a good attorney?" Bradley strode toward the porch to get another trunk.

"Yes, he's worked with Archer for the past three years."

"My concern is how he's going to manage without Cormack."

"Quite well, thank you," Eleanor snapped. The man had a penchant for getting under her skin. Clearly one of the most obnoxious men she had ever met, he seemed to have the habit of sticking his nose into matters that were none of his concern.

"He'd better be, if he expects to get Jeffrey out of this mess."

"And speaking of Jeffrey, I want to see him immediately. How is he?" Bradley turned his head and looked at her without saying a word. A little late to be inquiring about Jeffrey, she thought with a twinge of guilt, and Bradley's gaze told her as much.

He shrugged before he heaved the second trunk over his back. Then he grunted as he walked past her, "About as good as a man can be who's in jail on charges of cattle rustling."

"He's innocent!"

"So he says." Bradley settled the second trunk onto the wagon bed.

"You think otherwise?"

On his way for the last trunk he called over his shoulder, "I think according to American law, Miss Hunt, a man's innocent until proven guilty."

Eleanor's skin prickled with irritation. "I'm glad you know that, Mister Smith, but you're evading the question. I have the feeling you think Jeffrey is guilty."

Bradley gave his attention to the trunk as he wedged it between the other trunk and a bag of grain. "In

23

something like this, Miss Hunt, feelings don't really count for much, and the evidence is stacked heavily against him. That's why Prescott wanted an *experienced* attorney. To give the boy a fair chance to prove his innocence. And he's going to need the best defense he can get if David Lang dies."

"He has the best defense possible," she replied.

"Good."

With the one word Eleanor felt as if he had dismissed her completely. Not deeming to reply further, she stood there quietly and observed Bradley as he piled the valises one by one onto the wagon. Jeffrey was twenty-eight years old, but Bradley had called him a boy. And he was right. In so many ways Jeffrey had never matured, probably never would. Having grown up in immeasurable wealth as an only child to older parents, he had been pandered to and spoiled the first twelve years of his life.

Then Jeffrey's father had lost his fortune. A few weeks later he committed suicide, and a year later Jeffrey's mother died. Against his older sister's advice, against his wife's angry protestations, Alexander Hunt had taken Jeffrey under his wing. "The son I never had," the meat-packing magnate had said, and his nine-year-old girl—a silent protester—had overheard.

From that day forward Alexander Hunt gave all his attention to Jeffrey Masterson, molding him to one day take over the Hunt Meat Packing Company. As her father grew closer to Jeffrey, Eleanor had grown closer to her mother—and both of them had grown away from Alexander and Jeffrey.

A thud caught Eleanor's attention. Her gaze shifted to the man who threw two of the valises on top of the grain sacks. Judging by appearances, he was only a few years older than Jeffrey—five or six at the most—but he was a man. His shoulders rippled beneath the tight expanse of checkered material. Her gaze lingered on the perspiration

24

stain that ran down the center of his back. He was every inch a man.

When he looked up to find her staring at him, he returned the gaze for a few seconds, then grinned. Although Eleanor had a fleeting fear that Bradley Smith could read the secrets of her soul, she neither surrendered to nor quailed before him. Defiantly she returned the stare. No man was going to make her lose her composure.

His grin slowly disappeared, and the green eyes darkened with an emotion Eleanor could not identify. "Are you ready?" he finally asked.

The implications of his question coupled with the husky tones of his voice wrapped Eleanor in a cocoon of sensuality—a cocoon from which she had no desire to escape. Without moving, without touching her, he seemed to draw her very soul to him. The man was dangerous, dangerous indeed!

"Yes, I am," she answered. With great reluctance she smiled and looked at the precarious piling of hay, grain, and luggage on the wagon. In a voice that was unusually loud, she asked, "Do you honestly think we'll make it to the station with all our goods intact?"

Bradley lifted his hat, an errant lock of dark brown hair falling across his forehead. "Had I known you were coming, Miss Hunt, I would have driven the buggy, but we weren't expecting a woman. That's why I drove the work wagon. Your letter simply stated that Masterson's defense counsel would be arriving, leaving us to believe that Shea was arriving by himself. I figured a man wouldn't mind riding in a work wagon."

Eleanor had the grace to lower her eyes. She was guilty of being deliberately evasive in her letter. She had known what conclusion they would draw when they received it. She was afraid if she told them the truth, they would contact her father in New York and stop her from

25

coming. She could not allow it to happen. Destiny drew her to Blissful.

She lifted her head and, blinking against the brightness of the morning sun, looked Bradley directly in the eye. Softly, assuredly, she said, "I'm part of Jeffrey's defense counsel, Mister Smith."

His expression never changing, Bradley asked, "What part?"

This was not the reaction Eleanor had anticipated, certainly not the one to which she had become conditioned during the four years she'd been working for the law firm of Archer Cormack. "I'm one of his attorneys."

For a long minute Bradley stared at her, then whistled faintly. "Well, Miss Hunt, congratulate yourself. You've set me back on my heels."

A smile hovered on Eleanor's lips. "I hope I have, Mister Smith. That was my intention."

Bradley raked his hand through his hair and resettled his hat. He walked around the wagon until he stood in front of her. His voice husky, he said, "Bradley is my name, Miss Hunt."

Eleanor found herself staring first at the firm, bronzed neck, then at the crisp, brown hair revealed in the opened neckline. She watched the pulse beat in regular cadence at the base of his neck. His breath warmly touched the lower part of her face.

"Say it."

As if his hand had caught her beneath the chin and lifted her face, she raised her head. Unconsciously she licked lips gone suddenly dry and stared mesmerized into forest green eyes. "Bradley," she murmured.

His eyes brushed back and forth across her lips, his caress more potent than a kiss. His gaze traveled all over her face. "Your eyes are an unusual shade of blue."

Instinctively Eleanor knew he was simply uttering a

26

statement. Flattery was not his intention. "Cobalt, my mother told me," she murmured.

"I'm sure you've been told on many occasions that you're a beautiful woman." He paused, but she said nothing. Still he did not touch her with anything but his expressive eyes. "You are. I can easily see how you could break through a man's defenses."

Excitement skittered through Eleanor's body. Her bones seemed to turn to butter, and she felt as if she were melting at his feet. Her heart pounded erratically; the blood pumped through her body in such proportions she felt giddy. And she honestly did not know why. Whereas the man's tone was a fragile caress; his eyes were hard and condemning; his words subtly accusing.

"I can't imagine you being Masterson's defense counsel."

Eleanor marshaled her errant emotions and took a step away from him, but was stopped when the side of the wagon jabbed into the small of her back. Irritated with herself for being attracted to an uncouth man like this—her eyes inadvertently meandered down one of the muscled legs, over the revolver in the leather holster to the thongs that tied it securely around his thigh—she said rather sharply, "Although most *men* don't recognize it, I *am* an attorney, Mister Smith. And quite a good one."

His eyes never left her face. "I would imagine that you are quite good at anything you do, Miss Hunt."

The words were innocent, but the inference was blatant.

"I am. In fact, I would imagine that I am better in my chosen field of work than you are." She grinned, suddenly feeling herself on surer ground. She could tell by the flicker in his eyes that her assertion took him aback.

Not for long. A dangerous gleam entered his eyes, and

his lips moved into an enigmatic smile. "I think you had better save your judgment until you see how good I am in my chosen field of work." He laughed, the seductive sounds wrapping themselves around Eleanor. "Of course, I prefer my chosen work to be done in bed . . . but if one is not available, I'll take the field."

Although she considered herself a modern woman and quite forward most of the time, Eleanor was horrified at Bradley's presumptuousness—even if his words were said in jest. But she refused to give him the satisfaction of knowing it. "We're wasting time. Shall we go?"

"I wouldn't call this a waste of time, Miss Hunt. I'd like to think of it as time well spent. We're getting to know one another better."

"If you think I want to know you any better, you're quite pompous, Mister Smith."

Before she knew what had happened, his hands spanned her waist, and as if she were a fragile China doll and weighed no more, he easily swung her through the air. Before he deposited her on the wagon seat, he held her suspended for a brief second that stretched into eons. "Pompous, no! Arrogant and confident, yes. And honest with myself."

"Are you implying that I'm not?" she asked in a rather breathy voice.

"Yes, I am, Miss Hunt." He tucked her skirt about her feet. "I think you're as interested in knowing more about me as I am about you."

"What you think, sir, is none of my business, and I would very much like to keep it that way."

"I give you fair warning, Miss Hunt, it'll be up to you to do so, because I certainly intend to know you better." When she gasped her outrage, he winked and chuckled. Then he was gone, and for the second time in a while she felt bereft. Long strides carried him around the wagon. "I think, Miss Hunt, you're going to find that you're quite interested in me also."

"I think, Mister Smith, that you are going to be a disappointed man, if that's what you think."

Bradley laughed softly. "I've proved my point, madam. If you were not interested already, you would not have issued such a challenge."

Chapter 2

By the time Bradley had settled himself in the wagon, Eleanor had regained a semblance of composure. Remembering the lewd man who had peered into the train window, she kept telling herself that all frontiersmen were made from the same mold, but somehow she could not convince herself. Despite his common name of Smith, he was not like the other man.

The other man leered with his eyes; Bradley caressed. Everything about the other man repulsed her; Bradley exuded a quality that drew her to him without question, without hesitation. Where he was concerned, Eleanor had absolutely no control over her emotions; they were running truant. But she could control her body. Angling her parasol over her shoulder, she sat rather stiffly, her back ramrod straight and her eyes fixed directly ahead.

Soon they were rumbling down the dusty street, nothing more than an outdoor corridor between two long rows of saloons and brothels. Although it was only mid-morning, the town was teeming with people, mostly men.

"I see that Blissful is nothing more than a raucous frontier town." Eleanor lifted her kerchief to her face and primly daubed a drop of perspiration from her brow.

Bradley smiled, an almost imperceptible movement of

his lips that softened the hardness of his countenance. "Raucous and frontier," he agreed, "but Blissful is more than nothing, Miss Hunt. To cattlemen and drovers, it's everything. It's the end of the line. From here they ship their cattle to markets in the East."

Distastefully, Eleanor's eyes surveyed the row of rough, unpainted buildings. "It's so crude."

"It's just a baby," Bradley defended. "Give her time. She'll smooth out."

Eleanor turned her head and studied the man sitting next to her. He was not an average frontiersman. "You like the frontier?" When he nodded but said nothing more, she asked, "How long have you been out here?"

Bradley clucked the horses and steered them around a group of rollicking cowhands in the middle of the street. "How do you know I haven't been out here all my life?"

"You're educated," she returned matter-of-factly, "and you don't talk with the same kind of accent these people do."

"I went to school in the East."

"What did you study?"

He chuckled quietly. "I didn't. That's why I'm out here, working as a cowhand for the Hunt Cattle Station."

"No," she returned quietly, adjusting her parasol to block out the glare, "you're out here because you like it."

Now he turned his head and gazed at her. His expression seemed to soften. "I like it out here," he drawled. "And you're right, I'm from back East. After the war I stayed in the cavalry and served on the Texas frontier. After my discharge I sort of drifted from one place to another. Finally I arrived in Blissful."

"Strange. I wouldn't have thought of you as a drifter."

Bradley pulled the reins and stopped the wagon in front of a bare-faced building, where curling, yellowed posters were nailed indisciminately to the wall. "I'm not,

32

Miss Hunt. I'm gainfully employed by Hunt Cattle Station."

The door opened, and an older man, pulling his suspenders up over his shoulders, stepped onto the boardwalk. His white hair was disheveled, a clear indication that he ran his hands through it often. His gaze rested curiously on Eleanor. "Morning, Bradley, I'm right glad to see you. Masterson's about to drive me crazy, wanting to know when his lawyer's getting to town. Thought maybe you had him with you."

"Well, not exactly the *him* you were looking for, but I have someone for you to meet. I found her at the depot this morning." Bradley leaped down, tied the reins to the hitching post, and started around the wagon.

"And who's that?" The deputy craned his neck to see her better.

Eleanor dropped her parasol and shut it briskly, slipping her hand into the leather loop so that it could hang from her wrist. She hated it when men talked about her as if she were not present, and all those she'd met so far did just that. Irritably she moved, wanting to climb down before Bradley reached her, but she was not quick enough. His big hands circled her waist, and for the second time he lifted her as if she weighed next to nothing and set her down. Briefly his eyes smiled teasingly into hers. His hands remained on her, and they stood for a moment and stared at each other. Casual as his touch was, a fire seemed to emanate from each of his fingers to radiate through her body.

"This is Miss Eleanor Hunt," Bradley murmured, only now dropping his hands and stepping back.

"Miss Eleanor Hunt!" Tully exclaimed. "You mean—Hunt Cattle Station?"

Drawing on her reserve strength, Eleanor swept around the wagon and beamed at the deputy. She placed the metal tip of her parasol on the sidewalk and leaned on the parasol as if it were a cane. "The same, Mister Tulford."

Embarrassed, he grinned and combed his hand through his hair. "Gosh, Miss Hunt, don't nobody call me *Mister* Tulford. I'm just plain ole Tully."

Liking the man instantly, Eleanor laughed. Then she felt Bradley's hand lightly cup her elbow—a most innocent and courteous gesture. Again she was assailed by a giddy feeling; her stomach fluttered uncontrollably. But quickly following these emotions were disgust and anger. She wondered if she had the same effect on him that he had on her.

"Not only is she Alexander Hunt's daughter, Tully." Bradley looked at Eleanor and grinned. "She's Masterson's attorney."

Evidently he was not so aware of her as she was of him, she thought, and it made her quite angry. He seemed to be in perfect control of himself and seemed to be bent on proving that his mere presence could upset her. Damn the man!

Tully's eyes rounded in disbelief. "My Gawd! You mean to tell me that a woman can be a lawyer?"

Bradley laughed and winked at Eleanor. "Well, now, that's what she's been telling me all the way over here from the depot."

"What does your paw think about this?" Tully asked.

"As little as possible," Eleanor answered.

Tully scratched his head. "Always figured this trial was gonna get a lot of attention. Now I'm sure of it. People will be coming from all around to see a woman lawyer."

"That's true, Deputy, they'll come to see me, but when they get here they'll hear me and find that I'm quite capable of defending Jeffrey."

Bradley's hand tightened on her elbow, and Eleanor

looked up into his face. At first her gaze fastened to his mouth, then moved to his eyes, where to her amazement she saw admiration. He might not like her, but he did respect her. Warm pleasure slowly suffused her body. "Now, may I see Jeffrey?"

"Yes, ma'am, you sure can." With an easy gait Tully led the way into the office to stop at the desk, where he picked up a large ring of keys. They jangled together, the sound echoing ominously through the small room as he crossed to the inner office door. "Right this way."

When Eleanor entered the long, rectangular room and saw Jeffrey unfold from the narrow cot in his cell to walk to the barred door, she gasped. This was not the same person she'd known in Chicago. In dismay she stared at the ghost of a man who hung onto the door and laid his face against the rusted bars. This could not be Jeffrey. She had never seen him so disheveled. He had a two-days' growth of beard, his hair was uncombed, and his shirt and trousers were rumpled.

At first Jeffrey did not recognize her either. Finally, when he did, he grabbed the bars with both hands and pressed his face closer against the rusted metal. "Eleanor!"

Pulling away from Bradley and the deputy, she raced down the aisle. "Jeffrey!" Tears coursed down her cheeks, and she covered his hands with hers. She stared into the dull eyes of the man who was like a brother to her.

"I knew you'd come." His hands slid through the bars to cup her face. They were rough and calloused, so different from what they had been when he lived in Chicago. His fingernails were short and dirty. He flicked a tear off her cheek with his thumb. "Oh, God, Eleanor! I'm so glad to see you."

"Me too." She sniffed, and a tentative smile touched the corners of her lips and lingered in her eyes.

"Archer? What about Archer?" Jeffrey searched the room wildly. His voice escalated in fear. "He's here, isn't he?"

"No." Eleanor gently pulled away from Jeffrey and brushed the tears from her face with a gloved hand. "He—"

"He is coming, isn't he?" Jeffrey demanded shrilly. Stark terror dulled his eyes; exhaustion blackened the skin around the sockets and gave them a sunken, hollow look.

"No," she whispered.

"Oh my God!" Jeffrey staggered back, his hands going to his temples. His face contorted as if he were in horrible pain, and he collapsed onto the cot. Lifting an ashen face to her, he cried, "Without Archer to defend me, I'll be hanged, Eleanor."

"No, you won't. I'm going to be here with you, and so is Allen."

Like a pouting child, Jeffrey swatted the covers contemptuously. "Allen! What good is he going to do me, and why the hell isn't he here with you?"

"He—had to go to Springfield first." As she stared at Jeffrey now, so different from the boy she'd grown up with and the man she'd known in Chicago, Eleanor again had that sinking feeling and wished she'd done as Archer had instructed, rather than sending Allen. "He'll be here as soon as he can, Jeffrey."

"Yeah," he muttered.

"He's an excellent attorney, and Archer has trained him well," Eleanor defended, though her defense was weak.

"My God! Allen Shea will be little more help than you in the courtroom."

"Jeffrey!" Eleanor thought she was prepared for Jeffrey's reaction, but quickly discovered she was not. Her heart ached, and she wanted to be reassured herself.

No one was here to do that for her. Not Mama, even . . . she was dead, and Aunt Edna was in Chicago.

Bradley shoved away from the door frame and walked to where Eleanor stood. He laid a hand on her shoulder and squeezed lightly as if he understood her anguish.

Jeffrey smiled lamely and shrugged. "You're a woman, Eleanor."

Eleanor passionately hated those words but had come to endure them with a nonchalance that fooled many. She felt the bite of bitter tears in her soul, but had learned long ago not to pity herself. "Yes, Jeffrey, I'm a woman and quite proud of it, but I'm also an attorney. One of the best, and you'll do well to remember that. I'm not here because you're like a member of the family. I'm here as part of your defense."

"Yeah," Jeffrey slurred.

Bradley said softly, "I know you must be tired, Miss Hunt. As soon as you're ready, I'll take you to the station so you can rest. You can talk with Masterson tomorrow, when you're feeling better."

The obvious concern in his voice and his gentle touch were Eleanor's undoing. She looked at the tanned fingers that spread over her shoulder. The hand was also calloused, the fingernails short, but they were clean. The grip was friendly and warm, with no sexual overtones. Strength and protection and reassurance flowed from him. For once, she wanted to give in to someone else's ministrations, to leave the thinking and the decision making to them.

"Thank you," she murmured, "I'll stay a while longer. I need to talk with him."

"I'll wait for you in the sheriff's office," Bradley said, but still he did not move away from her.

Sneering, Jeffrey leaped to his feet and rammed his fist into the air. "She's here to help me, Bradley, and don't you forget that. Get away and leave her alone. You're not

37

going to take her away from me. Eleanor belongs to me."

"Jeffrey!" Eleanor exclaimed. She turned so that she was looking fully into his furious countenance. "What's the matter with you?"

Jeffrey pointed his finger at Bradley. "Him. That's who. That's what. You took my job away from me, but you're not going to get Eleanor."

Puzzled, Eleanor now looked to Bradley. His face was hard and closed, and she was unable to read it. Not once did she think of moving away from his touch. At the moment, it was vitally important to her. In a world of their own, the two men stared at each other for a long time.

Eventually Bradley said, "I've always thought you were short on common sense, Masterson. Now I think you're blind. Miss Hunt is not an animal to be bought or sold or given away. She's a woman. And assuming that I want her, I think it's up to her whether I get her or not."

Bradley dropped his hand from Eleanor's shoulder and walked away. She missed the warmth of his touch and the protection his proximity promised. Feeling abandoned— an emotion she was experiencing altogether too much today—she stared dumbly at his retreating figure.

Jeffrey taunted her, "How do you think a drifter like Bradley Smith got to be manager of Hunt Cattle Station?"

"Manager," Eleanor murmured. The taunt destroyed the tender emotion Bradley had evoked in her.

Bradley stiffened and slowed his gait, but did not stop.

"Since you're my counsel, I might as well begin my confession, Eleanor." Jeffrey's petulant tone echoed through the room. "I think Mister Bradley Smith is one of the people who framed me. Him and Prescott."

"You can say what you want about me, but don't involve Harry," Bradley said.

"Why not? Both of you hate me and want to get rid of

38

me. Watch out for Smith, Eleanor. He's dangerous. From the minute he showed up at the station, he started wheedling his way into Harry's good graces, and he's hoping to do the same with you."

Not wanting this to be true, Eleanor walked to stand in front of Bradley. "Why didn't you tell me you were the manager?"

An invisible shutter seemed to lower over his eyes; his expression was bland. "It didn't come up in the conversation."

"It should have." Her voice was flinty. "After all, Mister Smith, I happen to own Hunt Cattle Station."

His eyes moved carefully over her upturned face again, over each feature, as if he were placing them in memory. "I thought your father did."

"It's all the same," Eleanor countered.

"Even if you *do* own Hunt Cattle Station, Miss Hunt, you don't own me."

"I never said I did."

"You're acting as if you do."

Hurt by this abrupt change from warmth to coldness, Eleanor recoiled from him and wished she had never allowed her feelings toward him to soften. He was no different from other men. He simply played the game differently and with more expertise. "You're fired, Mister Smith!"

Bradley grinned mockingly. "I would advise you to wait to make that decision until you get to the cattle station, Miss Hunt. Otherwise you're going to find yourself in a passel of trouble."

The man's arrogance goaded her like nothing else had. "I said you're fired." She spoke no louder, but her voice throbbed with intensity. "And I mean it. I don't need anyone to take care of me. I'll do it myself, Mister Smith."

Their expression enigmatic, Smith's green eyes flicked

39

down then up her, finally settling on her face. Again—and to her great discomfort—he thoroughly studied each feature. Finally he shrugged. "I have to drive the wagon back anyway and get my horse and gear. I might as well wait for you. Now, if you'll excuse me, Miss Hunt—" he caught her by the shoulders and gently set her aside— "I'll be waiting for you in the sheriff's office."

She watched him stride to the door and brush past Tully. For a brief second, Eleanor fought with herself. She wanted to do something drastic to shake the man's composure—run after him and scream . . . double her fists and beat his chest . . . kick his shins with the toes of her shoes . . . slap his face. Childish, yes, but she would do anything to destroy that shield of imperviousness.

"Uh . . ." Tully cleared his throat, his feet dragging over the floor as he stepped into the room. The key ring swung precariously on the end of his finger, the keys jingling together. "Are you gonna want to be talking with Masterson a little while, ma'am?"

"Yes, Deputy, I will." Eleanor drew in several deep breaths and relaxed. She fixed a smile on her lips—a difficult ruse to maintain, but one she had mastered well—turned, and walked back to the cell. By the time the door clanged behind her and the lock clicked into place, she was sitting in the small upright chair next to Jeffrey's bed. She slipped the leather loop over her hand and laid the parasol on the cot.

"Just give me a yell, Miss Hunt, and I'll be back to let you out." Tully withdrew from the room.

"Thank you, Deputy."

Jeffrey lounged against the front bars of the cell and watched Eleanor. She opened her leather handbag and withdrew paper, pen, and a small bottle of ink. She tugged loose the cork stopper.

"You carry that around with you all the time?" Jeffrey asked.

40

"Always." Eleanor ignored the sarcasm and unscrewed the cap from the pen. Dipping it into the ink, she poised it above the paper in her lap. "Now, tell me exactly what happened."

Jeffrey threw his head back and laughed, the mocking sound completely devoid of humor. "Who'd have thought a year ago, Eleanor, that Jeffrey Wayne Masterson would be accused of cattle rustling?" He rolled the back of his head against the bars. "Possibly murder."

"Stop it, Jeffrey," Eleanor snapped. She felt sorry for Jeffrey, but could not have him losing his composure, not this early in the game. "If I'm to build you a defense, you're going to have to quit feeling sorry for yourself and help me."

Jeffrey's eyes narrowed. "If you knew all I know, Eleanor, you'd feel sorry for yourself too."

"I would not," she snapped. "You ought to know me better than that, Jeffrey. I'm that much like my father."

"Yeah," he drawled, "maybe you are."

"Tell me everything you know."

Jeffrey laughed, but again the sound held no mirth. "No, Eleanor, you don't wnt to know everything I can possibly tell you. Believe me, you do not."

Eleanor elected to ignore Jeffrey's strange mood. She attributed it to his being alone and accused of a crime he did not commit. She must convince him that she and Allen were his advocates. They would get him out of this predicament. Writing the date across the top of the page, she said, "Explain the situation to me, Jeffrey."

"My God!" Jeffrey exclaimed. "Do you have to write while I'm talking to you? It gives me an eerie feeling . . . like I'm making my last confession."

Despite the gravity of the situation, Eleanor felt a certain pride in herself. For once during the sixteen years, since Jeffrey had come to live in their home, she was the

41

one in control. "I think a hangman's noose would give you an even eerier feeling, and this isn't so far different from a last confession. It may very well be. A lot depends on it."

Jeffrey stared at her, his eyes narrowing. Slowly he moved to sit on the bed in front of her. "What's happened to you, Eleanor? You've changed. You're not the girl I knew when I left Chicago to come out here."

The only sound in the room was the scraping of the pen across the paper. Finally Eleanor lifted her face and gazed solemnly into his. "You're right. I'm not the same person, Jeffrey. First, I'm a woman now, not a girl. Second, I'm an attorney, not your life-long friend, certainly not the little girl you think of as a sister, so I don't have time for reminiscing. I'm here to save you, and we have precious little time. Now let's get down to business."

Petulantly Jeffrey slouched back on the cot and propped himself up on an elbow. "All right. What do you want to know?"

Looking him directly in the eyes, Eleanor asked, "Did you rustle the cattle?"

His eyes rounded in disbelief, and his nostrils flared. Then he leaped to his feet. "My God! You, too! Tulford!" he shouted. "Miss Hunt would like to leave now." He whirled around. "I can't believe you would ask that of me."

"Jeffrey"—Eleanor leaned back in the chair and sighed heavily—"as long as you fight me, I can't help you. You must understand I'm your attorney, your advocate. The only person who is absolutely on your side. I must ask you these questions. I must know beyond a shadow of a doubt. In order to exonerate you of this crime, Allen and I must be apprised of all the facts."

Tully poked his head around the office door. "You ready, Miss Hunt?"

"Not quite," she raised her voice to answer. "Jeffrey is letting off a little steam. I think he's cooled down now."

"You're gonna stay, then?"

"When I'm ready to leave, Deputy," she said, "I'll call you myself." The door closed with a resounding thud, and Eleanor spoke to Jeffrey. "Now sit down and tell me everything that has happened."

"You and Allen," Jeffrey said, raking his hand through his hair. "You're the only ones who are going to be defending me?"

"Yes. We're your only hope of getting out of this."

He nodded his head. "When your father sent me here about a year ago . . . damn him, Eleanor, I hate him for sending me out here. I started as a cowhand, working my way up in the company, like Alex wanted. About six months ago, I started handling the accounts. That's when I noticed that the purchase of certain cattle corresponded to times when local thefts were reported. I began to save the newspaper articles. In every instance it was cattle we'd bought from David Lang, but I had no proof."

"Did you talk to anyone about your suspicions?" Eleanor asked.

Jeffrey shook his head.

"Why didn't you go to Prescott or send word to my father?"

He rubbed the back of his neck and paced back and forth. "I wanted more proof. You don't know the Langs, Eleanor. They're almost worshiped in this country. You don't point a finger at them unless you're sure of what you're saying."

"Did your suspicions stop you from buying cattle from David?"

"When I told David I wasn't going to buy any more, he was angry and demanded to know why. I told him we were already over inventories, but he knew I was lying." Nervously he rubbed the side of his face, then slid his palm down the outer leg of his trousers. "On the night that I was caught and framed for rustling, I was working in the office with the window raised. It was quite early, around eight o'clock, when a rock landed in the room. I thought it had been thrown at me, but when I picked it up, I found a note tied to it."

As Eleanor wrote, he continued to talk. "The note said David Lang was stealing cattle from local ranchers, and to take the suspicion off himself he was going to steal from his own father. If I wanted to catch David in the act, I should be at the Rocking W Ranch around midnight."

Only the scratch of the pen point on the paper could be heard in the cell as he stopped to think.

"Who sent the note?"

"I . . . I don't know." His back to Eleanor, he gripped the bars with both hands. Closing his eyes, he leaned his forehead against the door. "Stupid! How could I have been so stupid?"

Eleanor leaned back and flexed her shoulders. She was exhausted; her journey was catching up with her. "Why did you go, Jeffrey? You have more sense than to believe such a note."

"There was something about it, Eleanor, that made me believe it was true." His eyes had a faraway look to them, and his voice sounded mysterious. "Something that made me go."

Intrigued with Jeffrey's reaction to his own story, Eleanor studied him. "Who do you *think* wrote the note, Jeffrey?"

Abruptly Jeffrey stopped pacing and turned to pierce her with a cold gaze. "I told you, I don't know—"

"Who do you *think* wrote the note, Jeffrey?" she insisted, her cobalt blue eyes fixed on his.

He sighed and sat down to drop his head into his hands. "I can't be sure, but it looked like a woman's handwriting."

Eleanor edged forward on the chair. "Why a woman? Who could she be, and why would she be telling you this?"

"I don't know," he muttered.

"Why did she choose *you*, Jeffrey?" Eleanor thought aloud. "The sheriff would have been the logical person for her to go to, not you . . . unless she was working with David, and they were both framing you."

His head jerked up, and he glared at her. "I really didn't stop to think when I received the note, Eleanor. I knew I had to investigate to see if it was true. I decided on the spur of the moment to look into it. I had nobody I could tell. Harry was gone for the evening, and Bradley was only an extra hand. He happened to be working in the barn that night. To satisfy his curiosity, I told him I was going for a ride. I was just going to witness the scene for myself before I told anybody about my suspicions."

"But the rustlers knew you were there. They were waiting for you."

He nodded his head. "Although I didn't go to the place the note specified, they knew I was there, as if someone had told them. Then the shooting started—I don't know how or why—and David was wounded. The next thing I knew, I was arrested for rustling and for wounding David."

"Where is the note?" Eleanor asked, and her eyes locked with his. "That would be evidence in your favor."

"I . . . I put it in my shirt pocket." His gaze dropped. "I must have lost it during the fight."

"Oh, Jeffrey," she exclaimed. Disappointed, she stared at him for a long while before she asked, "Do you know any of the women in David's life?"

Jeffrey shrugged. "No. I didn't know him that well."

"Is there anything else you need to tell me?" she asked.

"An account was opened in my name at the Blissful

Bank. Large deposits were made regularly, and on the day David was killed, the money was withdrawn and the account closed. The clerk, Early Dobson, swore I was the one who did it."

"Where's Dobson now?"

Jeffrey shrugged. "I don't know."

"Don't worry . . . I'll find him. Anything else?"

"Not that I can think of."

Eleanor wiped the pen and placed it in its case; then she stuffed the cork into the ink bottle. "I'll be going now. I'll see you tomorrow."

Jeffrey knelt in front of her, taking both of her hands in his. Holding them tightly, he said, "Eleanor, please believe me. I'm telling you the truth."

"I believe you. Don't worry. Allen and I are going to help you. Now I must go." Withdrawing her hands from his, she folded the sheets of paper and tucked them and her other writing apparatus into her handbag. "I have work to do."

"I know I sounded ungrateful a while ago, but it's this place." He rose and waved his hand at the walls. "I'm glad you're here and that you're representing me."

"Thank you, Jeffrey. I'll do the best I can." Moving to the door, she called, "Deputy Tulford, I'm ready to leave."

"Eleanor!" Jeffrey's eyes were bright with tears. "Please get me out of here. Don't let me stay here another night. I'll go insane. I can't stand being cooped up in this little space."

Eleanor's heart went out to her friend. In some ways he was the brother she'd never had. Jeffrey had never been a strong person, and now, the one time in his life when he'd chosen to take a stand, he'd been betrayed. She reached out and brushed the tousled hair from his forehead and cupped the nape of his neck with her hand. He was such a lovable little boy and always had been.

Jeffrey, like her, had been a disappointment to her father. Whereas she was strong and wanted to follow in Alexander Hunt's footsteps, she was still just a woman. Jeffrey, on the other hand, was a man whom Alex had chosen to be his protégé, but Jeffrey did not want it. He had fought a losing battle against coming to the cattle station. Eleanor would have willingly taken the assignment.

"I'll see what I can do." Her voice was husky with tears.

As the office door opened, Jeffrey pulled her into a tight embrace and buried his face against her shoulder. She cradled him in her arms and comforted him. "Oh, God, Eleanor, I do love you," he sobbed.

Over Jeffrey's shoulder, Eleanor saw Bradley walk into the cell room. When he saw them clinging in an embrace, he stopped in his tracks. His face was closed and unreadable. "My apologies, Miss Hunt. I wouldn't have intruded, but I thought you called."

"I did." Eleanor met Bradley's blatant stare as she slowly released herself from Jeffrey's embrace. "I'm ready."

Chapter 3

"Please, Deputy Tulford," Eleanor pleaded.

Tully gazed longingly at the proffered money, then shook his head. "No, ma'am . . . can't no amount of money buy Masterson's freedom."

"I'm not buying his freedom," Eleanor explained. "I'm offering you this money as collateral to guarantee that if you release Jeffrey into my custody, I will guarantee his appearance for trial."

Tully yanked open the desk drawer and dropped the keys into it. "Why, ma'am, the sheriff would have a fit if I turned a prisoner free for no cause. Sure as the world he'd lynch me, and if he didn't, the Langs would."

"You're not turning him free," Eleanor repeated as she leaned closer. "He'll still be a prisoner, but he'll be in my custody. I'll be responsible for him, not you."

"Well, ma'am, I'm *supposed* to be responsible for him. That's my job."

Staring out the window and remaining silent during the exchange between Eleanor and the deputy, Bradley stood on the other side of the office, a foot propped up on a chair, an arm slung lazily over his raised leg. In the other hand he held a cup of coffee. "Maybe you do this sort of thing in Chicago, Miss Hunt, but out here it's

49

better for Masterson to be in jail. Tully's right . . . this is a job for him and the sheriff."

Eleanor whirled around and glared at his back. The material of his shirt was stretched tautly over his broad shoulders. "It suits your purposes just fine for Jeffrey to remain in jail, doesn't it?"

Without turning to look at her, his attention riveted to something outside the room, Bradley lifted the cup and took a swallow of coffee. "It'll be better for him."

"How do you know what will be better for him?" she retorted. "Even though you act like it sometimes, you're not God, Mister Smith."

"No, I'm not, but I do have a fair amount of sense. Take a look over here," Bradley drawled, pointing a finger. When she stood behind him looking out the window, he said, "Lang's men have started riding into town, and they're drinking heavily. I'd say David's condition must be getting worse, certainly not better."

Eleanor moved past Bradley and continued to peer through the window at the crowd that had quickly gathered. Tully followed, his thick brows drawn together in consternation.

"I know you're thinking of Masterson's welfare, Miss Hunt"—Bradley lowered his foot and set his cup on the shelf behind him—"but the boy is safer in jail. Let Tully and Carl look after him. They're better equipped to deal with the men out here."

"Yessir, Miss Hunt, we sure are." Tully bobbed his head.

"Surely those men wouldn't take the law into their own hands!" Eleanor scoffed.

"Sure don't want to tempt them none, ma'am." Tully heaved a sigh of relief when the group broke up and the cowboys walked into the saloon. "Sure hope Whittier keeps a tight hold on them boys, Bradley. They can be pretty rough, especially Haggarty."

"At least he's not here yet." Bradley tugged at the brim of his hat.

"Was earlier," Tully said. "Him and that whiny feller Neb that always rides with him. They left a few minutes ago. Headed north."

"I don't like Haggarty," Bradley mused. "I can't imagine why Lang ever hired the likes of him in the first place."

"Guess with all the cattle rustling, we're all getting kinda jumpy," Tully said. "Whittier probably hired whoever he thought could help him."

"Reckon so." Bradley turned to Eleanor. "Well, Miss Hunt, you've done all you can for Jeffrey right now. The way things are shaping up, I'd say it's high time for me to get you to the station. I'll have someone bring you back in the morning, and you can talk to the sheriff." His hand casually closed around her upper arm, and he started to guide her to the door.

When Eleanor jerked to free herself from his grip, his hand tightened on her arm. But he did not hurt her. "I'm not through talking with the deputy." She glared at him.

"Way I figure it, ma'am," Tully said, "we've done about as much talking on the subject as we can. Never heard tell of buying a person like this, ma'am. Why, sheriff's gonna be plumb mad when he hears that you want Masterson released to your custody. Meaning you no harm, but I never heard tell of a man being accountable to a woman."

"An attorney, Deputy Tulford," Eleanor said tightly. "You are releasing him into the custody of his attorney, not just to some woman."

Tully scratched his head and looked at her in bafflement. "Meaning no disrespect, ma'am, but it's kinda hard for me to forget that you're a woman."

"And impossible for you to remember that I'm an attorney."

Tully looked shamefaced. "Only the sheriff can turn Masterson loose, ma'am. I just can't do it for you."

Bradley guided her forcefully to the door. "Miss Hunt, I need to get back to the station. I have work to do. Now you can come peaceably, or—"

"Or what, Mister Smith?"

Bradley grinned. "I'll carry you, Miss Hunt."

"You wouldn't dare!"

Tully chuckled from behind Eleanor. "Yes, Miss Hunt, I reckon he *would* dare. Don't know much about Bradley Smith, but I do know this: when he says something, he means it."

Eleanor dug her heels into the floor, and she clawed at his fingers with her other hand. "You're not carrying me out of here, nor am I going of my own free will. In case you don't remember, Mister Hunt—"

"Bradley—"

She grunted. "Mister Smith, you no longer work at Hunt Cattle Station."

Bradley grinned. "We'll see what Harry says about that."

Like fuel on a fire, his words stoked Eleanor's anger. Temporarily forgetting she was imprisoned by his hand, she thumped her finger against her chest. "Harry Prescott has nothing to say about this. *I'm* the one who says, Mister Smith. Me. Eleanor Hunt. And *I* say I'm going to stay in town until the sheriff gets here. I won't let Jeffrey spend another hour in this miserable place. He's frightened out of his wits."

Tully's face screwed up in surprise, and he looked around the room. "Well, ma'am, I wouldn't say it were miserable. This is one of the nicest buildings in town. And we ain't done nothing to scare the boy. We're just trying to keep him alive until his trial."

"I'm sorry, Deputy Tulford, I didn't mean to criticize your jail or your service," Eleanor apologized over her shoulder, all the time glaring at Bradley. Between clenched teeth and in a staccato voice she said, "I'm staying. Do you hear me?"

Bradley sighed deeply and dropped his hand from her arm. "You're a stubborn woman, Miss Hunt."

"At the moment, I'm a stubborn attorney working for my client."

Bradley's voice lowered to a seductive drawl. "Pardon me, ma'am, if I prefer to think of you as a woman. I don't mind your being an attorney, but thinking of you as a woman does a lot more for me"—the right lid lowered in an audacious wink—"if you know what I mean."

Eleanor's eyes widened with surprise, but with supreme effort she retained her composure. "You are the most insufferable man I have ever had the misfortune to meet."

"But at least we met, Miss Hunt, and are getting to know each other quite well. In time I hope to see 'insufferable' change to 'desirable' and 'misfortune' to 'fortune'." His voice became even more husky, and his green eyes sparkled with promise. "And we'll probably get to know one another even better on the way home."

Realizing that she was making no headway with him, Eleanor knew it was time for her to change tactics. Although Bradley irritated her, she did not wish to be left to her own devices in Blissful. Neither did she intend to return to Hunt Cattle Station just yet. She must stall. "The deputy said the sheriff would be here in a couple of hours. Please . . . Bradley . . . wait with me. I really want to talk to him about Early Dobson."

Bradley's eyes narrowed as he scrutinized her. The face remained immobile and unreadable for what seemed like forever. Finally the hard lines of his mouth eased into a smile, and his eyes laughed at her. Eleanor was a tad uncomfortable. He reinforced the idea that he could read her thoughts and understand her strategy.

He walked out of the office, saying over his shoulder, "A couple of hours, Miss Hunt . . . no more. I'll be back for you later."

Eleanor stood for a second, staring after him; then she rushed out of the jail onto the boardwalk and into the bright afternoon sunshine. "Where are you going?"

Bradley never stopped walking. "To get me something to eat. I'm hungry."

His words reminded Eleanor that she had not eaten since dinner the night before. Suddenly she was quite hungry. "Wait!" She moved so quickly she stumbled over the hem of her dress and fumbled with her parasol. "I'll join you."

Bradley turned around and reached up to shove his Stetson back on his forehead. Folding his arms over his chest, he waited for her. When she stood in front of him, he asked, "What makes you think I'd like for you to join me? I may have other plans."

"Oh!" Eleanor stopped unfurling her parasol and looked at him rather blankly for a second. "May I? Do you?"

He rocked back on his heels.

"*May* I join you?" Eleanor smiled disarmingly, but her eyes glinted mischievously. "Since you're now an unemployed person, I'll even buy your lunch."

Bradley's eyes twinkled also. "Although I disagree with you about my employment status, Miss Hunt, I am not about to turn down your invitation. If anything, I am a business man, and a shrewd one."

"A man who makes the most of his opportunities."

"A man who creates his opportunities," Bradley corrected.

"I admire you, Bradley. And under other circumstances I could like you."

"Well, thank you, Miss Hunt. That's the nearest you've come to complimenting me. Should I feel dishonored, or do you move this slowly with everyone you meet?"

"Not everyone," Eleanor answered thoughtfully and slanted the parasol over her right shoulder. "After all, I'm a woman who's made it in a man's world, Bradley. I've had to make some very quick decisions. As the old saying goes, I've had to like the unlikable and love the unlovable."

Although she said the words lightly, Bradley scowled as if he did not like their implication. "Meaning me?"

"If you're unlikable or unlovable." Feeling as if she had scored a point, Eleanor wrapped her hand around his extended arm and began to walk. "Lead the way to the dining table, kind sir."

Bradley was preoccupied as they moved down the street to the nearest hotel. After they had seated themselves near the window, he removed his hat and ran his fingers through his hair. An errant lock drooped beguilingly across his forehead. Eleanor smiled as he swiped it back several times, the wave always defying his touch. She liked him without his hat, and she was glad he did not control the lock of hair. He looked more human and less indomitable.

After they ordered their food and the waitress walked away, Eleanor stared through the window at the man who was hitching his horse to the railing across the street. Dressed in a black suit, he was tall and lean and weathered. Truly a product of the West, she surmised. From the way he carried himself when he swaggered down the sidewalk, Eleanor knew he was important . . . or at least, that he thought he was. "Who is that?" she asked.

Bradley turned his head to watch the man. Eventually he answered, "Lang. Whittier Lang. David's father. One of the most influential ranchers in the area."

The father of the man Jeffrey was accused of shooting!

Lang moved between two of the buildings, climbed the stairs, and soon disappeared behind a door.

"Where did he go?" Eleanor asked.

Bradley was silent for so long that Eleanor thought perhaps he did not intend to answer. Finally he said, "If you want to know, ask him the next time you see him. I don't keep up with his business. I have enough of my own to take care of."

She dragged her gaze from the window and looked at Bradley. "Do you think David will die?"

Bradley squirmed into a more comfortable position. "He has a pretty bad gut wound. During the war I saw plenty of men die from less."

Eleanor clenched her hands together in her lap. "Jeffrey did not shoot him!" she whispered, then added, "He couldn't have. He was framed, Bradley. Surely you can see that—the note telling him to go to the Rocking W and the bogus bank account . . ."

"Here you are." The waitress set their food in front of them. "The best beef stew in town. Coffee for you, sir, and milk for you, ma'am. Anything else I can get you?"

"No," both of them replied.

When she walked away, Bradley reached for the sugar bowl in the center of the table. As if they had not been interrupted, he said, "It looks pretty bad for Jeffrey. And his story just doesn't make sense. Why would David be stealing cattle from his own father, when he gets everything he wants anyway? Why on earth did Jeffrey happen to pick this night to ride to the Rocking W to confront David with his suspicions that he was the thief?"

Her food forgotten, Eleanor leaned forward. "You're discounting the note Jeffrey received that tipped him off to the rustling."

"The anonymous note that no one saw. That Jeffrey can't produce because he seems to have lost it in the

56

shootout." Bradley swirled the spoon in his coffee, the metal gently tinkling against the china.

"Someone deliberately sent Jeffrey that note," Eleanor continued, "because they wanted him on the scene at the time of the crime. The note and the bank account were part of the frame-up."

"How ironic for Jeffrey that Dobson swore he was the one to open, make deposits, and close the account." Bradley set his cup down and broke off a piece of the freshly baked bread, which he spread liberally with butter. "You'd better enjoy your food while it's hot."

For a minute Eleanor watched him eat. Slowly she lowered her head and looked at her stew—chunks of beef and vegetables in a thick brown gravy. Her concern for Jeffrey seemed to dispel her hunger. Yet she knew it would be a long time until supper. Picking up her fork, she ate a bite or two, but mostly shoved the food around her plate. Finally she laid her fork down and picked up the glass to take several swallows of milk.

"You're deep in thought," Bradley said.

She raised her head and nodded.

He smiled broadly. Napkin in hand, he leaned across the table. Eleanor dodged his touch.

"Milk," he explained and drew back, holding up both hands innocently. "You have a moustache of milk."

"Oh!" She was momentarily disconcerted. Quickly she wiped her mouth.

"Now, where were we? Oh, yes—you were deep in thought. Want to share it with me?"

Eleanor folded her napkin meticulously and laid it beside her plate. "Were you in the barn that night?"

Picking up his cup, Bradley pushed back in his chair. "Meaning what?"

"You were the only one who could have known he was going to the Rocking W."

Bradley leaned forward and put the cup down with

57

such force that it clattered against the saucer. "Look, Miss Hunt, I'm happy that you're going to be legal counsel for Masterson until Allen Shea gets here, and I'm glad you're doing your job. But I want you to hear me, because this is the only time I'm going to say this. I did not frame Jeffrey, and I did not know he was going to the Rocking W. He told me he was going out for a ride, and I accepted him at his word. I don't care what the pup thinks."

"The pup! You can't be too much older than Jeffrey."

"In years, five," Bradley answered. "In experience, an eternity. How old are you?"

"We're not talking about age."

"I wasn't. You are. Now, since you introduced the subject to find out how old I am, I want to know how old you are."

"Twenty-five." Eleanor braced herself for the clucking of the tongue that generally followed her announcement. Although she did not really mind being a spinster, it did have its drawbacks, at times.

"Masterson is too young for you."

"He's three years older than I am!"

"He may be older, but you're more mature." Bradley cocked his head to the side. "Matter of fact, you *look* older."

"Well, thank you!" Eleanor fairly spat out the words.

Bradley chuckled. "You're taking it the wrong way, counsellor. Looking older doesn't necessarily mean looking worse."

"Nor does it necessarily mean looking better."

"Now you're fishing for a compliment?" His eyes teased her.

"Will I get one?" The pulse at the base of her neck beat erratically.

"If you fish long enough."

"Then I won't," she declared. "I've just hauled in

58

my line."

"Too bad. It could have been fun."

"I'm not here to have fun, Mister Smith. I'm here to protect Jeffrey and to prove his innocence."

"Do you love him?"

Eleanor ran her finger around the rim of her cup. When she answered, she raised her head. "Our families have been friends since we were small children. When Jeffrey's parents died several years ago, Papa took him under his wing. That's why Jeffrey ended up out here. Papa was teaching him Hunt Meat Packing from the ground up."

"In order for Jeffrey to take the company over someday," Bradley supplied.

Eleanor sighed. Time had done nothing to ease the hurt. "I suppose Papa hoped that one day Jeffrey would take over the company."

"And marry you."

"Yes."

"And will he?"

Eleanor grinned. "That, Mister Smith, is none of your business."

"I'd like to know."

"Good." Eleanor chuckled. "Keep wondering."

Bradley's expression was somber, his mouth compressed into a fine line. "Do you think perhaps you're too emotional to represent Jeffrey's best interests?"

"Speaking of Jeffrey's best interests"—Eleanor crossed her arms on the table—"I would like to return to the point I was making when you so adroitly distracted me from the subject. Isn't it ironic that you just happened to be in the barn the night Jeffrey was caught supposedly rustling Lang's cattle and that you were at the station in time to get Jeffrey's job?"

All the friendliness faded from Bradley's eyes. His voice was harsh. "I have been working at Hunt Cattle

Station for the past eight months, Miss Hunt, a long time before Jeffrey Masterson was arrested for rustling. I happened to be the best qualified person for the job of interim manager. At the risk of sounding arrogant, I'll add that Harry *begged* me to take the position." He picked up his napkin and wiped his hands. "Now eat your dinner and quit trying to make me out to be your culprit. Isn't it enough to feed your ego by firing me? Do you have to find me guilty of a crime also?"

"You're angry." Eleanor's lips twitched into a smile.

"Irritated," Bradley clarified and reached for his coffee. "You're a frustrating woman, Miss Hunt. I can only imagine what kind of attorney you are."

Eleanor laughed softly. She could not remember when she had felt more challenged and also more feminine. Bradley brought out the best in her . . . and the worst. The first was nothing unusual; the latter was exhilarating. She picked up her coffee cup and held it in both hands.

"A damn good one, I might add."

Despite his resolve to keep a stern face, Bradley grinned. "If you don't watch your language, young lady, I'm going to wash your mouth out with soap. Ladies don't use words like that."

Eleanor laughed again. "That, Bradley Smith, is one thing I don't claim to be. And don't ever call me *young lady* again." Setting the cup down, she balled her hand into a fist and extended it playfully across the table. "I don't take kindly to it. I have a name, and I prefer to be called by it."

Bradley's hand closed over hers. "And this is what I think of your resistance."

The laughter faded from her face, and she stared at the huge hand that engulfed hers. Crisp brown hairs stood out against the sun-browned skin. She felt the warmth of his touch radiate down her arm and through her body.

"Are you asking me to call you by your given name?"

The husky tones brought Eleanor's gaze up to his face. "Yes," she murmured, and wiggled her hand from his. Even freed from his clasp, she was not free from his touch. "I am."

"Eleanor . . . named for whom?"

"My grandmother on my father's side."

"How does this grandmother react to her namesake being an attorney?" Bradley asked.

"She died when I was a small child, and never knew society would classify her granddaughter a disgrace."

"What about your mother?"

"She fought me in the beginning, but when she realized I was determined, she became my strongest supporter." She looked up. "She died eighteen months ago."

"And how does your father cope with a daughter who is determined to enter a man's world on a man's terms?"

Eleanor's smile did not touch her eyes. "He's proud of me, but I think his greatest disappointment is my not being a man."

"I'm glad it's his disappointment, Eleanor, and not mine. I find you—a—"

"Yes?" Eleanor raised one eyebrow curiously.

"—an extremely challenging woman."

"And you, Bradley Smith, are an extremely irritating man." About that time Eleanor turned her head and saw Whittier Lang and a woman descending the steps of the building across the street. "Business!" Eleanor exclaimed, her head quickly turning back to Bradley. She laid accusing eyes on him. "You said he was taking care of business. Why, that woman is—she's a—"

Bradley shrugged. "She works hard for a living."

Eleanor's gaze returned to the bright red gown, trimmed in gaudy black lace. The woman took a roll of bills from Lang and dropped them into her reticule. "I don't know that I'd call that working for a living. You can tell exactly what kind of woman she is by looking at her."

61

"You sound as if you disapprove."

"Personally, I do, but it's really none of my business how the woman earns her living, or with whom Whittier Lang associates." Eleanor eased the strap of her handbag over her shoulder and started to stand, but Bradley caught her hand. She jerked, but he held it tightly.

"You're quite judgmental, aren't you?"

"I wouldn't describe myself as such," she said. "I think of myself as being quite a progressive woman, but even *I* draw the line on certain occupations that denigrate one's integrity."

Green eyes compelled her full attention. "Have you ever been a . . . woman of the street, Eleanor?"

She drew in a deep breath. "You must know I have not!"

"Then how can you make such a sweeping statement?"

"The woman uses her body as a means of making a living. She sells herself to the highest bidder. While she has a perfect right to live her life as she chooses, I cannot and do not approve of her actions. Nothing you can say, Bradley Smith, will make me change my mind. Now if you'll turn my hand loose, I'll be going."

"Sorry." He loosened his grasp. "I just wanted to remind you that you said you would pay for lunch. I didn't want you to leave without—"

Eleanor wanted to slap the smug grin off his face, but instead she only glared. Heaving an angry sigh, she unsnapped her handbag and pulled out her pocketbook. "How much did your lunch cost?"

"Smith!" a man's voice boomed from across the room.

Eleanor turned to see Whitter Lang striding toward them. When he reached the table, he brushed past her without an acknowledgment. He was taller and thinner than he appeared at a distance. His face was gaunt, his features sharp. "Tell Alexander Hunt that if my son dies, I'll hold him personally responsible, and I'll see that

Masterson hangs for murder."

Bradley rose, the two men standing about the same height, and said quietly, "Mister Lang, I understand your grief, but—"

Lang's hand darted out, and he flattened a calloused palm against Bradley's chest. His sharp gray eyes caught and held Bradley's. "Have you a son, Smith? No, I didn't think so. You have no idea how I feel. You can't begin to understand my grief."

"You're making a scene," Bradley said.

"Nothing like the one I'm going to make if David dies. I know Alexander Hunt is behind this rustling, Smith. Masterson is one of his errand boys. One of these days, I'll have the proof I need. Until I do, I'm going to drive Hunt into bankruptcy. He'll rue the day he ever touched a Lang. I'm just sorry that someone as smart as you got mixed up with a man like Hunt. Be sure to give him my message."

Before Bradley knew what had happened, Eleanor had insinuated herself between him and Lang. She glared into the older man's face and thumped her index fingers against his chest. "And you, Mister Lang, are going to rue the day that you slandered the name of Alexander Hunt in public."

Surprised, Whittier stepped back and gazed first at Eleanor, then at Bradley. "Who the hell is she?"

"Don't speak about me as if I'm not here," Eleanor said. "I can hear and I can talk. So speak to me. If you want to know who I am, ask me."

The head lowered, and the gray eyes narrowed. "Who are you?"

Bradley grinned. "Mister Lang, it gives me great pleasure to introduce you to Eleanor Hunt."

"Hunt," Lang murmured.

"Eleanor Hunt, Mister Lang. Alexander Hunt's daughter and Jeffrey Masterson's attorney." Eleanor regained control of the conversation.

"Attorney!"

"Is that all you can do, Mister Lang? Just repeat what other people say?" Eleanor demanded. "Now that you know you're speaking to a Hunt, have you suddenly been struck dumb? Well, let me tell you something—my father is not behind any rustling, nor is Jeffrey, and I don't know why you want to accuse either of them."

Bradley's hand closed over her shoulder, and he tried to move her, but she twisted loose.

"I can understand your grief," she continued, "and yes, Mister Lang, I understand death. My mother died only eighteen months ago. But grief does not give you an excuse to behave as you are. It's not a license to take your anger and hostility out on innocent people."

She wagged her index finger in Lang's face. "I will not tolerate your threats and accusations against either my father or Jeffrey. As far as I'm concerned, your son is guilty. He's the one who stole the cattle, and he's lying about Jeffrey."

Catching Eleanor by the hand, Bradley firmly pulled her out of Lang's face. "I think it's time for us to leave, Miss Hunt. Whitter, if you'll excuse us—"

Eleanor thrashed in his grip. "I'm not through yet."

"For now, you are," Bradley grunted and dragged her a few steps with him, stopping only to let her grab her parasol. "The sheriff has just ridden into town."

"He did!" Eleanor exclaimed, automatically turning her head to see through the window the lone rider in the street. Her argument with Lang was quickly pushed aside. Her gaze swung back to Whittier Lang. "Well, yes, that takes precedence over this. I have some unfinished business to take care of at the sheriff's office. We'll conclude this conversation at a later date. Now good day, sir. Meeting you has indeed been an interesting experience."

"At least it's an experience I will not soon forget," Whittier said. "You'd better hope you're a damned good attorney. Masterson is going to need one. I've employed the best."

"You better have, Mister Lang. You're going to need one." She felt Bradley's fingers bite into her shoulder. She was still fuming when she and Bradley stepped into the street. "Who does that man think he is, to speak about my father like that?"

One hand clasped tightly about Eleanor's wrist as he jerked her along the sidewalk, Bradley reached up with the other to adjust the brim of his hat. "He doesn't have to think. He is. Whittier Lang just simply is. He's to Blissful what your papa is to Chicago."

Eleanor spun in front of him so quickly he stumbled into her. "Don't you ever mention that man's name in the same sentence with my father's. My father is nothing like him." Out of the corner of her eye, she saw the woman who had been with Whittier Lang across the street. "My father is a gentleman. He would never associate with a woman like that."

Bradley looked across the street. When the woman noticed him, she smiled and lifted her hand, but did not stop walking. Also continuing to walk, Bradley waved and called out, "Good morning, Maude. How are things going?"

"Could be better. Could be worse."

Eleanor cast reproving eyes on Bradley. "How dare you speak to that tramp when you're my escort!"

Bradley stopped walking and jerked Eleanor up short in front of him. "Look, lady," he said softly, angrily, "I feel sorry that you're so judgmental. With your being the kind of woman that bucks false standards, I'd have thought you'd be more charitable in your opinions of others. I'm rather disappointed. How you feel about other people is none of my business. But don't you tell

65

me to whom I can speak. And let's get something clear right now. I'm not your escort, or even your friend. I'm your father's employee, sent to town to pick up Masterson's attorney. And that's all." He turned her arm loose and spun around, striding angrily down the sidewalk.

Speechless, Eleanor stared after him. This time, however, she did not try to catch up with him. Feeling guilty, she lingered behind and slowly unfurled her parasol. By the time she arrived at the jail, Bradley and the sheriff were deep in conversation. As she stepped through the door, the talking ceased and both men stood. In a cool voice Bradley introduced Eleanor to the sheriff.

"Right pleased I am to meet you, ma'am. Tully"—Carl Hix waved his hand toward the deputy—"said you were wanting me to free Masterson into your custody."

"Yes, Sheriff, that's my request." Eleanor moved to stand in front of the desk. The sheriff was a large man, taller than Bradley, and heavier. Thick black hair, liberally streaked with white, framed his friendly face. "As his attorney, I'll be responsible for his behavior and will see that he's present for trial. The deputy didn't have the dates, but I assume you do."

Carl chuckled and lowered himself into the chair. "Ma'am, it doesn't pay anybody to assume anything out here."

Placing both hands on the desk, Eleanor leaned forward, "Are you telling me—"

Carl opened the top drawer of the desk and pulled out a small piece of wood. Flicking open his pocketknife, he began to whittle, slivers of wood flying through the air. "We have a circuit judge, ma'am. We've already sent word we need him, but we haven't received an answer yet. Soon as we do, we'll set the date."

"Then by all means you must release Jeffrey to my custody," Eleanor said. "At this rate, no telling how long he'll be in jail."

The tip of Carl's tongue jutted from the corner of his mouth, and his eyes narrowed as he trimmed the wood. "Reckon he'll be a mite safer in here than out there. Besides, the folks wouldn't take kindly to my accepting money for Masterson's release."

"Yep." Tully nodded. "That's what I told her, Carl."

"Surely, Sheriff," Eleanor scoffed, "you're not going to let Lang's men tell you how to run your business?"

Carl's whittling stopped. He lifted his head and stared at her. Although his dark brown eyes were sunken in the weathered face and underlined with dark pouches, they were sharp and alert. "No, ma'am. Lang's men don't tell me how to run my business, but neither does a sharp-tongued tenderfoot woman lawyer. I do what's best for my town and my prisoner."

Eleanor backed away. "I'm sorry," she murmured and lifted a hand to brush a tendril of hair from her temple. "I didn't mean to insult you, Sheriff. I'm—I'm extremely tired."

"It's all right," Carl said and concentrated on his whittling again. "Everybody makes a mistake or two during a lifetime."

A light knock on the door caught Eleanor's attention, and she turned to see a young woman, whom she judged to be about nineteen, standing in the door, a lunch basket draped over her arm.

"Hello, Carl." Although the woman spoke to the sheriff, her bright blue eyes gazed curiously at Eleanor. Soft brown tendrils escaped the confines of the straw bonnet to curl around her cheeks.

"Howdy, Sarah," Carl said. "Come right on in. Reckon Masterson will be right glad to see you."

Sarah turned her head and smiled at the sheriff. "Sorry I'm late, but we had a minor catastrophe this morning that held things up."

"Quite all right. Sarah, I want you to meet Miss Eleanor Hunt."

The smile disappeared from Sarah's lips. "Eleanor Hunt," she repeated.

Eleanor stepped forward. "That's right. My father owns Hunt Cattle Station."

"I know." Sarah began to fidget with the handle of the basket. "What—what are you doing in Blissful, Miss Hunt?"

"She didn't exactly come all the way from Chicago to Blissful for a holiday," Carl answered dryly. "She's here because of Masterson."

Sarah's face paled, and she edged closer to the door that led to the cell room. "What Jeffrey needs is a good attorney, not a . . . a woman . . . not you," she blurted.

"Sarah Craven here!" Carl exclaimed. "Miss Hunt is—"

"Let me, Sheriff," Eleanor said and smiled at Sarah. "You're right. Jeffrey does need a good attorney, and that's why I'm here. I *am* his attorney."

The belligerence slipped from Sarah's face, a smile playing at the corners of her mouth. "You mean—you're not—you and Jeffrey aren't—"

"Jeffrey and I are good friends," Eleanor assured her. Out of the corner of her eye she watched Bradley to see how he would react to her confession. As if he hadn't heard a word she'd said, he stared out the window.

Sarah set her basket on the desk and finally said, "This is marvelous. I'm so glad you're here, Miss Hunt. Now Jeffrey has someone to defend him"—she looked directly into Eleanor's eyes—"and to believe in him. You do, don't you?"

"I do."

Sarah smiled. "I think it's grand that you came. I'll do anything I can to help you. Of course, I don't know anything about the rustling and the shooting."

"Thank you, Sarah."

"I hope you and I have an opportunity to visit, Eleanor. There's so much I'd like to talk to you about." Her eyes lingered on Eleanor's hat, then moved to her gloves. "Jeffrey told me that you frequently go to New York to do your shopping. Did you buy these there?"

Carl threw his hands up in the air. "Wouldn't you know it! No matter how bad the situation, women are bound to talk about clothes."

Eleanor laughed softly and nodded.

"At Newland's?" Sarah's eyes began to glow. "Do you shop there?"

Eleanor held out her hands. "Bought these there."

"Oh!" Sarah reached out to touch the soft red leather. "They're so pretty. And they match the berries on your felt hat."

"Well, now, Sarah"—Carl slid both hands into his hip pockets—"I reckon you better quit ogling them gloves and git in there and feed that boy."

"Oh, yes!" Sarah exclaimed with a start. "We'll visit later, Eleanor. If you're Jeffrey's attorney, I'm sure you're going to spend a lot of time in town."

"Not if I can get him released to my custody," Eleanor said. She turned to the sheriff. "Is there any way I could get word to the judge to ask if he would release Jeffrey into my custody?"

Carl reached up and rubbed his chin. "Don't rightly know where Judge Neely is. That might be a good idea if we did."

"Papa would know where Uncle Ted is," Sarah answered and rushed to the sheriff's desk.

Eleanor's head flew up, her eyes bright with interest. "Is the judge your uncle?"

"Not really my uncle," Sarah explained. "But he and my father have known each other all their lives. They're just like brothers."

"Good." Eleanor grabbed Sarah's arm and pulled her

69

to the door. "Let's go see your father."

"Can't," Carl said flatly. "He's still at the Stanwood Ranch, same as I was—only he stayed for the barbecue."

As if she could not quite believe the sheriff, Eleanor looked at Sarah, who nodded. "That's right. He probably won't be home until late this afternoon."

"Well," Eleanor said, "then we'll just—"

"No," Bradley answered, his expression as thunderous as his voice, "we won't. Harry is expecting me to bring home the grain and hay this afternoon. We're going home. One more night in jail won't hurt Jeffrey."

"Won't hurt none to let the little lady talk to Carver." Hix surprised Eleanor with his support. "If anybody can help her git Masterson out of jail, it's him."

"I don't mind her talking with Barber," Bradley said, "but I can't wait in town with her all day. I have to get these supplies back to the station."

Remembering the loaded wagon, Eleanor did not doubt Bradley's words. "I know you have to get back," she said, "so I'll stay here. You can come back later for me."

Bradley was breathing pure fire. Eleanor could not see the flames, but she could feel the heat of his wrath.

"I'm not leaving until I've talked with Dobson."

"I don't think you'll be doing that, Miss Hunt," Carl said. "Dobson left town about a week ago."

"How convenient," Eleanor snapped. "Right after his testimony, I'll wager. And what are you doing about it?"

"We're looking for him," Carl answered.

"There's no reason for you to stay," Bradley said, "so let's go."

"There's still the matter of getting Jeffrey out of jail."

"I have plans for tonight . . . personal plans."

"I'll stay at the hotel, if necessary." Eleanor stared unflinchingly into his face.

"I have plans for the morning, too."

Anger flashed in her eyes. "If you can't come get me,

then send someone in your place."

Sarah moved to stand beside Eleanor. "You can spend the night with me."

Eleanor stared at the younger woman for only a second before she said, "Yes, I will—it is best, Bradley. This way I can visit longer with Jeffrey and start work on his case. Now that the sheriff's here, I can question him. Send someone to pick me up tomorrow afternoon. I'll be at the Sarah's house."

"If you want to come to Hunt Cattle Station tomorrow afternoon, Miss Hunt," Bradley said, "you'll be at the General Store at three, or Cook and the grub wagon will leave without you."

"Then, Bradley, you had best let me get one of my valises off the buggy. The rest of the luggage you can take to the station today. When I arrive tomorrow, I expect my room to be ready and my clothes unpacked."

"If you're expecting me to do all this for you," Bradley said, "you'll be waiting a mighty long time. I'll take your luggage to the station, but I'm not getting your room ready, and I'm not unpacking your clothes."

"Then have one of the servants do it."

"For your information, Eleanor Hunt," Bradley ground out, "we don't have any house servants, only a cook—who does nothing *but* cook. You'll just have to do like the rest of us and clean up after yourself."

Chapter 4

Wearing an ecru cotton suit, Eleanor sat in front of the dresser and arranged the pale blue lace jabot about her neck. Satisfied that it was right for the delicate ensemble and that it truly did enhance the color of her eyes, she gave it one last pat. She lifted her hand and flipped the curls on her temples. Then her fingers strayed to her cheeks.

Glad for the bright morning sunlight, she eased forward to scrutinize her reflection in the mirror. Bradley had said she looked older than Jeffrey; now she wondered if she really did. Intent with her education and causes, she had not been preoccupied with the concept of age before, nor with men, for that matter.

One day in Blissful had completely changed her outlook on life. Quite truthfully, Blissful had not changed her. Bradley Smith had. She had lain awake for hours last night thinking about him. Even now he occupied her thoughts. With no effort at all she heard the husky sound of his voice as it wrapped itself around her to remind her that she was a woman first, an attorney second. She saw the thick brows above rich, vibrant green eyes. The rugged face looked as if it had been hand-hewn from granite. Although he closed her out at times,

Eleanor knew that Bradley was dependable. Remembering the errant lock that fell across his forehead, she smiled. The formidable Bradley Smith could be most vulnerable.

An emptiness aching in the bottom of her stomach, Eleanor rested her face in her hands. Bradley Smith was having absolutely too much of an effect on her. It angered her. The idea of someone—especially a man—having such control over her emotions frightened her. She would do well to stay away from the man while she was in Blissful. When she heard the soft knock, she lifted her head and called, "Come in."

The door opened, and Sarah poked her head around it. "Good. You're already up. How did you sleep last night?"

"Marvelously." Eleanor resolutely pushed away all thoughts of Bradley Smith. Feigning an interest in her attire, she stood and ran her palms down the form-fitting bodice that flared over the bustle. Despite the sweeping pleats that ended in lace and frills, the suit was rather conservative and tailored.

Eleanor assumed her brightest tone and said, "Nothing does more for the body than a bath and a good night's sleep. Has your father arrived home?"

Sarah closed the door and moved into the room. As she stood in front of the window, bathed in sunlight, Eleanor noticed for the first time how truly pretty she was. Her brown hair was pulled gently from her face and coiled into a chignon at the nape of her neck. She seemed to walk in an aura of innocence and gentle beauty.

"I'm surprised you didn't awaken when he came in last night."

Eleanor stared incredulously at Sarah. "Actually, I didn't. I must have slept more soundly than I thought."

"You must have," Sarah gurgled. "Papa was quite loud and happy. He had one drink too many."

Although Eleanor laughed with Sarah, she was concerned. "Does this bode well for me?"

Sarah shrugged and rubbed her palms nervously down her skirt. Hesitantly she said, "I . . . don't know. He likes Jeffrey." Then she rushed on, "Really, he does. It's just that Mister Lang has done so much for Blissful."

Eleanor leaned back against the dresser and said quietly, "You've already talked with your father about my wanting him to let Jeffrey out?"

Sarah nodded, and her voice softened. "He had to leave early this morning and couldn't wait to talk with you. So I told him what you wanted."

Eleanor picked up her hat and played with the pale-blue serge ribbon. Already she had her answer.

"That's a beautiful hat," Sarah murmured. "Did you get it at Newland's?"

Not really interested in the hat, Eleanor lightly fanned her fingers over the ostrich feather. "They have a huge millinery shop. My favorite in all of New York. Rosette, the lady who supervises it, made this one especially for this suit."

"I'm heading east one of these days. I really am," Sarah promised softly, then her eyes began to glow. "Jeffrey's been telling me all about Chicago and New York. And Nowland's Fashion Salon."

Eleanor fanned the feather again. "You and Jeffrey are quite close, aren't you, Sarah?"

Sarah's lids lowered, and she dropped her face. "I've gotten to know him quite well since he's been in jail," she answered.

Her gaze on the hat, she asked quietly, "Has he told you about me?"

Nodding, Sarah raised her head.

"Then why were you worried about my being here?"

Sarah shrugged and gave Eleanor a small smile. "I thought maybe he—was just telling me that you and he were friends because I was here and you were

75

in Chicago."

Eleanor laid the hat on the dresser. "My father wishes it were different. He would like for me and Jeffrey to marry someday. But Jeffrey was telling you the truth."

"Oh, Eleanor," Sarah breathed. "I'm so glad to hear you say that."

"Are you and Jeffrey in love?"

Delicate color fused Sarah's face. "I'm in love with him," she confessed softly, "and I think he's in love with me."

"I'm glad for you," Eleanor said. "I'm sure the two of you will be happy together."

Sarah's eyes darkened, and she turned to walk to the window. Picking at the curtain, she looked across the lawn. "No matter what Whittier Lang claims, Jeffrey is innocent, Eleanor."

"I know."

Sarah turned around, tears sparkling in her eyes. "But Whittier is determined that Jeffrey will hang for cattle rustling."

"I'm as determined that Jeffrey won't hang."

"Can you save him?"

"Yes," Eleanor replied, "I can, but I'm going to need some help."

"I'll help," Sarah said. "What do you want me to do?"

"Did Jeffrey tell you about the note?" Eleanor asked. Sarah reluctantly nodded.

"Who could have written it, Sarah? Jeffrey thinks maybe it was a woman. If so, it would logically be one of David's friends."

Sarah nervously trailed her fingers down her cheek. "I don't know."

"How long have you known David?"

"Since we were small children," she answered. "Our parents settled out here about the same time."

"Then you know David quite well?"

"I know him," she answered quietly, "but not all that well, because he's so much older than me."

"Well enough to have some idea who might be close enough to him to write this note to Jeffrey."

"David had no one particular woman in his life," Sarah said. "He liked them all. Try the saloons and dance halls. The women there will attest to his popularity. All of them knew him—quite well."

Eleanor thought she heard a thread of bitterness in Sarah's voice. "But there had to be someone—he trusted with this task. If you think of anyone, will you let me know?"

Sarah nodded. "I'll see what I can find out."

"Good." Eleanor smiled and picked up the hat. "Do you like this?"

"Very much."

Holding it out, Eleanor said, "I'd like to give it to you."

"Oh, no!" Sarah's head flew up, and her face registered shock. As if to resist temptation, she clasped her hands behind her back. "I couldn't."

"Of course you can take it. It's mine to give away, if I choose," Eleanor insisted and stepped forward. Sarah also took several steps. "This is my way of thanking you for your hospitality."

A tentative hand reached out, the fingers delicately touching the tip of the feather. "It's very expensive."

"It is," Eleanor agreed. "Everything was imported from Italy."

Sarah's hand dropped.

"Please take it," Eleanor said. "It's only a hat, and I have many more. I would consider it a great honor for you to have this one."

"You're going to need it today." Sarah's eyes went to Eleanor's face. "The sun will bake you alive."

"I have my trusty parasol," Eleanor countered.

"Oh—I know what!" Sarah's face brightened, and she

77

rushed out of the room, the hat in hand. "Wait right here. I have a gift for you." Within minutes she was back in the bedroom, holding out to Eleanor a navy-and-cream-colored parasol. "I made this myself, and it will just match your dress. See—even the lace fringe matches your jabot."

Eleanor took the parasol and unfurled it. Then she lowered it and inspected the delicate handcraft. Looking up at Sarah, she said, "This is beautiful."

"I design hats and dresses as well." Sarah blushed.

"You don't need to go to Newland's to buy your clothes," Eleanor exclaimed with candor. "Newland's needs to come to you so you can design clothes for them."

"That would be exciting." Sarah's face glowed with anticipation, and she hugged herself. "Maybe someday I'll be famous enough to go to New York."

"Or Europe?"

As quickly as the dreamy expression came to Sarah's face, it left it. "I probably won't ever get away from Kansas."

Eleanor came to stand behind Sarah. "You can if you want to. Only yesterday Bradley Smith—"

There he was, back in her thoughts again!

Eleanor inhaled deeply and said, "Only yesterday Bradley told me that he's the kind of man who makes his opportunities. You can be that kind of woman, Sarah."

"Like you?"

Eleanor thought a moment, then nodded her head. "Yes, like me."

"I don't know that I'm that strong."

"All of us are, when we're fighting for something we really want. You just haven't found a goal worth fighting for."

"Sarah." An older woman's voice called from the landing. "Your breakfast is ready."

"Your mother?" Eleanor asked.

"No—my mother's dead. That's our housekeeper."

"Sarah, do you hear me?"

"Yes, Clementine, we'll be right down." Sarah turned to Eleanor. "You are hungry, aren't you?"

"A little," Eleanor said, "but I'm more interested in getting Jeffrey out of jail. Where did your father go?"

Sarah picked at her skirt. "To visit a friend."

"Do you have any idea when he'll be home?"

"It won't do any good," Sarah replied.

"Perhaps not." Eleanor smiled reassuringly. "But I want the opportunity to talk with him myself."

"Probably not until late this afternoon."

"That's not so good," Eleanor mumbled. If she intended to arrive at Hunt Cattle Station today, she would have to be at the general store at three o'clock. She did not know Bradley Smith well, but she knew him well enough to know he was a man of his word. Cook would leave her if she were not at the store on time. And she did not relish the idea of facing Bradley Smith if he had to make a special trip to town to get her.

"What are you thinking?" Sarah asked.

"That I'm going to have to devise an alternate plan." Eleanor caught Sarah's arm, and the two of them walked out of the room. "Now, let's see what we have for breakfast. Today I'll need all the nourishment I can get."

The two women descended the stairs and walked into the large kitchen. The curtains were pulled aside, the shades up, and sunlight poured into the room.

"About time you got down here, young lady." Her thick white hair pulled into a tight coil on the nape of her neck, Clementine O'Darby had a fist firmly planted on each plump hip. "Food's getting cold quick."

Sarah kissed the housekeeper on her cheek. "Sorry, Clemmy." Then: "I'd like for you to meet Eleanor Hunt."

79

Shrewd eyes moved from the top of Eleanor's head to the bottoms of her feet. "Morning, Miss Hunt. Right glad I am to meet you. What brings you to Blissful?"

"Her father owns Hunt Cattle Station," Sarah supplied as she pulled a chair from the table and sat down. "And she's Jeffrey's attorney."

"Hrumph!" Clementine bustled to the table and began to serve the meal. "That young fool is gonna need a good 'un, he is. Got hisself in a passel of trouble. Lord, help poor Mister Lang."

The lament piqued Eleanor's interest. She sat down across the table from Sarah. Picking up her napkin, she unfolded it and laid it across her lap. "Why poor Mister Lang and not poor Mister Masterson?"

"Appears to me that anybody with a mind wouldn't have to ask that question," Clementine returned. "And to add to his grief, David is much worse. As soon as word came this morning, the mayor headed out to the Rocking W."

Eleanor held the navy blue and cream parasol above her head with one hand and dabbed a lace kerchief against her cheeks with the other. She was thankful for a restful night at the Cravens' home. But even a bath and the delicate cotton dress afforded little relief from the heat. The bonnet she had chosen to wear was doing precious little to shield her from the sun, the parasol doing only a fraction more. Already she had discarded her gloves.

"How much farther, Mister Ebersteen?"

The old man leaned his head over the side of the buggy and spit. Shifting the cud of tobacco around in his mouth, he mumbled, "About three miles. We still got to go by the cutoff to Stanwood Ranch."

"Everybody seems to live off this road," she commented and unconsciously ran the kerchief around her neck. "We've already passed the turnoff to Hunt Station."

"Yep, reckon that's why it's called the main road." He gently slapped the reins across the horse's back. "Giddap, Bertha."

Frank Ebersteen was rude, insufferably rude, and had been from the minute Sarah Cravens had introduced him to Eleanor at the livery stable. But Eleanor soon discovered if she wanted to get to the Rocking W in order to question David Lang, even to see him alive, she had no choice but to hire the man, his trusty buggy, and the horse.

Eleanor twisted on the wooden seat, trying to find a more comfortable position. When she found none, she sighed. If she were not so stouthearted, she would be disappointed. No one in Blissful except Sarah was inclined to help Jeffrey, and even Sarah was hiding something. Eleanor suspected this morning that Sarah knew more than she was telling, perhaps even knew whom Jeffrey thought had written the elusive note. The mayor had done an excellent job of letting her know where his interests lay. Openly uncooperative!

Eleanor figured that both Barber Cravens and Sheriff Hix were in Lang's back pocket. Well, she was not! And she was not going to let any of them stand in the way of her investigating the facts of Jeffrey's case. She would question David Lang . . . despite Frank Ebersteen and Bertha. And she would eventually find Early Dobson.

Suffocating in the dust and heat, Eleanor opened the first three buttons of her suit and pulled the lace collar aside. "Can't we go any faster, Mister Ebersteen?"

"Nope." Although he never raised his voice, his tone was emphatic. "Bertha's accustomed to this speed. Wouldn't want to upset her. She's like me. Old and constitutionalized."

81

Slowly the miles clicked by. By midday they reached a small creek, and Ebersteen pulled the wagon aside. "Not much farther to go, but Bertha wants to stop here awhile," he announced. "We'll refresh ourselves with some cool water."

Eleanor stared at the narrow stream. Only one tree was in sight, and that was quite a ways from the creek. The afternoon sun bore down. But she did not contradict Frank Ebersteen. After all who was she to deny Bertha an opportunity to stop for the midday meal? She merely hoped that when she was old and constitutionalized, someone would be as considerate of her. Eleanor climbed off the wagon and walked around, while Frank and Bertha headed for the water. She fluffed the bows and lace trim on her gown as best she could, but the heat had wilted them too.

After he drank, Ebersteen filled his hat with water and poured it over his head. Raking his thin, wet hair out of his face, he asked, "You really a lawyer?"

Eleanor started. This was the first time the man had initiated a conversation with her since she'd employed him. "Yes."

"Your paw don't care that you're doing a man's job?"

Eleanor made no attempt to keep the sharpness out of her words. "He cared, Mister Ebersteen. Like you, I just happen to have a strong constitution."

"Yep, I reckon so." Ebersteen pulled a piece of tobacco out of his pants pocket and cut himself a plug. "Guess you're gonna find it easier out here to be yourself and not worry much about whether you're doing a man's or a woman's work. Most of the time we're doing a lot of both."

Eleanor was rather surprised at the old man's philosophy. She moved to the foot of the tree and sat down on a crop of dying grass. "Why are the people of Blissful so prejudiced against Jeffrey?" she asked.

Frank chewed for a long while, then spat. Eventually he said, "Mister Lang done a lot for us out here. Because of him we finally got the railroad. Folks don't take kindly to a city slicker coming along to steal our cattle and kill our people."

"But Jeffrey says—"

"He says! That's all! Again the old man spoke emphatically without ever raising his voice. "Nobody found that note Masterson kept talking about. And Rocking W hands found Jeffrey with cattle from their herd."

"Maybe they were helping David with the rustling," Eleanor suggested.

"Nope." Frank spat again and wiped the back of his hand across his mouth. "Whittier respects his men and pays them good. They don't need to rustle cattle."

"Maybe they lied to protect David."

"Maybe."

Frank looked up at the blue sky, sparsely dotted with small white clouds, and squinted. Grunting, he pushed to his feet and shuffled to the wagon. "Reckon it's time for us to be moving on, if we expect to make the Rocking W today. Sure don't know what you wanted to prove driving out here. I can tell you one thing, you ain't gonna be well received, ma'am. You sure ain't."

"I'm sure I won't." Eleanor walked to the wagon. Climbing aboard, she unfurled her parasol. "But I didn't take this job because it was easy, Mister Ebersteen. I became an attorney because of the challenge. I'm quite accustomed to dealing with difficult people."

The wheels turned, and the wagon jostled to a start. "Maybe in Cheecago, but not out here on the frontier."

"People are people, and, Mister Ebersteen, I *do* understand human nature." Eleanor primly patted a loose curl into the black snood that bound her hair. "I know Whittier Lang was rather nasty yesterday, but he

83

was speaking as a bereaved father, nothing more. Although he'll probably be angry and withdrawn, he'll understand that it's my duty to question his son."

"Tell you, ma'am, them human natures you been studying in school and in Cheecago sure are different from the ones we have around here. Kinda makes me think of a kid learning to shoot a gun. He starts with a target, and soon he gets to where he hits the bull's-eye all the time. When it comes time for him to kill something that's alive and moving, the story is altogether different."

Eleanor laid her palm on the leather handbag that held her paper, pen, and ink. She was quite ready to interview David Lang. It would not take her long to trip him up in his lies. Archer Cormack had taught her quite well. "I've graduated from target practice. I'm quite accustomed to dealing with people from all walks of life."

"Lady, out here we don't walk through life. We fight through it. And speaking of fighting—" Frank pulled the reins and stopped the horse as four riders approached "—looks like we done met some of them human natures you're such an expert at dealing with."

The approaching men were rough—even rougher than the ones Eleanor had seen in Blissful—and she thought she'd seen the worst. Their hats, pulled low over their bearded, unkempt faces, were dirty and stained, as were their worn clothes. Each wore a gun belt with two revolvers.

"Howdy, Ebersteen," one of the men called out. "Where you headed?"

"Rocking W," he answered.

As if ducking out of the sun, Eleanor moved on the seat, subtly pulling her handbag so that it rested in her lap. She unfastened it and slipped her hand into the front pocket.

The men drew nearer, two staying in the middle of the road, one moving to Ebersteen's side of the wagon. Another stopped his horse close to Eleanor. In horror she stared at the man—the one she had seen through the window of the train yesterday when she arrived in Blissful. Up close he looked even more dirty and repulsive.

Although he was astride the horse, it was evident he was short and squatty. His face, unusually ugly, was cold and aloof. The eyes were a cutting gray—the same color as the leather vest he wore—and at the moment they were fixed on Eleanor. "Well, well," he drawled. "Look who we got here. Who's your passenger, Ebersteen?"

"Eleanor Hunt," she answered, returning the blatant stare without a quiver. "Who are you?"

The man laughed. "Right feisty, ain't you, lady? Thought so yesterday when I saw you on that train. Yes, sir, I was ready to come inside and get you right then."

Eleanor never smiled. "I asked who you are."

The man pulled his soiled hat off and flourished it through the air. "Haggarty, ma'am. Saul Haggarty, foreman of the Rocking W, at your service."

"I'm glad to have made your acquaintance, Mister Haggarty. If you'll have your men remove themselves, Mister Ebersteen and I shall be on our way."

"Hunt, you say?" Haggarty squinted at her. "You belong to the Hunt Cattle Station?"

"No, I don't belong to the cattle station," Eleanor answered, "but my father owns it."

"Alexander Hunt's daughter?"

"I am."

"That low-down manager of yours wounded Mister Lang's son." Haggarty seemed to snarl the words. "We don't know if the boy is gonna live or not."

"I'm on my way to the Rocking W now to visit with

85

David," Eleanor said.

"Mister Lang don't want any of you Hunts on the place."

"Whether he wants me to visit is not the issue, Mister Haggarty. I intend to do so. This isn't a social call. I'm on my way to question David about the rustling and the shooting."

"Look, lady," Haggarty snarled, "just turn this buggy around and head back to your place. The Langs don't want nothing to do with the Hunts."

"Come on, Miss Hunt," Frank said, "let's me and you turn around and head back to town."

"No." Eleanor laid a calming hand over Frank's. "This man is not going to frighten me with his blustering."

"Well," the driver muttered under his breath, "he does me."

"Now, Mister Haggarty, as I said before, I want you and your men to remove yourselves."

"What if me and my men don't want to, ma'am?" Again Haggarty laughed, and the others joined him.

Eleanor whipped a derringer out of her purse and leveled it at Haggarty. "I should hope to persuade you, sir, that you and your men *do* wish to remove yourselves."

Haggarty eyed the small pistol. Reaching up, he tugged the brim of his hat. "You shouldn't point a gun, ma'am unless'n you intend to shoot it."

"I don't and I do, Mister Haggarty."

One of Haggarty's men kicked Bertha's rump, causing the wagon to lurch and knock Eleanor off balance. She dropped the derringer, and it slid under the wagon. Laughing, Haggarty reached out and snaked an arm around her waist to swing her in front of him. Her bonnet slipped off, and she gagged as she inhaled his foul breath.

"Well, pretty lady, seems like you're gonna have to be

86

right nice to me, now, ain't you?"

Frank leaped to his feet and grabbed for Eleanor, but old age and stiffness caused him to stumble and fall. "Put her down. She ain't done nothing to you."

Although Eleanor struggled, Haggarty held her firmly against him with one arm and guided the horse away from the wagon with the other. "Now, old man, if you know what's good for you, you'll settle down. I'm gonna take the little lady for a ride."

"No, you ain't." Frank reached for his rifle.

One of Haggarty's men whipped his revolver from the holster.

"Don't," Eleanor screamed, but already it was too late.

The shot echoed through the air. The driver groaned and clutched his chest. Slowly he crumpled over the seat, blood oozing between his fingers and staining his shirt.

"Mister Ebersteen!" Fear for the old man's life gave Eleanor an extra rush of adrenalin. Kicking herself free, she fell to her feet, scrambled up, and ran to the wagon. Out of the corner of her eye, she saw Haggarty dismount and pursue her. His men laughed and egged him on. As she reached the wagon, as her hands touched the old man, Haggarty's hands clamped over her shoulders; he jerked her around into a painfully tight embrace.

Her nostrils filling with the stench of him, Eleanor twisted her head from side to side. "Please," she begged, her hands clawing at his, "let me take care of Mister Ebersteen. He may be dead."

"Just relax. He ain't hurt all that bad." Haggarty was breathing heavily, his chest heaving from exertion. Sweat ran down his cheeks onto his neck.

"Make one of your men look at him."

"Neb,"—Haggarty laughed—"look at the old man."

One of the men rode closer to the wagon and peered at the prostrate body. Complying to the letter with

87

Haggarty's command, he did no more than look. "He ain't hurt bad," he whined. "Just a flesh wound, I figure."

"See there, he's all right. Even if he wasn't he's getting to be pretty old. It's time he met his maker."

Still Eleanor pounded her fists against Haggarty's chest. His grip tightened, his head lowered, and his lips moved directly toward hers.

"Fight me," he begged, his eyes wild with pleasure. "I love a woman with spirit."

Eleanor was filled with revulsion when she felt Haggarty's body responding to hers. As quickly as she'd begun fighting, she ceased and went limp in his arms. Haggarty laughed and his grip loosened. Eleanor carefully eased her hand behind her, groping for the parasol.

"Now, then," Haggarty mumbled, a hand sliding down her midriff to rest on her stomach, "that's more like it. Just relax. You're going to enjoy this."

"Yes," she murmured, "I think I shall." Her fingers circled the handle of the parasol. Before he knew what she was doing, she swung her hand in front of her and hit him squarely across the face. He yelled, more from surprise than pain, Eleanor guessed, and released her to stumble backward. Eleanor took the opportunity to lunge forward to freedom.

Quick to recover his wits and balance, Haggarty was after her. He caught a handful of nainsook and pulled so hard that he ripped the cotton. Her heart pounding furiously, Eleanor tripped on the hem of her gown and sprawled across the road. In the distance she heard the cowboys laughing.

"You shouldn't have done that." Haggarty dropped to his knees and knelt over her, his hands busy unfastening his gun belts. He tossed them aside. "I was gonna be kind to you, but not now."

His eyes greedily devoured her, and Eleanor recoiled in revulsion. His hands yanked the lace collar and jabot out of her dress. Eleanor wanted to claw his eyes out as he ogled her exposed breasts. Snarling low in his throat, he pressed his wet lips against her skin.

She shuddered and tried to wiggle out from under him, but could not. With one hand he locked her wrists above her head; with his leg, he pinned her body to the ground. She felt his hardness press against her and tossed her head, her bonnet rolling to the side, her snood coming loose. Tendrils of black hair brushed across her face.

"I like a spirited woman," Haggarty repeated as he lifted himself and unfastened his belt. "Fighting makes it more worthwhile."

"I swear I'll kill you," Eleanor spat.

Haggarty threw back his head, his laughter drowning out that of his men. He clawed at his breeches, pulling them down to reveal his arousal. "Maybe. But it'll sure be worth it if you do. Ain't had me a nice piece in a long time."

"Think there'll be enough to go around, Saul?" one of the men called out, the question followed by more raucous laughter.

"Don't know if I want to share this one or not, boys. But I reckon we'll be doing Mister Lang quite a service. Why, he'll be thanking us."

"If we live to tell about it," another of the men yelled. "There's a rider headed this way. Riding like a bat out of hell, and straight for us."

Cursing, Haggarty pushed up on his knees and began to fumble with his breeches. While he did this, Eleanor gained her second wind. Then she rolled over away from him, grimacing when something hard dug into her back. She lifted herself up and turned to see Haggarty's guns. Moving quickly, she grabbed the guns and scooted beneath the wagon. Haggarty was close behind her when she heard the shooting.

Over her shoulder she saw him turn and run; his men also scattered in different directions, leaving him alone.

Taking advantage of the diversion, Eleanor closed her fingers over the handle of his pistol and withdrew it from the holster. Although it was larger and heavier than hers, she felt no qualms about using it. Now was her opportunity to have her revenge; she determined that Saul Haggarty would pay for humiliating her. She looked around for him, but he was hidden. She crouched behind the front wheel of the wagon.

The stranger rode closer. "Well, Haggarty—" She could not see the man, but felt relief when she recognized that familiar husky tone; it was Bradley Smith, come to her rescue. "Looks like your men didn't think enough about you to stay around."

"They gone to get help. Don't shoot, Smith. I ain't got no gun."

"That's not like you." Bradley nudged his horse forward.

"That fool woman was fighting so much, she knocked it out of my hands."

"And just why was the woman fighting?" Bradley asked, an edge of steel in his voice.

"Don't rightly know," Haggarty said. "When she told us she was heading for the Rocking W, we was trying to persuade her to change her mind. All of a sudden, she whipped this derringer out of her purse and started shooting at us."

As he talked, Haggarty moved from behind the scrubby bush, his hands raised, and Eleanor saw he had no revolver. He edged toward his horse and slowly dropped a hand. Then she saw the brilliant reflection of silver. He had a knife and was going to kill Bradley. Concern for him overrode her own sense of humiliation and her desire for revenge. Without thinking, she shoved away from the wagon and the protection it afforded her. Aiming the revolver, she fired at Haggarty.

The bullet hit him at the same moment that he released the knife. He groaned and lurched forward, catching the side of the wagon to keep from falling. With horror Eleanor watched the knife sail through the air. While her shot did not deflect Haggarty's weapon, it warned Bradley, who dodged the knife. Instead of the blade penetrating and fatally wounding him, it merely grazed his abdomen. Cursing, Haggarty clutched at his shoulder and ran toward his horse. Bradley gasped in pain and caught his stomach. Haggarty mounted the sorrel and galloped away.

Eleanor ran from behind the wagon toward Bradley. Then she heard Ebersteen's faint moan. Unsure which to help first, she looked from the wagon to Bradley.

"Take care of him." Blood seeped through Bradley's fingers. "I'll be okay. It's just a scratch."

"Are you sure?"

"I wouldn't say so, if I weren't," he gritted between clenched teeth. "Are you all right?"

"I'm fine," Eleanor said.

"Good. I'm going after Haggarty."

"No, you're not," she shouted and raced to his horse, grabbing at his leg. "You're wounded. You don't even know where Haggarty's headed, and I need you here. Mister Ebersteen is badly wounded, if he isn't already dead."

"He . . . ain't . . . dead," Ebersteen said weakly.

"He's hurt, Bradley, and we need you." She could not have him going after Haggarty in his condition.

"How are you, Miss Hunt?"

"I'm fine, Mister Ebersteen." She looked up at Bradley. "Please, don't go."

"Go see about him," he muttered and slipped off the horse.

Not wasting a second, Eleanor raced to the wagon as the driver sat up. He reached up and touched a huge knot on his forehead.

"I . . . reckon I'm all right. Where's them varmints? I'm gonna tear them apart limb from limb."

Relieved, Eleanor laughed. "They're gone. What about your chest?"

Ebersteen looked at her rather blankly for a second, then lowered his head and gazed at his shoulder. He pulled the blood-soaked material aside. "Just a scratch. My head hurts worse than this." He looked up. "What made them leave?"

"Bradley," Eleanor answered.

"Let's get you to the house so we can take care of your wound, Frank," Bradley said. "You feel like driving?"

"I'm fine," the old man insisted, his gaze landing on Bradley's bloodstained shirt. "You're the one who needs doctoring."

"I'm okay."

Eleanor looked from one to the other, her gaze finally coming to rest on Bradley. "Neither of you is okay. You're both wounded and in need of medical attention."

Still holding a hand across his stomach, Bradley stooped and picked up the parasol and bonnet, both of them soiled. Tossing them into the bed of the wagon, he looked disapprovingly at the disheveled woman who stood in front of him.

"What are you doing out here by yourself? I thought you were in town with the Cravens."

"I'm not by myself." She sounded slightly defensive.

"It's only by the grace of God that you're not," he said. "Because of your stupidity, both of you could be dead."

Eleanor chafed beneath his anger. "But we're not."

"No thanks to you." Bradley snapped. "I told you yesterday that I didn't want you going off by yourself."

Eleanor drew to her full five feet, seven inches. Still

92

he was taller than she, and she had to look up at him. "Bradley Smith, I am accustomed to doing what I please, when I please. You are my father's employee, not my bodyguard or my keeper. Is that clear?"

"Oh, yes, ma'am, it's quite clear. You really had the situation under control, didn't you?" He grimaced.

"I was doing all right by myself," Eleanor retorted. "If I hadn't shot Haggarty, this wound could have been even worse than it is."

Bradley's eyes softened. "That's true, ma'am. Because of you, I only have a scratch."

"For God's sake, it's more than a scratch," she snapped and caught him by the arm to lead him to the back of the wagon. "You're going to stand here and bleed to death."

Bradley jerked his arm loose. "Frank, take Miss Hunt on to the station. When you get there, Eleanor, send Frisco into town to tell Carl what happened."

"Why can't you?" she demanded.

"Because I'm going to the Rocking W. Lang has to assume responsibility for his men's actions."

"You'll do no such thing," Eleanor exclaimed. "Haggarty roughed us up a bit, but he didn't really hurt us any." Worried about him, her eyes anxiously scanned his pallid complexion. In his present condition she was not about to let him know the indignities Haggarty had made her suffer. Futhermore, this was her score to settle. "We have more important things to worry about right now. Get into this wagon, and let us take you to the station."

Taking Bradley unawares, Eleanor pushed him into the wagon, "Mister Ebersteen—" she tugged Bradley's shirt out of his trousers "—take Bradley's horse and ride into town. Tell the sheriff what happened. I want him to go to Hunt Station and take a statement. I'll drive Bradley home in your wagon."

"Yes, ma'am." Frank moved more quickly than he had all day.

"I said I'm okay," Bradley muttered.

"And *I* know you're not." Already he was too weak to fight anymore. Helping him sit on the back of the wagon, she unbuttoned his shirt to pull it aside. Nauseated by the thought of blood, let alone the sight of it, Eleanor felt her stomach churn, and her throat knotted. "Your—your gut is split open."

His face twisted in pain, Bradley laughed. "I have a cut, but my gut is not split open."

Remembering what he'd said earlier about men dying from such wounds, Eleanor did not find his words reassuring. She leaned down and ripped off the bottom of her petticoat. Kneeling in front of him, she took a deep breath, eased one hand around his waist, and with the other began gently to swab blood from the wound. "I'll try not to hurt you," she reassured him.

When the flow had been checked, Eleanor lifted an ashen face to find Bradley staring intently at her. "I'm—" she licked her lips "—not hurting you, am I?"

"No," he whispered. He pushed a strand of hair out of her face, his fingers brushing against her cheek. "Did—did Haggarty—"

"No."

Eleanor was not about to tell Bradley how the man had physically and sexually abused her. Haggarty belonged to her; she would exact her own revenge. She hated him anew each time she thought about his touching her, but he was not worth thinking or talking about. Bradley was.

She had been aware of his virility from the moment she saw him at the depot, but this was her first encounter with the enormity of the attraction between them. Her head dropped, and she gazed at his torso. Forgetting the wound, she became fully aware of his naked, warm flesh beneath her palm. With each breath he drew, his body

94

moved against her.

"I'm so glad you happened to be riding by."

"I didn't 'happen' to be riding by. I rode into town to get you." He moved the lace jabot, making her aware that the upper swell of her breasts was clearly exposed. She felt heat rush to her face. "Sarah told me where you had gone."

His touch infinitely tender, without any sexual overtones, was the sweetest caress Eleanor had ever experienced. Her heart thudded loudly; she was sure Bradley could hear it. She swore he could feel it. Beneath her hand she felt the warmth and the gentle movement of his body as he breathed. "What about your business?"

"It can wait. I was worried about you." His voice was soft. "David Lang's condition has worsened."

"I heard," she murmured, raising her head to stare into his face.

"Yet you were headed out to the Rocking W?"

"I had to." Silently she pleaded for his understanding. "Jeffrey's life depends on it."

He nodded. "Promise me you won't travel anywhere without an escort. Feelings are running too high now for safety."

Eleanor rose and reluctantly removed her hand from his body. Hoping he did not notice her trembling, she tied the ends of the bandage around him. She was much too close to him. She felt his breath against her face. She focused her eyes on the pulse point at the base of his neck.

"Promise me," he said.

"I promise."

She went to step away, but his hands caught her waist, and he pulled her close. She lifted her face to stare into his eyes; yet their bodies never touched.

His voice was husky. "I owe you my life."

"Not really."

95

"You're a pretty good nurse."

"Doctor," she murmured, mesmerized with the passion that burned in his eyes.

"Doctor?"

She smiled at his confusion. "I wasn't sure if I wanted to be a doctor or an attorney."

"What motivated your choice?"

The conversation was pedantic, but the current between them was strong and vital. They communicated on a much higher level.

"Blood." She felt herself swaying closer to him. "I can't stand the sight of blood."

"Then I owe you more than my life, Miss Hunt."

When he leaned forward, Eleanor knew he was going to kiss her. And she wanted him to. She hungered for the taste of him; she wanted to know the sweet touch of his lips on hers. But she would not . . . experience had taught her the difference between love and desire. She doubted she would ever find love, and what Bradley Smith felt for her was simply desire—no more. Once, in her innocence, she would have settled for less than love, but not now. Because she had wanted a man, she had compromised herself. Still he had refused her, and it had taken a long time for her to regain her integrity.

She flattened her palms against his chest and, careful not to hurt him, pushed back. Distance served to strengthen her resolve. "You owe me nothing, Bradley. I would have done it for anyone. And please . . . call me Eleanor." She forced her stiff lips into a smile. "Now, I think it's time for us to get to the cattle station."

"We haven't known each other long, Eleanor, but it's definitely time for us to do this."

Bradley caught her shoulders in his and pulled her closer to him. His lips gently brushed against hers—not a kiss, but rather a promise of a kiss.

Shaking from the onslaught of emotion caused by his

96

touch, Eleanor pulled away from him. When she spoke, her voice quivered. "Don't ever do that again."

"I won't."

They stared at each other for what seemed like eons. Then Eleanor dropped her face and turned away. That was not the answer she had wanted. Grabbing the side of the wagon, she hoisted herself into the seat and picked up the reins. She heard Bradley shuffling in the back and knew he was lying down.

"No, Eleanor Hunt." His voice seemed to float over her shoulder, "I shall never do that again. That was merely an introduction. Next time, I promise I'm going to kiss you properly."

Chapter 5

Next time, I'm going to kiss you properly!

Bradley's promise, as potent as the caress itself, skittered deliciously through Eleanor's body. Her expression softened; her lips trembled into the tiny beginning of a pleased smile. Then she pulled tight her running emotions. She would not allow herself to respond to this man. Wounded or not, he was a man—a most desirable man—and as such a mortal enemy.

She knew that giving in to Bradley, no matter how insignificant the giving might be, would irrevocably alter her life. A kiss—a real kiss—had the potential of changing everything and she was not yet ready for that. Futhermore, Bradley Smith would never settle for mere kisses.

Soft, husky laughter teased her ears.

"There won't be any next time." Her voice did not carry as much assertion as she would have wished, but it was calm. "I choose the men I allow to kiss me 'properly,' as you put it."

He laughed again, the sound accusing her of lying. She brushed it aside.

"Because you're a wounded man, I let you take liberties I otherwise would not have allowed." Instead of

99

reaching for the reins, she straightened her snood and pinned it in place.

"You didn't allow me anything," Bradley answered. His voice sounded weary now. "I took what I wanted."

Worried, Eleanor squirmed on the seat and looked over her shoulder at him. Her concern, however, did not keep her from responding to his audacity. "No man ever takes from me, Bradley Smith. Never be so foolish as to think otherwise. I haven't made it as far as I have by allowing men to take advantage of me or my sex."

"You wear quite a chip on that shoulder of yours, don't you?"

"Yes, I do." Defensively she added, "I didn't put it there. Men like you did. But I wear it proudly."

"I'm sorry," he said quietly. He paused, then added in those same quiet tones, "Since a man put it there, it's up to a man to take it off. I guess you know what that means, don't you?"

Eleanor quickly averted her face. The kindness in his voice touched her deeply, too deeply for her to make a banal retort. She did not wish for him to see the tears that filled her eyes. "It can mean anything you want it to mean."

"A man has hurt you, hasn't he?"

Yes, a man hurt me. Several men have hurt me. Not deeming to answer aloud, Eleanor reached for the reins and twined them through her fingers. For a moment she stared at her hands—usually soft, with beautifully manicured nails. Now they were scratched, with traces of dried blood on them. Her nails were broken and ragged. Two days on the frontier, and she was changing, internally and externally, whether she wanted to or not. She frowned, and a slight shudder ran through her body. She was frightened for herself. No longer was she in control of her life; she seemed to be a victim of her destiny.

"Who was he?"

100

Her low *giddap* set Bertha into a slow gait down the dusty road. "It doesn't matter." But it did matter. Every time she thought about Radford Vaughn, she felt a heavy weight settle on her heart. "I've gotten over it, and I've forgotten him. I'm a tough woman."

"A fighter," Bradley added.

She thought she heard admiration in his voice. "I think so. Aunt Edna says I'm a survivor."

"Who's Aunt Edna?"

Now Eleanor grinned. "My father's older sister. She came to live with us when my mother died."

"She doesn't have a family of her own?"

"No . . . she—she never married," she answered a mite defiantly as she prepared herself for some sort of retort. When none came, she added lamely, "She worries about me because I'm an extremist."

After another silence, Bradley said, "It's all in the way you look at it. I prefer to think of you as an extremely passionate woman."

Her laughter was hollow. "Men must always reduce everything to a sexual experience."

"Some men may, but not me. I was thinking more about life than sex. Any woman thrust into a situation can fight the odds and win. But only a passionate woman will always try to fight and win, no matter how many battles she's lost along the way."

"In addition to being a drifter and a cowboy, you're a philosopher." Eleanor changed the subject; the discussion was getting entirely too uncomfortable for her. Bradley was too close to the truth. Emotionally she was treading on new territory and was unsure of herself.

"I believe there's a little of the philosopher in all of us."

Bradley shuffled in the wagon, and Eleanor looked over her shoulder. He pulled his hat over his face.

"I'd offer to drive for you, Eleanor," he murmured,

101

"but my stomach is hurting dreadful, and I'm getting weaker."

"Thanks for the thought," she replied. "Try to get some rest. Bertha and I will do just fine."

Slowly, so slowly time seemed to pass. By now the mid-afternoon sun beat relentlessly down upon them. Eleanor's bonnet afforded her little protection against the blistering rays, and already her skin was burning. Lying still in the wagon, Bradley seemed impervious to even the weather.

When she thought he was surely asleep, he spoke and startled her. "The other fellow was someone in your past. What about Jeffrey?"

She did not equivocate this time. "You heard me tell Sarah he's like a brother to me."

"I wasn't sure whether to believe you or not. He seems to be a rather possessive brother, if you ask me."

Eleanor laughed. "If you're referring to the scene in the jail, he was trying to irritate you. I gather he succeeded."

"Do you have anyone waiting for you in Chicago now?"

"That's none of your business." She turned to look at him.

Bending his knee and planting one foot firmly on the floor, Bradley pushed himself closer to the seat. But he did not sit up. "I'm making it my business."

"You're in no condition to make any demands."

Bradley's raspy chuckle touched her ears. "Lady, you have no idea what my condition is." Grimacing against the pain, he scooted closer to the seat, this time pushing into an upright position. "I asked if you are courting anyone in particular."

Eleanor's breath caught in her chest. Unable to look at him and fearful that he would read her expression, she turned her head. After a long minute, she said, "No,

I'm not."

He shuffled more. "Good."

"I don't see that it affects you one way or the other."

"Then you can't see too well, Eleanor Hunt. Or maybe you're more of an innocent than I thought, and I need to spell it out for you. I'm interested in you."

Eleanor tightened the reins and guided the horse around a huge hole in the road. Several seconds elapsed. "I'm sure you are. It's simple curiosity. You're probably wondering about a twenty-five-year-old woman who's an attorney and never married."

Again he laughed; again the sound titillated Eleanor's nerve endings to send shivers of pleasure over her body. "That, Eleanor Hunt, is no mystery. Any woman with your drive and ambition would frighten most men."

"Most men, but not you?" she asked over her shoulder, a strange feeling settling about her. When he did not answer, she looked around.

One hand firmly planted over his abdomen to hold the wad of material in place, he climbed to the front of the wagon. When he sat down, he clamped his hand more firmly over his cut and grimaced.

"You shouldn't be stirring," she snapped. "You're going to start bleeding again."

"Probably. But I'll have to be moving about pretty soon anyway. We're almost home. Just over the rise."

"I can hardly wait," she breathed.

Eleanor had often imagined the first time she saw Hunt Cattle Station, but none of the scenes she'd played out in her mind could equal the magnitude of the moment itself. She caught her breath and waited impatiently as Bertha slowly clopped up the hill.

"This is the first time you've been out here?" Bradley asked.

"Yes." Her eyes eagerly scanned the horizon for the first sign of . . . the house. Strange, she had wanted to

103

call it home. Yet she had never been here and knew virtually nothing about it.

"How come?"

"Whenever my father came out here, my mother and I would take a trip to New York or to Europe." Her answer was casual enough that she hoped he would not prod any further to learn the real reason she'd never come west.

"Oh, yes," he drawled, "forever buying clothes."

Eleanor smiled and nodded her head. The wagon crested the small hill, and she saw Hunt Cattle Station for the first time. Unable to control a small gasp of pleasure, she gazed at the maze of pastures and fences on one side of the road. On the other sat the main house and the fields that stretched to the horizon and were ribboned with waterways.

"It's so huge," she breathed. "I never dreamed of it being like this."

"Wouldn't be, if it were not for Harry." Bradley's gaze idly ran over the buildings and land that comprised Hunt Cattle Station.

"I never realized how much he contributed to the company."

Bradley scrutinized her strangely for a second, then said, "It was Harry's dream to convert the station into a functioning ranch." His hand swept over the pastures to the left of the road. "We breed fine cattle, horses, and mules."

"What kind of horses?"

"The Scotland's Glory and Gladis."

Trees were planted around the main house; otherwise the landscape was flat and seemed to stretch for miles in every direction. Huge barns, stables, and feeder pens were so numerous that Eleanor lost count of them.

"Over there—" Bradley pointed to the other side of the creek that ran through the middle of the property— "we have our crops."

"Your own private world," Eleanor murmured.

"Not quite, but each rancher likes to think it is. No matter what we do, civilization is catching up with us with amazing speed."

They drew nearer the main house, an imposing two-story frame structure with a veranda that wrapped around three sides. Orchards had been planted on both sides of the house, and trees lined the wooden sidewalk that led to the main road and the driveway.

"It's so different from what I had imagined," she breathed. "Rather than a cattle station with miles and miles of feeder pens, it looks exactly like a home."

"It *is* a home," Bradley said. "This is the only home Harry Prescott knows."

Bradley's words irritated Eleanor. While she had heard nothing but good about Harry Prescott, from her father on down, Eleanor had her doubts. By not riding into Blissful himself, Prescott had made it clear that he was unconcerned about the arrival of Jeffrey's attorney. Now Bradley was telling her this was the only home Prescott knew and in fact, was giving Prescott credit for creating the cattle station.

"It looks like a woman had a part in the planning of this," Eleanor quietly explained.

"Yeah . . . well, perhaps she did," Bradley said disinterestedly.

"No," Eleanor said, then felt compelled to add, "my mother would have been the only woman involved."

"And she wasn't, because you and she were always trotting around the world, buying clothes," Bradley added.

Eleanor cut him a sharp gaze. "It's really none of your concern, but Mama had no interest in Papa's business, especially this part of it in Kansas. She really despised Kansas. She refused to come out here and never allowed me to. However, before you make any more disparaging

105

remarks about Mama's or my interest in the cattle station or our trips to Europe, let me tell you, my father was most satisfied that Mama didn't wish to come out here. He encouraged our traveling."

"Did you inherit your mother's dislike of the place?"

Eleanor's head slowly turned, and again she stared at the house. No, she thought, always honest with herself, it was cultivated carefully through the years. Papa had discouraged any interest she showed in the business and had forbidden her to travel to Kansas with him. He had always taken Jeffrey with him. Always Papa had taken Jeffrey, never her or Mama!

Mama had always been there to kiss the hurt away. The closer Papa and Jeffrey had become, the closer she and Mama had grown.

Eventually she said, "I suppose I allowed Mama's dislike to influence me. If I hadn't, I would have come sooner."

"What do you think about the place, now that you've seen it?"

"It's beautiful. I can hardly wait to meet Prescott."

Bradley grinned. "Me too."

Eleanor guided the horses up the road past the bunk house to the elegant home. A ranch hand out in the yard raced across the lawn through the orchard grove to the driveway to unlock and open the gate.

"What happened?" He looked directly at Bradley.

"Trouble with Lang's men, Arty," Bradley answered. To Eleanor he said, "Stop here."

"Here, ma'am, let me help you." Arty rushed forward to assist Eleanor. On the other side Bradley slowly climbed down. "Hey, Boss, you been hurt?" Arty asked, concerned.

"Yes, he's hurt." Eleanor moved around the wagon to Bradley. "One of Lang's men wounded him with a knife. He has a gut wound."

Bradley laughed shortly, then grimaced in pain. "Don't worry, Arty. It's just a cut."

The ranch hand raced toward the house. "I'd better get Harry."

"No," Bradley called, "I'm all right."

"You are not," Eleanor said and insinuated her shoulder under Bradley's arm.

Looking over her head, Bradley said to the hired hand, "Take care of unloading this wagon."

"For God's sake, Bradley," Eleanor exclaimed, looking down at his bandages, which were now saturated with blood. She coaxed him forward. "You're dying, and all you can think about is unloading my luggage."

"It's not your luggage I'm thinking about. It's the supplies," he gritted between clenched teeth. "But I don't know why. You've fired me, haven't you?"

"Don't be silly." Eleanor's head jerked up and she stared into his pain-whitened face. Her voice softened, and she said, "I can't fire you. As you said, you work for my father, not for me."

"Thank you." Although his lips twisted into a semblance of a smile, his voice was tight. "You're so magnanimous, Miss Hunt."

"I try to be, Mister Bradley."

By this time they were at the steps that led to the side entrance. The door opened, and Eleanor looked up. Standing on the veranda was one of the most beautiful women she had ever seen. Tall and slender, she wore a blouse, a leather vest, a split riding skirt, and boots. Her hair, a deep, rich auburn except for a white streak, was swept into a chignon on the crown of her head, the austerity of the style broken by gentle waves that softened the classical lines of her face. Blue eyes framed with long, dark lashes moved back and forth between Eleanor and Bradley.

"What happened to you?" Her voice was husky.

"Tangled with Haggarty and came out on the short end of the stick." He straightened up and looked from the older woman to Eleanor. "Miss Eleanor Hunt, I'd like for you to meet Harry Prescott, superintendent of Hunt Cattle Station."

The abrupt introduction was like a slap on the cheek. Eleanor gaped at the woman. "Harry Prescott."

"I was christened Harriet, but my name is Harry." She pressed her hand against the base of her throat and stared at Eleanor in amazement. As if she realized she were staring, her cheeks flushed with color, and she dropped her gaze.

Slightly embarrassed herself and curious about the woman's perusal, Eleanor said, "I—I thought you were a man." She looked at Bradley. "And you allowed me to think this."

"I did." Offering no apology, he walked into the foyer, the screen door slamming behind him. Through the wire netting Eleanor stared after him. He untied the thongs of his holsters, then unfastened his gun belt to hang it on the rack just inside the door. "I guess I was a little upset that you were acting so uppity and knew nothing about our operation out here."

"Here." Harry abruptly opened the door and moved into the washroom to the long table, where she picked up the pitcher. "Let me take a look at your cut. Do I need to send for Doc?"

"I already have." The woman's concern irritated Eleanor, who joined them.

"Oh?" Harriet turned, the pitcher suspended in the air, and looked at Eleanor.

"I sent Mister Ebersteen back to town on Bradley's horse," Eleanor said, unaware of her proprietary air. Slipping past Harry and taking the pitcher from her, Eleanor moved to Bradley's side and filled the basin with water. "He's to bring the doctor and the sheriff."

108

After she set the pitcher down, she turned to Bradley. Fighting her aversion to blood, she determined to be the one to take care of him. She did not understand her motives, but knew she was not going to take the time to analyze them now. Her hands were gently pulling the checkered material from his shoulders when she said, "Here, let me help you out of your shirt, so I can change the bandage."

Bradley grinned at Harry. "Like I told you, she's quite efficient . . . and headstrong."

"So I see," she said dryly. "I'll go get some medicine and clean bandages."

"It's going to need some stitches, Harry," Bradley said, "and I don't think we ought to wait for Doc. No telling when he'll get here."

"Probably not any time soon," Harriet said as she disappeared through the door. "I understand Irma Jane's delivering today."

Eleanor unwrapped the bandaging material from around Bradley and swallowing the bile that rose in her throat, then thoroughly examined the cut. After she wrung the water out of the washcloth, she lightly sponged the wound. "It's not bleeding nearly so much."

"Stands to reason." His voice was weak, and she raised her head and looked into his pale face. "I don't have much more blood to lose."

"Am I hurting you?"

His eyes settled on hers. "Yes," he whispered.

As she stared into those green eyes, darkened with pain, Eleanor knew he was not talking about physical hurt. As he had done since the minute she first met him, he was speaking on a sexual level. Clearing her throat and averting her gaze, she said, "You need to lie down."

"You're right, lady," he said in a husky voice. He grabbed a towel from the peg and clamped it against his midsection, then moved past her. Long strides carried

109

him down the hallway. "That's where I'm going."

"What about the medicine and some clean bandages?" Eleanor trotted behind him.

"I'm getting pretty weak and will soon be lying down. I'd rather it be on my bed than the floor of the washroom." He opened a door and stepped into a large bedroom.

His, Eleanor thought as she lingered in the doorway and looked at the heavy masculine furniture. When Bradley sat on the edge of the bed, he groaned. Eleanor rushed into the room and knelt in front of him, both her hands resting on his knees. His eyes darkened, and Eleanor felt she was drowning in the eddy of swirling emotions.

"What can I do to ease the pain?" she asked.

Bradley chuckled softly and reached out to tweak an errant lock of hair that defied her hair net. "Eleanor Hunt, if I were to answer that question, you'd take fright and run away from me."

She returned his smile. "I said pain," she murmured, "not passion."

"Is not passion the sweetest pain known to man?" he countered.

"And is not man the greatest pain known to woman?" Her hands slid down his legs. "Here, let me help you out of these boots."

Again Bradley chuckled and extended a leg. "Are you afraid of love, Miss Eleanor?"

"No, Mister Bradley, I'd welcome love." Eleanor tugged the boot off and moved to the other foot. "But I do abhor lust, and I'd say that nine times out of ten, that's all a man offers a woman."

"That many times for you?"

His voice compelled her to look up, but she did not. "I learn my lessons quickly. Once was enough for me."

"Surely there have been countless men who've wanted

110

to marry you."

"Yes." She stripped the socks from his feet and tossed them aside. "But I found that a man offers less than lust when he proposes marriage."

"You're bitter?"

"No, resolved that I want more out of life than most women do. I would never be happy keeping house and knitting and quilting."

Bradley stood and laughed shortly. "With your wealth, I can't imagine your ever having to do that." He unfastened his belt and began to unbutton his trousers.

Eleanor's eyes widened. "What are you doing?"

Taking these bloody clothes off," he answered. "From the way you talk, I assume you're not an innocent."

"Perhaps not," Eleanor conceded and stood to her feet, "but I'm not a wanton, either . . . and I do choose whom I look at."

"Then you'd better decide real quick if you're going to choose to look at me, lady." His hand brushed carelessly over the swirl of stomach hair, beneath the waistband of the trousers.

"You're most indelicate!" Eleanor hastily averted her head.

Bradley laughed. "Untrue, and one of these days I'll prove it to you."

She heard the swish of material as he stepped out of his trousers. The belt buckle hit the floor with a ping. The bedsprings creaked beneath the weight of his body.

"I'm covered. You can look now."

Eleanor turned and he sat on the edge of the bed, the sheet draped over his midsection. He held the towel to his abdomen. In the hallway she heard footsteps.

It's Harry," Bradley announced and lay down. "You'd better leave if you're squeamish. This isn't going to be pleasant for either of us."

"I'll be all right."

Harry walked into the room and set a large tray on the night table. She opened a bottle of whiskey and poured a glass. "This is mine," she said and handed him the bottle. "This is yours."

"Thank you." He took a long swallow.

"Drink it down. You're going to need all of it." Harry smiled grimly and began to lay out her instruments: scissors, a large needle, leathery-looking string.

Eleanor felt her stomach begin to churn. Her palms grew clammy, and perspiration beaded on her upper lip. She turned gray around the mouth. "What's that?"

"Sinew," Harry answered. "About the best thing to bind a cut. Learned it from the Indians. Get on the other side of the bed and help me."

"Let her go, Harry. She's not good at this." His hand tightened around the neck of the whiskey bottle as he settled into the mattress.

"Good or not," Harry said, "I need help, and she's it."

"I'll be all right," Eleanor promised and moved to the other side of the bed to clasp Bradley's free hand in hers.

Harry picked up the glass and began to pour whiskey over the cut. Bradley gasped and tensed, his grip almost breaking Eleanor's hand.

"Sorry," Harry murmured, "but it has to be done, Bradley."

"I know." He spat the words. "It burns like hell."

"Your sojourn in the netherworld has just begun. This isn't going to be any better for a long time." Harry threaded the needle, then held the tip over the candle flame. Bradley took several long drags of whiskey.

"What are you going to do?" Eleanor felt the color drain from her face; her legs felt as if the bones had melted and she was going to crumple to the floor at any moment.

"Sew it up," Harry answered.

"If she doesn't," Bradley said between clenched

112

teeth, "I'm going to have an ugly scar and women won't love me."

"If I were you—" Eleanor's voice was a mere whisper "—I'd take my chances."

"Can't," he grunted as Harry pushed the needle through his flesh. He perspired profusely and grasped Eleanor's hand more tightly. "I—I don't—have a wife yet."

Eleanor felt no pain as his fingers nearly crushed hers. She wanted to close her eyes, but found she could not. While she felt nauseated, she was fascinated at the skill with which the woman treated the wound. By the time Harry was through, Bradley had finished the bottle of whiskey and was asleep. Eleanor was standing at the window, deeply breathing in the fresh air.

"Let him rest for a while," Harry said and gathered up her things and placed them on the tray. "Sleep will do him good."

When Harry left, Eleanor returned to the bed to reach down and brush a lock of hair from his forehead. Her gaze moved to the beard-shadowed cheeks and chin. She could not resist touching him, delighting in the feel of his whisker stubble against the tips of her fingers. She lowered her hand and let it rest lightly on the mat of crisp hair above the bandage. She felt the rise and fall of his chest and the steady thump of his heart against her hand.

"Sweet dreams," she murmured and tucked the sheet beneath his chin.

One of his eyes opened and he grinned drunkenly at her. "They will be, if you'll kiss me good night."

Eleanor returned the grin. "Then you'll have to dispense with sweet dreams."

A hand slipped from beneath the covers and caught hers. "Is that any way to treat a wounded man?"

"No," she whispered and delighted when his fingers gently squeezed hers, "I think not." She leaned down

113

and planted a chaste kiss on his cheek.

"May I have more?" His grip did not tighten, nor did he pull her closer.

She straightened. "No, a wounded man could stand no more."

"Is that a promise that when I'm better I can expect more?"

Eleanor smiled and pulled her hand from his grasp. "I make no promises, Bradley Smith. Now get some rest."

Chapter 6

"It's beautiful. In fact, the entire house is." Eleanor walked around the guest bedroom on the second floor of the house, trailing her fingers over the lovely furniture. Strangely enough, she was jealous, jealous of this woman who seemed to be more a part of her father's life than she was . . . a woman he had hired to handle his cattle station. A woman whose identity he had kept secret from her and her mother. Eleanor turned to face Harry, who stood in the doorway.

"Even from the outside, the station obviously has a woman's touch. I had a feeling that a woman had contributed a lot to all this. How long have you been running it?"

"About seven years. You can't begin to imagine how things have changed around here during that time."

Papa allowed Harriet Prescott to manage the cattle station, but would not allow her to become a part of the Chicago office. He had closed her out altogether when Jeffrey had become his ward. That old familiar pain of rejection shafted through Eleanor; she found it difficult to reconcile, and even more difficult to accept. Eleanor moved to the window. Her back to Harry, she caught the curtain in one hand and pulled it aside to gaze at the front lawn. "Bradley said it was the fruition of your dreams."

"In a way, it is." Her arms folded over her chest, Harry leaned against the door frame. "But most of the credit goes to your father."

Eleanor tensed. Although Harry's words were innocent enough, they bothered her. "Papa has never talked much about the station."

"Perhaps he didn't think you were interested."

Oh, yes, he knew, Eleanor thought, but only said, "Perhaps." She turned and with that piercing stare she learned from Archer, looked directly into Harry's eyes. "I was quite surprised to learn that you're a woman."

Not appearing to be intimidated, the older woman returned the candid gaze. "Most people are."

"Papa never told us."

Harry pushed away from the casement. "Perhaps he thought there was no reason to since I was . . . only an employee."

"Perhaps," Eleanor replied thoughtfully. When she thought about it, her father had discussed none of his business with her or her mother. "It's different out west. I guess it doesn't matter if you're a man or woman."

"Does your father know that you're out here?"

Eleanor did not answer immediately. While Harry was not unfriendly, the woman was not friendly either. "No,"

"Why are you here?"

"To—help Allen defend Jeffrey."

"Archer Cormack couldn't come?"

"No—" she licked her lips "—not at this time."

Harry's blue eyes were piercing. "There were no other attorneys in Chicago who could have taken the case?"

Eleanor had come to expect censure from a man, but not from a woman. She automatically squared her shoulders. "There were, but Allen and I are the best for

116

the case. Both of us have been trained by Archer Cormack."

"You keep referring to Allen. Even in your letter you led us to believe that it was he who was coming. Yet you're the only one who arrived."

"I'm sorry about that," Eleanor apologized. "I wanted desperately to come and was afraid that if Papa found out, he would—"

"Stop you," Harry concluded.

Eleanor nodded. "Allen is coming after he finishes some work he's doing in Springfield. But I had to come also. You see, I believe in Jeffrey's innocence."

Harriet smiled; her expression softened. "I'm not questioning your being an attorney or your coming here. I'm proud of you. Being an independent person myself, I admire your having defied the conventions of society. I'm questioning your reason for having come. I know as well as you that it was not altogether to defend Jeffrey, was it?"

Unwilling to answer, Eleanor continued to watch the older woman. Harriet walked into the room to stand in front of the dresser. She idly ran the tips of her fingers over the brush set. "Do you believe in fate, Eleanor?"

She shrugged. "I suppose so."

"I do. I believe you were destined to come to Blissful."

An eerie feeling swept through Eleanor, and she hugged herself. The woman seemed prophetic. "Blissful is a fairly new town."

Her gaze on the brush she now held in her hand, Harriet fanned her thumb over the bristles. "You have a date with destiny. Jeffrey's defense was merely the excuse you needed."

"Are you saying I don't care about him?"

"No. I'm saying that you would have come eventually—with or without Jeffrey." She laid the brush down and moved closer to Eleanor.

"Yes, I think so. I've wanted to ever since I was a small child." Her eyes glowing with excitement, Eleanor said, "I know this sounds strange, but when I drove the buggy up to the house, I felt as if I'd been here before."

Harriet chuckled softly, and her eyes twinkled. "I know the feeling, but I guarantee you've never been here. Probably your father or Jeffrey has talked about it so much that you feel as if you know it."

Eleanor smiled wistfully. "No, he never discussed it with me, nor did Jeffrey. He wrote to me occasionally but it was only to complain."

"He's never been happy out here. I've tried to persuade your father to let him return to Chicago, but Alex is a stubborn man." Her voice became indulgent. "Once he's made up his mind about something, there is absolutely no changing it."

"You know my father quite well, don't you?" Eleanor asked.

"I—I suppose I do. We've worked together for many years." She smiled, and her voice became crisp. "Well, I'll leave now. I'm sure you're tired and want to rest."

"I am tired," Eleanor agreed, "but you needn't rush on my account. I . . . don't know much about this part of my father's life. I'd like to learn about it. Please, tell me all about Papa and Hunt Cattle Station."

"Another day," Harry said kindly and moved across the room. "Get some rest now."

Not wanting to be alone, Eleanor asked, "What about the sheriff? Someone will need to talk with him."

"Don't worry." Harry stopped at the door. "By the time Carl gets here, Bradley will be awake. I'll have a tub and some water sent up so you can bathe."

"I'd appreciate that."

"We've already eaten lunch. Shall I have Gaspar bring you something?"

118

"Gaspar?"

Harry's eyes twinkled. "Gaspar Jones, our cook."

"Yes, please, I'm quite hungry."

"Harry!" A gravelly voice called up the stairs.

"That's him now," Harry said.

"Whittier Lang's here to see you."

Harry raised a brow. "I'll go see what he wants."

When Harry walked into the parlor, Whittier was standing in the center of the room, holding his hat in his hand. She was surprised at how old he looked. At least ten years had beed added to his fifty-five. He stepped forward and said without preamble, "I rode over to apologize for what happened to Miss Hunt and your manager."

"I expect more than a few hollow words, Whittier," Harriet said. "I expect you to get rid of those gunslingers you hired. They're dangerous."

Whittier's eyes narrowed. "Ever since I've known you, Harry Prescott, you've been like this—never grateful for anything."

"Haggarty wounded Frank Ebersteen and Bradley and frightened Eleanor. And you think you can walk into my house and casually say 'I'm sorry' and everything will be all right! Well, it isn't."

"A man must do what he must," Whittier answered. "I'll protect the Rocking W at any cost, Harry."

"And you are." Harry had no doubt he meant what he said. Whittier Lang was not known for idle threats. "I want you to know that my men are armed and will protect Hunt interests at all costs, too."

"If only it wasn't for all this damned rustling," Whittier muttered. "Look what it's done to us—making enemies out of friends."

"Not all of us," Harry returned. "Some of us have left this in the hands of the proper authority and are willing to let them apprehend the wrongdoers."

"Well. I'm not willing to sit around and let my cattle be stolen. I'll be leaving now, Harry. That was all I came to say." He walked to the door, stopped, and turned around. Reaching into his shirt pocket, he pulled out a letter. "Almost forgot . . . Fanny asked me to deliver this to you, since I was coming this way."

Harry stepped forward and took it. She looked at the writing, but did not recognize it. "How's David?"

"No better. He's still in a coma," Whittier said, his shoulders sagging slightly. Then he straightened his back and spun around to wag a finger in her face. "Tell that Miss Hunt to stay away from my place. I won't have her disturbing me or my family. Do you hear?"

"She's only defending her client," Harry answered.

"He's still in a coma. And I mean it, I don't want her coming near my place."

After Whittier Lang left, Harry walked over to the window and opened the letter.

A man, tall and lean, wearing an obviously expensive suit, opened wide the door to his hotel room. "Hello, Harriet."

"Hello Lyle." Harry tried to keep her voice calm, yet it had a certain breathless quality to it. The door closed softly as she walked to the center of the room, her silk skirt rustling gently about her feet.

"I wondered if you'd come."

Standing beside a large oval reading table, she turned to look at him. "When I received your message this afternoon, my first inclination was not to."

His thick white hair gleamed beneath the overhead lamp. Age had not dimmed the startling beauty of his blue eyes or the masculinity he exuded. Lyle Pearce was as attractive today as he had been twenty-seven years ago,

120

perhaps even moreso.

"I'm glad you had second thoughts . . . whatever the reason."

She relaxed a little more, even managed a small smile. "Curiosity . . . I wanted to see how you'd changed since I saw you last."

His lips curled into a beguiling smile. "Have I changed that much?"

"No."

"Neither have you." His eyes ran the length of her silk gown. "You've always looked lovely in green, and particularly that shade. It reminds me of the forest in springtime."

"I didn't wear it because of sentiment, Lyle." But even as she uttered the words, Harry wondered at their truth: she'd no doubt spent hours going through her wardrobe before she'd chosen this particular gown. "I wore it because I like green, because I feel lovely in green."

His eyes darkened. "You've never forgiven me, have you?"

She averted her head and laid down her black and green parasol. "Yes, I've forgiven and had almost forgotten—until I received your message today. Then it seemed as if I'd been carried back in time." She remembered the frightened, unwed eighteen-year-old who'd given birth to her first child in a brothel. Her lover had abandoned her in her hour of greatest need.

"I'm truly sorry, Harriet." His voice was husky, and she knew that he was moving toward her.

Before he'd taken many steps, she turned around. Coolly she said, "Call me Harry."

He stopped and stared at her sadly. "You've always been Harriet to me. Somehow I can't think of you as a Harry."

"I've been Harry for the past twenty-five years," she answered.

121

"We were only kids," he said. "I was scared silly of the sheriff and his threats."

Finger by finger she pulled the black gloves from her hands and dropped them over the parasol. "You were a kid," she admitted, "but you were also an outlaw who had every right to be frightened of the law."

"I couldn't come to you at first," he explained.

"I know, but later you could have. I lay awake at night, wondering where you were and when you were coming back. It was the waiting and not knowing that nearly drove me insane."

"If I could do it all over again, Harriet . . . Harry, I wouldn't leave you. I've missed you."

"Have you?" Her head down, she gazed at the gloves, running the tips of her fingers over the soft material.

He walked to a table on the far side of the room and poured two glasses of wine from the crystal decanter. Retracing his steps, he handed one to her. "For old times' sake."

She took the glass, making sure their hands never touched, and lifted it to stare at the golden liquid for a second. Then she looked at him and said softly. "For old times' sake."

The years had been kind to him, she thought, her gaze curiously running over his physique. His body, still lean and straight, modeled his suit well. The dark blue material contrasted nicely with his white hair, the only evidence of his forty-four years.

He sipped the wine, then said, "It's too late for us, isn't it?"

"Yes."

"You're the only woman who's ever meant anything to me."

Harry smiled sadly. "If I'd meant that much to you, Lyle, you'd have come back to me. You'd have been there to console me."

"I knew you'd think that." He spoke rather brusquely and strode to the desk. Opening the tobacco box, he picked up a cigar. "You'll never know how many times I rode in this direction and always turned away."

"Why, Lyle?" Her fingers curled tightly around the stem of the glass. "Why didn't you come back to me?"

He leaned over the candelabrum to light the cigar and said between puffs, "I couldn't come back until I had something to offer you. I had to prove myself, prove that I could be something more than a petty thief."

"And now you have?"

He nodded, his face reflected in the glow of the candlelight. "There's nothing petty about me now, Harry. I'm a wealthy man. I own five thousand acres of ranchland and have investments in the east. I even have foreign investments."

"You've—never married?"

He shook his head. "You spoiled any other woman for me, Harry. I could never forget the time we spent together." He rubbed his fingers up and down the gold watch chain that dangled from his waistcoat pocket. "Have you thought of me?"

"Yes." She lifted the glass to her lips, never tasting the flavor of the wine as it slid down her throat.

"Harry, will you marry me?"

She turned from him as he spoke the words she would have given her life to have heard twenty-six years ago. "No."

He laid the cigar in an ashtray and moved to where she stood. Her back was to him, as he placed a hand on each shoulder. She felt the heat of his touch all the way to the bottoms of her feet. Even now, so many years later, Lyle Pearce had the ability to tear her up emotionally. "I love you, and you love me."

"You may be right, Lyle, but I still can't marry you."

"It's Hunt?"

"How did you know?" She lowered her head and stared into the wine, watching the bubbles as they surfaced one by one.

"There's little I don't know about you. You're going to marry him?"

"He's asked me."

"Do you love him?" He turned her around, his blue eyes piercing hers as they searched for an answer.

"He's been good to me, Lyle. He was there after you left."

He took the glass from her hand and set it on the reading table. Then he caught her shoulders and brought her close to him. "It didn't take you long to find solace in another man's arms, did it?"

She twisted out of his grip. "It took me a long time, Lyle."

"Does he know that you were a sporting lady who ran a brothel?" he asked softly.

"Yes," she whispered, then added in a louder voice, "and he also knows I lived with an outlaw for several years."

Lyle's shoes clicked briskly over the floor as he walked to the table and filled another glass, this time with whiskey. He quaffed the liquid in a single gulp. "Do you ever think about the baby, Harry?"

She wrung her hands. "Yes, I find myself thinking of her more and more, the older I get."

"I'm sorry," he apologized and walked to where she stood. Taking her hands in his, he squeezed gently. "I didn't mean to upset you. Does Hunt know about you and me?"

"Yes, I told him," she lied, looking at him steadily. She pulled her hands from his.

"Could it be that Alexander Hunt's daughter is adopted?" He paused. "That she is really our daughter?"

"No," she gasped and caught onto the back of the chair

124

to keep from falling.

Lyle continued to speak. "Eleanor Hunt recently celebrated her twenty-fifth birthday, was supposedly born in Kansas, and has blue eyes . . . like me. Hunt has never allowed her to come near the cattle station. Why, Harry?"

"Lyle, please believe me, our daughter died." Harry sank down into the sofa and nervously pleated the material in her skirt.

"That's what you told me, Harry, but I have reason to believe otherwise."

"Why?" she asked through numb lips.

"Someone who knows told me so," he said with a satisfied smile.

"Whoever told you Eleanor is our daughter is lying." She spoke quietly, marshaling her composure. "They don't know what they're talking about."

"*He*, Harry—not *they*. Jeffrey Masterson."

"Jeffrey." The word trailed into silence as she stared at Lyle in bewilderment. "How would he know this?"

"You're forgetting that he's the son Hunt never had, the son-in-law that Hunt wants . . . or at least thinks he wants," Lyle snapped.

"How did he find out?" Harry demanded, her voice rising.

"He found a loose key in your bedroom one day and soon discovered that it unlocked your personal safe."

Harry's legs gave way, and she fell onto the sofa.

"In it he discovered a diary that belonged to Abigail Hunt."

"Oh, my God!" Harry gasped, her hand fluttering to her breast.

Briskly Lyle crossed the room to pour another glass of whiskey, which he pressed into Harry's hands; then he sat down beside her. She lifted the glass to her numbed lips and swallowed the fiery liquid.

125

"Don't worry, Harry. He hasn't told anyone but me."

"Why you?" she whispered. "Why not me or Alex or Eleanor?"

"Masterson's smart, Harry. He's out to make a fortune, and to make it off others. He's not satisfied to steal a few cattle here and there. He's after big money, quick." The blue eyes caught and held hers. "Blackmail, Harry. He's planning on blackmailing you and Alex to keep him from telling Eleanor the truth. He's just biding his time."

"I won't be blackmailed," she said finally, "because it's not the truth."

"Part—if not all of it—is true," Lyle said gently. "Eleanor is adopted, and Alex has hidden the fact from her all these years. He doesn't want her to find out."

"I won't pay," Harry insisted. "I'll take my chances with the truth."

"You don't have to take a chance, love," Lyle said, his voice softening considerably. "I'll take care of the matter for you. I've dealt with men like Masterson before. If you give them enough rope, they always seem to hang themselves."

"I'll take care of myself," Harry said.

"No," Lyle said, "this time I'll do it."

Harry heard the promise, but not the significance of the words. For years she'd been waiting for the moment when she and Alex could build a life together; it looked like she would never know it. First it had been Abigail; now it was Jeffrey. "It seems like death and destruction follow in Jeffrey's wake," she murmured. "Because of him, Alex and Eleanor's happiness and my future are threatened, and Gideon's dead."

"Your Gideon?" Lyle's hand curled into a fist.

Harry smiled. "My Gideon."

From the first moment Gideon Davenport had set eyes on Harriet Frazier, he had been her champion. Until the day he died he'd have done anything in the world for her. A big, burly man, he was all soft and warm and friendly on the inside. Unsuited for a life of crime, he had refused to run with Lyle and the gang. Apprehended and sentenced, he served his five years in the penitentiary, then returned to work for Harry. Through the years he had been her dearest and closest friend—always there when she needed him.

"About two years ago he went to work for Whittier Lang as foreman of the Rocking W."

"What happened?"

"No one really knows." She leaned her head against the back of the divan and thought back to that night so long ago. "Gideon knew something was wrong. The day before David was shot, Gideon came to me and told me something strange was going on between Jeffrey and David. He figured it was the cattle rustling. I assured him that everything would be all right, that I would take care of it."

Her voice was teary. "But everything was not all right. I went to bed, and after that I'm not sure what happened. Jeffrey claims someone threw a rock in the office window and warned him about David's stealing cattle from his father at the Rocking W. He rode over there and was soon involved in a shoot-out. Gideon was killed, David wounded, and Jeffrey arrested."

"Did you see this note?" Lyle asked, his eyes glinting with interest.

She shook her head. "No one has."

Lyle took the empty glass from Harriet and placed it on the table beside the divan. "Beware of Masterson," he said. "He's dangerous."

"You and I know that, but Alex doesn't. As you said before, he wants Eleanor to marry him."

"I'm not going to let him," Lyle said. "I'll kill Masterson before I let him marry my daughter."

127

Harry sat forward, her fingers clinching the armrest of the divan. "Lyle, I don't want him to marry her either, but you must understand and accept that Eleanor is not your daughter. Please understand that. And don't worry about Eleanor. Jeffrey wouldn't be stooping to blackmail if he thought he had a chance of marrying her. Eleanor Hunt is not about to marry him."

"I want to see her," he finally said.

"No."

He laid a silencing hand over her mouth. "I'm not going to disturb her world, Harry. I promise. I won't tell her a thing about you and me. Under the circumstances, you did what you thought was best for her. She would have had no future as the daughter of a whore and an outlaw. I merely want to see her."

"Not if I have my way about it." Harry answered, then said, "I find it strange that Jeffrey would tell you about Eleanor's birthright."

"Not really. The world is quite small, when you think about it, Harriet—Harry. I met him and David Lang several months ago. I was negotiating to buy some prize bulls from them, imported from Europe for the purpose of interbreeding."

"Whittier's bulls," Harry murmured dryly.

"I didn't know that," he said. "I thought we were working on a legitimate deal. Masterson seemed to like me. Said I reminded him of his father. One night he got drunk and began to talk about Alexander Hunt and his daughter, laughing about the way he was going to pull the rug out from under the cattle baron. With a little more liquor and coaxing, he told me the story as he'd read it in Abigail's diary. I immediately knew that it was you and our daughter."

"Yes," Harry murmured, "I'm sure you did."

The ride home was long and thoughtful and painful for Harry. Lyle brought back the past too vividly and forcefully, and it frightened her to think that he was quickly becoming a part of her present. Damn Jeffrey Masterson! Because of him, Lyle Pearce could bring heartache to Eleanor as he had to Harry so many years ago. She would not allow that.

The thought that he'd gone through her personal safe angered her. He'd been careful to return everything to its original place, because she'd never suspected. In no way had he betrayed himself. While his deviousness angered her, his knowledge of Eleanor's birthright frightened her. She would not allow Jeffrey to hurt the child. She would not!

No matter what she thought of Jeffrey, however, Harry did not worry that he would tell Eleanor that Alex was her adopted father . . . that would not suit his plans at all. Thus, while he was biding his time, Harry would make the best of hers. She would find that note Jeffrey was talking about. Lyle was right; Jeffrey was smart. He had told the sheriff about it, but since then he had played it down. She wondered if it was a deliberate strategy on his part for people to discount the story altogether. For a while she had not believed in it, but now she did.

Evidently Jeffrey had hidden it quite well, holding onto it until the right moment, the same way he was holding onto his knowledge of Eleanor's birthright. He was unconcerned about the lives he might shatter or the devastation he might wreak when he produced it.

Well, Harry thought, she would take care of Jeffrey Masterson. He would not hurt another soul, nor would he take Hunt Cattle Station away from her. She would guarantee that.

The buggy clattered up the drive, and Harriet glanced up to see Eleanor silhouetted in the window of the study. She would not allow Jeffrey to hurt Eleanor.

Chapter 7

Eleanor had spent the first half of the evening studying the general ledger; now she read newspaper clippings. Preoccupied with taking meticulous notes, she was unaware several hours later that Bradley had walked into the office until he spoke.

"Are you planning to sit up all night?"

Looking at the clock, she laid down her pen and stretched. "I didn't realize it was so late. But you're a fine one to point an accusing finger at me. What are you doing up?"

"I spent the entire afternoon and evening sleeping," he answered, "but you didn't."

Eleanor leaned back in the chair and bridged her hands together in front of her. "How are you feeling?"

"Better." He sat down stiffly in the chair opposite the desk. "I'm hungry."

"I would imagine. You missed lunch and dinner. I wanted to awaken you, but Harry said you needed your rest."

"Where is she?"

"She had some business to take care of in town and left soon after dinner," Eleanor answered. "I wasn't sleepy, so I came in here to do some work."

131

"I've been quite worried about you." She leaned closer and peered into his face. "At least you have some color now."

"You do too." He smiled. "Or maybe it's that blue dress bringing out the color of your eyes."

Pleasure suffused Eleanor, and she smiled. Bradley grinned, and before she knew what he was doing, he leaned forward to touch her cheek with the pad of his thumb. The lamplight flickered golden on his face.

"First milk. Now ink. You should know by now that you write on the paper, not your face."

Feeling as if her blood were hotly racing through her body, Eleanor rose and walked to the wall mirror, where she pulled her handkerchief out of her pocket and dabbed at the ink. She had to put some distance between herself and Bradley. "Look at the notes I've been taking."

Bradley picked up the sheet of paper and scanned the figures in the three columns. "Are you doing all of this for Shea or yourself?"

"For both of us and for our client." Eleanor returned the handkerchief to her pocket and, still looking in the mirror, tweaked the curls that framed her face. "As Jeffrey said, he did purchase the cattle immediately after recorded rustling attempts. The number of cattle and dates of theft correspond with the purchase orders."

Bradley turned loose of the paper to let it flutter to the desk. "Could be coincidental."

She spun around. "Don't be obtuse. Only a fool would set himself up like this. And whatever else he may be, Jeffrey is no fool."

"Are you sure about that?"

Before she could answer, she heard a noise and looked up to see Cook standing in the doorway, tray in hand. "How about a cup of coffee before I go to bed?" he asked. "Freshly brewed just for you, Miss Hunt."

"I would love it, Gaspar. You seem to be a mind

reader." Eleanor moved to the desk and cleared a spot for the tray. "Thank you."

The bewhiskered face beamed. "Why, thank you, ma'am."

"I'm not Miss Hunt," Bradley said dryly, "but if you don't mind, Gaspar, I'd like a cup also."

"Just so happens I thought about you, too, Bradley. Saw you hobbling down this way. Brought you a cup and something to eat, too." He cast them a toothless grin as he quietly slipped out of the room.

Eleanor unwrapped Bradley's sandwiches and handed them to him, then served each of them coffee. Her cup in hand, she walked to the window. After several swallows, she said, "It's too blatant, Bradley! I can't believe Jeffrey is guilty. Does anyone else have access to the books?"

Swallowing his food, Bradley shifted his weight carefully. "Not at the time Jeffrey was keeping them."

"David is guilty."

Bradley finished off his sandwich and set the half-empty cup on the tray. "Maybe both of them are guilty."

Not taking exception, Eleanor nodded slowly. "I've been thinking that myself."

"But you must take the bank account into consideration," Bradley said thoughtfully. "It looks like Jeffrey accumulated a great deal of money during the time he's been out here."

"Anyone could have made it look like that, Bradley. The town belongs to Lang. Everyone I talked to yesterday told me as much. Maybe he persuaded Early Dobson to testify against Jeffrey. You know how loudly money talks."

"Say you're right." Bradley spread his hands out. "Why would someone go out of his way to frame Jeffrey?"

Her eyes narrowed, Eleanor returned to her chair. "To

133

protect David Lang. That's why. Why did you say out of *his* way? Perhaps it may be out of *her* way."

Bradley grinned and lazily lifted a hand to run it through the thick brown hair. "Equality all the way down the line, Attorney Hunt, even to rustlers."

Shaking her head, Eleanor leaned forward, closer to him. "I was thinking about the note Jeffrey received."

Bradley sighed. "Back to the note."

"I know you doubt the note, but I happen to believe Jeffrey. He said it could have been written by a woman."

"Man or woman, what difference does it make?"

"It makes a great deal of difference," Eleanor explained. "This woman may have been working with David to frame Jeffrey."

"The whole thing is preposterous! I don't know of a woman David was particularly interested in. Furthermore, I don't know why Jeffrey didn't go to Harry or the sheriff with his suspicions." Bradley rose, his hand protectively hovering over his wound, and moved to the window.

"Jeffrey wasn't sure. He was going to investigate, to find out for himself. As influential as the Langs are, Jeffrey would have been a fool to have gone to the sheriff or to anyone with only his suspicions. And simply because you do not know of a particular woman in David's life does not mean there isn't one."

"No," he agreed wearily, "it doesn't."

"If you're honest, Bradley, you'll admit that no matter how much evidence Jeffrey might have had, sentiment would have been against him. He's an outsider." She did not know why she was trying to persuade Bradley to believe in Jeffrey. She only knew she had to.

Again Bradley raked his hand through his hair. "You're right. A woman, you said?"

"That's what Jeffrey thinks. Who could it be?"

"How should I know?" He shook his head, then turned

134

around. "I didn't monitor David's personal life."

"I talked with Sarah about it today," Eleanor murmured. "She said there was no particular woman in David's life. Yet I have the feeling she knew more about it than she wanted me to know. She was extremely nervous when I questioned her about it."

Bradley was quiet for a long time before he said, "What about Sarah and David?"

Eleanor shook her head. "I thought of that, but dismissed it quickly."

"How about jealousy? Maybe she and David were friendly before Jeffrey came out here, and Jeffrey took her away from David."

"Jealousy is always a good motive," she admitted, "but Sarah said there was nothing between her and David, and I believe her. How about fear as a motive?"

Bradley hiked a brow. "Whose would that be?"

"Harry's," Eleanor replied. "I could see where she might fear Jeffrey."

"Harry!" Bradley exclaimed incredulously. "That makes absolutely no sense at all."

"Yes, it does," Eleanor answered. "It's obvious that Papa is training Jeffrey to take over the business, beginning with the cattle station. Harry stands to lose her position, and she might be willing to do anything to keep it, especially if this place means as much to her as you and she have led me to believe."

"Not Harry. I grant she does not like Jeffrey, and it's true she wanted your father to take him away from the station, but she's not a rustler and would never do this to him. Harry Prescott is not that kind of woman."

"Perhaps she would. Hunt Cattle Station is probably all she has in her life, Bradley. And she could see it slipping through her fingers when Papa refused to send Jeffrey back to Chicago." Eleanor emphasized her point. "That is bound to have angered her and perhaps drove

135

her to extreme measures."

"Why don't you ask Harry about it?" he said scathingly. "I heard the buggy a while ago. I imagine she's had time to get to her room."

"I shall. I don't put as much stock in Harry Prescott as you do."

"I'm a good judge of people, Eleanor, and I know Harry Prescott. She wouldn't frame Jeffrey, no matter how despicable he might be and no matter how good her reason."

Eleanor returned the even gaze. "You don't like Jeffrey either, do you?"

"No. He's a weak man, hiding behind lies and deceit. I see nothing in him to admire."

"And because he's weak, you think him guilty."

"I repeat, counsellor, I don't know if he's guilty or not. For Harry's sake, I hope not."

"What about my father?" Eleanor's eyes blazed.

Bradley's eyes glinted fiercely. "Your father is well able to take care of himself. He wasn't concerned about Jeffrey's innocence or guilt. His only concern seems to have been Alexander Hunt and his meat-packing empire."

Eleanor's hand clenched into a fist. "You have no right to say that."

"I read the telegram he sent. His orders were to hire the best attorney she could for Jeffrey—one who, no matter what the evidence or circumstances, would prove his innocence. Money was no consideration. At any cost, Alexander Hunt's reputation has to be saved."

"You seem to have a low opinion of your employer. Does it extend to his daughter also?"

"Does it matter what I think?"

"No." She unclenched the hand and automatically began to straighten the papers on the desk. "It merely puts matters into proper perspective."

"Perspective, maybe. But I doubt you know what proper perspective is. Thank God, Shea is going to handle this case. Maybe he won't be so personally involved that he can't see an inch in front of his nose."

"Since you're so damned intelligent, Mister Smith, why don't you tell me what proper perspective is?"

In one greedy motion, Bradley caught her in his arms, locking her hands between their bodies. "I'll show you, woman." He crushed her mouth with his and trapped the words between their lips. For one fleeting second before his face lowered to hers, Eleanor stared into eyes that were hot, intense, and filled with a hunger that was angry because it was so urgent. So bittersweet was the kiss that it singed Eleanor to the very bottom of her soul.

His mouth guided hers to open wider, and his tongue slid into her mouth. Her palms against his chest, she tried to push against him, but when she felt the bandage beneath her fingers, she pulled back. If he felt the pain, he never showed it. His grip tightened; his kiss became more desperate. Against her will, Eleanor gave herself up to the delicious insanity of the moment, to the wonderful delirium that engulfed her.

The kiss was hard and harsh like the man—explosive. Inside she burst into a million tiny particles, all of them light and fire. She was aflame, burning to the very core of her being. She clung to him, afraid she would die if she did not. His energy seemed to flow into her, but she knew that when he withdrew she would be hollow, in need of him again. He was creating a void in her that only he— Bradley Smith—could fill.

As abruptly as he'd brought her into his arms, he threw her aside. The force of his shove sent Eleanor off balance, and before she could regain her equilibrium, she felt herself falling backward. In the next instant she collided with the wall, her hair coming loose to tumble about her shoulders. Her chest hurt as she took long-needed oxygen into her lungs.

Without a backward glance, without a word, Bradley Smith strode out of the room. The door slammed, and Eleanor stood alone in the jarring silence. His words rang in her ears. Bradley Smith not only seemed to hate her father, but was transferring that hatred to her. Although she'd have liked to think differently, she knew her father's first interest was to save his reputation and his financial empire. That was a characteristic of Alexander Hunt she accepted. But she did not appreciate Bradley's so contemptibly throwing it in her face.

She straightened up and gently daubed her bruised lips with her fingertips. He'd been rough, but the kiss had pierced her very soul. Bradley Smith had touched her where no one else had ever dared to reach. She almost hated him for that.

She drew in several deep gulps of air to steady her heart and regulate her breathing. Unable to stand on her trembling legs any longer, she melted into the chair, moments later to catch her hair and repin it to the crown of her head. Very slowly she regained her wind, and her sanity returned.

Of course, she was emotionally embroiled in Jeffrey's case, but not to the point of losing her objectivity: she knew what proper perspective was. She was merely gathering information that she would eventually pass on to Allen. She was fully aware that he, not she, would be the defending attorney.

Part of you might claim that, a small voice said, *but you don't really believe it, Eleanor. This is your case. None of what you've been doing can be classified as research for Allen. You want this case; you want it so much you've gone to great lengths to get it, and will go further, if necessary.*

Disturbed by the direction of her thoughts, Eleanor moved to the desk and straightened the papers. When she was through, she picked up the lamp and walked out of the study. Automatically her gaze shifted to the room down the hallway, to Bradley's room. Eleanor was drawn to him as if he were a magnet.

With a determination born to only the strongest, she pulled her gaze from his door and slowly walked up the hallway to the bottom landing. Lamplight pooling around her, her left hand on the banister, she climbed the stairs without a backward glance.

When she reached the upper landing, she stopped and looked down the hall. A sliver of light radiated from beneath Harry's door. Eleanor had told Bradley she would talk with Harry, and she would.

As soon as she set her lamp on her night table, she moved down the hall and hesitated only momentarily before she tapped lightly on Harry's door. She had been braver with her accusations when she was talking to Bradley. She felt some trepidation at the thought of facing the woman herself.

"Harry," she called, "I know it's late, but if you're not too tired, I'd like to speak with you."

The door opened, and Harry stood in the wedge of light, wearing her cotton dressing gown and holding her hairbrush in one hand. "It must be important."

"I'm worried about Jeffrey. I wanted to ask you about the note."

Closing the door, Harry stepped into the hallway. "The note?" she repeated.

"The one Jeffrey received the night David was killed."

"What about it?"

"Jeffrey told me a woman wrote it."

"The mystery thickens," Harry said softly. "First there is a note that no one but Jeffrey has seen. Now the note was written by a woman. This is news to me."

"You know nothing about it?"

Harry folded her arms over her chest and leaned against the door. Her eyes narrowed. Without answering

Eleanor's question, she asked, "Who wrote the note?"

"I don't know, and I don't think Jeffrey does, either," Eleanor answered.

Their eyes locked. In a dangerously quiet voice, Harry said, "What are you really asking me? What do you want to know?"

"The person who framed Jeffrey had to be someone with something to lose. Since the note was written by a woman, I believe it was one who cared about David or—"

"—was a woman who stood to lose her position on a particular cattle station," Harry finished.

Refusing to break visual contact with Harry, Eleanor nodded.

"I don't know if the note exists or not, but this you can believe: I did not write it, and I am not trying to frame Jeffrey Masterson. I am not a cattle thief or a murderer. This station means a great deal to me, but my integrity means more. Had I wanted to frame Jeffrey, I would have done a better job of it."

"I'm sorry, Harry," Eleanor said, not understanding why she had pushed the older woman so hard.

Harriet's voice softened when she said, "Please stay out of this. You're getting much too involved. Let Allen Shea handle Jeffrey's defense."

Her eyes wide, Eleanor backed away, "First Bradley . . . now you. Of course I'm involved, but not so much that I can't be objective where he's concerned. I happen to understand him . . . you don't."

Harry returned to the dresser and began to unpin her hair. "Perhaps not."

"He didn't want to come west, Harry. Jeffrey is not like Papa. His life will never be a company. Yet, to please Papa, he came."

"Why didn't he stand up to your father?" Harry asked coolly. "You did."

"Jeffrey's more sensitive than I am," Eleanor said, "but he's not as bad as you and Bradley are making him out to be. I know him, Harry. He's been like a brother to me for the past sixteen years. Why are you staring at me like that? If you have something to say, say it!"

Harry sighed and shook her head. "No, I have nothing to say. If you search long and hard enough, you'll find the truth. Now, if you don't mind, Eleanor, I'd like to go to bed. I'm tired . . . I have a headache,"

"Say that the note does indeed exist, Harry. What woman could have written it?"

Harry turned, her hand closing over the doorknob. "I don't know, Eleanor. David has always been a popular boy. It could have been any of his female friends—or any of Jeffrey's enemies."

"You do not think it curious and more than coincidental, Sheriff Hix, that Early Dobson abruptly quit his job and headed for parts unknown, never to be heard of or seen again?" Up for hours herself, Eleanor was in the sheriff's office the next morning at eight o'clock. "The only man who can identify Jeffrey as the person who opened this account, made periodic deposits, and closed it?"

"No, ma'am, I do not!" Carl pushed back in his chair and crossed his hands behind his head. Morning sunlight poured into the office. "If you knew anything about the frontier mind, ma'am, you would know that people are constantly moving on. All of them are running from something in their past and are looking for the pot of gold at the end of the rainbow. Of course, you can't know this because this is only your third day in Blissful."

"I'll ignore your sarcasm, Sheriff," Eleanor snapped.

"It wasn't sarcasm, ma'am, and for your own good,

141

I hope you don't ignore it. If you're gonna defend Masterson, you're gonna have to learn to think like people out here."

Instantly repentant, Eleanor said, "I apologize, Sheriff. My outburst was uncalled for. I'm so frustrated."

"I think all of us are. Tully and I haven't found hide nor hair of Dobson since he left town. It's as if he's disappeared from the face of the earth without a trace."

Irritable steps carried her to the window, and she looked down the lonesome street, filled, as usual, with raucous cowboys. Carl moved to the potbellied stove and picked up the coffeepot.

"Does anyone in town even remember Dobson?" she asked. "Or has Lang, with his money, wiped their memory clean?"

"Don't reckon nobody could forget Dobson once they saw him. He was a tall, slender man. Quite ordinary, except for that shoulder-length blond hair. He was quite vain about his hair. Looked like spun gold in the sunshine." Carl lifted the cup to his lips and blew the hot coffee before he took a swallow. "Dobson was real popular with the womenfolk hereabouts. He spent a lot of time at the Two Bits Saloon and Dancing Hall. You know, Maude Livingston's place up the street. Well, when I questioned her, she didn't know where he had gone."

"There must be something we can do."

"If you really want to help Masterson, go home and leave the investigating up to me and Tully."

Eleanor glanced down the street to see a buckboard racing into town, followed by a huge cloud of dust. The horses, skillfully navigated by a young woman—in her mid-thirties, Eleanor guessed—stopped in front of Bundy's General Store. The woman was tall and slender and wore western garb: broad-brimmed hat, long-sleeved

142

blouse, leather vest, and riding skirt. Lithely she climbed down and with gloved hands reached up to flip the hat from her head. Deep brown hair, gleaming richly in the afternoon sunlight, cascaded down her back. She tied the reins to the hitching post.

"Who is she?" Eleanor asked.

Carl moved to stand behind Eleanor and to look out the window. "Julia Stanwood. She owns the ranch adjacent to your father's cattle station. She's a widow. Her husband was killed about a year ago in a shoot-out."

"By a gunman?"

"A gunslinger," Carl murmured. Lou was in town for a council meeting. Some cowboys were drunk and started shooting up the town. One of the stray bullets killed him instantly. Julia's been running the ranch single-handedly since then. She's a mighty tough lady. In fact, if it weren't for her, the Stanwood would still be a small one-man operation. Yep, she's some kind of woman."

Fascinated, Eleanor stared until Julia disappeared into the store. Walking to the desk, she picked up her gloves and began to slip them on. "She hasn't been interested in any man since her husband died?"

Carl thought a minute, then shrugged. "Not that I know of. Sho and David were friendly at one time."

"How friendly?"

"I figure you ought to ask Julia about something like that," Carl said.

"Well, Sheriff," Eleanor announced, "there's nothing more I can do here. I guess I'll be heading home."

Carl lifted an eyebrow in surprise. "Good. I'm glad you're taking my advice."

Once she was out the door, Eleanor unfurled her parasol and climbed into the wagon. As she and Frisco traveled down the street, she glanced curiously at the second story of the Two Bits Saloon. Her gaze bounced from one window to the other. Then with a jolt, she returned it to the middle window in time to see a person dodge back. At first she thought it was a woman, but then she remembered Carl's description of Early Dobson.

In the sunlight his shoulder-length hair glistened like spun gold!

Chapter 8

"I don't know that Bradley's gonna like this, Miss. You running around in them britches with a gun belt around your waist . . . just inviting trouble, if you ask me." Frisco lined empty bottles along a fallen log.

"Harry dresses like this. In fact, the hat, vest, and britches are hers. Thanks to Bundy's General Store, the shirt, boots, and revolver, of course, are mine."

"Well, that's Harry, not you. She's lived out here most of her life, and you haven't." Turning, he clamped his hand over his eyes and glared at her. "Guns are dangerous, and with you being from the city and all—"

"Thank you for your concern, Frisco. I've been trained in the use of firearms. I'm not the least concerned about Mister Smith's opinion of the way I choose to dress."

Grinning, Eleanor looked down at the trousers she wore. While they were a little looser on her than on Harry, they fit well enough. She was glad she had seen them on the clothesline when she and Frisco had arrived at the house. She wanted to do some target practice with a weapon other than her derringer. Harry's trousers provided her with the freedom she needed.

She lifted the nickel-plated .45-caliber revolver in her

right hand, her fingers curling around the gutta-percha handle, and aimed at the target. It was heavier than the derringer, but with a little practice she could handle it easily enough. "It's easy on the trigger, and the front sights are a little higher and thicker than on most guns."

"And the barrel is about as long as the ejecting rods," Frisco mumbled. "The kind of revolver that a gunslinger carries around. Ma'am, you just don't—"

The blast of the revolver cut Frisco short, and he stared open-mouthed as she shot four of the six bottles. She sighed and shook her head in frustration. Sliding the .45 into the holster, she said, "I'm not as comfortable with this as I am with my derringer, but before the afternoon is over, I'll feel better with it and much safer. Set up some more, Frisco. Farther away this time. And make them more difficult to hit."

"I hope you know what you're doing, Miss Hunt."

"Believe me, Frisco, I do." She muttered to herself, "And I'll do it."

Clad in the clothes she'd borrowed from Harry, her hair twisted into a coil and tucked under the Stetson she wore, Eleanor rode into Blissful after dark. She dismounted in front of the Two Bits Saloon and Dancing Hall, and shying away from the light that filtered through the windows and doors, she tied the reins of the sorrel to the hitching post. While she did not expect to pass for a man, she did think it was possible that if she remained in the shadows and attracted no attention to herself, most people would assume she was a young boy. As such, she would be able to walk through the saloon and slip upstairs without attracting undue attention.

She stepped onto the sidewalk and moved through the swinging doors into the crowded saloon. Her right hand poised above the handle of the Colt .45, she threaded her

146

way to the spiral staircase. Up the stairs she moved, the palms of her hands growing clammy the higher she climbed. She reached the landing just as one of the doors opened.

"Hey, kid," a woman called, "what you doing up here? Ain't you a little young for a place like this?"

Eleanor stopped but did not turn around.

"Leave him alone, Louise." Another door opened and another woman called out. "As long as he's got the money, who cares how old he is?"

The woman called Louise laughed. "That's right, kid. As long as you have the money, nobody cares how old you are. If I wasn't expecting company in a few minutes, I'd invite you into my room."

"I'm on my way to see Maude," Eleanor said rather gruffly in an effort to disguise her voice. "Can you tell me which room is hers?"

"Oh, la-de-da," the first woman mocked. "He's Maude's baby. First door to your right, little one."

"We know better than to rush in on Maude's territory."

Both of the woman laughed, then the doors closed. Eleanor ventured a peek over her shoulder to find herself alone again. Heaving a sigh of relief, she quietly moved down the carpeted hallway until she stood in front of the door to Maude's room.

Her heart thumping against her rib cage, she leaned her ear against the oak panel. She could hear voices—one was a man's; she could not be sure about the other. Early Dobson was here. She was sure it was he whom she'd seen this afternoon, and Maude Livingston was hiding him. That was the reason why it appeared he had dropped from the face of the earth. Archer had always said the safest place to hide something or someone was always the most obvious one.

She knocked on the door. The talking inside ceased; a

deep, husky voice called sensuously. "Yes?"

"Miss Livingston?"

Brittle laughter was her answer. "Been a long time since someone called me Miss Livingston. You must be a stranger in town."

"I need to talk with you."

"I don't have time for talking. I'm a working woman." Her voice grew louder as she neared the door.

"I'll pay for your time."

Maude opened the door to stare suspiciously at Eleanor. Her red dressing gown was unbuttoned and billowed to the side to expose her cotton undergarments. She held her hand out and said, "You sure will. Two dollars in advance."

"May I come in, please?"

"After you give me the money."

Eleanor dug into the pocket of the trousers and extracted a wad of bills, two of which she handed to Maude. The door closed, and Eleanor moved to the center of the room.

"Miss Livingston—" she said.

"Maude. Call me Maude." The woman crossed to a desk, where she tucked the money into a drawer. Then she picked up a sliver of paper onto which she sprinkled tobacco from a small pouch.

"I'm—"

Tracing her tongue along the cigarette, Maude said, "I know who you are, Miss Hunt. You can't hide what you are in them clothes. What do you want?"

"To find out some information."

"My price may go up."

Eleanor wanted to ask the woman how well she knew David and Whittier, but she knew to ask would be foolish. If the woman was criminally involved, the question would merely serve to warn her. "I need to talk with Early Dobson."

Maude lifted the chimney from the lamp and lowered her face to the burning wick. After she lit the cigarette, she inhaled deeply, then exhaled. Her face veiled by a cloud of smoke, she finally said, "Why come to me?"

"I saw him here this afternoon."

"I doubt that."

"He was standing over there." She pointed to the window.

"You've made a mistake," Maude insisted. "Early Dobson isn't here."

"Miss Living—I mean, Maude, I must talk with him. He's the only person who can help clear Jeffrey."

"Why can't all of you leave him alone? He's already told the sheriff that Masterson set that account up and closed it himself."

"But that's a lie," Eleanor insisted, "and Early knows it."

"Why should he lie?" Maude asked.

"For money," Eleanor returned evenly. "I think Whittier Lang paid him to lie in order to protect his own son."

Maude ground the cigarette into an ashtray. "Our conversation is at an end, Miss Hunt. If you'll excuse me, I have business to attend to."

"I heard a man's voice in here earlier."

"Of course you did," Maude snapped. "I earn my living by pleasing men, Miss Hunt. Now get out."

A door opened, and a man walked into the room. He raked his hand through long silken tresses.

"No—" Maude exclaimed.

He sighed wearily and held up his hand to silence her. "It's all right, Maude. She's right. I'm the only person who can testify who opened the account, made the deposits, and closed it. I'm not going to spend the rest of my life running and hiding, always looking over my shoulder. Nobody paid me enough to do that."

Eleanor could hardly contain her excitement. Finding Dobson was her first breakthrough in Jeffrey's case. This was her witness. "Come with me to the sheriff's office," she said. "Let him witness your story. No one would believe me."

"You're the attorney for Masterson?" he asked, and Eleanor nodded.

"Early," Maude snapped, "you're making a mistake. You should never have returned to Blissful, and you shouldn't be taken in by this woman."

"Maybe." He walked into the other room and returned wearing his coat. Standing in front of the mirror, he shoved his hair beneath his hat. He crossed the carpeted floor to stand in front of Maude, catching her face in both hands. He smiled. "I'll be back directly."

Maude laid her hands over his; her eyes shimmered with tears. "Don't do it, Early. They'll get you for sure."

He pulled his hands from beneath hers. "I'll be all right . . . I promise. No one knows I'm here."

Maude followed them out of the room and down the corridor. As they descended the stairs, Maude remained on the landing, but Eleanor could feel those eyes drilling a hole through her back.

"Did Jeffrey open the account, Early?"

"No." Delirious with happiness, her heart seemed to do somersaults.

"How about the deposits? Did he make them?"

"No, an unidentified man made several of them. I always reckoned he was from the east—taking into account the way he spoke and dressed."

His answers proved her suspicions. Someone had framed Jeffrey. "Did David make any of the deposits?"

"Nope."

"Who closed out the account?"

"The Easterner."

"Who was this man, Dobson? Surely you must know

150

something about him."

"Howdy, Dobson. Too bad you returned." A huge man stood in the middle of the saloon. His hat was pulled low over his forehead, and his lower face was shadowed with several days' beard. His black coat was covered with a thick layer of dust and was pulled behind his holsters. His hands were poised above the two Colt .45s he wore, and a sudden hush fell on the people and they scattered. "I came to have a talk with you."

"Oh, my God!" Dobson exclaimed. In turning to run up the stairs, he hit Eleanor and knocked her hat off.

"Look," someone yelled. "It's a woman!"

"Why, it's that woman lawyer!" a man added.

Seemingly oblivious to the crowd around him, the gunslinger called, "Really been better if you'd done like you was told, Dobson."

"Don't!" Eleanor's hand dropped to her revolver, but she could not clear leather before the man whisked out his guns and fired. Shots rang out. Moaning, Dobson fell down on the stairs. Eleanor screamed out in pain as fire blazed through her shoulder and burned down her arm. Blood quickly stained the front of her shirt. Gasping against the pain, she pulled the trigger, her bullets flying into the killer's chest. In the background, she heard someone cry, "Get the doctor." Breathing deeply, her left hand hanging limply by her side, she crawled up the stairs to Dobson. His moaning had ceased, and he lay quite still.

"Early!" Maude screamed and flew down the stairs to where he lay. His hat had fallen off, and his hair lay in gentle waves about his shoulders.

Blood trickling from the corner of his mouth, he lifted his head and said, "Maude—"

"Don't talk," she begged. "The doctor will be here soon."

He coughed, spit up more blood, and opened his eyes

151

wide. "I love you, Maude," Then his head rolled back and he gasped deeply.

"Dobson!" Eleanor cried. "Are you—"

Maude's eyes were dull. "He's dead. All because of you, he's dead." She cradled Dobson in her arms, her tears spilling onto his cheeks.

Pressing her hand against her shoulder to stop the flow of blood, Eleanor muttered, "I'm sorry. I didn't mean for this to happen."

"If you had stayed home where you belonged, it wouldn't have," Bradley said, his hands clamping over her shoulders as he jerked her to her feet.

"How did you—"

"When you didn't show up for dinner, I figured you were up to some harebrained scheme." His voice throbbed with anger. "Then Frisco told me about your afternoon of target practice. Why did you do this, Eleanor? You promised me—"

Dizzy from the loss of blood, Eleanor swayed toward him, and he looked down, his eyes focusing on the dark circle of blood. "My God! You've been wounded."

Before Eleanor knew what was happening, he swung her into his arms and carried her up the stairs. He kicked open a door and carried her to a bed, where he gently lay her down. With his pocketknife he cut the vest off. He unbuttoned her blouse to pull the soaked material aside.

Her head turned from the wound, her eyes closed, she said, "How bad is it?"

"Just a flesh wound." His voice was softer now; any signs of anger were gone, replaced with tenderness and concern. "But you're going to be pretty sore for a while, and we're going to have to make sure mortification doesn't set it."

"I'm already mortified. We don't have to wait for it to set in. I didn't mean for Dobson to be killed." She wadded the sheet in her fist. "I came prepared to protect him, but

152

couldn't even do that."

"It takes more than a day's practice to be good enough to fight a gunslinger," he said and smiled. "But he underestimated you. Probably figured you didn't know how to handle your gun."

Eleanor laughed weakly. "I guess I fooled him."

"You sure did."

Bradley uncorked the whiskey bottle and held it over her chest. Remembering the way Harry had tended him, Eleanor's eyes widened, and she watched as he poured the liquor over her wound. She bit her lips and dug her hands into the sheet to keep from screaming aloud. Before he replaced the bottle, he filled a glass and held it to her mouth.

"No," she muttered and twisted her head away from him.

He caught her chin and held it in place. "Oh, yes," he said, "you're going to drink all of this. You'll need it before the night is over."

She tried to twist her head away from the burning liquid, but he held her firmly in place. Finally, when she had swallowed all the whiskey, he set the glass down and caught her shivering body in his arms and held her. When the convulsing had stopped, he lay her back down and brushed the hair from her face.

"I'll be back. I need to find something to use for bandages."

"You're not going to have to sew me up, are you?"

"I don't think so. It's just a graze."

When Bradley returned, Eleanor was rather groggy. She could hardly bring him into focus. "Dobson said Jeffrey didn't open the account."

"I know," Bradley answered.

It took a few seconds for his words to penetrate the pain-ridden fog that enshrouded her. "How—did you know?"

"Carl and I located him in Dodge yesterday and persuaded him to return to Blissful with us. We thought he would be safer here."

"Why?"

"Maude's place had already been searched, and we thought no one would think about his returning."

"The safest place being the most obvious one."

Bradley chuckled. "That's right. Only this time we figured wrong."

Eleanor lifted a hand and idly played with the buttons on Bradley's shirt. "Maude loved him. Oh, Bradley—" Eleanor's chin quivered, and tears brimmed in her eyes. "I'm so sorry. I didn't mean for this to happen."

"I know," he said softly, his lips brushing gently against her forehead.

"Bradley," the sheriff called, knocking, "can I come in?"

Bradley hastily covered Eleanor with the sheet. "Come on in."

Opening the door, Carl walked to the edge of the bed and looked down at Eleanor. He twirled his hat in his hands. "Well, Miss Hunt, I see you didn't take my advice."

Swallowing her humiliation, Eleanor said, "I wanted to question Dobson."

"And in the process you got him killed and damned near got yourself killed."

"Who was the gunslinger?" Bradley asked.

Carl shrugged. "Nobody we know of or heard about."

"Dobson said some Easterner opened Jeffrey's account, made deposits, and closed it," Eleanor said. "Perhaps it was him."

"Yeah, maybe so." Deep in thought, Carl picked at his bottom lip. Finally he said, "What are you going to do with her tonight?"

"We'll stay here," Bradley answered. "I'll send word

154

to Harry where we are so she won't be worried."

Her shoulder throbbing less now, Eleanor eased herself more fully into the softness of the pillow. Closing her eyes, she wondered why someone from the east would deposit such large sums into Jeffrey's bank account.

Eleanor knew she was going to have to talk with David Lang. He was the only person alive who could clear Jeffrey.

She awakened much later in the night to find Bradley lying next to her. Her head was just under his chin, and his arm was wrapped around her. She gave a contented sigh and squirmed, brushing her cheek against his chest. Bradley's embrace tightened.

"Where are we?" she whispered.

Bradley chuckled softly. "At Maude's."

"Does—does anyone know that we're—we're sleeping together?" Again she kept her voice low.

"Why are you whispering?" he asked. "No one's in here but you and me."

Eleanor tried to sit up, but a sharp pain sent her back into the shelter of his arms. "Answer my question."

"Carl. Maude. Most of the people who work for her. Harry."

"They all know that we're sleeping together!" Her voice escalated with incredulity.

"It's not quite as bad as you think," he said. "Your the only one who's been asleep. I've been awake."

Eleanor laughed faintly and lifted her face to look into his. "Little difference that makes. We're sharing the same bed."

"Umm," he droned, as if he found the idea pleasing. "That's true."

"You—you'd better go."

"Yes, he murmured, his lips gently finding hers. "I should."

The kiss was her undoing. She pressed herself against him, opening her mouth to his, demanding his intrusion. Bradley groaned, and careful not to hurt her, shifted under her weight until they lay together. Eleanor felt for the first time the urgency of his desire as he allowed the kiss to deepen; each kiss becoming hotter and more demanding.

Her shirt twisted, and his hand touched the exposed flesh above her waist. His fingers lingered, then slipped along her skin like liquid fire to find the softness of her breast. Eleanor arched beneath his touch. She pulled his shirt from his trousers and slipped her hand beneath the cotton to touch the magnificent body.

He lifted his mouth from hers and muttered hotly against her cheek, "Eleanor, forgive me. I stayed to take care of you. I didn't mean for this to happen."

"Don't talk," she murmured.

Desire snapping her will and thought, her hand moved down to brush against his thigh. She only knew she never wanted this sweet, wonderful moment to stop. At the intimate touch, Bradley shuddered convulsively, and for an instant he ground himself into her palm. Then he caught her wrist and held it to the mattress as he buried his face in her throat, drawing long, gasping breaths. Eleanor shook helplessly.

"I have to stop," he whispered raggedly. When she did not answer, he said, "You would have hated us both in the morning."

Drawing in deep gulps of air, Eleanor pushed away from him. In a strained voice she said, "I don't know what came over me."

Bradley hauled himself up and crossed the room. A match grated against a piece of abrasive paper; it flared to light and touched off the lamp wick. In minutes the dim

156

light of the lamp flickered through the room. Bradley stuffed his shirt into his trousers and stood, leaning against the dresser, staring at her.

Propping herself on an elbow, Eleanor brushed her hair from her face and rounded her lips gently with her tongue. They were sore and bruised. She felt naked and vulnerable . . . and confused. Gathering the sheet, she held it beneath her chin.

"I want to make love to you, Eleanor," he said, "but this isn't the right time or place."

"You don't have to speak in such delicate terms for me, Bradley. What we just shared was lust . . . not love."

"There's a great difference between lust and love, Eleanor. I want to teach it to you."

Embarrassment heating her entire body, Eleanor said, "I'm tired, Bradley. I want to rest now."

He opened his mouth, sighed, then closed it. Impatient strides carried him to the chair across the room. "I'll be here if you need me."

Curling under the sheet, she lay down but could not sleep. She was all too aware of Bradley's presence in the room, and her body ached . . . not from her wound, but from a need that had been growing altogether too familiar to her since she'd met Bradley.

Chapter 9

"What did you want to see me about?" Whittier Lang demanded as he walked toward the creek where Bradley stood hidden in the thick foliage.

"Two reasons." Steady green eyes coolly surveyed the older man. "First, Dobson's dead."

"I heard."

"Did you also hear that Dobson was ready to admit that he had lied about Jeffrey being the one to open the account?"

Whittier gave Bradley a thin smile. "No, and if you're insinuating that I had him killed, you're wrong."

"According to Dobson, Masterson did not open the account, nor did he make any deposits or withdrawals from it."

"You heard Dobson say this?"

"He told Miss Hunt. He also claims he was paid to make this false statement."

"We have only the word of Masterson's attorney?"

"Dobson was going to give the sheriff a written statement."

Lang laughed. "But he died before he did that, didn't he, Smith?"

"Extremely convenient for you, wouldn't you say?"

Lang stared long and hard at Bradley before he said, "I told you I didn't have Dobson murdered. I had no reason to kill the man. His testimony won't help Masterson in the least."

"He was going to change his testimony, and the change would make it evident that Jeffrey was being framed. That would constitute reasonable doubt as to his shooting David, wouldn't it?"

Lang's hand clenched into a fist, and he moved closer to the creek. "I didn't know Dobson was in town. Furthermore, my boys were all at the ranch last night. You can't lay the blame on one of them."

"No," Bradley agreed, "I can't."

Lang said curiously, "Then why this secret meeting?"

"None of this is making sense to me," Bradley said. "Your son's being connected with the rustling, the accident, or Jeffrey's being framed."

"It may not make sense," the older man grated between clenched teeth, "but the fact remains my son was shot, and witnesses—witnesses who are alive and who will testify to the truth—saw Masterson gun him down. There's no denying that."

"I'm not." Bradley moved closer to the older man. "Harry told me that you'd apologized for Haggarty's mistreatment of Eleanor and Ebersteen, but I'm giving you fair warning if your men bother Miss Hunt or anyone from Hunt Cattle Station again, I'll hold you personally responsible."

Whittier's face twisted bitterly. "You better think a long time before you tangle with me, Smith. And for your information, that damned female got what she deserved. Haggarty was doing his job."

Years of discipline calmed Bradley. "Remember, I won't tolerate a second incident."

The two men stared at each other for a long time before Lang averted his gaze and said, "I heard that Hunt has another lawyer on his way to Blissful to defend Masterson."

"Maybe so." Bradley wondered in what direction the conversation was headed.

"Talk says it's Allen Shea, a promising lawyer trained by Archer Cormack himself." Lang laughed. "Evidently Hunt doesn't trust his daughter to get Jeffrey out of this mess. Maybe he has more sense than I've given him credit for."

"Miss Eleanor, I tell you, you're gonna get both of us in trouble," Frisco grumbled. Carrying her valise in one hand, he led her out of the Two Bits Saloon to the waiting buckboard. "Bradley gave me orders to take you straight home."

"If you're worried about what Bradley will do, you may go home, Frisco," Eleanor said and adjusted her arm in the improvised sling the doctor had made that morning when he'd checked on her wound. "He's your boss, but certainly not mine. I'm going to go to the Stanwood Ranch—with or without you. If you won't take me, I'll hire Mister Ebersteen to drive me."

Frisco shook his head in exasperation and tossed her luggage onto the back of the buckboard. "I'd better go with you, ma'am. No telling what sort of trouble you'll get yourself into. Look what happened the last time you had Frank take you somewhere. Here, let me help you up."

"I expected Bradley to be the one to drive me home," Eleanor said as she sat down and straightened her skirt. Her hand lingered on the material, and she smiled. Bradley was gone when she awakened, and so were the clothes she'd worn the night before. Laid out on the chair were this blue cotton dress, straw bonnet, parasol, and black patent leather shoes. The colors were so well

161

coordinated that she wondered if Harry had selected them for her, but secretly she hoped it had been Bradley.

"He has some business to take care of," Frisco answered as he rounded the buckboard and climbed in on the other side. "Sure wish it had been him."

Eleanor laughed. "Don't worry, Frisco. Nothing is going to happen today."

Muttering under his breath, Frisco guided the buckboard out of town, the miles clicking off quickly as they headed north. About an hour later they arrived at the Stanwood Ranch. Stopping in front of the house, he jumped down and hurried to Eleanor's side of the wagon to help her down.

"Thank you, Frisco," she said.

He pointed to the corral, where several hired hands were breaking horses. "I'll wait for you over here, ma'am."

As she nodded and walked onto the porch, the front door opened and Julia Stanwood stepped out of the house. She wore a checkered shirt and divided riding skirt. Her eyes ran over Eleanor curiously. "Good morning."

"Hello, I'm Eleanor Hunt."

"I know."

Eleanor smiled. Up close Julia was even more beautiful than she'd first thought. "I guess my visit must be something of a surprise."

"Nothing comes as a surprise out here." Julia's large green eyes twinkled. "Not even your escapade at the Two Bits Saloon last night."

"News travels fast."

"Extremely. I'm glad you didn't wait. We don't stand on ceremony here at the Stanwood. And quite frankly, I'm delighted to see you. I always enjoy talking with a woman who has so recently been in the east. That sling must be cumbersome. Here, let me take your parasol

162

and purse."

"Thank you," Eleanor said.

"You should be grateful you weren't hurt worse."

Turning, Julia opened the door and led the way into the parlor. The shades were drawn and the windows open. Sunshine poured into the room, giving it a glow of warmth and comfort. Even with its heavy furniture, it was roomy enough to accommodate easily a large number of people. Grouped in front of the fireplace was a divan, a coffee table, and two wing chairs—dark walnut furniture, upholstered in plush black leather. Julia laid Eleanor's purse and parasol on a table, then stopped behind the divan.

"But I have a feeling that you didn't come all the way out to the ranch to talk about fashion, did you, Miss Hunt?"

"Eleanor—and no, I didn't."

"Please call me Julia." She waved Eleanor to a chair and said, "I'll go get us some lemonade."

When Julia returned, she set the tray on the coffee table and handed Eleanor a glass of lemonade. "Whether you know it or not, you're the talk of the town."

Eleanor smiled. "Me, my being an attorney or my being the attorney to defend Jeffrey, or my escapades?"

Sitting herself opposite Eleanor, Julia laughed softly, then took a long swallow. Holding the glass in front of her and studying the pale yellow liquid, she said, "All three."

"And which are you the most curious about?"

Julia's gaze shifted from her drink to Eleanor. Their eyes caught and held in a candid gaze, one of mutual respect. "As a woman—as a widow—not much older than you, I'm interested in you, the woman. After all, you are my competition. As a businesswoman and the owner of the second largest ranch in the area, I'm also interested in your career as an attorney. Which one brought you to the Stanwood?"

"Curiosity," Eleanor admitted. "I saw you in town yesterday and wanted to get to know you better."

Julia smiled. "I asked *which* brought you—not *what*."

"The attorney," Eleanor replied. "I wanted to know how well you knew David Lang."

Julia lowered her head and traced a droplet of water on the glass. "Why?"

"I believe Jeffrey is being framed."

"But why did you come to me to find out about David?"

"The sheriff said you and David were friends."

"Yes, we were."

Julia set her glass down and rose. Moving to the window, she leaned against the sash. "When I married Lou and moved here three years ago, David was very lonely. I felt sorry for him. In so many ways, he reminded me of my younger brother. Ever since I've known him, he's had a wild streak in him. I guess that comes from his being an only child. After Aubra—Whittier's wife— died, Whittier doted on David, giving him everything he wanted and more."

"Do you think David was involved with the rustling?"

Julia hugged herself, rubbing her hands up and down her upper arms. "He certainly didn't need the money."

"Given his personality," Eleanor prompted, "is it something he would have done out of sheer pleasure?"

"Possibly," Julia said grudgingly.

"Do you know anything about the note Jeffrey received on the night of the rustling?"

"Nothing more than that Jeffrey claims to have received one."

"Last night Dobson told me that Jeffrey was not responsible for the bank account. Someone paid him to say that, and that someone is trying to frame Jeffrey."

Julia pushed away from the window. "I don't know if this person to whom you're referring is David, but I have

164

the feeling that Whittier did buy Dobson's testimony. That angers me. I don't like the idea of his controlling and manipulating everybody in Blissful."

"Anyone who knows you, Julia—" from the hallway Bradley's deep voice echoed through the room to startle both women "—would say Lang has no control over you *or* the Stanwood. It is rumored around here, my dear lady, that you are in control of every available bachelor's heart for miles around."

"Bradley!" Julia whirled about, her face immediately brightening.

At the same time Eleanor also turned to see him lounging insolently in the doorway, his hat in his hands. Eleanor was both glad and irritated to see him. All morning she had been thinking about him and remembering last night; she had wanted to talk with him but found him gone when she awakened ... tending to business, Frisco had said. Yet here he was at the Stanwood, with no way of knowing she would also be here. His visit had nothing to do with her.

"What a pleasant surprise. What brings you out this way?" Julia asked.

"Just riding by," he answered casually. "I let myself in. Hope you don't mind."

"Of course not." Julia gave him a special smile and patted the sofa. "Have a glass of lemonade with us, Bradley. It's quite refreshing."

"Believe I will." He strode leisurely across the room, where he sat down next to Julia.

Eleanor's hand tightened around the base of the glass. She found herself extremely irritated because he was sitting beside Julia, although there was a prudent distance between them. She disliked the camaraderie they seemed to share. She would have enjoyed disliking both of them, but that pleasure was denied her. Although she was uncertain how she felt about Bradley, Eleanor definitely liked Julia.

He smiled at Julia. "Sure you two don't mind my joining you?"

"Absolutely not. I want to see that heart of yours that I manipulate." She leaned across the sofa and lightly laid a slender hand on his thigh. "Can you imagine any woman not wanting you to join them?"

He laughed, and his eyes, a deeper, richer green than Julia's, flitted over to Eleanor, who had managed by supreme effort to keep her face emotionless. "I can think of one or two."

Julia rose. "The two of you visit while I get you a glass, Bradley."

He waved her down. "No need to. I've already stopped by the kitchen. Hoping the two of you would invite me to join you, I took the liberty of telling Flora to bring me one."

Again Julia laughed, the melodious sound echoing trilling through the room. "That's more like the Bradley Smith I know. You certainly do make yourself at home around here."

Eleanor liked Julia; she really did. But she did not like the response the woman seemed to evoke from Bradley. Feeling a twinge of jealousy, Eleanor gazed at Julia's hand resting casually on Bradley's thigh and wondered what the "Bradley Smith Julia knew" was like. His big hand curled over Julia's, the sun-browned skin a virile contrast to her creamy whiteness . . . the same hand that had touched her so intimately last night. He held Julia's hand a moment; the gesture, both simple and friendly, seemed one of great sensuality to Eleanor.

Then he moved to place his other arm across the back of the sofa; muscles rippled beneath the dark green shirt fabric. As vividly as if it had been last night, Eleanor imagined herself touching him, feeling the warmth of his flesh, the movement of his body. Inadvertently, inexplicably her eyes lowered, again to rest on the sinewy length of his legs . . . up the thigh . . . to the . . . So vivid were her thoughts, heat suffused her body.

Deeply engrossed, Eleanor did not join the conversation, nor did she hear the knock on the front door until Julia walked out of the room. She heard Bradley chuckle softly and lifted her head to stare into his mocking green eyes, eyes that seemed to read her every thought and to enjoy every second of her discomfort.

"How's your arm this morning?" he asked.

"Fine," she replied stiffly, then added, "Thank you for the clothes."

"Harry brought them in for you."

"Oh," Eleanor murmured, disappointed that he had not selected them for her himself.

"I wanted to be there when you awakened," he said, "but I had to leave."

Finishing off her lemonade, she set the glass down. "I know. Frisco told me."

Julia's voice drifted into the parlor from the veranda. "Hope this isn't an official visit, Carl."

"It is. I need to see Miss Hunt."

"Oh! She's in the parlor. Follow me."

The door slammed too; footfalls echoed in the hallway. Eleanor rose when Julia and the sheriff entered the room. Carl quickly took off his hat and held it in front of him. Eleanor's heart thudded anxiously.

"Morning, Miss Hunt, Bradley."

"Morning, Carl," Bradley said.

"How nice to see you, Sheriff," Eleanor said, "although I am rather surprised that you knew I was here."

"Don't be. After last night," Carl said, "I had you followed. I don't want any more surprises from you."

"You had me followed," Eleanor sputtered indignantly.

"Yes, ma'am. That's about the only way I know to keep

167

you out of trouble—or at least, to be close by when trouble occurs." Carl's eyes went to Bradley, and he nodded. "I wouldn't have been as worried about her if I had known you were with her."

Bradley grinned. "I wasn't."

"Would you care to join us for a glass of lemonade, Carl?" Julia asked. He shook his head. "Perhaps some coffee."

"No, ma'am, not today. Afraid I'm here on business." Carl twisted his hat nervously and shuffled his feet. He looked at Eleanor. "It's about Mister Shea."

"Allen! What's happened to him?" she exclaimed.

"Well, ma'am—" He seemed to be having a hard time finding his words "—he was traveling on the morning train when it was held up by outlaws. He's badly wounded."

"No!" Eleanor exclaimed. She had never meant for all this to happen when she told Allen to go to Springfield. She had only intended to delay him long enough for her to arrive before him. "He can't be. Jeffrey needs him."

"He's in town, ma'am, at Doc's place."

"How badly is he hurt?"

"Pretty bad. Doc doesn't know if he'll make it through the day."

"I must see him." Eleanor hated the frontier—it was taking away everyone who meant anything to her. First Jeffrey. Now Allen. With her uninjured arm, she grabbed her purse and slung the strap over her shoulder; then she picked up her parasol, buit did not bother to unfurl it. "Does Frisco know where Doc's place is?"

"Eleanor—" Julia rushed after her. "You ought to be in bed yourself."

Bradley strode across the room, his hand gently cupping her arm. "I'll take you," he said. "I'll send Frisco back to the cattle station with the news."

Eleanor nodded. She could not believe this was

happening. She had always depended on Allen; he had such a promising career ahead of him.

"Uh, Miss Hunt—" the sheriff followed Eleanor and Bradley out of the house "—the mayor finally received word from the judge. He'll be in Blissful in two weeks to try Jeffrey."

"Did he say anything about bail?" she asked over her shoulder.

"Don't know that you want him out on bail, ma'am."

"Of course I do," Eleanor exclaimed. "He's only charged with rustling."

"Not anymore, ma'am." They walked onto the veranda. "David Lang died late last night."

"My God!" Julia exclaimed. "Do you know what this means?"

"It means Jeffrey might hang," Eleanor said. The responsibility for saving his life rested entirely on Eleanor's shoulders now, and she did not have one shred of evidence to prove his innocence. All her strength drained from her, and she did not know if she could bear the weight of her responsibility.

"It means all of us are in for a rough time from Whittier Lang," Julia said. "He'll go on a rampage."

Eleanor whirled around and demanded, "Are all of you so selfish you think only of yourselves?" The three of them looked at her in surprise. "None of you has uttered one word about Jeffrey. You're too worried about what's going to happen to you and to Whittier Lang. Does Jeffrey not mean anything to you?"

"I'm sorry." Julia's face softened with apology. "I didn't mean to sound callous. I am worried about Jeffrey, but to be quite honest, I'm more worried about the rest of us. Whittier will have a score to settle."

"That he will." Carl gave his head an emphatic nod. "Good thing Masterson is in jail."

"Well, he won't be for long, if the judge said he could

be released into my custody," Eleanor declared.

"You can't mean that, ma'am!"

"Did the mayor ask the judge about it?" Eleanor demanded.

Carl opened his mouth to answer, but Bradley spoke rather roughly—in a tone that Eleanor interpreted to be a command rather than a suggestion. "Masterson will be safer in jail, Eleanor. Leave well enough alone."

"That's right," Julia added. "You don't understand the attitude of frontier towns, Eleanor."

"Did the mayor ask the judge?" Eleanor never took her eyes off Carl.

"Yes, ma'am. He set bail at five thousand dollars and said you could get him in the morning. But that was before David died, Miss Hunt."

"It doesn't matter. He gave his permission; that's all that counts."

Bradley moved to stand in front of her. Using that same authoritative voice, he said, "Didn't you hear what Carl said? When the judge gave his permission, David was alive. His death changes circumstances, Eleanor. Carl can't let Jeffrey go now."

Eleanor tilted her chin loftily. She had dealt with attitudes like this for years. She would show Bradley Smith who was in control of the situation. "I'm going to get him out, Bradley. Nothing you say will make me change my mind."

Carl clenched his jaws together in disapproval. Clamping his hat on, he said, "Just remember, ma'am . . . the responsibility for him is on your shoulders."

Thinking of Allen, she said, "How well I know that, Sheriff."

"Eleanor," Bradley said, "for God's sake, be reasonable!"

"I won't presume to tell you how to run your business, Mister Smith. Don't presume to tell me how to

170

defend Jeffrey."

Carl took a step toward the door. "Guess I'll be heading back to town, too. Things are going to be rough. I can expect the boys to start drifting into town in droves. The saloons are going to be filled to overflowing."

"Want me to send in some men, Carl?" Bradley asked.

"I'll send some, too." Julia said.

"No, thanks." The sheriff shook his head. "I have enough for tonight, and once Masterson is released, Bradley, he'll be your problem."

"Eleanor," Allen whispered, his lids fluttering open, "is that you?"

Sitting in a chair beside the bed, she leaned forward and smiled. "It's me."

He grimaced and his hand touched the bandage across his abdomen. His eyes closed again. "I don't know when I've ever hurt so bad. I'm burning all over. Now . . . I know . . . why Archer sent me. He . . . didn't want to . . . get hurt." His effort at laughter ended in a hacking cough.

"Oh, Allen! It's all my fault." She rose, but he held her hand up. "Archer told me to go to Springfield, but I wanted to come out here, and I—"

He managed a weak smile. "Don't you think I know you well enough to know what you were doing? I know what Jeffrey means to you."

Two large, hot tears rolled down her cheeks. "Oh, Allen."

"Please don't cry," he said, taking a few deep breaths. "It's not your fault. Tell me—tell me about the case."

Eleanor sat back down and began to talk quietly, but the medicine the doctor had given him began to take effect, and he went to sleep. From the next room the doctor called, "Would you care for a cup of coffee or tea,

Miss Hunt?"

"I'd like a cup of coffee," she replied and rose to join him in the small parlor adjacent to his surgery.

"How is he, Doctor Williford?" she asked.

"The wound is pretty bad, but he's strong. He's held on longer than I expected. Cream or sugar?"

"Black," she answered. *The color of my world today,* she thought. "Do you mind my staying here with him?"

Williford shook his head. "Not at all. I have some house calls to make, but Mrs. Shubert, my housekeeper and nurse, will be here. She'll be glad for the company, and so will Shea."

Eleanor was sitting on the railing on the front porch of the doctor's house when Bradley walked up. He quickly sprinted up the stairs to stand beside her.

"How is he?"

"He's sleeping right now. The doctor said he was holding his own. Only time will tell."

"I'm sorry," Bradley murmured.

"I know I can't prove it, but I believe Whittier Lang was behind this."

"You can't hold him responsible for every crime that takes place, Eleanor."

"It isn't coincidental that this one took place mere hours after David's death and to Jeffrey's attorney. Mister Lang didn't fear my being Jeffrey's legal counsel, but he did Allen."

"I think you're jumping at shadows."

She rubbed her shoulder and sighed. "Maybe I am. I don't know anymore. I suppose I ought to walk over to the jail and set bail for Jeffrey."

"Don't do it, Eleanor."

"Bradley, nothing you can say or do will make me change my mind."

He moved closer to her. "Don't be a fool!"

Eleanor was too weary to fight with him. "I *would* be a

fool if I didn't do what I thought was right for my client."

"You're not thinking about what's right for Jeffrey. Right now you're not even thinking about him as a client. You're concerned about your childhood friend. You're caught up in worry over your associate."

"And I suppose you're thinking about what's right for Jeffrey?" Her blue eyes, the color of a steel blade, pierced his.

He did not shrink from her gaze. "Whatever I'm thinking, it's more than you're doing at the moment. You women are all alike. Your entire lives are predicated on emotion. I knew from the first day that you wouldn't be any good at defending him."

She cringed, and her hand tightened around the railing. These words—or a variation on them—had been thrown at her all her life, and most frequently by her father. Still they hurt her. She continued to gaze at him.

"Despite what you believe, I'm the best hope Jeffrey has. You'd better pray that I'll be good at defending him. Now, if you'll excuse me, Bradley, I'm going over to the jail and speak with the sheriff."

"I'm sorry, Eleanor. I didn't mean that."

He pulled her gently against his chest, careful not to hurt her shoulder, and she felt the heat of his body through the thin fabric of her dress. She felt the anger slowly draining out of her to be replaced by another emotion—one with which she was quite familiar—lust. She had succumbed once, but wouldn't again.

"You're such a stubborn woman."

"Determined," she returned.

His grip loosened, even softened, but his expression was guarded. Yet he held her close. "Spoiled and determined to have your own way, no matter what the consequences. Daddy's little darling."

Bradley thought she was so shallow that she never weighed the consequences of her decisions. In so many

173

ways he was like her father. Alex loved her . . . Eleanor had no doubt of this. But she had not been his little darling. His little darling was his meat packing company; it filled his heart and his time. It seemed to be his very soul.

"Howdy, folks," the sheriff called out as he opened the gate and moved up the sidewalk. "How's the patient?"

"Holding his own," Eleanor answered as she moved out of Bradley's embrace. "I was on my way over to arrange for Jeffrey's release."

"I've sent the papers to Tom for him to sign. As soon as Tully returns, you can have Jeffrey."

"How long do you think that will take?"

"Several days," Carl said and pushed back his hat. "I forgot to tell you earlier when I was at the Stanwood—Radford Vaughan will be the prosecuting attorney."

Eleanor gripped the banister.

"He's a New York lawyer, hired by Whittier," the sheriff continued. "Don't suppose you know him."

After what seemed an eternity, Eleanor said through numbed lips, "Yes—I know him . . ."

Carl touched his fingers to the tip of his hat and nodded. "Well, I'll be off on my rounds. See you in the morning."

A good ten minutes had passed since the sheriff rode off, yet Eleanor had not moved. Bradley's curiosity was thoroughly piqued. At the mention of Radford Vaughan's name, she had gone deathly still, and all color drained from her face. Even now she continued to stand on the porch and stare into the distance, her hands still tightly gripping the banister.

Bradley walked up behind her to lay his hands on her shoulders. He felt her tension. Careful not to hurt her wounded shoulder, he began to knead the tight muscles

174

with his hands. "Who is he?"

"Radford Vaughan," she answered perfunctorily.

"Has he had that much of an effect on your life?"

"Tend to your own business, Bradley." Eleanor moved away from his tormenting touch.

"Right now, I think this *is* my business."

Bradley did not know what perverseness compelled him to probe into Eleanor's personal life. Of course, he was attracted to her and had been from the first second he'd laid eyes on her. While he did not like the poor-little-rich-girl part of her, he was attracted to Eleanor Hunt, the woman who dared to march to a different drummer and to defy society and its strictures.

In the short time she'd been at the cattle station, he'd discovered that she loved challenges, especially the getting over and around obstacles; she thrived on opposition. When she was set against, she did her best. At the same time, Bradley knew that Eleanor Hunt was sharp-tongued and impulsive. She could be stubborn—as he had just witnessed.

"I knew Radford a long time ago," Eleanor finally said. "He's—he's no longer a part of my life."

"Must be, or he wouldn't be having this adverse effect on you."

"You have no idea what you're talking about."

"Yes, I do. Outside you appear to be composed and calm, but inside you're all torn up because of this Radford Vaughan."

A brittle smile touched her lips, and she took a step to move past him. "Excuse me. I'd like to be alone."

He caught her hand in a firm clasp and blocked her way. "What does he mean to you, Eleanor?"

"I loved him."

Bradley frowned but said nothing.

"But he didn't love me."

Careful not to hurt her arm, he took her fully into his

arms, pressing her face gently against his chest. Rocking her back and forth, he held her. Finally she pulled back her head and looked into his face.

"You think I'm silly, don't you?"

"I've thought you were a lot of things during the past week, Eleanor Hunt, but silly isn't one of them." Bradley dropped an arm lightly over her shoulders and guided her down the steps and across the lawn. He opened the back gate and closed it after they passed through.

"Where are we going?"

"To a quiet spot," he answered as they continued to walk.

They lapsed into a comfortable silence as he led her to a secluded spot on the creek behind the doctor's house. She sat on a large clump of grass beneath the low, spreading branches of the tree, and he moved to stand on the creek bank.

"How did you happen to settle in Blissful, Bradley?"

His back to her, he bent and picked up a handful of pebbles.

Softly she teased, "Now it's your turn to be silent. Are you hiding a hurt, too, Bradley Smith?"

Bradley swung his arm and loosened a rock that skipped across the creek, leaving a rippling path in the surface of the otherwise tranquil water. The others he tossed away as he turned to walk back to Eleanor. He dropped to the ground at her feet and plucked a blade of grass that he pulled between his fingers. His face mottled with sunlight, he looked up at her.

"I've had my share of disappointments, but I'm not hiding any hurts."

"Or running from your past?" she quizzed lightly.

"No." Lying on his back, he stretched out and stuck the blade of grass in the corner of his mouth. "I joined the Cavalry during the War Between the States and started creating the past that I wanted."

176

"How old were you?"

"Twenty-one, going on forty."

"What was your past like before you started creating a new one?"

He grinned. "I was working at Newland's in New York."

Eleanor's eyes widened in surprise, and she exclaimed, "Newland's! You worked at Newland's!" Her gaze raked over his entire frame. "Somehow I can't imagine you being employed at a fashion salon."

Bradley laughed and crossed his hands beneath his head. "I couldn't either. That's why I joined the army and set my own course."

"You've never had any regrets?"

"Not really." He closed his eyes. "Afterward I chose to remain in the service, my tours of duty bringing me to the west."

"How long have you been out of the army?"

"About five years."

"And you're thirty-three."

Slowly he turned his head to look at her. An easy grin touched his lips. "You remembered."

"Of course I did," she returned jauntily. "Whatever condition my heart may be in, my mind is totally intact."

"Oh, I think your heart's in excellent condition," he drawled. "Once you talk to someone about this Radford Vaughan, you'll find that you don't even have any scar tissue. Absolutely no permanent damage."

"Are you so sure you want me to tell you about him?"

Bradley sat up, his face very close to hers, his green eyes steadfastly contemplating her. Finally he said, "To be honest, Eleanor, a part of me does; another part doesn't."

She reached out to brush a lock of hair from his forehead. The touch was light and gentle, completely innocent. Yet its innocence was the stroke that set off a flame of desire that seared through his body. As quickly as she'd touched him, she withdrew her hand and stood to walk to the creek bank.

"Isn't it strange, how false our society is, Bradley? In what other society does one's reputation hinge on sexual relationships prior to marriage? A man can have many lovers, and they only enhance his masculinity; a woman can have only one lover, and her reputation is ruined . . . she is promiscuous."

"You're right." He rose and moved to stand beside her. Slipping his hands into the back pockets of his trousers, he rocked back on his heels. Tiny wrinkles puckered his brow.

Eleanor glanced at him. "Are you sure you want to hear my confession?"

"Yes."

Yet she paused before she said, "I met Radford on one of my trips to New York to visit my grandparents. Mama and I went about four times a year . . . whenever Papa came out here to check on the station. It was love at first sight."

She stood and walked closer to the tree to pluck on the leaves, pulling them off one by one. "At least, I fell in love with *him* at first sight. We began to court and secretly talk about marriage. Of course, I knew I would have to wait until he completed his schooling, but I didn't mind. I thought we shared many common goals. He told me he wanted an educated and intelligent wife. I believed in women having the same rights as men, and he did too. Or so he said at the time."

Tears burned her eyes, and she sniffed, then continued, "He always wanted to be an attorney. Because he was away at the university and I lived in Chicago, I didn't get to see him as frequently, but we continued to write. As his studies intensified, the letters came less regularly. I also entered college and fought for my education."

178

"You really believe in challenges, don't you, Eleanor?"

"I believe in equality." A twig snapped between her fingers. "I have as much a right to an education and a career as a man. You have the right to be a cowboy; I should have the right to be an attorney."

"You should."

"But a woman doesn't. I don't."

"What happened between you and Radford?"

"He came to Chicago one year on a case." She walked to the edge of the creek, knelt down, and drew her fingertips through the water. "He came to see me. He said he was proud of me and happy that I'd become a lawyer. We spent the whole summer together, and I thought we were going to be married."

She closed her eyes tightly, yet tears coursed down her cheeks. "He never said anything, but I thought . . . I thought he really meant all those things he'd been saying about women being equal. When the trial was over, he left. Without a word, he simply left. I couldn't believe it. I followed him to New York and went directly to his office."

Her voice was bleak, and she stared blankly into the blue mirror of the creek. "He was angry with me for coming and asked how I could have thought he would ever marry a woman of my kind. He wanted a wife, not an attorney. I—I told him that I loved him so much I was willing to give up my career for him. That's when he informed me that he was already married and had been for over a year."

Bradley took a step toward her. "I'm sorry that your first experience with love—"

Her head jerked up. "Lust!"

"—was so—"

"Are you *finally* at a loss for something to say, Mister Smith?"

"Only for the proper words with which to say it,"

he answered.

"Have I properly shocked you?"

"No, I think this happens to more women than you know."

"I'm sure it does, and they can't talk about it, because their lives would be ruined. To keep their reputation intact, they carry the grief hidden within their hearts for the rest of their lives."

"I'm sorry," he murmured.

"There's no need to be," she said.

"You've kept this bottled up inside you all these years?"

"Yes, I have. I had already disappointed Papa many times during my life . . . I couldn't do it again."

"Do you find that talking has helped you release some of the pain?"

Eleanor smiled and nodded her head. "I'm over the heartbreak itself. I just haven't come to grips with my weakness and stupidity."

"No one is weak or stupid for having loved someone. That's one of the marvelous emotions we feel because we're human."

Eleanor laughed bitterly. "I can do without that 'marvelous emotion.' I chased Radford from Chicago to New York; I begged him to marry me; I went so far as to offer to give up my career for that—"

"Bastard," Bradley supplied easily. "But look how the gods have favored you, Eleanor Hunt."

"Favored me! Whatever do you mean?"

"You didn't give up your career, and now both your integrity and your heart are intact. Last time you met him, you were on his territory. That placed you at a slight disadvantage. This time when you meet Radford Vaughan, it will be on your territory, on your terms."

"If this were a confrontation between Radford and me, I wouldn't mind, but it isn't. He's here to prove that

Jeffrey is guilty of cattle rustling and murder. I'm here to prove Jeffrey's innocence."

"I have no doubt in your ability to win against him in court," Bradley said.

"He's one of the best, Bradley. He commands a large fee, and people are willing to pay it. In fact, only those who are willing to pay it can retain him. Next to Archer, Allen is the only person who can hold his own with Radford, and he—he—" Her voice thickened with tears. "Now it's up to me."

"You're underestimating yourself," Bradley said.

Eleanor shook her head. "No, I'm confident of my ability, but I also know that I haven't had the exposure and experience he has. Archer hired me to be an attorney, but at best, I'm just his assistant, Bradley. People don't take female attorneys seriously."

Bradley moved to stand in front of her. He caught her chin with the tip of his finger and lifted her face. His gaze locked with hers. "This is your chance, Eleanor. You can win."

Drowning in the green depths, she murmured, "Yes, I can. I must win. I must. So much is at stake."

He gently folded her into his arms and gave her a warm hug, one that went no further than reassurance. Minutes later they turned and walked back to the house.

Chapter 10

The morning was beautiful. The sun, a golden orb of warmth and brightness, rested against a backdrop of blue sky and lacy white clouds. Although it was not cool, a gentle breeze stirred through the leaves and caressed Eleanor's face. Standing on the edge of the veranda, she gazed into the distance at the tranquil countryside—such a contrast to her life.

She was glad to be home. When Doctor Williford had announced that Allen was past the critical point, Bradley had insisted on her returning to the cattle station. After her three day vigil, she had offered no resistance. As confused and worried about all that had happened recently, she had thought she would never be able to sleep. Surprisingly, after a hot bath and a cup of that strong herb tea that Gaspar brewed for her, she was asleep almost before her head touched the pillow.

Eleanor felt better today. Her arm was healing nicely, and Allen was improving. The sheriff had promised that he would send word as soon as Tully returned with the signed papers for Jeffrey's release. Most important, Eleanor had gotten over her initial shock that Radford Vaughan would be the prosecuting attorney in Jeffrey's trial. In fact, she was quite excited about Radford's arrival. She felt as if she were being given a second chance to redeem herself.

Like a child she circled the porch column with a hand and swung around, the skirt of her yellow dress billowing about her ankles. She threw back her head, lifted her face to the sun, and laughed. She felt wonderful and alive. Although she would be working with Allen as much as his recuperation allowed, she would plan a defense for Jeffrey that would boggle the mind of Radford Vaughan.

The screen door creaked and the bottom grated across the veranda floor. "Well, Miss Eleanor," Gaspar said, "I'm sure glad to see you're home and feeling so pert this morning. We was worried about you. You ought to know better than to go off by yourself like that. You'll get yourself killed if you ain't careful."

The breeze ruffled tendrils of hair about Eleanor's cheeks. Brushing them aside, she smiled kindly. "Thank you for your concern, Gaspar. I promise I shall be more careful in the future. I guess you heard that Jeffrey is going to be released from jail?"

"Don't know that Mister Jeffrey's coming home is something to be happy about," he mumbled, and hobbled to the edge of the porch to set down a large food basket. "The longer Carl Hix keeps him in jail, the better. Seems to me with Lang's men drunk and on the loose that would be the safest place for the boy. I'm gol-darned worried about what Whittier Lang is up to. He's liable to have somebody ride down here and shoot us all."

"Gaspar!" Eleanor exclaimed. "Surely you don't believe that!" But even as she uttered the words, she knew in her heart of hearts that Whittier Lang was responsible for Allen's close call with death.

"Yep! Reckon I do, Miss Eleanor. Out here a man believes in his own justice, and Whittier believes in that eye-for-eye stuff. 'Sides, the man has lived around here since before Blissful was a town."

184

"Well," Eleanor said, "if he or his men come, we'll just have to show them who's boss at Hunt Cattle Station."

"And speaking of the boss," Gaspar said, "I need to get this basket out to him. I don't reckon Frisco is anywhere around, is he? Probably not . . . not when I need him. I don't have time to deliver this to the fence line where Bradley is."

"I didn't know he was gone," Eleanor said, her eyes looking toward the basket. "He must have been up early this morning."

"Was," Gaspar said. "The fence was down on the bottom forty. He was the only one who could go. Told me to tell you if'n he didn't get back in time and word came from Carl about Masterson's release, Frisco or me was to drive you into town." He moved to the edge of the porch and turned his head in both directions, muttering all the time, "Now where's that good-for-nothing son of a gun? Never around when I need him."

Still eyeing the basket and ready for a romp in the glorious sunshine, Eleanor said, "Gaspar, I would love to go for a ride. Why can't I take Bradley's lunch to him?"

His pale brown eyes rested on Eleanor, and Gaspar raised a hand to stroke the beard around the corners of his mouth. "Well, now," he drawled, "I don't know. How's your arm?"

She flexed it. "Almost as good as new."

He pursed his lips. "Harry might not—"

Eleanor sighed. "I'm really all right, Gaspar, I'm an accomplished horsewoman. If you'll just point me in the right direction, I'm sure I can locate Bradley." She smiled. "If you'll let me take it, you can get back to your work."

The man's eyes narrowed, and he continued to ponder, plucking at his beard. Finally he chuckled and bobbed his head emphatically. "Well, all right."

185

Eleanor reached for the basket, but he caught it away from her. "Since you're going to be riding a horse, it needs to be repacked. You go on over to the barn and let Arty saddle you up. I'll be over directly." He turned and marched into the house.

Bradley was unaware of the sun burning down on his bare back as he pounded the post-hole digger into the ground. The handles vibrated in his gloved hands as the sharp metal pinged through the hard, dry earth. Yet he found the work to be a blessing. While it did not take his mind off Eleanor, it did keep his body from responding as quickly.

He had done nothing but think of her since the night she was wounded, his feelings vacillating between acute disappointment that she and Vaughan had been lovers and an elation that she was not an innocent. Without turning loose the handles to the digger, he flexed his muscles and sighed. So much to do and so little time.

He had promised to drive Eleanor into town as soon as word came from the sheriff. If it came today, he wondered if he would be finished with his work in time to take her. He pushed his hat farther back on his head; then pulled the faded bandanna from his hip pocket and wiped the perspiration from his face.

When Jeffrey had been arrested, Bradley had thought taking the manager's position was a godsend. Now he was not so sure. Most of his waking hours were spent working on the station, and it left little time for his investigation. Now that Eleanor was here, he found his interest in her growing as his interest in his work diminished. With a careful glance that quickly skirted the nearby buckboard from which dangled his long-discarded shirt, he measured the fence line he had yet to complete. Another two hours should do it. He gripped the handles of the post-hole

186

digger in both hands.

Then he heard an approaching horse. He turned and in the distance saw a rider top the gentle hill. He thought it was a man. He pulled the brim of his hat lower to block out the midday glare. Then he saw the yellow dress flared over one side of the huge gray and knew it was Eleanor, riding sidesaddle. For a moment, her broad-brimmed hat had fooled him. The horse galloped closer, and Bradley never moved. He simply watched.

Even at that distance their gazes locked. No longer wearing the sling, she slid off the horse, the basket on her arm. A gust of wind blew the hat from her head to reveal black hair burnished richly in the sunlight. Smiling tentatively, she brushed a few strands out of her face. After taking several steps, she stopped.

He felt her gaze move over his naked torso like a sweet caress, up the thin line of his scar on his abdomen, up to his face again. When her eyes once more caught and locked with his, she licked her lips . . . intentionally or innocently? He did not know; he did not care. He only knew she was the most provocative creature he had ever known.

He turned loose the post-hole digger, and it thudded to the ground behind him. He moved toward her; she moved toward him, her lips curving into a gorgeous smile. He stripped off his gloves, dropping them as he walked.

He wondered if she were a figment of his imagination. Was Eleanor really here? Each moved toward the other until he was close enough to feel the heat from her body.

He could hardly believe the object of his thoughts was here. To reassure himself that he was not dreaming, he reached out and touched one of the shining curls, then twined the silken strand about his finger. As his knuckles grazed her cheek, he felt the softness of her flesh. She trembled, and her lips parted to emit a sigh that sweetly floated up to his ears. He pulled his finger from the curl

187

to let it dance about her face.

"What a wonderful surprise." Although the sun had been shining brightly all morning, she brought a glow of happiness and a warmth with her that had been missing in his life for a long time.

"I brought your lunch."

"Thank you."

"Frisco was gone, and Gaspar had work to do. I—he—I told him I would bring it to you."

"I'm glad you did." Bradley had always thought her eyes beautiful, but today they were swirling with sensuality, dark with mystery, sweet with promise. They moved from his face down his neck to his chest. As her eyes lowered, so did her lids, her dark lashes a contrast to the creamy smoothness of her cheeks. "Any word from Carl?"

She shook her head and allowed him to take the basket from her. "I just came to bring your lunch. I guess I had better get back to the house."

"No!" Bradley reached out and caught her hand. He was not going to let her take this away from him by leaving. He smiled at her. "Have lunch with me. Gaspar always fixes too much for one person."

"All right," she murmured without thought of argument.

Their fingers entwined, and he led her to the shade, where he set down the basket. She knelt beneath the tree and reached for the tablecloth. While she spread the lunch, he tethered her horse to a nearby tree, then went to the brook and washed off. Returning to the buckboard, he slipped into his shirt and buttoned it up, but did not tuck it into his trousers. Eleanor's soft laughter reached him.

"What's funny?" he asked, sliding a glance over his shoulder.

She set the bottle of wine aside and held up two

delicate glasses. "Gaspar. When he asked me to deliver this basket, I'm sure it didn't contain both of these. That's why he went back into the house."

Sitting down opposite her and uncorking the wine, Bradley smiled. "You'll have to forgive him. He's a romantic old soul and a matchmaker by trade. In fact, he's probably a better matchmaker than he is a cook."

"Why do you keep him on?"

Bradley poured the wine into the glasses before he picked up a piece of fried chicken and waved it through the air. "I didn't say he wasn't a good cook."

He had not realized how hungry he was until he bit into the drumstick. Later, after two pieces of chicken and three slices of freshly baked bread, he stretched out in the shade and propped up on an elbow to sip his wine.

"You're not eating much?"

She smiled. "One piece of chicken and a slice of bread. That's quite a bit when you consider I recently ate a large breakfast."

Bradley laughed. "You're going to spoil Gaspar. He loves to have someone to coddle."

"He's probably lonesome," Eleanor said and began gathering the remains of their lunch and placing them in the basket. "You and Harry are gone most of the time."

"Work."

After Bradley drained the glass, his studious gaze ran the line of fence. "Ranching is hard, Eleanor . . . damned hard. And never ending. About the time you think you're through, it's time to start over again. Yet I love it. This is my life."

Her gaze also shifted to the fence. "What happened?"

Bradley's gaze returned to her face. "The fence was down. It's a good thing the men discovered it when they did. Otherwise we'd have lost a lot of cattle."

"Deliberate?" she asked.

He shook his head and said, "Probably not." Sitting

up, he handed the glass to her. "You know what I've been doing all morning. Now, tell me what you've been doing."

Eleanor pulled her legs up to her chest and rested her chin on her knees. "Working on Jeffrey's defense. Unless I can find that note, he doesn't have one. It'll be no contest; Radford will win." She paused and added, "I must know who the woman was."

"Have you narrowed down your suspects yet?"

"I know for sure it wasn't Sarah. The night in question, she was ill in bed; Clementine and her father took turns sitting up with her most of the night."

"Did you ever talk with Harry?" When Eleanor nodded, he asked, "And?"

"I don't quite understand Harry's relationship to Papa, but I'll stake my life that she's loyal to him."

"I think you're putting too much stock in this note." He flipped over and caught one of her hands in his. "I don't mean to tell you how to do your job, but you're running out of time. You need to concentrate on the evidence at hand. Maybe you can work out a deal."

"Never!" Horrified, Eleanor pulled away from him. "Jeffrey's not a rustler or a murderer."

"I didn't say he was, but he has done something or knows something that involves him in the mess."

Eleanor leaped to her feet. "If it's the last thing I do, I'll prove his innocence to you. To the whole community! To Radford Vaughan! Wait and see."

Bradley smiled and rose lazily. "I know you can do it. You don't have to prove it to me. Now you'd better get back to the house and let me get this fence mended, or you'll have just cause to fire me."

Delicate color shaded Eleanor's cheeks as she remembered her idle threats the first day she met Bradley. "How much longer before you're finished?"

He thought he heard a wistfulness in her voice, or

maybe he simply wanted to hear it.

"A couple of hours," he promised and walked her to her horse. He stooped and picked up the hat. Putting it on her head, he tied it beneath her chin. "Now you won't lose it so easily."

He stepped back and watched as she mounted. Then the gray galloped away. At the top of the hill she stopped the horse, turned, and waved. He waved at her, watching until she disappeared in the distance. Then he walked to the buckboard, where he unbuttoned and slipped out of his shirt.

Strange, how quiet it seemed now that she was gone. Already he missed her. He walked back to the fence line, stopping to pick up his gloves and to slip them on his hands. It took him about fifteen minutes to settle the last post into place and to fill the hole with dirt. He was about to pack it when he sensed her presence.

He did not move for what seemed like centuries. Then he felt as if she were silently commanding him to turn; he did so to find her standing behind him. Mesmerized, they stared at each other.

"I forgot the basket," she whispered.

"I would have brought it home."

"I was—afraid Gaspar would be angry if I left it." Her eyes never leaving his face, she moved toward him.

"You shouldn't have returned." He dropped the shovel and walked to her.

"I had to," she whispered.

Finger by finger he stripped the leather gloves from his hands. Never missing a step, he dropped them at his feet. He lifted his hand, removed his hat and tossed it to the side.

The basket forgotten, he clasped her in his arms. She felt good against him, her softness molding to the length of his hard frame. His arms tightened about her and she did not fight him. Her face lifted; his lowered. Her lips

191

welcomed his.

Soft, fluttering like the petals of a flower opening to the rain, her lips moved under his. The tangy taste of wine blended into the sweetness of the kiss, the tentative introduction quickly, surely moving into the warmth of desire. Her hands slid under his arms and around his back. When she pressed herself more firmly against him, Bradley moaned softly.

Eleanor's hands slipped up his back and twined together at the nape of his neck. She pushed up on her toes. Breathing deeply, Bradley lifted his mouth from hers. Eleanor's eyes were closed, her lashes a black lace fan over her elegant cheekbones. Her mouth was soft, her body pliant against his. Desire burned through Bradley's body. He knew he had been waiting for this moment of ultimate possession since the first day he had met her at the depot in Blissful. Again his mouth brushed softly against her parted lips; they settled into a warm, full kiss; they teased and stroked the fires of desire that flamed between them.

"Eleanor," he muttered thickly and trailed kisses along her arched neck to the base of her throat, "if we keep kissing like this, you know what is going to happen, don't you?"

"Yes," she whispered and pulled back to look at him with dark, passionate eyes.

"I won't let you go this time."

"I know."

With a small groan, he pulled her into the warm circle of his arms and held her close. He felt her warm breath against his naked chest. He lifted a hand and began to pull the pins and combs from her chignon. When her hair hung loose, he brushed his fingers through the long strands.

"I've wanted to do this ever since I met you," he said. "It's so beautiful. Soft, like the finest silk."

192

"And having worked at Newland's Fashion Salon, you would know," she murmured.

Newland's Fashion Salon. The words reverberated through Bradley's mind and shattered the fragile spell that held him entranced. The words that so epitomized Eleanor's life. He wondered what her reaction would be should she ever learn he'd been hired to investigate her father, to find out if he was the mastermind behind the rustling ring. He had told her he did not like Jeffrey Masterson because he hid behind lies and deceit. He too hid behind a veil of secrecy.

How many years ago had he denied his family and chosen to go by his first and middle name? How easy it had been to lose himself in anonymity as Bradley Smith and to forge a new life.

Still Bradley could not, would not let her go. She was sweetness returned to his life. He removed his hand from her hair and caught her in a tighter embrace. She moved her head, her cheek and hair brushing against his chest. The movement sent a flutter of passion into his lower body.

"Have you no desire to return to New York?" she murmured. With the tip of her finger she traced the swirl of hair up his stomach to his nipple.

"I like the city every once in a while," he answered, "but I like the frontier even better."

Her finger brushed across the tip of his nipple. It hardened. "Does it never bother you, having to give up the amenities that civilization affords?"

He caught her hand in his to stop the torment. "No. Does it bother you?"

"Yes. There are only two general stores in town, and Bundy's has more hardware and livestock than dry goods."

"He's a supplier for wagon trains headed west, so his goods are more functional than ornamental."

"I know," Eleanor sighed, "but there are days when I wish I had more choices for shopping."

She would, he thought without rancor or judgment as he stared into her star-struck eyes. She had been born into wealth and had been giving orders to servants since she learned to talk. What most frontiersmen considered amenities, she took for granted.

But again he refused to be dissuaded from their purpose. He swung her into his arms and moved toward the shady shelter of the tree. She nestled against him, laying her cheek on his chest. Strands of hair wrapped around his arm.

"Are you really happy being a cowboy?" she asked.

He laid her on the ground and stretched out beside her, propping up on an elbow. "Yes," he said, "I am. Does it bother you?"

Reaching up to cup the back of his head with her hand, she smiled. "Yes, you bother me."

He let her guide his head to hers. Pleasure wafted through his body when their mouths touched, when her lips pouted beneath his, when they teased and coaxed a response. His hand settled on her waist; he felt the rise and fall of her abdomen as she breathed. His fingers moved, leisurely unbuttoning her dress. Then he pulled her bodice aside.

He touched the soft white fabric of her chemise. He moved slightly, his head lowering until his mouth was moving in brushlike strokes up and down her throat, finally to stop at the pulse point in the center of her collarbone. He felt her pulse flutter against his lips.

"You bother me, too."

"Should I apologize?" Her hand lightly brushed over his cheeks.

"Absolutely not." He nuzzled his face into the creamy swell of her breasts, exposed by the chemise. "This is the most delicious kind of bothering I've had in a long time."

He felt her tense, but he did not remove his face. He simply turned his head and rested his chest against her breasts.

"You've . . . had many women in your life, haven't you?"

"I'm experienced," he admitted, adding nothing else. Now he lifted his head far enough that he could look into her face.

"I'm . . . I'm not, really," she confessed. "I've only . . I mean . . . just Radford . . ."

Pursing his lips and shushing her, Bradley laid a silencing finger over her lips. "What happened to either of us before this moment doesn't matter. We're here now. That's all that matters."

"Yes," she murmured and arched to press her mouth against his.

While they kissed, his hand drifted from her hair along the delicate curve of her jaw. His fingers lightly whispered over her skin, over the line of her throat, and down to her breasts. He felt and heard her sharp intake of breath. She tensed beneath his touch; her breast pulsated to life. He felt the nipple go taut beneath his palm.

Bradley loved her with his mouth and tongue and hands until she trembled and writhed beneath him. He kissed her eyes, her nose, and the tip of her chin, his lips forging a trail from there to her ears. He seared a path of kisses down to the taut peak of her breast, still protected by the delicate chemise. He blew against the delicate fabric and felt her swell and tighten in his mouth. She quivered violently.

Reluctantly he lifted his head and gently removed the undergarment. Now he looked at her breasts, and she trembled anew. He lowered his head to touch the throbbing tip with his lips and tongue; Eleanor moaned softly beneath the gentle onslaught of the caress. His other hand pulled the hem of her skirt up. Hard callused fingers touched her flesh. She gasped and started; her hand stopped his, and her eyes opened, rounded and full of fear.

"Don't." He pulled his hand from hers. "I want to make love to you."

For long seconds they stared at each other in a battle of wills. His lips slowly spread into a tender, persuading smile. An answer trembled on her lips and she went limp again. "Yes," she murmured, "make—make love to me."

Holding her head between his hands, his mouth settled on hers, but the kisses were no longer gentle and tentative. They were hot and moist, designed to prepare her for ultimate possession.

His hand traveled up the soft skin inside her thighs. Her hand rubbed his jaw, tracing the line from ear to chin. He could hear the tips of her fingers rasp as they scratched over his beard stubble. Her blue eyes traveled back to his.

"Make me forget," she said and lifted her face to his. "Everything and everybody."

Bradley tensed and pulled away from her. Nothing had deterred him from his purpose. He had even told her that this time he would not let her go, but the words "make me forget" were too much even for him. He glared into her startled blue eyes. She wanted him to make her forget! Forget who? Forget what? Catching her hand in his, he jerked it from his face.

"No, thank you." His stomach churned nauseously. God, but he was angry . . . angrier than he could remember having been in a long, long time. "You're not going to use me to wipe Radford Vaughan out of your mind."

Before she had time to think, Eleanor slapped him, the imprint of her palm red on his cheek. Already Bradley regretted his impulsive reaction, but he said nothing. He leaped to his feet and walked away.

Eleanor lowered her head, and her hands shook as she buttoned up her bodice. Clumsily she rose, and after brushing the twigs from her dress, she tucked her hair back into her chignon. Her head high, her back straight, she walked to the gray that grazed nearby.

His desire abating along with his anger, Bradley said, "If Carl sends word about Jeffrey, wait for me. I'll be home in a couple of hours to drive you into town."

She mounted and twined the reins through her fingers. "I'll manage."

Although she was one of the most beautiful, desirable women he'd ever known, Eleanor Hunt was also one of the most frustrating. In a few long strides he closed the distance between them. "You're not to go into town without me or one of the men."

Sitting regally astride her horse, she looked down at him. "Mister Smith, I've told you before and I'll tell you again: you may be the manager of Hunt Cattle Station, but you are not the manager of Eleanor Hunt. I shall do whatever I deem is best for me, with or without your advice."

"Damn it, woman! You're insufferable."

"If I am, it's only because of men like you."

Bradley stood and watched as she rode away, twice in one afternoon. This time she did not stop on the hill to turn around and wave. She did not smile at him. Her back was straight, her shoulders squared. She was angry.

He gathered his tools and tossed them haphazardly onto the wagon bed. The end of the post-hole digger slid into the lunch basket, and it rocked back and forth. Muttering under his breath, he jerked on his shirt and fastened his gun belt around his waist. He tugged his hat in place and walked around the buckboard.

Right now he was feeling like a consummate fool! He had work to do and was leaving it undone. Sure, the fence was up—but not as securely as it should be. What the hell! He would send one of the men back later. He was not about to have Eleanor hike out to town by herself. No telling what she would do in her anger . . . with sentiment running as high as it was, she could be killed.

With Haggarty on the loose, she was not safe. True, he had warned the man off, but Bradley knew Haggarty's kind: he was quick on the draw, but slow on intelligence. He always acted before he thought.

But, Bradley thought, how could he point a finger at Haggarty when he himself had overreacted? There was no reason for him to have taken exception to the fact that Eleanor wanted to make love to him to forget Radford Vaughan. How many women had he used to help him forget?

Dear God, Eleanor was a woman in every sense of the word. Her body had been awakened to a man's touch. She had enjoyed sexual pleasure and wanted it just as much as he did. Yet he found himself victimized by the same double standard that he had always condemned.

With passion his guiding emotions, he could simply want Eleanor Hunt's body; but it was not so for her. He demanded that she want him and him alone.

He hated Radford Vaughan. He had never met the man, but he hated him!

Chapter 11

As if pursued by a deadly enemy who was quickly gaining on her, Eleanor pushed the gray at full gallop. The wind, hot and dry, blew the hat from her head and whipped strands of hair across her face. She only wished it could whip away her shame and condemnation. She'd known better than to return. Bradley had easily seen through the ruse; he'd known, just as she had, that her return was not simply for the basket. He'd known that she desired him, enough to pursue him . . . a mistake she'd made not just once, but twice. How could she have been so stupid?

Her entire body burned with shame, which in turn angered her. Why should she feel shame for giving expression to her sexual desires? After all, they were a natural part of any human being. Men were free to revel in their sexual desires, whether married or not. Yet for centuries, these same desires, both in and out of wedlock, were considered reprehensible in women.

Because of her belief in suffrage, Eleanor readily accepted—in fact, was even proud—that she was more emancipated than most women. She agreed whole-heartedly with Abigail Adams, who had advocated women's suffrage during the Revolutionary War period.

Eleanor thought society and its demands were hypocritical, especially those made on women. She should be free to experience all emotions—desire included.

Her most painful confession, the one slowest in coming and the hardest to accept, was that if this philosophy were true, she should be experiencing no inner conflict. She would not care that Bradley Smith thought her promiscuous—or that he had rejected her.

Rejected her! She felt as if someone in her brain shouted the words. The sound echoed through her mind, driving her to the brink of insanity. How swiftly she ran the gamut from humiliation to anger to hostility, from shame to castigation to self-hatred and bitterness.

Rejected again, and by a man! She could not believe her stupidity. It did seem as if she'd have learned her lesson from Radford. Men had one standard for themselves, another for women.

She had lived and moved in a man's world long enough to know this. Yet she had foolishly allowed her heart. . . . Her heart! The words jolted her, and she actually straightened up on the gray. She could not imagine herself thinking such a thing; her heart had not been involved. She tugged the reins, slowing to a trot.

Eleanor's thoughts had come full circle, and she was able to step out of herself and to evaluate them a little more objectively. She could accept that she had returned to Bradley Smith because she desired him, but she absolutely refused to entertain any thought that there might be more than just a physical attraction between them.

Eleanor Hunt was not about to revert to subterfuge, no matter how embarrassed she was. She had learned early in life to accept responsibility for her actions, and she would do just that. Her body and its needs had compelled her to return. Her heart had definitely not been involved.

Pleased with her assessment of the situation, Eleanor

breathed deeply. Indeed, she had matured since she had last seen Radford. It had taken her a long time to admit that her emotions were involved with him. But today she could admit that she desired Bradley Smith. She actually smiled. Her heart had not been involved at all, only her pride, and she had learned through the years how to mend her pride so that its ravages were not even discernible.

The gray easily covered the miles home, and Eleanor slid comfortably into bitterness. Always, where men were concerned, she returned to this feeling. It was numbing and comforting, and somehow brought a sense of control to her shattered self-image. She was not sure how long it would take her to regain her dignity . . . probably not long. Besides, no one would know but her. She was quite adept at hiding her feelings.

By the time she reached the creek that ran behind the house, she had her thoughts under control. She lifted a hand and pressed it against her chest; it was tight. She wondered if her heart were the seat of all her self-respect. If so, that would explain the pain. Oddly, she could despise Bradley Smith and at the same time ache for the fulfillment of his possession. In all her experiences with Radford . . .

Dear Lord, she thought, her face flushing warmly with the rush of memories unbidden, she had lied outright both to herself and to Bradley. In comparison with Bradley, she had had no real experiences with Radford . . . a few kisses that she had been wise enough to stop before they matured into passion.

Never had she allowed Radford to touch her as intimately as Bradley had . . . not even when she had traveled to New York to tell him she loved him and wanted to marry him, that she was willing to give up her career for him. Yet for some perverse reason—a reason she clearly did not understand—she wanted Bradley to

201

think she was worldly-wise and experienced.

"Miss Hunt!" Frisco Ingram's greeting interrupted her train of thought. He ran down the sidewalk to wait for her. "You been gone so long we was worried about you."

Eleanor blinked her eyes and looked around in surprise. She had been so preoccupied, she did not realize she was riding through the front gate toward the house. She slipped off the horse and gave the waiting hired hand the reins.

"We have company." Frisco's eyes followed her as she moved up the sidewalk. "Sheriff Hix. And Miss Sarah. And—"

"Jeffrey!" Eleanor screeched his name and raced up the steps onto the veranda. Rising, he held out his arms, and she ran into them. After a quick hug, she pulled away, her hands quickly examining him. "Oh, Jeffrey."

"I'm fine, Eleanor. Really I am." He laughed, and catching her by the shoulders, he swung her around playfully as if they were children again. Eleanor was happy. For the first time since she had arrived in Blissful, Jeffrey's countenance was bright, his eyes glowing. He looked like the Jeffrey Masterson she had known all her life, the man who was like a brother to her.

"Yeah." The sheriff, leaning his chair on its back legs against the wall, had his arms crossed over his chest and his hat pulled over his face. "He's all right now, Miss Hunt. Cattle being stolen all over the place. David Lang dead. Allen Shea almost killed in a train robbery. But Jeffrey Masterson, accused of rustling and murder, is all right. That is, if you don't consider Whittier's Lang promise to kill him, and if you don't think about Lang's men being angry and drunk enough to do it."

Jeffrey cast a reproving glance in Carl's direction. "All of you are being too pessimistic. Nothing is going to happen to me. No matter what he says, Whittier knows I didn't kill David."

"Maybe his head knows, but his heart doesn't, and right now Whittier Lang is a man ruled by his heart. Besides, the man really believes in an eye for an eye, a tooth for a tooth."

"Yet you were the one who suggested bringing him here when Tully rode in with the papers, Carl." Sarah's eyes twinkled, and she winked at Eleanor.

Carl lifted a hand and pulled his hat down a ways. His laughing blue eyes teased Sarah. "Well, now, I reckon I did. And I reckon I had my reasons."

"And they are?" Eleanor asked.

"Knowing you were determined to have Jeffrey out of jail and that most people in town were at the graveyard attending David's funeral, I figured this was the best time to bring him to you. And, when a young gentleman learned that I was riding this way, he sent you this." The legs of the chair thumped to the floor as Carl leaned forward and slid his hand into his shirt pocket to pull out a note.

"Thank you," Eleanor murmured, taking it from him. She unfolded the paper, and when she saw the familiar scrawl, her heart thudded erratically in her chest. After all these years, she still recognized his handwriting. After all her rationalizing, Radford Vaughan still had the ability to reach out of the past and affect her. Her hands trembled as she held the paper in front of her eyes.

In the distance—the far, far distance—she heard Sarah say, "I'll wager you're wondering about my reason for coming."

"To bring his lunch," Eleanor said absently, her concentration on Radford Vaughan. The years had not changed him. He was as conceited as ever. After what he had done to her, he now sent her a note to blithely announce his presence and his desire to see her at the Blissful Hotel dining room at seven o'clock for dinner tomorrow night. He had not asked, but had simply stated his plans, as if he expected her to comply without question. Her brow furrowed. Surely he did not expect her to appear in answer to such a summons!

"Eleanor!"

Jeffrey's call caught her attention. "What?" she murmured.

He laughed. "You're so lost in thought, that must be an important letter."

She dropped her arm, crumpling the paper in her hand. "It is," she answered quietly, wondering if the blood would ever flow through her veins again. "This is my first communication with the prosecuting attorney."

Jeffrey tensed. "Vaughan?"

Eleanor lowered her head and meticulously folded the note. "Radford arrived in town today. He's sure that Allen and I will want to meet with him so we can discuss a deal. The evidence is pretty much stacked against us."

Sarah gasped and leaned forward. Jeffrey's eyes filled with fear, and he caught Eleanor's arm. "No deals, Eleanor. I'm not guilty. *I did not shoot David.*"

"I know."

"Oh, Jeffrey," Sarah sobbed, hiding her face in her hands. "What are we going to do?"

"Don't let this attorney jargon fool you, sweetheart. We're going to do exactly what we talked about." Jeffrey walked to the swing to take Sarah into his arms. "Eleanor, in case you don't know, Miss Sarah Craven has agreed to marry me."

Radford Vaughan forgotten for the moment, Eleanor stared at the couple in the swing. Sarah looked up into Jeffrey's face with adoring eyes. Eleanor knew how Sarah felt about Jeffrey; nevertheless, the announcement took her by surprise.

"Congratulations!"

"Congratulations aren't the issue." Carl crossed his legs. "Don't know what Barber's gonna say when he

204

finds out."

Eleanor cast a reproving gaze on Sarah and Jeffrey. "Your parents don't know?"

"I talked with Clementine, but I haven't told Papa yet. But it doesn't matter what he says." Sarah continued, her voice growing stronger and more defiant, her eyes never wavering from Eleanor's. "I'm going to marry Jeffrey. I love him."

Jeffrey squeezed her and murmured, "I love you, too, sweetheart."

Grimacing, Carl walked to the edge of the porch. "Spare me the lovebird stuff! Where's Bradley?"

"Down there." Eleanor pointed in the direction from which she had recently ridden. "He's repairing the fence."

Carl flipped his hat on and walked down the steps. "Reckon I'll ride out a ways and see if I can find him."

"You don't have to. I passed him on the way up. He'll be here in a few minutes." Harry's voice could be heard from the hallway before she opened the screen door and walked onto the porch, her gaze flicking over Jeffrey and Sarah. "What a surprise!"

"You didn't think I'd get out of jail?" Jeffrey asked, feigning disappointment.

"I knew you would if Eleanor had her way. I'm surprised to see Sarah here with you."

"Might as well know, Harry." Carl turned around. "Sarah is planning on marrying the young man."

Planting her gloved hands on her waist, Harry once more returned her gaze to Sarah.

"It's true, Harry," Sarah said and clutched Jeffrey's hand tightly.

The screen door grated a second time against the floor, and Bradley, not having taken the time to change his clothes, stepped onto the veranda. Evincing no surprise, he looked at the couple in the swing. "Did I arrive in time to hear a wedding announcement?"

"Yep, you sure did." Carl crossed his arms over his chest and rocked back on his heels. "That is, if we can keep him alive that long. But then, I reckon that responsibility is yours now, Smith."

"Not mine," Bradley drawled. "That honor goes to Miss Hunt."

"That's right." By sheer force of will Eleanor kept her gaze fastened to Bradley's face. She refused to acknowledge the sensuality of the man or to let him know that he was having any affect on her emotionally. "Jeffrey's been released into my custody."

Carl's hands swept open. "Well, folks, I'm leaving. You can decide what you're going to do and how you're going to do it. As for me, I'm heading back to town. I figure it's gonna be a mighty peaceful place now, and a lot safer than Hunt Cattle Station."

"Why don't you stay for supper, Carl?" Harry asked. "There's always room for one more at the table."

"Sounds tempting, but not tonight. I have some work to catch up on." He smiled and waved. "Be seeing you."

Jeffrey stood and swaggered to the banister. Hitching his hands into his trouser pockets, he looked at Bradley and smirked. "Well, Smith, guess your stint as station manager is about to come to an end."

Harry slid Jeffrey a disapproving glance. "I guess that depends on me."

The cocky grin slipped from Jeffrey's face. "What do you mean?"

"You may be out of jail, but you're certainly not a free man yet," she said. "And while you're involved in the trial, I need a full-time employee. I think we'll wait awhile to return your job to you."

Jeffrey glared coldly at her for a long time before he relaxed and smiled. "You're right, Harry. I'm sorry. I've been in jail so long, I'm not thinking straight."

Harry smiled. "You just take it easy . . . enjoy your vacation. Now, Miss Sarah, would you like to join us for dinner?"

"I can't," Sarah answered. "I promised Clemmy that we'd be home for dinner."

"We?" Bradley asked, scowling deeply at Jeffrey. "You're going into town tonight?"

"I'm not going to let her drive home by herself," Jeffrey answered defensively.

"That's not a wise decision." A small frown furrowed Harry's brow.

"She can ride with me," Carl said.

"Absolutely not!" Jeffrey exclaimed. "I'm her fiancé, and I'll take her home."

Jeffrey's contemptuous gaze bounced from Bradley to Harry. "Neither of you has ever given me credit for doing anything right, have you? I've never been anything more than a tenderfoot! You've put up with me simply because you thought I was going to be Alex Hunt's son-in-law. Well, now you don't even have to do that, since you know I'm not going to be."

While Eleanor understood Jeffrey's aversion to Bradley and Harriet, she also recognized the wisdom in what they said. "You're not going into town, Jeffrey."

He spun around. "You too, Eleanor?"

She steeled herself. "Me too, if it's in your best interests."

"Well, let me tell you something—" Jeffrey's voice rose in anger "—I'm going into town with Sarah, and that's all there is to it. I'm not going to run scared because of Whittier Lang and his men."

"Then you're a bigger fool than I gave you credit for," Bradley said.

"Jeffrey—" Sarah laid a tentative hand on his arm; he caught her hand in his and squeezed. "Perhaps you'd better listen to them."

"You're out of jail because of me," Eleanor said, "and you're staying out depends on me. So help me, if you don't stay here and obey me, Jeffrey, I'll have Carl lock you back up."

Jeffrey said nothing, but his face was set in hard unyielding lines. Eleanor marveled that even now he did not look or act like a man. He reminded her of a spoiled, petulant child, determined to have his way regardless of the consequences to him or anyone else.

As she watched him lead Sarah down the sidewalk to the waiting buckboard, Eleanor wondered if she'd ever really known Jeffrey. Although she'd never admit it to Bradley, she was rather surprised with his astute assessment of her and Jeffrey. She was younger, yet more mature.

When she thought about it, she was more ambitious than Jeffrey. She'd been the one who wanted to study at the university, who wanted a career. Her father had practically coerced Jeffrey into coming to Kansas in order to learn all about the meat-packing industry. She sighed: if only Papa had given her the opportunity! She had begged, but Papa had not listened. He preferred a son to a daughter.

Still, Eleanor had to protect Jeffrey. First he was her childhood friend; now he was her client. She walked down the steps. Bradley, folding his arms over his chest, leaned against one of the porch columns. Harry stood next to him. Both of them calmly surveyed the scene below.

"Sheriff," Eleanor said, "will you escort Sarah back to town?"

"Yes, ma'am, be right glad to."

Jeffrey swung Sarah onto the buggy seat, and she leaned down to kiss him quickly. He whispered something, and she laughed softly, nodding her head. Eleanor returned to the porch, waving to Sarah until the buggy

208

was out of sight.

"Jeffrey," Harry said, "why don't you make yourself useful. Frisco can use your help in the stables. You have plenty of time before supper."

Jeffrey gave her a cold, hard stare, but said nothing. After he disappeared around the house, Harry opened the screen door and walked into the foyer. "I'm going to take a bath and rest awhile before supper."

"That sounds like a good idea," Bradley said.

Footsteps shuffled down the hall and stopped before they reached the foyer. Gaspar called out, "Boss, if you're gonna take a bath, you better hurry. I got the cistern filled with water, but if'n someone beats you to the stall, you'll have to fill it yourself. I ain't gonna do it more'n one time in one day."

"Our outdoor bathhouse," Bradley said, by way of explanation.

"I know."

"You're welcome to use it anytime." Bradley's eyes twinkled.

"I'd rather have the privacy of my bedroom and warm water," Eleanor returned.

"Better get out there," Gaspar called again. "I ain't gonna tell you another time."

"I'm on my way," Bradley answered over his shoulder. To Eleanor he said, "I'll see you later."

She nodded and waited until he disappeared down the corridor before she ascended the stairs and walked into her bedroom. A tub filled with water was sitting in the middle of the room. She smiled; Gaspar had really taken her under his wing.

While she unbuttoned her dress, she walked to the window and stared through the filmy curtains onto the lawn. The window open, she heard the splash of water from the backyard and knew that Bradley was taking a shower.

She bunched the curtain in her fist, closed her eyes, and leaned her forehead against the windowpane. She could see him tug the handle to lower the chute. She heard the water splash as it sluiced down his body and imagined skin browned by the sun, muscle finely textured by hard work.

She felt that ache begin anew in her lower body. She wanted Bradley Smith, and if she remained at Hunt Cattle Station, she would one day allow him to make love to her.

Eleanor was quite pleased with the way she looked when she walked into the parlor. She had taken great care with her hair, a mass of curls atop her head. Even greater care had gone into the selection of her dress, a blue silk one designed by Madame Louise Devereaux of Newland's Salon. The style was more daring than Eleanor ordinarily wore—straps rather than sleeves, and a scooped neckline that exposed the upper swell of her breasts—and one that she had ordered expressly to wear to an opera in New York.

"Eleanor—" Bradley's gaze swept appreciatively over her body, lingering on her breasts before it returned to her face "—as usual, you are lovely. That shade of blue enhances the beauty of your eyes."

His eyes darkened as they explored her face, then lowered to her breasts. Her earlier lesson forgotten in the wake of renewed desire and excitement, Eleanor felt herself grow tight beneath his searching eyes. His gaze was as potent as a caress. She sucked in her breath.

"Thank you." She could hardly utter the words. She had never seen Bradley in evening clothes before, and she was quite speechless. From the first moment she'd seen him, she'd been aware of his masculinity and a raw, rugged sensuality. But now, he was one of the most debonair she had ever seen—and her wealth and status in society had guaranteed that she had seen many. "You look quite handsome yourself."

"Thank you." The smile deepened, and his eyes twinkled as if he knew this sudden sophistication had startled her. He delighted in her reaction.

Eleanor would not have believed that black evening dress could change a man's appearance so drastically. She had seen hundreds of men dressed this way, and they had done nothing in particular for the clothes, or the clothes for them. Still, Bradley exuded masculinity and sensuality; he was sophisticated and suave.

"I suppose Harry and Jeffrey will be joining us?" she asked.

"Not Jeffrey. Like a child, he's pouting. He said he would be eating at the bunkhouse. Harriet is still dressing. Would you like a drink while we wait for her?"

"Oh . . . yes, please." Eleanor hastily averted her gaze and moved to sit down on the sofa, careful not to muss her dress. When he did not immediately move, Eleanor looked at him questioningly.

"I don't know what you drink." His eyes were the shade of the forest in springtime. "As emancipated as you are, I wonder if I should offer you whiskey and a cigar."

"And then sit down and talk about the business of the day," Eleanor added.

Bradley's eyes narrowed; his voice lowered. "Well, I really hadn't thought about that. You and I can find other, more interesting things to . . . er . . . talk about."

Eleanor could not mistake his meaning. She laid her hand in her lap. "I'm sure if one looked long enough, one could find other, more interesting things to do besides talk, Bradley, but between you and me, talk is all we're going to do. And right now, even talk is running thin. I prefer sherry to whiskey, and I can't abide cigar smoke."

He walked to the table on the other side of the room.

211

One hand curled around the crystal decanter; the other picked up a delicate glass. "Eleanor, I'm sorry about this afternoon."

Eleanor clasped her hands. "I'm not. I don't know what possessed me to return for that basket."

"Don't lie to me," he said softly. "Both of us know why you returned."

"Regardless of why I returned, you quickly reintroduced me to male hypocrisy."

"You're right, and I apologize for that."

He brought her drink to her. His eyes blatantly roved over her face, moved down her throat, and rested on the swell of her breasts exposed by the scoop-necked dress. Eleanor wanted to reach up and cover herself, to hide from his penetrating gaze. Instead, her smile widened, and when his face lifted, their eyes locked together.

"Ironically, I like the west because people are not so restricted by society's hypocrisy. Yet today I victimized myself by the very society I tend to loathe and ignore."

Eleanor reached for the glass, her fingers brushing against his, lingering a little longer than she should have let them. The confession disappointed her.

"While I wanted to enjoy an amorous afternoon with you, I wanted you to feel more for me than mere desire."

Despite her best intentions, Eleanor lowered her head. She felt the heat rush to her face and only hoped she was not turning red also. All her life she had demanded emancipation and cried for equality, but she was unprepared for an open discusson on . . . sex. She could hardly think the word, much less say it.

"After you left, I realized what a fool I'd been, and I guess you were laughing at me. You've been accustomed to such urbane men in your life, men like Radford Vaughan, that I must have appeared rather gauche."

Eleanor looked up so quickly that she almost spilled her drink. "No," she hastily denied.

He sat down beside her and laid his hand on her arm, his fingers warm to her flesh. "You'll have to be patient with me, Eleanor. I've never dealt with a suffragist before." His eyes intimately brushed each feature of her face. "In fact, I don't know that I've dealt with a woman who can be as honest about herself and her feelings as you."

"Bradley—" Eleanor's voice was husky. "I—"

As he had done earlier in the day, he laid a finger against her mouth to silence her. Excitement skittered through her body when she felt the callused texture of his skin against her lips.

"Let's start all over again," he said. "Neither of us will make any demands on the other. We'll enjoy the moment."

Eleanor shook her head; this had gone too far. Bradley did not understand her at all. Although her thoughts were chaotic, there was enough coherence in them for her to realize that she did not understand herself either.

He smiled tenderly; his face softened. He eased the untouched glass of sherry from her hands and set it on the nearby table. He caught one of her hands in his and pressed it against his chest. She felt the steady beat of his heart against her palm.

"No?" He laid his hand over her breast. "Your body is telling me differently."

Fearful that Harry would walk into the room, Eleanor withdrew her hand and pulled her body away from his palm. But she continued to gaze wistfully into his eyes. She longed for his heart to race beneath her hand; she longed for some indication that he was as excited by her touch as she was by his. But all he was offering her was lust, not much more than Radford Vaughan had offered. At least he was honest; Radford had not been.

"I always listen to my body when it speaks," she said, "but I don't always obey it."

213

Her gaze never wavered from his. Disappointment flickered in his green eyes. "You're determined to make me suffer."

"Don't be so melodramatic. Whether I make—" Still having some difficulty discussing sexual intimacies with Bradley, Eleanor paused and leaned over to pick up her glass of sherry. After several bracing sips, she angled her face rather arrogantly and cleared her throat. Continuing in a steady voice, she said, "Whether we make love or not, Bradley, I have a feeling that you're not one to suffer from a woman's rejection."

A new, unfamiliar emotion flickered through his eyes. Eleanor was sure of it.

"Anyone, whether it's a man or a woman, suffers when rejected, Eleanor." His voice lowered and softened. The sensual lips curled into a beautifully gentle smile that was as beguiling as his tone. "I apologize for hurting you and for demanding more than I'm willing to give."

The apology was Eleanor's undoing; her entire body trembled. She had determined to hate this man, to hold him at a distance, yet she could not. Being so much more worldly-wise than she, he was manipulating her body, her mind, her emotions as if she were a lifeless puppet dangling on a string.

She drained her drink, then leaned over and set the glass down, hoping her trembling hand would not betray the depth of her emotions. She rose. She had to put some physical distance between herself and Bradley. The hard, indomitable man she could easily fend off, although her body yearned for the passion his ultimate possession promised. This gentle man touched her in places she had never been touched before. He was treading too near her heart, and while she wanted this and had always longed for it, she was frightened. No longer was she in control.

She walked to the fireplace, the swish of blue silk about her legs a delicate caress in the otherwise silent room.

Her back to Bradley, she said, "Radford's in town."

"That's no surprise."

"He wants to see me . . . and Allen."

"You I can believe, but not Allen."

Eleanor heard Bradley's footsteps; she felt him behind her. Before the hands could settle on her shoulders—yes, she knew, something inside her knew, he would catch her by the shoulders—she turned around to face him.

"Any man in his right mind would want to see you," Bradley said.

Breathing was difficult; Eleanor felt as if a heavy weight had been laid on her chest. "He—wants to see me about the case, I'm sure."

Bradley hiked a brow skeptically. "I'm sure, and you're to talk business over at a candlelight dinner."

"Dinner, yes," Eleanor returned. "But not candlelight. We're eating in the hotel dining room."

A look of pure disgust crossed Bradley's face. "If you think that, you're a fool. Don't take me for one. You and I both know why Radford Vaughan wants to see you, and we know how he intends the evening to end."

His hands settled firmly on Eleanor's shoulders. She winced.

"My concern is how *you* intend the evening to end."

"As I see it—" Eleanor shrugged free but did not move from in front of him "—what I do with my life is my concern, Bradley, not yours."

His eyes narrowed, the sooty lashes almost but not quite hiding his somber eyes. "As of this afternoon, when you rode back to me—"

The pause was deliberate, but uncalled for. Eleanor understood exactly what he was saying; she could not deny the truth of his words.

"—You became a part of my life. Thus, what you do that affects you and me *is* my concern."

Separated only by inches, neither moved. They simply

stared at each other. Bradley's breath, lightly scented with whiskey, brushed warmly over her face.

Finally Eleanor said, "You're right, Bradley. I rode back to the fence today because of you. I was drawn to you. Giving in to my base desires was a mistake that I'll readily admit, a mistake that I'll not make again. You're quite presumptuous to assume that you mean more to me than you do. And although it is none of your business, I'll let you know that both you and Radford Vaughan share the same place in my life. You are business associates, nothing more."

Chapter 12

His hands sunk in his pockets, Lyle Pearce stood on the front porch of the house and stared into the distance. Night ribboned its approach across the sky in vivid colors as the sun settled below the horizon. Soon substance would lose its reality to shadows, and loneliness would settle its coat unequivocally on all things, human or not.

Lyle despised the land and everything it stood for. With everything within him he fought to turn the wasteland into a paradise. Yet despite all his struggle, despite all the thousands of dollars he poured into his effort, he was losing. This angered Lyle, who was not a man to lose frequently or easily.

His recent visit to Blissful served only to remind him of how much he had sacrificed in order to attain his goals. Harriet was still one of the most beautiful women he knew. He wanted her more now than he had twenty-seven years ago. He also wanted his daughter. His greatest loss was not having his family. They lent credibility to a man's claim for respectability.

He walked down the steps into the yard and gazed at the white frame three-story house he had built for himself and his servants. It was a grand structure with spires and gables reminiscent of European architecture.

Majestically it imposed itself on the rugged, uncivilized terrain of western Kansas. Lyle had dared defy this barbaric country with touches of grandeur and civilization. On one hand, he could be lauded for having succeeded; the house was there, in the evening a dark silhouette against the dusky skies. But deep down he knew he had failed. His house was as much at variance with its surroundings as a nun in a brothel.

He turned his head and gazed one last time into the distance, then extracted his watch from his waistcoat and looked at it. He sighed and clicked it shut. The hour was getting late.

He walked into the house, directly to his study. Masculine in design, it was large and comfortable. Lamplight gleamed brightly on the dark mahogany desk that stood in the middle of the room. Hanging neatly on the back of the chair was a black suit coat that matched the trousers he wore. On the desk lay his cravat.

No one was up but Lyle. He sat at the desk for a while and filed some papers; then he wrote a letter. When that was finished, he stood and flexed his shoulders, then walked to the window to stare into the darkened yard.

Eventually he returned to the center of the room, his brow furrowed in thought. Locking his hands behind his back, he began to pace the floor in front of his desk. Every once in a while he deviated from this to walk to the window and peer onto the moonlit lawn. Then he stopped in front of the wall mirror to comb his thick white hair. Anxiously his eyes would dart to the huge grandfather clock in the corner of the room, tirelessly ticking away the hour.

He was sitting in a wing chair, his legs stretched out, when he heard a horse gallop up to the house. In one easy motion he leaped to his feet and rushed to the window. He held his hand over his eyes and pressed his face against the pane. He saw the rider, and his face brightened. Before the servants could be awakened by the visitor, he rushed to the door and answered the knock himself.

"Come on in," he said, relief evident in his voice. "I'd just about given up hopes that you were coming."

"Sorry, Mr. Pearce." A rugged cowboy swaggered into the foyer. He whipped his hat from his head and raked his stubby fingers through flattened hair. "What with the funeral, I had a hard time getting away from the old man."

"I figured as much." Lyle moved down the corridor into the parlor; the visitor followed. Lyle waved his hand to a reading table on the other side of the room. "I kept supper for you."

"Thanks, Mister Pearce. That was mighty kind of you." He dropped his hat on the back of the sofa and headed for the food. "I'm really hungry."

"Would you like some coffee, Haggarty?" Pearce moved to the table to sit opposite the man.

His mouth already full, Haggarty simply nodded his head. As soon as Lyle handed him a cup of coffee, he drank greedily. "They let Masterson go today."

Lyle hiked a brow. "Freed him?"

"To that woman lawyer." Haggarty crammed his mouth full again, talking as he ate.

Pearce nodded, his brow clearing. "Tell me something about her."

Haggarty swallowed, then took several gulps of coffee. "Right nice-looking woman," he said. "Right feisty, too. She ain't scared of nobody."

Pearce smiled. "I've been hearing quite a bit about this young lady. She's causing quite a stir in Blissful, isn't she?"

"Yep," Haggarty drawled, "that she is. She's a mighty

purty woman. Black hair and blue eyes. But she's a snooty little thing. I'd like to bring her down a peg or two."

"I understand she's quite a spirited woman," Lyle said casually.

Haggarty leaned back in the chair. "I reckon she is. The day me and the boys stopped her when she was headed for the Rocking W, she whipped out that little derringer and pointed it right at me. Good thing Neb nudged the horse, or I might a been a dead man today."

"I hadn't heard about this," Lyle said, his voice dangerously quiet.

"Wasn't nothing," Haggarty said. "I was going to have me a woman, but that manager from the Hunt Cattle Station showed up and ruined the fun."

"Bradley Smith?"

Haggarty reached up to massage his upper arm. "Him all right. I would have got him out of the way, except that Hunt bitch shot me in the arm and caused me to lose aim. I'll get her one of these days."

"Leave Eleanor Hunt alone." Lyle barked the command. When Haggarty looked at him in surprise, he added in a much quieter tone, "I don't want you to get into any trouble that will mess up our operation at the Rocking W."

"Don't worry, Mister Pearce," Haggarty assured him, "I ain't."

Lyle was not reassured, but he did not want to press the issue. "I understand Hunt has hired another attorney to defend Masterson."

Haggarty nodded. "He did. The morning train he was riding on was robbed and he was wounded. He won't be defending anybody."

"I suppose you don't know anything about this robbery?"

Haggarty simply grinned, and Pearce shook his head.

"Lang seems to be short on intelligence. Now it's left up to Eleanor Hunt to defend Masterson."

"Yep. Sheriff delivered him to Hunt Cattle Station when we was at the funeral."

"This doesn't bode well," Pearce lamented. "I have a feeling that Lang will rue the day he had Shea shot, and ultimately I shall too."

"Don't worry, Mister Pearce, this woman can't hold a candle to the lawyer Lang done hired."

"I wouldn't be too sure about that, Haggarty." He leaned back in his chair and idly ran a finger around the rim of the cup.

Haggarty shrugged and shoved a biscuit into his mouth, swallowed, and wiped an arm across his lips. "His lawyer arrived in town today. City slicker from New York."

Disgusted with the man's lack of manners, Pearce dropped his gaze.

"Radford Vaughan." Haggarty leaned back in the chair and cradled his stomach with both hands.

"Yes, I know." A secretive glint in his eyes, Lyle stood and tugged on the bottom of his waistcoat. Then he walked to the desk to open a black lacquered box. Taking out a cigar, he said, "Mr. Vaughan and I have met before, Haggarty. He's done some work for me."

"Ain't that a coincidence!" Haggarty exclaimed. "Imagine you and Mister Whittier using the same lawyer."

"Hardly." Pearce struck a match and lifted it to the tip of his cigar. "You ought to know by now that nothing in my life is by accident or coincidence."

"You mean—" Haggarty's eyes widened.

As always, Pearce was amazed at the man's denseness. Yet Haggarty was reputed to be one of the fastest guns in the west. That expertise alone was Pearce's rationale for hiring him. "I mean, I'm responsible for Whittier Lang's

221

having Radford Vaughan as the attorney to prosecute Jeffrey Masterson." He puffed several times on his cigar before he said, "Vaughan's one of the best. I wanted to make sure Masterson doesn't get out of this alive."

"He couldn't anyway," Haggarty said. "Not when you look at all the evidence against him."

"With Dobson's death we lost our best witness. I wonder why the fool returned to Blissful."

"Don't matter none," Haggarty said. "Everybody figures Lang bought Dobson and that he's the one responsible for the whole thing."

Lyle lifted his hand and rubbed his chin. "Does anyone know who the gunslinger was?"

"Nope."

Lyle smiled and walked to a wing chair. As usual, he had worked carefully and diligently to set Masterson up with that bogus bank account. He had not been lying to Harriet when he told her that he was taking care of Masterson; he was. No one had known what Lyle was doing; therefore, blame could never return to him. The people whom he hired to carry out his orders were independent individuals who knew no one and were not known by anyone in his present operation.

Haggarty laughed. "I'll tell you, Mister Pearce, that Hunt woman ain't bad with a gun . . . when you consider she's a city gal. Reckon the man who gunned down Dobson didn't take her serious."

"No," Lyle mused, "he underestimated his foe . . . always a deadly mistake. I can tolerate so many killings if they're productive . . . but all of these lately have been a sad loss of lives. If Masterson and Lang had been killed that night as planned, instead of Gideon Davenport, all of this would be over and done with."

Haggarty jumped to his feet. His voice was shrill; his eyes round and rather wild. "Look, Mister Pearce, I've explained what happened. You've gotta believe me. I had

222

to kill Gideon Davenport. He figured out what we were doing. It was just a matter of time before he went to Old Man Lang or the sheriff."

"It's all right, Haggarty." Pearce pacified the man with a wave of his hand. Haggarty was too stupid to get riled over past mistakes. Lyle could be patient; he needed Haggarty a little longer. After this next job was completed, he would make sure Mister Haggarty was properly reimbursed for all his contributions to the cause. "All seems to be taking care of itself. David died without regaining consciousness, and our little secret is safe. With Vaughan I'm hoping we can correct your second mistake. We'll get rid of Masterson."

"We could always kill him."

Pearce clucked his tongue softly and shook his head. "That's barbaric, Haggarty. I like to do things legally— and civilized. If we play our cards right, the law will decide Masterson's fate, and our hands will be clean. In the meantime, I want you to get back to Blissful, and don't let Masterson out of your sight."

"Sure, Mister Pearce, if that's really what you want."

"That's what I want."

"Look, Mister Pearce, it would be much easier and safer for you to let me kill Masterson. I'm worried about how much he knows."

Pearce shot Haggarty a piercing gaze. "I do the thinking, Haggarty. You simply follow my orders." Settling the cigar into the corner of his mouth, Pearce folded his hands behind his back and began to pace again, the same route in front of his desk. "Don't think I'm not worried about Masterson. I wonder exactly how much he knows about us. How much did David tell him?"

"That's why I think—"

"But," Pearce said, "Masterson is smarter than David Lang. Whatever he knows he'll keep to himself. He has grandiose plans for himself."

223

"Look, Mister Pearce, you can't believe he really wants to become a cattle rustler . . . a man as rich as he is."

Pearce smiled. "I never used the word *rustler*, Haggarty. But yes, I do believe Mister Masterson wishes to join the ranks of those who earn their money outside the law. If he didn't, he'd have spilled his guts long ago. He would have played his trump card. And by the way, Haggarty, Masterson is not rich himself. Alex Hunt is the money behind him."

"What's his trump card?"

"The note."

"If there is one," Haggarty said.

"There is."

Before Haggarty could answer, the clock began to sound the hour.

Closing her book and laying it aside, Eleanor glanced at the mantel. But she did not have to look at it or hear the sounding of the hour to know what time it was. She had been aware of each passing minute since Bradley had announced at dinner that he had to leave for a business meeting immediately upon finishing the meal. .

"I love that clock." Harry folded the paper she had been reading and rose, "but it marks time much too fast for me. The older I get, the faster time goes. I had no idea it was ten o'clock. I think I'll go to bed. How about you?"

"No," Eleanor said and rose, "I'm not sleepy. I think I'll join Jeffrey in the study. I have some questions to ask him."

"Reckon he's speaking to anyone yet?"

Eleanor smiled and shrugged. "I'll soon find out."

"Better you than me," Harry said. "I'll see you in the morning."

Eleanor walked down the corridor to open the door to

224

the office. "Jeffrey—" she began, her voice soon trailing into silence. Although the lamp was still burning, the room was empty. Jeffrey was gone. "Gaspar," she yelled and raced toward the kitchen, "have you seen Jeffrey?"

"As he was leaving."

"*Leaving?*" Eleanor echoed.

"Yep." He shuffled out of the kitchen. "Left some time ago."

Rushing past him, Eleanor ran to the barn to find Frisco still working. "Have you seen Jeffrey?" she asked.

He threw the pitchfork down, grabbed the lantern, and walked closer. Nodding, he said, "He saddled his horse and left about an hour ago."

"Eleanor—" Harry stood on the edge of the porch "—what's wrong?"

"Jeffrey's gone," she called back as she returned to the house. "I should have known he'd do this. He has no regard for anyone, not even himself."

Harriet was quiet a long while before she said, "Don't concern yourself, Eleanor. I don't think there'll be any trouble tonight. It's too soon after the funeral. Furthermore, Jeffrey's a big boy now. Let him take care of himself."

"I think I'll sit on the front porch awhile."

"And wait for Jeffrey," Harry asked softly.

"Yes." *And wait for Bradley,* she added silently.

Eleanor moved into the foyer. When she pushed open the screen door, she called over her shoulder to Harriet's retreating figure, "By the way, did I tell you I'd probably stay in town tomorrow night?"

Harry stopped, the skirt of her dress swishing at her feet as she turned. "Oh?"

As if she were a child answering the implied why and resenting it very much, Eleanor explained, "I'm meeting Radford Vaughan."

"Is that wise?"

225

Eleanor released the door. "Radford and I happen to be old friends."

"And if you meet with him tomorrow night at the hotel, people are going to wonder exactly how friendly you are." Harriet gazed steadily at Eleanor, then said, "I'm not going to let you go."

Unable to believe her own ears, Eleanor gaped at Harriet.

"Your father wouldn't approve, and neither do I. I'm not going to have you traipsing all over the countryside ruining your reputation. Your father will have my hide if I do."

Eleanor laughed. "My father wouldn't care in the first place, and besides, how will he know?"

"He's scheduled for a visit in two weeks."

Eleanor almost staggered beneath the news.

"And word travels fast out here," Harry continued. "If you insist upon meeting with Vaughan tomorrow night, I'll have Bradley drive you into town and wait for you."

Eleanor opened her mouth to protest, then the irony of the situation hit her. She wanted to laugh; instead she smiled and said, "Thank you, Harry. That would be nice." Then she stepped closer. "When did my father decide to make a trip out here?"

Harry's lids lowered. "I'm not sure what prompted his decision."

"You know, Harry," Eleanor said faintly, "I think you know a lot more about my father than you're letting on. He's coming out here because I'm here, isn't he? You told him that Allen was wounded and couldn't defend Jeffrey. Papa *is* bringing another lawyer, isn't he?"

"He learned that you were out here from your Aunt Edna," Harry admitted. "And he was angry at you for leaving without letting him know."

Eleanor chuckled quietly. "He would have been even

angrier had I told him. What about the attorney?"

"I don't know," Harriet replied. "I told him about Allen's accident, but in his letter to me Alex said nothing about bringing another attorney."

The smile still lingered on Eleanor's lips. "Won't he be surprised when he arrives and the trial is over. I'm glad they set up the date. Now Papa won't be able to take away my opportunity."

"He wouldn't do that," Harriet argued.

"Not intentionally," Eleanor agreed and retraced her steps to the door. Pushing on the screen with her palm, she said, "But he would do it, and I'm sure he is. That sounds like something Alexander Hunt would do."

"You don't like your father?"

Standing still, Eleanor did not open the door any wider. "Yes, I like him very much. I love him, too."

"You don't sound as if you have a very high opinion of him."

Now Eleanor did turn, and she leaned against the door frame. "I have an extremely high opinion of my father. He doesn't have a high opinion of me."

Moving to where Eleanor stood, Harry lay a hand on her shoulder. "You're wrong about your father."

"How would you know?"

"You're his life. When he's out here, all he can talk about is you. He's proud of you, Eleanor . . . real proud."

"So proud he doesn't think I can live my own life or make my own decisions."

Harry laughed gently. "He's accustomed to having a little girl on his hands. You'll have to let him get accustomed to your being a woman, and a headstrong one at that."

"How long do you think that'll take?" Eleanor asked. "I've been a woman for a long time."

"I think perhaps this trip will serve to open his eyes."

Harry smiled and winked. "In fact, you've doen quite a bit of growing up since you've been out here."

Eleanor warmed under the compliment. "Thank you, Harry."

As if she were embarrassed by the intimate turn of the conversation, Harry dropped her hand and stepped away. "Well, Eleanor, I'm going up to bed."

"Good night. I'll see you in the morning."

Pleased with the conversation that had given her a little insight into the station superintendent, Eleanor smiled to herself as she pushed on the screen door and walked onto the veranda. Sitting on the banister, she stared across a yard full of black silhouettes and silver shadows. She had enjoyed the evening thoroughly, although some of the pleasure had diminished when Bradley had left for his meeting.

She was naturally curious about his meeting tonight. After their intimate conversation before dinner, she had expected him to tell her where he was going, but throughout the meal he had remained silent on the subject. When he did not volunteer the information, she had been tempted to ask, but had not. Through the years, pride or perhaps wisdom had taught her to temper her curiosity.

Where Bradley was concerned, Eleanor was too unsure of her feelings. Despite her wanting to, she knew that she cared about him. Moreover, she was infatuated with him—a feeling she had never felt for Radford—and Bradley was infatuated with her. Harder for her to understand and admit was this primitive fascination she and Bradley felt for one another.

This giddy feeling between them, this electrical current that seemed at once to draw them together and to push them apart was so different from the emotions she'd experienced with Radford. She and Radford had shared a loftier emotion. Theirs was intellectual and spiritual. She had thought herself in love with Radford, absolutely, unequivocally. Of course, the subsequent events of their courtship—if one could call it that—and the years had proved her wrong.

Now she was attracted to Bradley, and most of the time she did not even like the man. An intelligent woman, she identified these emotions he stirred up as mere desire, nothing more. Recognizing this for what it was, she could handle it . . . but could she handle Bradley?

Even as she sat on the porch, she promised herself that she would not wait long for him. The wind, hot and dry, blew against her as if to tell her to go in; yet she remained outside to wait a little longer. The half hour sounded, then the hour. Finally she could not convince herself to sit there any longer. Neither Jeffrey nor Bradley was coming home. She lifted her arms skyward and stretched. Renewing its strength, a gust of wind whipped her skirt around her ankles.

Her eyes locked on the road, and she reached up to brush a strand of hair out of her face. No one was in sight. Although she was hesitant to leave her vigil, she slowly crossed the porch. Her hand slipped into the handle and she tugged on the screen door, the bottom grating irritably across the floor. Seemingly out of nowhere she heard the galloping of hooves; she turned the door loose and rushed to the edge of the porch. Circling the porch column with an arm, she leaned over the banister to peer down the road. Her heart was racing. Then the cry "Gilmore's place is on fire" shattered the stillness of the night.

In a matter of minutes Hunt Cattle Station was a flurry of activity. Lights burned in every window; people ran in all directions; buggies headed down the drive and onto the road. No time to change clothes, no thought to do so, Eleanor found herself sitting in the buckboard beside Harriet. At the speed they were traveling, all of it against

229

the wind that was blowing furiously, she hung on tightly and figured it would be a miracle if they did not kill themselves en route to the Gilmores'.

Although she did not know the Gilmores' place, Eleanor could have found it tonight. The light from the conflagration arched golden in the air, an ominous contrast to the fragile radiance of the moon. Soon they merged with others who joined in the fire-fighting crusade. Those on horses rushed past; the buggies lined up and moved more slowly. People greeted one another, but did little talking afterward.

When Harriet stopped the buckboard in front of the Gilmores', a few people had already gathered to form a water line to fight the blazing house. The wind swept the flames in all directions.

"Hurry up," someone called out. "As dry as it is, and the way this wind is blowing, the barn is going to catch fire."

Men were running back and forth into the building to bring out the furniture and personal belongings. Disregarding their evening gowns, Harry and Eleanor leaped from the buggy and ran to join the water line.

Her eyes filled with dust, the wind biting against her cheeks, Eleanor passed the buckets until she thought her arms would break. She was wet; her face was covered with grit and perspiration, her dress torn and dirty. She reached for a pail of water as she saw another wagon drive up. She turned her head; it was Bradley. He was driving, and his passenger was Julia.

Eleanor was so startled she missed the bucket; it fell to the ground, and water sloshed all over her skirt and shoes. He had been with Julia Stanwood this evening. That was his business engagement. In the wake of discovery and disappointment, the fire was temporarily forgotten.

"If you're not going to watch what you're doing," the

woman next to her shouted, "get out of line, and let someone take your place."

Eleanor turned her head and brushed a falling strand of hair out of her face. "Sorry," she mumbled, her words lost in a howling gust of wind and cinder and soot.

"It's all right," the older man to her right said and handed her another brimming bucket, "Lemmy is always a little brisk. She don't mean no harm. We're all getting tired. After you pass that along, why don't you rest awhile?"

"I think I will." When the man stepped forward to close the ranks, Eleanor staggered back. The water was hardly affecting the fire. As if in defiance, the flames seemed to dance even higher in the blackened sky; the wind blew with even more gusto.

"Marty!"

Eleanor turned to see Letty Gilmore running wildly through the people. The scream, however, was lost in the commotion.

"Marty!" the woman cried as she bumped into Eleanor and looked wildly into her face. "Have you seen Marty?"

Eleanor shook her head.

"He's my five-year-old. I've lost him. I can't find him anywhere." Her eyes pivoted to the burning structure. "He—he can't be—"

Eleanor caught the woman's shoulders. "No, he's not. He's somewhere around here. I'll help you find him."

"Oh, my God!" Letty wailed, her small hand lifting to push stringy hair out of her face. "I haven't seen him in so long. What could have happened to him? You don't suppose he could be in the house . . ."

"Don't get upset, Mrs. Gilmore!"

The woman was hysterical. She was not listening to a word Eleanor said. She caught Letty as she lunged for the blazing building and held her until she ceased to fight. The wind, renewing its fury, carried sparks to the barn, and it soon ignited into a blaze. "Oh, my God!" the woman whimpered and wilted into Eleanor's arms. "The house and the barn!"

Eleanor led Letty away from the fire. "It's going to be all right, Mrs. Gilmore. You sit right here, and I'll find Marty."

"Marty," Letty repeated the name dully. Then her head jerked up and she screamed, "Marty! Where's Marty?"

"He's around here somewhere," Eleanor assured her. "I'll find him for you."

The woman centered her tearstained face on Eleanor, and one hand clamped like a vise around her arm. "You'll find him. You promise?"

"I'll find him. I promise."

Calling the child's name and moving through the hordes of people, she searched in front of the house, then back. Around and around she went. Then she spied a child running toward the barn.

"Marty!" she screamed, but it was too late. Already the five-year-old had darted through the doors, nothing but a flaming arch. Eleanor was after him. Before he had gotten very far, she grabbed him by the waist and tugged him into her arms.

"Hambone," he cried, his little fists pelting against her chest. "Hambone's gonna burn up!"

Hanging onto the fighting boy, Eleanor inhaled the gray smoke and coughed as she carried him out of the barn. "Who's Hambone?" she asked when her coughing had subsided.

"My doggie." Tears pouring down his cheeks, he pointed into the barn. "He's in there, and he's gonna burn up. He's just a puppy. He doesn't know what to do."

"I'll get him," Eleanor promised, taking the boy to a safe place away from the barn. "You stay here and wait for me, all right?"

Rubbing the tears from his eyes with two dirty fists, he nodded. Eleanor turned and rushed into the barn, moving to the very back, where the tiny mutt cowered. She scooped the puppy into her hands and turned to leave, but a blazing beam fell to the ground in front of her feet. She jumped out of the way in time to keep from getting burned, but her clothes were singed; she smelled them burning. Before she thought, she inhaled the thick black smoke. Coughing, she staggered in the direction of the door, but her lungs and throat were aflame. She could not breathe, nor could she see. Her eyes burned, and tears ran down her cheeks.

She fell once, using her free hand to push herself to her feet. She took another step and fell down again. Her hands frantically clawed through the dirt as she attempted to rise. Tears rushed down her cheeks as she gasped for breath. She kept the puppy beneath her body, protecting it from the smoke and the heat.

She was not going to make it out! She collapsed to the ground. As if he sensed the danger, Hambone whimpered and snuggled even closer.

Then Eleanor was enveloped in cool wetness. It was heavy and suffocating, but it felt good and safe. Never had she yearned for water more. She was swooped up into strong, protective arms. Her head rested against a bare chest; she nuzzled her cheek into a mat of soft, silky hair. She heard the steady cadence of a heartbeat. The puppy whimpered and squirmed into a ball between her and her savior.

"You little fool," a familiar voice murmured, the softness of his tone taking the sting out of the words.

Eleanor lifted her arms and wrapped them around Bradley's neck. Flooded with joy over his saving her, she forgot her disappointment and anger at his having spent the evening with Julia Stanwood.

"If I weren't so glad you're alive, I'd tan your bottom, woman."

The husky tones sounded thick with tears. Eleanor smiled and brushed her cheek up and down, burrowing a little deeper into the comfort and protection of his arms. His words did not bother her; she heard the care and concern behind them.

She was aching all over; she was exhausted. She lay in the shelter of his towering strength, luxuriating in the feel of his body as he moved. Her eyes were burning too badly for her to see where they were going.

"I'm going to put you down," he said. "Do you think you can make it now?"

She could, but certainly did not wish to. She wanted to remain in his arms forever.

"Eleanor?"

"Yes," she murmured.

"Can you stand up?"

"Do I have to?"

"I wish you didn't, but you do."

"Yes."

Slowly Bradley settled her feet on the ground, and his arms slipped from around her. The soggy blanket slid down her body to bunch at her feet. Holding onto the puppy, she stared up into Bradley's face. She felt alone and bereft.

"Thank you for saving me," she murmured.

Bradley groaned and caught her into his arms in a warm embrace full of care and concern. "Thank God I saw you in time."

"You're gonna crush Hambone!" The child clawed his way between Bradley and Eleanor. When they pulled apart, he said, "You're gonna hurt him."

Bradley took the puppy from Eleanor and handed him to Marty. "You take this dog and get away from the barn," he said sternly. "If I catch either one of you around here, no telling what I'll do. You hear me?"

"Yes sir, Mister Smith." Holding the squirming, whimpering dog in his arms, Marty solemnly nodded.

"Now get." When the child was gone, Bradley turned to look at Eleanor. They exchanged a tender smile as he wiped an ash from her face. He glanced down at the blue silk dress. "It's ruined."

"I can buy another," she whispered, and her eyes went from the house to the barn, the structure collapsing in front of them. "It's nothing compared to what the Gilmores are losing."

"Are you all right?" he asked.

Although it was unmercifully hot, she clasped her arms across her breasts. "I'm fine. Go on and help them."

Bradley stood for a moment longer, his green eyes piercing hers. His hand cupped her cheek. He smiled; then he was gone.

Later, when the buildings were nothing more than glowing embers and everyone had done all they could, Eleanor and Harry convinced the Gilmores to spend the night at the cattle station. Harry stood with Ira, the two of them talking in low tones with Bart Stevens, the banker. Marty and Hambone snuggled in her lap, Eleanor sat in the buckboard, waiting.

The other Gilmore children, Louella and Ginny, slept in the bed of the wagon, their clothing forming their mattress. Their mother sat beside them, staring blankly at the buildings that had once been their home and barn.

Holding the little boy close, Eleanor turned to see Julia sitting alone in a buggy across the yard. She too was bedraggled and exhausted. Her face and clothing were covered with ash and grime; strands of hair escaping the elegant coil on the nape of her neck wisped against her cheeks. Like Letty Gilmore, Julia seemed to be staring blankly into space.

Eleanor's gaze then wandered back to Ira and Harry. Bradley had joined them now and stood in the small circle, talking with them. Slung negligently over his shoulder was his suit coat, now bearing slight resemblance to the filthy wet trousers he wore. His white shirt, also wet, was torn and dirty; it was plastered to his body.

Now that all urgency and danger was gone, Eleanor thought about Bradley's saving her. Sheer pleasure seeped through her body. She remembered the protective warmth of his body as he swung her into his arms and swept her to safety. Almost with a will of their own, her eyes wandered over to Julia, and Eleanor felt a twinge of jealousy. Bradley had announced he was going to a business meeting, but a part of Eleanor had to wonder if it was more than that.

Eventually Bradley stepped away and lightly slapped Ira on the shoulder. His voice when he spoke drifted over to Eleanor. "We'll have a barn raising and have these buildings back up in no time."

Ira shrugged. "I don't know that I have the heart to begin again, Bradley."

Bradley squeezed his shoulder. "Sure you do, Ira. Everything will look better after you get a good night's rest. Bart, Harry—I'm leaving now. We all need to be getting home."

"You driving Julia home?" Harry asked.

Bradley nodded.

"Check before you crawl into bed," Harry warned. "I don't know where I'll have people sleeping."

Again he nodded and waved his hand as he walked toward Julia's buggy. Disappointed, Eleanor wondered if he intended to say good night to her. He slung his coat into the bed of the buggy and said something to Julia. She smiled wearily and nodded.

Then he turned to walk toward Eleanor, his gaze

236

locking to hers. The two of them stared at each other through the silvery glow of night. Their faces were shadowed; their expressions unreadable.

When he was close enough for her to hear, he said, "It's only business." She nodded, and he lifted a hand to brush her cheek. "Ashes."

She reached out and ran her fingers over the bridge of his nose. "You, too."

He caught her hand in his. "I'll need to take another bath when I get home."

Although she was so exhausted her body ached, and she thought her muscles would never obey any command again, Eleanor smiled. "Gaspar isn't going to fill the bath cistern with water again today, and it certainly isn't going to rain anytime soon."

She saw the flash of white teeth as he returned the smile. "There's plenty of water for me to bathe tonight."

Harry walked to the wagon and climbed onto the seat. "Thought you were leaving, Bradley."

"I am," he said. "I wanted to check on Eleanor to see if she was all right."

"I guess all of us are as right as we can be, under the circumstances." Harry took up the reins. "Well, Bradley, good night. Eleanor and I are taking the Gilmores home. We need to get these children into bed."

Bradley squeezed Eleanor's hand tightly. "I'll be home as soon as I can."

Chapter 13

"Well, Gaspar, I think we have all the Gilmores in bed, and Harry's on her way. That leaves you and me."

"And I'm just about on my way out," Gaspar said. "So's that leaves you, Missy."

"So it does." Eleanor walked through the kitchen into the washroom to lay her nightclothes on the oak stand. She was exhausted, ready to take her bath and retire for the night. She was also filthy, she thought, gazing at her reflection in the shaving mirror. In taking care of the children, seeing that they were bathed before going to bed, she had cleaned her hands and face, but that was all. Her gaze swept down the front of her sodden dress.

"I have two kettles boiling," Gaspar said, "in case you want to bathe in warm water."

"Thanks," she called out and returned to stand in the doorway between the kitchen and washroom.

Gaspar, using his apron as a pot holder, lifted a metal teakettle from the wood stove. Carrying it to the table, he filled a cup with a pungent-smelling liquid. "Got Miss Harry some herb tea here," he said. "It'll relax her and help her sleep better tonight."

Eleanor smiled at the old man. "You're a doctor now, Gaspar?"

He returned the pot to the stove. "Sorta. I learned about this from the Indians. It tastes as bitter as gall, but it shore works wonders on the old body. There's enough for you to have a cup after you take your bath, Missy." He picked up the small tray and turned to her, his mouth curved into a toothless grin. "Do you mind taking this up to Miss Harry? I'll clean up the kitchen while you're gone. By the time you return, you'll be able to take your bath in private and go straight to bed with a cup of hot tea."

"No, I don't mind. Is she expecting this?"

"Yes, ma'am, she sure is."

Eleanor took the tray from him, careful not to rest its weight in the palms of her blistered hands. To be honest, Eleanor was glad that Gaspar had asked her to serve Harry the tea. She was curious and wanted to know more . . . she certainly wanted to see the woman's bedroom. She felt she would learn more about the enigma called Harry Prescott. As she and Harry had passed in the hall, Eleanor had caught glimpses of the room, but she had never been inside to see what it was really like. Even the night she had gone to discuss the note with Harry, she had not been invited inside.

Quietly Eleanor climbed the stairs and moved down the hall to Harry's room. Balancing the tray on the fingertips of one hand, she lightly tapped on the door. She heard Harry's faint call, "Come on in. The door's open."

Eleanor entered to find the room empty. At the far end, a door stood ajar, and light spilled through the narrowed opening.

"Thanks, Gaspar. Just leave it on my night table," Harry said.

Eleanor heard the words, but she never moved. From where she stood, she slowly pivoted and stared. Quick glimpses had not prepared her for the elegant beauty. She walked to the night table at the head of the bed. In setting the tray down, her hand slipped, and the metal clattered against the night table to send a letter fluttering to the floor.

"Gaspar," Harry called in concern, "is something wrong?"

"Oh, no," Eleanor reassured her as she hastily stooped to retrieve the sheet of paper, "I didn't drop it."

"Eleanor!" Her light cotton gown billowing around her feet, Harry raced into the bedroom to come to a halt beneath the wall sconce. In the dim light, her auburn hair, hanging in a thick braid over one shoulder, glinted richly like copper. "What are you—doing here?"

Eleanor heard Harry, but was unable to answer. She stared at the familiar scrawl on the paper; she read and reread the intimate closing: *With all my love, my Darling, Alex.* The words careened through her brain; they made her want to read the letter.

"That's mine," Harry said. "Please fold and return it to the table where you found it."

Eleanor lifted her head and stared with lackluster eyes at the older woman. "Written to you by my father?"

"Yes."

Dropping her head, she obeyed Harry and laid the letter on the nightstand. She picked up the fallen picture frame and stared into her father's face. "I don't suppose . . . he was writing figuratively, was he?"

Her face drawn, as if she were angry, Harry walked to the armoire and threw open the doors. As she rummaged, she said over her shoulders, "You read the letter, didn't you?"

"No, it blew off the night table when the tray slipped from my hand. I was picking it up when I noticed the signature. I don't make it a habit to read other people's mail."

"I'm glad."

Eleanor whirled around and glared at the woman. "How long?" she asked.

"Does it matter?" Harry did not pretend to misunderstand.

"Of course it matters," Eleanor exclaimed and held out the photograph. Then her gaze automatically spanned the room—an expensive room that had been decorated with a couple in mind; a room that was neither masculine nor feminine, but a mixture of both. She looked at the huge four-poster bed, the covers invitingly turned back. Her eyes swept from the shaving stand to the dresser and beyond to the matching armoires.

"I suppose you're going to tell me that it began after Mama died." Clutching the photograph in one hand, Eleanor marched to the wardrobe. "And that in his grief Papa found solace in your arms?"

"Is that what you'd like to believe?" Harry asked.

"Yes," Eleanor admitted, snatching out a blue dressing gown and waving it in front of Harry. "But this tells me differently. Papa and I shopped together at Newland's for this. All those other gifts that he claimed were for the wives of his men . . . all of them were for you."

"Quite possibly some were, but your father is good to his people, and he does give them gifts on special occasions. I think you're exaggerating."

"I wish I were." Again her eyes riveted to the bed. She could not imagine her father sleeping in that bed; she could not imagine his making love to Harry there.

Harry walked to where Eleanor stood and took the picture frame and the dressing gown from her. "It's always difficult for children to acknowledge that their parents are humans, with the same foibles and urges that—"

"You're not my parent!" Eleanor shouted, unable to control her anger and hurt.

Harry's eyes darkened, and she bit her lip. Finally she lowered her head and stared at the photograph. "Of course not," she finally admitted. "But the truth still remains, it's difficult for you to admit that your father is a man, with a man's passions."

"And you're his—you're his—" Eleanor's head lifted, and she stared at Harry.

"I'm his mistress," Harry finished with quiet dignity. "Whatever you might think of me, Eleanor, I want you to know that I love your father."

"That's supposed to make adultery all right?"

"We're not going to stand here and talk about your father's morals—or mine. Many years ago I made a decision, and I accepted the consequences. Now you, Eleanor Hunt, are going to have to grow up and accept life as it is, not as you want it to be."

"I guess you're the reason my mother refused to accompany my father out here to the cattle station," Eleanor said bitterly, willing to blame someone else for her mother's shortcomings.

"I really can't speak for your mother," Harry said and moved to the night table, where she replaced the photograph. After she slipped into her dressing gown and laced it up, she picked up her cup of tea. "But I shouldn't think that was the reason. She should have known there was another woman in your father's life, but she had no reason to suspect me."

"And why should she have known?" Eleanor asked.

"A woman in love with her man would have known. If it'll make you feel better, I always knew I was the other woman in your father's life. Our life together, such as it is, has been predicated on that premise."

"You've been happy being the other woman?" Eleanor asked incredulously.

Harry cupped the tea in both hands and took several swallows before she said, "I love your father more than any other person in the entire world. I'm happy to have what part of him I can." She smiled sadly. "It's quite possible, you know, that I could have had nothing."

Eleanor covered her ears with her hands. "How could Papa have done this to Mama? How *could* he?"

Do you think perhaps the question could be rephrased? How could your mama have driven your papa to seek a mistress?"

"No," Eleanor said, but even as she shook her head in denial, she thought about the months that she and her mother spent in New York away from her father; their frequent trips to Europe; the separate bedrooms when they were home. "Papa was so disappointed when I turned out to be a girl. He wanted a boy, you know."

About to take a swallow of tea, Harry lowered her cup and looked at Eleanor in surprise. "No, that's not true! Alex has always been proud of you." She laughed softly. "Sometimes angry and irritated, because you're so headstrong and stubborn—but always proud. He loves you, Eleanor . . . you must believe that."

"Oh, I do," Eleanor said. "He loves me very much. That's why he went to such lengths to match me and Jeffrey. But Papa was disappointed that I was a girl. He wanted a son to take over the business and carry on his name."

Harry's countenance softened. "And believing this, you've spent all your life trying to be the son that Alex never had?"

"I wanted Papa to be pleased with me," Eleanor admitted, "and I wanted to succeed in his business. I have intelligence, and I wanted to use it to be something more than a—a fixture around the house."

"I agree, but you've defied your father at every turn— no matter what he suggests or asks you to do."

"He never invited me to accompany him to the cattle station. I guess that was because of you and him,"

Eleanor said.

"Maybe," Harry answered, "but more likely he didn't think you would like it out here. You spent so much time in New York and Europe, he thought life on the frontier would bore you."

"Papa never knew me," Eleanor said sadly. "He never took the time to understand what I really wanted out of life. He didn't know what bored or interested me. Maybe if he had spent as much time with me as he evidently did with you, he would have known."

Harry carefully replaced her cup on the tray. "I'll forget you said that, Eleanor. You're too angry and upset to know what you're saying."

"I meant every word I said, and I don't want you to forget," Eleanor said. "When my mother died, do you know where my father was? He was out here with you . . . with his whore. Do you realize that, Harry? You're a whore?"

"Yes," Harry answered, "I was a whore. I first met your father at a brothel."

The quiet admission startled Eleanor. She staggered back, bracing herself against the dresser.

"I fell in love with your father the first time I saw him, and he with me. But he was loyal to his family. As long as your mother was alive, he would not leave her."

"He had a strange sense of loyalty," Eleanor sobbed, her hand coming up to her mouth. "I'll never forgive him for this. How could he love a woman like you?"

Rushing out of the room, Eleanor slammed the door. Drawing in deep gulps of air and biting back the tears, she hurried into the kitchen. True to his word, Gaspar was gone, and a single lamp in the center of the table flickered dimly throughout the room.

She could not believe her father had been living with another woman all these years . . . not her father. The image of Whittier Lang emerging from the building with

245

Maude Livingston swam before Eleanor's eyes. Her father was no better, nor was Harry. She was a whore and his mistress. Any other man, any other woman, Eleanor could have accepted—but not her father . . . not Alexander Hunt. In one tiny instant, one bat of the eyelash, her father had tumbled from the pedestal on which she had placed him years ago.

With the back of her hand she wiped the tears from her eyes. Harry was lying; her father would not do this. He had always taught her to be so prudent. What had not been instilled as morals had been instilled as the ethics of good business.

Once again Eleanor saw the unfairness of it all: a man had his rules, a woman hers. Alex Hunt could philander without impunity, but not a woman.

Sitting down at the kitchen table, she pillowed her face on her arms and cried until she had the hiccups. When the clock on the far wall sounded the early morning hour, she sat up. Standing, she walked to the counter and opened a drawer to extract a large handkerchief. After she wiped her eyes and blew her nose, she poured a cup of tea and sipped it. Gradually the tension eased away, and she relaxed. The clock chimed the passing of another hour, and still Jeffrey had not returned. Nor had Bradley for that matter.

But why should they? They had to answer to no one. She sighed; she was exhausted and should not be condemning Jeffrey because she had learned a home truth about her father. But she was disappointed in Bradley . . . he had promised, and she had thought him a man of his word.

She slid her clothes over in order to scribble a note, telling Jeffrey and Bradley they had been assigned to sleep in the bunkhouse. She hoped they would read it before they barged into their rooms, especially Jeffrey, since the Gilmores were sleeping in his. Dropping the pencil, she leaned back in the chair and let her arms hang loosely by her side. She had so much on her mind; she was worried about Jeffrey, concerned about Bradley, and downright disappointed in her father. If only she had not taken that tea to Harry, if only she had not learned. If only . . . she would have been happy in her ignorance.

Then Harry's word came back to reassure her: Alex Hunt was a man, with a man's foibles and urges. Rather than being a father first, he was a man; and if she was going to love him, Eleanor would have to accept him as he was. But she could not, Eleanor thought, her heart twisting in anguish; she would not. Her father would have to make a choice: it was either her or Harry.

Her tears shed, her resolve firm, Eleanor stood and stubbed her toe against the table leg. Punishment for your thoughts, Aunt Edna would have said, but Eleanor paid the slight mental rebuke no attention. At the moment she took solace in her anger and in her ultimatum. It made her feel she was in charge again; she was once more in control of the situation.

Reaching for her clothes, she wondered where Jeffrey could be and what he could be doing. Surely he was not at the Craven's! Not at two o'clock in the morning! Yet she consoled herself that all was well.

And Bradley—where was he? Surely not at Julia Stanwood's! Somehow Eleanor could not console herself that all was well with Bradley. The visions of him and Julia together in bed tortured her. Perhaps his infatuation with her was all pretense and part of a game he played with women.

Her gaze wandered to the tub in the middle of the kitchen. She would take her bath and go to bed. Before she could do so, however, she would have to empty out the used water. She wished she could curl up and go to sleep as she was. At the moment she was beyond exhaustion and eaten alive with jealousy, disappointment, and anguish. With great effort she pushed out of the chair and walked across the room. Catching the tub by the handle, she dragged it out of the house to the edge of the porch.

As she tilted the tub to drain it, she looked around. What was nondescript in the daytime was unusually pretty tonight. The full moon cast the backyard into silver radiance. The tub empty, Eleanor set it down and leaned against a column. The wind had died down now, and the hot, dry breeze touched and oddly refreshed her. Her eyes moved from the barn to the cistern to the crude structure where the men bathed if they did not use the river. Certainly she had been tempted to use it herself.

This was where Bradley had bathed today, where he would bathe tonight, if he came home. She recalled having heard the whining of the chute as it lowered and the splash of water. A shiver ran through her body as she thought about him standing in that small building with water sluicing over his naked body.

What if he stayed and bathed at Julia's? The question tormented her further. Her gaze lifted, and she stared at the star-studded sky. Stubbornly she hung onto his promise. He had said he would be home tonight, and he would.

She could only wonder what detained him. While a small part of her was jealous of him and Julia, a greater part would not allow herself to be. She liked Julia. Eleanor also knew Bradley well enough to know that if he had said tonight's visit to Julia was business, it was. He was not a man to lie or to deceive her. She could count on his word.

She reached up to tuck an errant strand of hair into her chignon and winced as her muscles rebelled against the slightest movement. She had been so preoccupied with other matters this evening, she had not noticed her own discomforts or wounds. She held her hands out and looked at her blistered palms.

She walked into the washroom and glanced into the shaving mirror. She looked a sight! Her hair, loosened from the chignon, whisked around her face. It was dirty and needed washing. She touched her finger to a smudge on her cheek.

Her hand and gaze slid down her throat to her bodice. Wet, torn, and burned in places, her beautiful silk dress was ruined and would have to be discarded. She looked at the snag where it had caught in the barn when she had rushed in after Marty. She smiled.

A dress was a small price to pay for saving a life, even if it was a puppy's. Eleanor worried about the Gilmores. They had lost everything except their clothing and their furniture—their house, their barn, their livestock. According to Harry, they had no money for rebuilding. Letty, in a state of shock since they'd arrived at the ranch, had said nothing; she was not even crying. Eleanor was concerned about the woman.

All Eleanor had lost was one dress, easily replaced. She would talk with Harry tomorrow to see how she could help the Gilmores, perhaps loan them some money. She had enough from her mother's inheritance to do that. But she would have to be careful in making her offer. In the short while she had been out west, Eleanor had learned that these people were independent and proud. She did not want them to think she was extending charity or pity.

Tomorrow evening she would meet with Radford. That is, if she was going to meet with him. The trial began the day after. While Eleanor was glad that she was defending Jeffrey, she was also anxious and a little frightened.

When she had struck out here on another of her crusading adventures, she had been far too optimistic. She was going to save her childhood friend and prove herself an attorney of repute. Now, tonight, she was facing facts.

First, her father's infidelity to her mother. And next, Jeffrey. By representing him, she might be doing him a great injustice . . . she had no doubt in herself as an attorney; she was a good one. But she was having doubts about her being the attorney for Jeffrey. If only Allen had not been shot. Trained by Archer Cormack himself, he'd have brought with him expertise that comes from years of practicing law. He had the courtroom experience she lacked.

This isn't like you, Eleanor, she told herself. *You're not thinking straight because you're tired. Take your bath and go to bed. After a good night's sleep, you'll feel much better.* She shoved away from the post. *If only Papa were here to tuck her into bed and to kiss all her hurts and doubts away. But if Papa were here, he'd be tucking Harry into bed, not you!*

Then Eleanor remembered: Harry had said her father was on his way. He would be here soon. A child wanting him to tuck her into bed and kiss her goodnight was one thing; a woman confronting an angry father was another. Not ready to face Alexander Hunt, she drew in a deep breath.

One thought gave birth to another. She wondered where Jeffrey was, and why he had not returned to the ranch. She had expected him to help the Gilmores fight the fire, but he had not.

Perhaps there was a good reason for it; Eleanor hoped so. Again she relegated worry to the future. She was too tired to worry properly at the moment. After a good night's rest she could put everything into perspective. She leaned down, grabbed the handle of the empty tub, and dragged it into the kitchen. It was past time for her to bathe.

She quickly retraced her steps to the back porch, where she picked up two empty pails from the wash bench. She had not taken two steps when she heard a horse approach. Quickly she set the pails down and peered into the silvered shadows.

The rider stopped a distance away from the house to the side, where she could not see him, but soon she heard noises from the barn. A minute later Jeffrey opened the gate.

"It's about time you came home," she called.

"Hey!" he answered, far enough away that he was part of the dark curtain of night. "What a surprise. I didn't expect you to wait up for me."

"Didn't you?" Eleanor was too tired and disappointed to play games with him.

"All right." His voice grew louder as he neared the porch. "So I left when you told me not to. It's not every night that a man becomes engaged."

"It's not every night that a man is released from jail into the custody of his attorney," Eleanor reminded him. "Where were you? With Sarah?"

He nodded.

She sighed. "Of all people, surely you must know what is at stake."

"I know what's at stake, Eleanor, and I know damn well that these people have already tried and convicted me. I don't have a chance. I'm going to take every second of life I can and enjoy it to the hilt. I don't care what anybody says—you, Bradley Smith, Harry Prescott, or Barber Craven."

Jeffrey moved closer to Eleanor, and although the moon was bright, it did not fully illuminate his face. His features were clear enough, but she could not read the expression in his eyes.

"My God!" he exclaimed. "What happened to you?"

"Fire at the Gilmores'. Their house and barn burned down."

"Oh, my God!" His jaw went slack with dismay. "I didn't know. I should have been there helping."

"Where were you?"

Jeffrey sighed and raked his hand through his hair. "I didn't mean any harm, Eleanor. We just wanted to be together to talk about our future. I brought her to the deserted line shack at the bottom of the property."

Oddly enough, Eleanor did understand and sympathized with him. Exhausted and emotionally drained, she said, "I'm sorry it has to be like this. But it will be all right, Jeffrey. I know you're innocent."

"I only wish others in town believed that, especially the jurors. I swear to God, I didn't kill David, and I've never stolen cattle in my life."

"I need evidence, Jeffrey," Eleanor said. "Are you ready to tell me about the note?"

His brow furrowed momentarily, then cleared. "In the morning," he promised and walked to the door.

"Not in there," Eleanor said. "You'll be sleeping in the bunkhouse."

"Why?"

"The Gilmores are spending the night here. Ira and Letty are using your bed; the children are in mine."

"Where are you sleeping?"

"In Bradley's room."

"Without Bradley, I presume."

His proprietary tone irritated Eleanor, especially after he had slipped away without telling them and had spent most of the night with Sarah. "You presume correctly. I left a note on the kitchen table informing both of you that you would—"

"Where is he?" he interrupted, impatient.

"He had to drive Julia home from the Gilmores'."

Jeffrey nodded. "Ever the gallant one. That sounds like Smith."

"And what does that mean?" Eleanor's tone was sharper than she'd intended.

"Smith is determined to move up in this world,

Eleanor, any way he must, even if it means marrying into money."

"You think he has designs on Julia's ranch?"

"As well as on her body," he answered.

"I think you're wrong." Eleanor refused to entertain the thought that Bradley might want to marry Julia for her ranching fortune. But Carl's words returned to haunt her. The first time she had seen Julia, he had told her that many men wanted to marry her for her money.

Jeffrey's expression softened. "You like him, don't you?"

"Yes," Eleanor answered, not willing to lie to him.

Jeffrey gently pressed his palm against her cheek. "Don't like him too much, Eleanor. He's a hard man, used to taking what he wants, and he's not what he appears to be."

While Jeffrey's observation of Bradley was unsettling to Eleanor, she could not deny the truth in what he said. She had wrestled with the same thought herself. She found herself wondering what a man with his education was doing working on a ranch as a hired hand. If he was not actually interested in Julia, she could find no logical reason for him to be this late in returning from the Stanwoods'.

"Something about him makes me wonder: it is odd that he showed up just in time to become my replacement."

Shaking her ominous feelings aside, Eleanor forced herself to smile. "Coincidence, Jeffrey . . . simple coincidence."

"Yeah," he drawled and dropped his hand. "Maybe. But I'll keep my eyes open."

Eleanor laughed softly. "Not if you go to sleep tonight."

Jeffrey tousled her hair. "Good night, Eleanor. I'll see you in the morning."

He was moving in the direction of the bunkhouse when

he stopped and turned around. "Eleanor—"

"Yes?"

"Tonight wasn't what you might think. I don't want you to get the wrong impression about Sarah. We didn't do anything but talk."

"Whatever the two of you did is your business," she assured him.

"I know," he retraced his steps, moving closer to her, "but she's not like you, Eleanor. She's an innocent, and I didn't want you to think differently."

Jeffrey's words cut Eleanor to the quick. Before she could reply, he added, "She's a woman, Eleanor, and proud of it."

Slowly Eleanor descended the steps and walked out to meet him. "A woman who dares to be different from the pattern men set for her and to think for herself is automatically denied certain qualities and assigned others, innocence—whatever that ambiguous term may mean—being one of those denied. Well, Jeffrey Wayne Masterson, let me tell you, it's because I'm a woman and proud of it that I refuse to let others, *men in particular*, deny me my right to think for myself and to plan my life as I see fit."

"That's what I mean, Eleanor. Sarah is different from you. She's not . . . emancipated. She's a lady who wants to be married and have a family. She needs and wants a man in her life . . . you don't."

Dumbfounded, Eleanor could only stare at him.

"Good night. I'll see you tomorrow."

Long after Jeffrey had gone and the light in the bunk house had been snuffed, Eleanor continued to stand on the porch, fuming. The world was full of gross inequalities, and it looked as if it would always be that way.

She lifted a hand and rubbed her aching temple. She was too tired to think about it, about anything tonight.

She would take her bath, go to bed, and think about it all tomorrow. She looked at the buckets still perched at the edge of the porch; then she looked at the pump. Before she could bathe, she had to fill the tub in the kitchen.

She held her hands out and looked at her blistered palms. No! Absolutely not! She was not lugging one more bucket of water tonight. Her gaze lifted to the bath cistern. *Why not?* She could take a shower—a cool, refreshing shower. Swiftly came her answer: because Bradley would be coming home soon.

If she bathed quickly, she could be through before he arrived. *What if you're not through?* came a niggling thought that Eleanor hurriedly quelled. Bradley was no different from Jeffrey in his thoughts about the definition of womanhood, and he was attracted to her because she was different from the kind of women with whom he had been associating. That this attraction was based entirely on curiosity concerned Eleanor.

Sarah was a lady who wanted marriage and children, Jeffrey had said. Julia was a lady, Sheriff Hix had said. Jeffrey preferred Sarah. Did Bradley prefer Julia?

She questioned her purpose in life and wondered if in her fight for suffrage she had compromised herself, as Jeffrey had implied. Again she was too exhausted to be concerned. She was going to take a bath and go to sleep.

Gathering her clothes and washcloth and towel from the kitchen table, she blew out the lamp and quietly left the house to cross the lawn. When she reached the bath house, she laid her clothes on the bench.

With nervous anticipation she opened the door and peered for the first time into the crude structure that until tonight had been a sanctuary for men alone. The only noise to break the silence was an occasional plunk of water escaping the chute to drop onto the floor. The moonlight was bright, and she had no difficulty seeing. Cracks between the planks in the floor allowed the water to flow through freely. Pegs jutted out of the walls, and on the single shelf rested a bar of soap. Directly overhead stood the cistern, its chute locked into place, the handle extending into the bathing area.

Tingling with the excitement that goes with being the first to do something forbidden, Eleanor stepped into the room and closed the door. She hung the towel over a peg, then began slipping out of her dirty, sodden clothes. Piece by piece they fell to the floor. Quickly she unpinned her hair and shook her head so that it tumbled freely about her shoulders.

Her right hand curled around the handle and tugged. With a metallic whine the chute lowered, and clean, cool water spilled over her. At the first splash, she gasped, but welcomed its refreshing flow. Lifting her face, she closed her eyes and sighed deeply, allowing the water to rinse away her tension and exhaustion along with the grime and dirt.

When she was completely relaxed, she returned the chute to its place and picked up the bar of soap. Before she could lather her washcloth, she thought she heard a noise outside. Momentarily startled, wondering if it was Jeffrey returning . . . or one of the hired hands . . . or Bradley . . . she paused to listen. She had heard no one approaching. But she would not have, she quickly told herself . . . the running water would have drowned out any sound.

"Eleanor, is that you in there?" Bradley's words whispered through the closed door.

Her heart did an erratic drumbeat against her chest. *Bradley . . . Bradley was here.* "I didn't think you were coming home."

"I told you I was."

Joy trembled through her. "What kept you?"

"We had to take the Spencers home first. Their wagon broke down, and it was too dark for us to try to repair it, even if we could have. Please believe me," he said softly.

"I do," she murmured.

"I was afraid you wouldn't wait up for me."

"I didn't." The bench creaked, and Eleanor imagined him sitting down. He began to whistle softly, a haunting lyric that touched her heart.

"Give me a few more minutes, and I'll be through."

The whistling stopped, and he laughed softly. "Take your time. I'm in no rush."

As surely as if he had stated his intent aloud, she knew he was here undressing to take a bath. *Of course, idiot,* an inner voice reprimanded without mercy, *you knew when he returned home he would be taking a bath. That's one of the reasons why you argued with yourself about showering out here.* Still, thinking about his taking a bath was not quite like knowing he was here, right outside the stall, ready to shower.

Weak with anticipation, Eleanor felt as if she were going to melt through a crack in the floor. She carefully braced a hand against the wall to keep from falling. Closing her eyes, she was soon lost in her sensual fantasy.

She imagined Bradley pulling off his boots. One dull thud followed another. Then his socks. He stood with feline grace, his callused hands moving to his waist, his fingers deftly unfastening his belt first, the buttons on his trousers next. As clearly as if she were looking at him, Eleanor visualized the trousers sliding down his legs, lean, sinewy legs, shadowed with dark hair. His undergarments followed. He was naked, and at any minute was going to open the door to the bathhouse and enter.

At the thought she inhaled deeply and trembled with excitement.

257

Chapter 14

When the bathhouse door did open, Eleanor stood there, eyes closed, heart beating rapidly, pulse pounding. Although she'd known he'd return home soon, although she'd known he was undressing outside the stall, she was still surprised to see him face to face.

"I'm glad you are out here." His voice was thick and husky.

Feeling the intensity of his gaze, she slowly lifted her lids. In the moonlight his nakedness was clearly visible, but Eleanor's gaze was transfixed to his face. She could not bring herself to look any lower. She wanted to; really she did, but she could not. For all her talk of emancipation, she found that she was truly shy when it came to sharing intimacy with a man.

Bradley climbed the two steps that brought him into the building, but did not close the door. Blatantly his eyes feasted—and that was the only word to describe it—on her body. They leisurely moved from her breasts down her stomach; they lingered on the dark triangle at the juncture of her thighs before they moved thoroughly down the length of her legs and up again.

For one of the few times in her life, certainly in the last ten years, Eleanor was unsure what to do. She felt a sense of innocence that men in general had denied her since she'd begun working at a career, a sense of innocence that she had denied herself since her horrifying experience with Radford. Although she had not been branded with the scarlet letter for adultery, from that time forward she had worn the self-inflicted brand on her soul. She raised her hands to her chest, the wet washcloth dragging across her breasts, water droplets running down her stomach and legs.

"I had hoped to find you here." In shutting the door, Bradley pressed closer to her. Their bodies did not touch, yet Eleanor shivered. His very presence in the tiny sanctum unleashed years of pent-up passion within her.

"It wasn't by design." Even her voice trembled.

"Perhaps you didn't plan it, but it *was* by design." He took the washcloth from her, his fingers lightly brushing against her skin, and hung it on a peg. The bar of soap he returned to the shelf. "Fate is the master designer in all our lives."

"Why did he put Julia into your life?"

He laughed. "Believe me, she's strictly business."

"Like a marriage of convenience?" Eleanor prodded.

"Well, they do have their advantages." His teeth flashed as he grinned. "But to me Julia Stanwood is nothing more than a business associate. Now let's not talk about her anymore."

His hand went to her face, his palms resting on her cheeks, his fingers spreading into her hair. A sweet warmth permeated her entire being. He lifted her head at the same time he lowered his, and their lips touched tentatively. Desire instantly flamed between them, and their mouths bound together in mutual hunger.

His hands slid down to curl around her throat, his thumbs brushing evocatively against the pulse point at the center of her collarbone. Eleanor whimpered softly, the sound coming from deep within, and swayed closer to him, her breasts brushing his chest.

Bradley's hands moved over her shoulders, his fingers gently curling around her upper arms, always careful not to press the wounded area. The tip of his tongue played with the fullness of her lips, causing them to tremble and beg for total possession. His mouth urgently parted hers, and his tongue surged hotly between her lips to taste fully her sweetness. At his urging she moved closer, her breasts straining against his chest.

The crude bathhouse faded away in the glory of the intimacy they shared. Her hands slipped between his arms and around his back. Needing no further urging from him, she pressed the length of her water-slicked body against his nudity, their bodies touching completely. When she felt his arousal on her lower body, her desire turned into a burning ache in her belly.

His hands slid down her arms finally to circle her back. Her soft curves blended into the hard lines of his male physique as his hand flattened on the smooth roundness of her buttocks, as his fingertips traced the line of indentation. The kisses intensified to arouse Eleanor to the very core of her being. When his mouth moved from hers to travel along her jawline up to her ear, he left her aching for more . . . for more than kisses.

She was vaguely aware of the firm pressure of his fingertips as they slowly traveled up, then down her spine to stop at the curve of her buttocks. Beneath her palm she felt the crisp hair and warm texture of his chest.

He held her away from him and gazed into her face. "I've always known you would be beautiful, but in my wildest dreams I never imagined you being this beautiful."

"Thank you," Eleanor whispered, pleasure warming her face. Her thoughts incoherent, she said, "You're beautiful, too."

Bradley laughed softly, richly. "Can a man be beautiful, Elly, my girl?"

Coming from Bradley, the diminutive of her name sounded marvelous. "Yes."

"I'll take your word that he can, but how do you know that I am? You haven't looked at my entire body yet."

Eleanor closed her eyes, but she was aflame with pleasure, atingle with exhilaration. Again he laughed, the sound delightful to Eleanor. "Open your eyes and look at me. You have a right to see what you're getting."

When she did not open her eyes, she felt him lean against her, his lips to touch her closed lids lightly in brushstrokes. His warm breath, lightly scented with wine, blew against her desire-fevered skin.

"I'll not let you go to sleep on me now."

His lips settled sweetly over hers, but this time it was not light or tentative. The moment of discovery was gone. His mouth moved intimately against, then within, hers. Eleanor's hands gripped his shoulders; her fingers dug into his back. A thrill—unlike any she had ever experienced—ran through her.

Again Bradley traced the line of her lips with his tongue. He gently slid his tongue between them to savor her inner mouth in a way that made her knees grow weak and her heart beat thunderously.

He finally lifted his lips from hers. "Are you awake, princess?"

"Yes," Eleanor murmured. She slowly opened her eyes and gazed at him. Stepping back, she let her eyes run the full, hard length of him. When her gaze returned to his face, she said, "Just as I said, you're a beautiful man."

Bradley groaned low in his throat and pulled her into a tight embrace and held her, cradling his face in the curve of her neck and shoulder. "You don't know how frightened I was when I looked into the barn and saw you

262

there. You could have been killed or badly burned."

"Marty. Hambone," Eleanor said thickly. "I had to save them."

"Yes," he murmured. He lifted his head in order to look at her; his hands rose to her face again. "You had to. That's my Eleanor . . . out to save the world, whether it wants to be saved or not."

That's my Eleanor. Over and over the words echoed through her mind; she loved their rhythm; she loved their sound. She delighted in the promise.

"Now, little Elly, it's time to take a bath."

He reached up and pulled the handle, the chute lowering to spill its water freely over them. Then with a gentleness Eleanor had never imagined in her wildest dreams, Bradley began to bathe her. He massaged the soreness out of her shoulders and arms. The water ran through her hair, and he cleaned it, combing the tangles out with his spread fingers.

"I've always wanted to see your hair down," he said. "I've lain awake at night imagining what it would be like."

"Are you disappointed?" she asked.

"Nothing about you disappoints me," he answered. His fingertips firmly dug into her head to set her scalp atingle.

The coolness of the water and the magic of Bradley's hands eased away Eleanor's aches; at the same time they sparked the fire of her attraction for him. He closed the chute, then reached for the soap, liberally lathering it between his hands.

"What are you going to do?" she murmured.

"Bathe you." Even as he spoke the words, he began to wash Eleanor's face. "Considering your constitution of steel, Eleanor Hunt, you're one of the most delicate women I've ever met." Lightly he touched her cheeks,

263

her chin, her forehead, careful to keep the suds out of her eyes. He cleaned her ears, feathering his fingers in every nook and around every curve; he brushed his hand over the arched column of her neck.

"I've never—a man has—never bathed me before." She trembled beneath his touch and did not care that he knew.

"I'm glad. I enjoy being the first." His palms slowly worked over her collarbone, inching down over the wet smoothness of her breasts, every stroke starting a new fire of excitement in her until she was ablaze with desire. He lathered his hands freshly and massaged her breasts anew, his touch a silky caress that Eleanor could hardly stand.

He tenderly cradled the weight of her breasts in his palms; his hands slid up and around, his fingers rolling the nipples. Eleanor's breasts swelled beneath his caressing fingers; she felt the warm rush of desire settle in her pelvis. At the moment when she thought she could stand the torment no longer, his hands slid down her midriff, resting for only a moment on the flat plane of her stomach before they slipped on down to the dark triangle of hair.

His hand, now rinsed of soap lather, gently parted her thighs. His fingers entered and gently explored the most intimate part of her. Eleanor shuddered with raw desire, going hot and cold all over. Her eyes closed, soft sighs whispered through her lips, and her head rolled from side to side in sheer pleasure. Her hands locked about his neck as she simply melted beneath his searching touch. Her blood raged through her veins, pounding through her head, and caused her pulse to beat frantically.

But still this was not enough. Wantonly she begged for more. The tormenting longing seared through her. Her hips began to undulate, and she arched her lower body, straining against Bradley's hand. Her body trembled with the force of emotions he unleashed in her.

Eleanor writhed under his loving ministrations, all her feeling centered in the pleasure point under Bradley's hand. She felt as if heated passion ran through her veins to set her afire, and the furious beating of her heart caused her to gasp for breath. Her entire body screamed for relief.

When she thought she could endure the pleasurable torment no longer, an explosion occurred in her lower body, one that seemed to shatter her being into a million tiny particles of tingling delight. She arched against Bradley's hand, moans of sheer pleasure escaping through her slightly parted lips. Finally she wilted, her head falling against Bradley's shoulder. Dazed by the intensity of her climax, Eleanor dug her fingers into his shoulders and held on as if her life depended on him.

When her shudders had died and she was totally relaxed, he pulled away from her. When those hands that had worked such wonderful magic to her body were gone, she opened her eyes. "Don't leave me."

He smiled reassuringly. "I'm not. I'm going to rinse you off. Then we're going to find a nice soft bed and spend the rest of the night getting to know one another better . . . and better."

Eleanor gazed at Bradley's chest, lean but sinewy. Droplets of water glistened in the mat of thick black hair. Although she had experienced a wonderful climax, it was only the beginning of the pleasures that were shared between a man and a woman. She found herself again inundated with yearning . . . with a yearning for his complete possession.

His hand curled around the handle; he pulled; the chute groaned and whimpered, and finally obeyed; the water sluiced through to spill over both of them. He shoved the handle up; the flow of water stopped. "Now to dry you off."

He lowered his head and gently laved the water droplets from each of her breasts. Again he swiftly carried her to the heights of pleasure. What began as soft moans turned to passionate groans as his mouth closed around one of the hardened tips and he gently sucked. On and on, first one breast, then the other, the foray continued. Eleanor did not think she could endure the tormenting pleasure. She whimpered her pleasure and clutched him to her tightly.

He moved away from her, this time to grab her towel. "Time to dry off."

"Yes," she murmured, as his hands covered in the soft cotton material began to daub her body gently. When he was finished, he picked up her sodden clothes from the floor and wrung them out. Then he hung them on the pegs. Opening the door of the bathhouse, he stepped outside and returned shortly with her dressing gown.

After he helped her into it, he grinned. "Just hold it together with your hands, no need to waste time buttoning it, just to unbutton it again."

Spellbound, she grabbed the material in her fist at her neck and nodded. She watched in the glow of moonlight as he slipped into his trousers, fastening only the top button, and gathered under his arm the rest of his clothing. With his free hand he caught hers. "Time to go."

"Where?" she asked, although it did not matter. She was ready to follow him wherever he led.

"To bed. With all the company here tonight, I have a feeling my room has been assigned to someone."

"It has." She waited a moment, then added, "To me."

Bradley chuckled. "How delightful. And where am I supposed to sleep?"

"In the bunkhouse."

"That doesn't sound quite fair, does it?" His voice was a whispered caress. "You in my bed and I in a room full of snoring men?"

"No."

"But then, life is not always fair, is it?"

"No."

"Shall I take you to your—my room—and tuck you into bed?"

"Please." She wondered if she would ever speak in complete sentences again.

In the moon-kissed night, they walked hand in hand across the yard. Quietly they entered the house and moved to Bradley's bedroom. Eleanor knew she should not permit him to stay with her, but at the moment she was happily ensnared in a magical web, a willing victim of the night and its silver trappings. When Bradley closed the door behind them, he dropped the remainder of his clothes to the floor and picked Eleanor up in his arms to carry her to the bed.

Moonlight spilled through the room to bathe it in delicate radiance. Lying on her back, the material of her robe sliding to either side of her body, she gazed at him. Moonlight streaked his face, the soft light casting a hazy nimbus around his form, silhouetting his strong physique.

Leaning down, he pressed a sweet kiss to her lips. "I really should say good night and leave."

Yes, she thought, he should. She smiled into the craggy face that was so close to hers and said, "Should you?"

"If I were a gentleman, I would."

"That's one claim I've never heard you make."

Bradley shook his head. "No, but basically I'm an honest man."

"I know. That's the one trait I so admire in you,"

Eleanor returned, propping up on one elbow.

Bradley was silent for a few moments before he said, "Remember, I said basically honest. Don't deify me yet."

Eleanor ran her fingers down his chest to insinuate them beneath the waistband of his trousers. She wiggled them in the mat of soft pubic hair. "I'm not."

His hand clamped over hers. "If you don't stop that, Sweet Elly, I won't be leaving at all."

"Do you get the impression that I don't want you to leave?" She lifted her other hand and touched his cheek, loving the feel of the crisp beard stubble against her palm. She ran her hand over the hard, rugged features.

"Are you sure what you're asking, Eleanor?"

"I'm sure."

"In the morning you won't have any—regrets, will you?"

Her fingers stilled their movement as she looked into his face. "No. Why do you ask?"

"Now is the time to let me know," he said. "Now, while I'm willing to stop. If we continue, you know where it's going to end."

"Yes, I know," was her simple answer.

"That's what you want to happen?"

A shudder of anticipation for his complete possession ran through her. "Yes," she whispered.

Slowly his head lowered, and his lips touched hers again to light the flame of passion that had so recently flared between them. Again he set her desire on fire. His lips moved on hers, the pressure firm but gentle. Wanting more, she moaned and wound her arms tightly around him, her hands savoring the feel of the hard, bulging muscles of his back.

Leaning over her, Bradley's mouth traced the outline of her collarbone, and his hands explored her body leisurely to delight her with their discoveries. He thrilled her with his fevered search.

Eleanor pressed her body close to his, feeling the warm moistness of his skin. Her face raised and angled, her lips gently touching his as her other hand slowly moved down his chest, circling his nipple, arousing it to a hard point, moving down the line of crisp hair to his navel. She reveled in her power as a seductress when she felt his hard, masculine body tremble from her ministrations of love.

Her fingers unfastened the button on his trousers, and he stood, the material slithering down his legs to pool at his feet. Now she touched the thick mat of hair that pillowed his manhood, around and around the sensitive area but never touching his most intimate part. Bradley stretched out on the bed, and he took Eleanor into his arms, his lips coming down on hers. Yet her hand would not be stilled.

When the pressure of his mouth pushed her head back, when his lips opened hers, and his tongue invaded the sweet domain, Eleanor's hand moved to curl around his masculinity, the soft tips of her fingers caressing the area of greatest sensitivity.

His soft moan filled Eleanor with pleasure in her prowess as a lover. She moved her mouth from his and lowered her face to circle his nipple with her mouth. Finally Eleanor began to fondle the other nipple with her tongue. The fingers of one hand splayed through the thick brown hair of his head, the other one gently massaged his most intimate parts.

As Bradley's breathing became more shallow and labored, Eleanor's head lowered further, her hair and her lips brushing down his torso, her tongue flicking designs on the muscles of his taut stomach.

"Oh, God, Eleanor," he rasped, his voice thick with wanting, "I can't stand anymore of this. I—I haven't had a woman since I met you. Give me—give me a chance if you—"

Heady with her prowess as a lover, exhilarated with his confession, Eleanor lowered her head to plant multitudes of kisses across his stomach, to trail her long fingernails up and down his thighs.

With a feral growl, Bradley grasped her shoulders and pulled her up to his face, his lips coming down on hers in a warm, moist kiss. Eleanor's fingers dug into the muscles of his shoulders, and she opened her mouth to press her lips against his, sighing softly as he slid her down on her back and stretched out beside her. Her mouth opened beneath his and welcomed the thrust of his tongue. She quivered when his hands, warm and callused, began to journey slowly over her body.

Their kisses were long and drugging; his hands rediscovered all her curves. Welcoming the erotic exploration of his tongue in her mouth, welcoming his touch to her entire body, Eleanor begged for her own seduction.

He held her tighter as she pressed her lower body against him, seeing and searching for the fulfillment to the wanting that he had stirred up within her.

Eleanor's hands blatantly investigated the muscular terrain of Bradley's back; they swept up the indentation of his spine, across the flexed muscles of his shoulders and down again to the small of his back, lower until she felt the swell of his muscle-hard buttocks.

As Eleanor gave herself to the man's possessive touch, as she gave herself to the pleasure of exploring his body, the kisses deepened. She trembled anew when Bradley's hands slipped around her body and cupped her throbbing breasts. His thumbs stroked the nipples until Eleanor moaned. His hands journeyed over her flat stomach to the darkened juncture of her thighs, where the tips of his

270

fingers teased the point of highest sensitivity.

Eleanor pressed even closer, the touch of his fingers once again sending evocative messages through her body, making her one mass of emotion. Her mouth opened wider beneath his, and her tongue began a quest of its own. Bradley groaned and shifted so that he was above her.

Slowly he lowered himself, and Eleanor welcomed his weight. She arched until she felt him flatten his body against hers, the crisp hair on his chest rubbing against her nipples. She began to rotate her hips as she felt the hardness of his arousal. His fingers touched her, preparing her. They slipped in and out the moist portal.

Eleanor whimpered her pleasure, lifting her body to his when he removed his hand. She cried out to him, begging for his touch. Then he lowered the weight of his body over hers, his knee spreading her legs apart, his hand stroking the inner line of her thigh.

She felt his hardness as it touched her maidenhood, and she tensed. He withdrew, and his hands began to reassure her again. Although she yearned for his possession and would not deny herself any of the pleasure it promised, she was frightened and needed the reassurance.

Aware of the passion that pulsated through Bradley's body, Eleanor felt an answering fire spark to life within her. For the first time in her twenty-five years, she wanted the fulfillment of a man's possession; she must have this man's complete possession.

Bradley lowered his head, his mouth unerringly finding hers again. Again he possessed it deeply, demandingly. Hungry for total consummation herself, as she supposed him to be, Eleanor met his urgency with a sudden yearning of her own. This time when Bradley spread her legs apart, she followed his command. When

271

he levered over her, she opened her body to the virile thrust of his need and felt him slide within her. She momentarily tensed and gasped as she felt his bigness inside her, the strangeness of him, and she began to cry.

"Dear God!" he whispered and stopped his movement to hold her all the more tightly. He caught her chin and pulled her face up, his lips touching hers, tasting the salt of her tears. Alternately whispering endearments in her ears and kissing her, Bradley did not move for a few seconds. His hands explored her body, rebuilding the fire of desire, spreading the flames through her body.

At last Eleanor lifted her arms and locked her hands behind Bradley's head, and she began to move her hips around his hardness. Bradley slowly moved within her, gently at first, then more urgently as their desire mounted.

At last Eleanor tore her lips from his, and her head rolled to the side; her body drew taut as she reached the height of fulfillment. In that moment of explosive joy, she gasped with pleasure, then moaned softly. Almost at the same time Bradley reached his climax, and they held onto each other tightly as their bodies convulsed together. Eleanor turned her face to his shoulder, her teeth softly biting into his burning flesh, her fingers digging into him. She felt the small beads of moisture that had formed on Bradley's hot skin and rubbed her cheek against the dampness of his chest.

He propped up on one arm and looked down at her. "Why didn't you let me know you were—"

"Does it matter?" she asked.

"Hell yes!" he exploded and raked his hand through his hair. Abruptly he leaped from the bed and walked to the wall lamp just inside the door. "I wouldn't have made love to you had I known you were a virgin!"

His apparent anger hurt Eleanor, but she controlled

272

herself. Quietly she said, "I would have made love to you had I known you were a virgin."

"My God, Eleanor—" he seemed to spit the words at her "—this is no time for joking."

"I wasn't."

"It's different for men."

"I know," she replied in that same low tone. "Perhaps women like me will bring about a change."

"Are you so sure we need a change?" Reaching into the small metal container, he extracted a match and struck it, the sulfur odor quickly permeating the room. As soon as the lamp was burning, he moved to the washstand to pick up the pitcher and fill the basin with water.

"Yes."

"You want to be a man."

"Don't be ludicrous. Of course I don't want to be a man. I simply want the same rules to apply to women that apply to men." She laughed softly, enjoying the play of light on the muscularity of his flexed buttocks. "After tonight, I've discovered that men have their place in a woman's life."

He turned and Eleanor hastily averted her eyes. She was not quite so brazen in her actions as she was in her talk. Returning to the bed, basin in hand, he set it on the nightstand. After he wrung out the washcloth, he sat beside her and began gently to wipe her thighs.

"Bradley," she murmured, humbled by his caring ministration. Tears pricked her eyes.

"We'll be married as soon as we can," he said matter-of-factly.

Eleanor smiled and reached up to touch his cheek. She loved the feel of his beard stubble beneath her fingers. "Is it possible to fall in love at first sight?"

Never looking at her, he said, "I don't know. I've

never been in love before."

Eleanor pushed up on both elbows disbelievingly. "You mean—you asked me to marry you, and you don't—"

Bradley threw the cloth back into the basin, water splashing onto both of them. "For all your talk, Eleanor, I thought you were—well, you've been so forward." He cut himself off and shrugged, clearly at a loss for words. He raked his hand through his hair. "I'm as angry as hell. You've played me for a damn fool!"

Shocked, Eleanor sat up and pulled the sheet over her nudity. "How?"

"All this talk about your being an emancipated female and your affair with Vaughan was nothing but lies. You led me on deliberately, knowing that if I thought you were not an innocent, I would make love to you." His eyes narrowed, and he glared furiously at her. "Maybe, Eleanor Hunt, I've been played for a double fool. You went to bed with me in order to spite Vaughan."

"Don't feel so smug, thinking you have things all worked out," Eleanor exclaimed, "because you don't. Let me add another truth to this: you've made it easy for me to make a fool out of you."

Eleanor slid off the bed and picked up her dressing gown. With an aplomb she certainly did not feel, she said, "Thank you for an enjoyable evening, Bradley. Now if you don't mind, I'd like to get some sleep. I'm—I'm rather tired, and I have an appointment with Radford tomorrow evening that I don't intend to miss."

He walked up to her and caught her by the shoulder. "Oh, no, you don't," he gritted between clenched teeth. "Two can play this game, Miss Eleanor Hunt. No one plays fast and loose with me."

Despite her anger, Eleanor had to laugh. "Me?" she finally said. "You're accusing me of playing fast and loose with you!"

Bradley's hands bit into the tender flesh, and his face hardened. "You're not going to meet Vaughan tonight—or any other time."

"And who's going to stop me?"

"I will."

She jerked her shoulders trying to free them from his grasp, but his grip only tightened. "Turn me loose," she said in a low voice.

"We're going to be married."

For a second she stared at him in surprised silence. Finally she said, "No, we're not."

"For God's sake, why not? Any other woman I know who happened to find herself in the same circumstances would be begging me to marry her."

"First of all, Bradley, you've made a mistake thinking I'm like any other woman you know. Second, I don't beg. Third, the circumstances were of my own making. And fourth, I'll never marry a man for less than love."

He threw up his hands in the air. "You could be pregnant."

Eleanor drew back in dismay. She had not even thought of that possibility; she had allowed herself to become totally caught up in lust. A baby! She could have a baby!

"And with my luck you probably are."

"There's the possibility," Eleanor returned, "but it certainly isn't your problem . . . it's mine. If I'm pregnant, I shall take care of myself."

Walking toward her, he said in a low voice, "The hell you will! If you're pregnant, that baby is mine too."

"The hell I will." Eleanor jerked away from him. "Mark my words, Bradley, and don't ever forget them: the man I marry will love me more than life itself. I'll be his life. I won't take second place to anyone or anything."

He moved closer and once again she became aware of his magnetic presence, made all the more sensuous by his nudity. Her eyes strayed down the flat, muscled plane of stomach to the dark triangle. Remembering the pleasure his body had given her, she swallowed and quickly lifted her head.

When she encountered his smug grin, she frowned. "Put your clothes on and get out before someone finds you here."

"I shouldn't imagine that an emancipated woman would care what people thought."

"I would hate for them to think I had stooped so low," she countered.

His hands flew out to clamp around her arms, and he dragged her against his chest. His warm breath blew against her face. "Lady, you'll have to do a lot of climbing before you reach me, and don't you ever forget that."

"I won't," Eleanor said. "But don't think you're going to use marriage in order to marry into the Hunt fortune."

"Misfortune, not fortune, has everything to do with my proposal of marriage," he snarled angrily. With that, he tossed her away, and she fell against the bed.

Already regretting her impulsiveness, Eleanor watched him. Quickly he slipped into his clothes, buttoning his trousers but leaving his shirt open. He sat down in the large wing chair in the corner of the room and tugged on his socks and boots. When he was dressed, he stood and walked to the door. His hand on the knob, he began to laugh.

"I fail to see the humor in this situation." She rose.

"You would." His lips curled into a sarcastic grin. "May I remind you that you're kicking me out of my room?"

"If you think I'm going to invite you to stay the night—"

276

She squared her shoulders and rested her hands on her hips. When his gaze shifted from her face, she looked down to see that the material of her wrapping gown had separated to expose her breasts. Quickly she grabbed the cotton in a fist and pulled it together. When she lifted her head, he was laughing at her; her cheeks burned with embarrassment.

As abruptly as his laughter had begun, it stopped. His face softened, as did his voice. "Eleanor, for all your bravado, you're such an innocent. A sweet, lovely innocent."

"I am not." She drew to her full height and tilted her chin arrogantly.

"The offer still goes."

She looked at him in surprise. "What offer?"

"Marriage."

Inwardly Eleanor recoiled. He was proposing marriage to her with the casualness with which her father negotiated business deals. In fact, her father was generally a little more impassioned than Bradley was. The flickering light of the lamp played across his rugged countenance.

"I care about you," he added.

"You care because you're the first man to have made love to me, isn't that it?"

"Well, yes, I guess it is," he finally admitted. "When I first—in the beginning I thought that Vaughan—had—" He smiled and nodded his head. "Yes, Eleanor, I *am* glad that I'm the first man in your life."

While the admission made Eleanor happy; it hurt her more. "Go on and brag about your conquest. But remember this, you may be the first man to have penetrated my body, Bradley Smith, but you're sure as hell not the first to penetrate my heart." Not far from tears, she pointed to the door. "Now get out."

277

Still he made no effort to move. "I'm not going to brag about my conquest, Eleanor. First I'm not that kind of man. Second, I don't think I've made any conquest. I think this may be the biggest mistake of my life."

No words could have hurt Eleanor more. "Bradley, I'm exhausted. Please go."

"Not until we set the record straight." He moved closer to her and caught her face in his hands. "Let's begin all over again. I don't care about the Hunt fortune. I do care deeply about you, and I know you care about me."

"How do you know?" She blinked back the tears.

"Because you're that kind of woman. As much as you seemed to care about Vaughan, you never let him make love to you. Yet you allowed me to. You would never have done so unless you cared about me."

"A minute ago, you said—"

"I know what I said."

"What made you change your mind?"

"I'm thinking a little more clearly now." He wiped away the tear with his thumb. "Now, what do you say to our starting all over again? Let's be rather old-fashioned and go through the courting ritual. Will you, Eleanor Hunt?"

"I'll . . . have to think about it," she answered, smiling through her tears.

"Don't think too long," he murmured and leaned forward to plant a light kiss on her lips, but she turned her head away. "Eleanor, if you should—if you should be pregnant, you'll let me know, won't you?"

"Yes, but I won't marry you just because I fear that I am."

Bradley dropped his hand. "Then I'll have to convince you that you can't live without me."

He did not have to. She already knew she did not want to live without him. Neither did she want to live with him

278

if he did not love her. She could not bear it if Bradley were to have a mistress, as her father had. She was the product of a marriage of convenience and refused to accept one for herself.

Her father had cared for her mother, but he had never loved her. Eleanor would not have that kind of marriage. She had seen what it did to her mother. Her father had been caring and tender, but not loving.

"No," she murmured, "you're going to have to convince me that I can live with you."

Chapter 15

Angry and frustrated and absolutely confused, Bradley walked out of the room and closed the door. He had not taken three steps before he heard a soft thud followed by a click and knew the door was not only closed but also locked. As if she thought he would force himself on her! That added to his irritation. He had offered to make an honest woman out of her. Did she want it? Hell, no! She was content to run around the countryside and flaunt her emancipation. What the hell did she think emancipation meant?

The question jarred him to the point that he stopped and turned around, ready to head back for another encounter with her. To be emancipated brought a certain amount of freedom with it, but not to the extent of shirking responsibility. And if she was pregnant and did not marry him, she was shirking her responsibility to him, the father.

Furthermore, he could not understand why she did not want to marry him. Through the years women had thrown themselves at him, begging him to marry them. Now that he had found one that he wanted to marry . . . again his thoughts pulled him up short, and he quickly began to run from the truth. Even as mature as he was, Bradley knew that truth in its purest form was often startling, if not downright frightening. He had proposed to Eleanor because he had taken her virginity and she had nothing now to offer in marriage to another man.

Even as the excuses flitted through his mind, Bradley realized their absurdity. He had not proposed to Eleanor because he was the first man to make love to her. He wanted to marry her because he cared—really cared—about her. In the short time that he had known her, she had insinuated herself into his life and had done it so subtly that he did not realize how deeply ingrained a part of him she was until tonight. Until she had turned down his offer of marriage.

His hand on the knob of the back door, he stopped. He would not delude himself into thinking he would not have cared for Eleanor if she had not been a virgin. He would have. To know that he would have the joy of teaching her all about love was an added pleasure, but not *the* pleasure. He cared for Eleanor because she was strong and enthusiastic . . . quick, imaginative, and inventive.

He had found her to be a forward-looking person, not easily discouraged by temporary setbacks. Eleanor was the kind of woman who never said die, no matter what the odds. Her whole approach to life was youthful and optimistic, the kind of attributes a woman of the west had to have in order to endure. These were the pleasures of caring for Eleanor, and he should have told her so.

Maybe he did not care for her in the sense that she wanted or expected to be loved, but he was sure they had a foundation strong enough for marriage. Respect. Admiration. He smiled, his mind and body inundated with pleasant memories. And they were definitely physically attracted to one another. That could only enhance their relationship.

He would tell her so. He took two steps, but stopped, immediately checking himself. Eleanor was definitely a product of civilization. When the trial was over, she would be on the first train back to Chicago.

Even if she does return to Chicago, a small voice said, *you could still have her. It's within your power.* In conflict with himself, Bradley stood in the hallway for a minute before he turned and walked out of the house.

On his way, he stopped in the washroom at the linen closet. He did not intend to sleep in the bunkhouse tonight. Eleanor had wanted to be by herself, and so did he. While he recognized and admitted his attraction to Eleanor, he was also confused and frustrated. He had been hired to come out here; he had a job to do. But since he had met Eleanor Hunt, he had done more lusting than work.

Pulling out a couple of spare sheets, he slung them over his arm and walked out of the house. He would sleep in the barn tonight. It was bound to be cooler and quieter there than in the bunkhouse. As he rounded the corner of the house, he felt cold metal shoved against his temple.

"Stop right there, Smith, and don't make a sound." Shrill laughter quickly followed the command. "Or maybe you should. I'd love to put a bullet through your skull."

"Yeah, I imagine you would," Bradley drawled.

The man moved from behind Bradley to stand in front of him, the gun pointed at his stomach. Squinting through the dark, Bradley saw Phineas Grosse, one of Whittier Lang's men. "What's the meaning of this?" he asked.

"The old man wants to see you."

"Right now!" Bradley exclaimed.

The man laughed again, the shrill sound echoing loudly through the dark silence. "Didn't have the heart to bother you sooner, Mister Smith," he drawled sarcastically. "If I found myself a woman, I'd want her all to myself to. So I gave you some time with her."

The sheets slid off Bradley's arm and landed at his feet, and his hand clenched into a fist. "I wouldn't, Mister Smith." The man laughed again. "'Cause I'd just as soon kill you. The old man may trust you, but I don't. Not one little bit. You're a mite too slick for me. Me and Haggarty figure you're mixed up in this rustling with Masterson."

"As long as you and Haggarty are doing the thinking," Bradley said, "I don't think I have too much to fear." He bent and retrieved the sheets. "Let me put these up—"

"No, you ain't." Grosse cocked the hammer. "You're not getting away from me."

Bradley sighed and shook his head. "I'm not trying to get away, Grosse. If I leave these here and I'm not back by daylight, somebody will figure that some ill deed has been done and will launch a search party. If I put these up, they will simply assume that I'm up working bright and early."

"Yeah. Yeah." The gunman eased the hammer up. "You're right. Where do they go?"

"Linen closet in the washroom," Bradley answered. "Give me a minute."

With Grosse on his heels, Bradley slipped in and out of the house, then went to the barn to saddle his horse. Soon the two of them were riding toward the Rocking W. They did little talking as they rode, which was fine with Bradley; he had time to ponder the situation with Eleanor.

He also worried about telling her the truth about himself. Several times she had referred to his honesty as if it were the virtue she admired most in him. Every time he had been careful to qualify his measure of honesty. Yet he could not help but wonder what her reaction

284

would be when she learned who and what he really was, when she learned for whom he was really working.

When Grosse opened the door to the study at the Rocking W, Bradley walked into the room. Huge black wrought-iron lamps attached to the wall just inside the door and on both ends of the mantel burned brightly. The top buttons of his shirt undone, Whittier Lang sat at his desk, poring over his books. He never looked up or acknowledged the presence of the two men. Bradley's gaze wandered around the room, truly a reflection of Whittier Lang. The walls were covered with hunting trophies and Indian memorabilia. After a moment Lang closed the ledger he was working in and laid down his pen.

Lifting his head, he said, "Thank you, Grosse."

"Anything else, Mister Lang?"

Pushing back in his chair, the leather and wood creaking as he shifted his weight, Whittier lifted a glass and finished off his drink. "Has Haggarty returned yet?"

"No, sir." Grosse shuffled his feet slightly. "Said he would need a couple of days, sir."

"Yes. Yes, I know. I'm so tired I forgot." Using his first three fingers, he squeezed his forehead at the top of his nose as if to ease a headache. Rising, he walked to the center of the room to stand in front of the blackened fireplace. The lamplight flickered over his gaunt face, even more drawn with his grief. "Goodnight, Grosse. Stay close by in case I need you."

"Yes, sir, Mister Lang, I sure will." Grosse backed out of the room and closed the door.

"Care for something to drink?" Lang asked, already on his way to the oak liquor cabinet.

"I don't think so," Bradley answered and sat down

on the sofa. "It's a little too late or a little too early to be drinking, I'm not sure which."

Lang laughed softly and refilled his glass. "For those who are living, I'm sure it is, but for those of us who are not quite dead and not quite alive, time ceases to exist."

"Mister Lang—" Bradley twirled his hat around in his fingers "—I appreciate your loss, but you're not the first man who has—"

Whittier held up a silencing palm. "I've heard this sermon too many times lately, Smith, to tolerate it once more. How I while away my time is my business. Is that clear?"

Bradley tossed his hat onto the coffee table and leaned back into the softness of the cushions, extending one hand along the back of the sofa. "That's clear, Mister Lang. What was so urgent that could not wait until tomorrow, that made you send a hired gun to get me?"

"I suppose you've heard I hired Radford Vaughan to prosecute Masterson?"

Bradley acknowledged this with a curt nod.

"After what Masterson has done to me and my family, I'm determined that he won't live, Smith."

"I thought Alex Hunt was the man you wanted."

"I did, until Masterson killed my son."

"What if he didn't kill David? What if he's innocent, as he claims?"

Lang's fingers curled tightly around the glass, his knuckles turning white. "He's not innocent."

Bradley would not let the subject drop. Since he had met Eleanor, he was seeing the entire scene through a different perspective. "What if he's telling the truth about someone having thrown a note through the window of his office, warning him about the rustling?"

"Look, Smith," Whittier said, his voice a low growl, "you work for me, and don't you ever forget that! A man

286

who works for me owes me blind loyalty."

Bradley tensed, his arm slipping down as he leaned forward slightly. With deceptive grace, like that of a cat of prey, he eased into a position of attack. "Mister Lang, I'm making a lot of concessions because I know you're grief-stricken over the death of your son, but even under these conditions, I won't let you go this far with me. I am a professional investigator whom you hired to locate rustlers in this area. I am not one of your employees, and I do not owe you any allegiance. I give no one blind loyalty. If you'll remember, when we signed the contract, I told you even if the rustler turned out to be you, I would turn you in."

Whittier lifted the glass and quaffed the liquor in one swallow. "My God! You're beginning to sound like Hunt's daughter! So you think Masterson is innocent, huh? Next thing, you'll be telling me is that Hunt isn't behind this entire operation."

Bradley was exhausted and wanted nothing more at the moment than to be asleep. He had enough to think about as it was without adding an old man's imaginings. He shifted his weight and raked his hand through his hair. "Mister Lang, I don't know who the rustlers are. I do know that you have a motley crew working for you, any one of whom could be responsible."

"Maybe by your Eastern standards we're motley," Lang sneered and thumped his index finger on his chest, "but my men are tough, and they're loyal to me."

"Only so long as it pleases them," Bradley pointed out.

"As long as I pay them top dollar." Whittier moved back to the liquor cabinet. "I've always found money to be a proper *incentive*. And speaking of incentive, I have a proposition to put to you, Smith."

"I have a feeling this is why you brought me here."

Whittier poured another glass full of whiskey,

recapped the bottle, and replaced it on the silver tray. His back to Bradley, he said, "Vaughan is one of the best attorneys in the east, but even he cannot work miracles without the proper materials. He says we have a strong case." Whittier took a swallow. "Our only weakness is the note Masterson keeps harping on."

"The note you don't believe in?"

"I don't, but I believe Hunt is smart enough that he had Masterson create that story, and I also believe that there may be someone else out there who is motivated by money, Smith, who might step forward and claim to have written such a note."

"Like Dobson?"

Lang ignored him and he went on, "You see, Alex Hunt and I are quite similar. We both know the power of money, and we use it freely to get what we want."

Bradley did not like the direction in which the conversation was headed. When Whittier had hired him, he had not liked the man. Now he was finding out that he did not even respect him. "What are you proposing?"

Whittier crossed to his desk and set down his glass. Opening the top drawer, he extracted a small metal box, unlocked it, and began to take out stacks of bills. "I want to buy some information, Smith."

"I'm not an informant, Lang—you know that. You and I have already agreed upon a price for my services."

"This is a new contract," Lang said. "I want you to get close to the Hunt girl and find out what her case is."

The pile of money grew higher; still Bradley did not move, nor was he tempted to. "What is this, Lang? Double protection?"

Whittier's hand stilled, and he looked up. "What do you mean?"

"You hired Radford Vaughan because he's one of the best attorneys in the east, but wasn't there another reason?"

288

The old man's eyes narrowed, and he peered out from beneath his heavy white eyebrows. "What do you know about Vaughan?"

"More than you know about Eleanor Hunt, if you think she's weak enough to let either Vaughan or me get close enough for her to reveal her defense of Masterson."

"I understand that you're quite friendly with Miss Hunt." Whittier grinned.

"Depends on what you mean," Bradley returned, not liking the feeling that was crawling up his back.

"I keep a close eye on you, Smith. One of my men saw you and Miss Hunt in the field together, and from the story he tells me, the two of you were rather intimate."

Damn! Bradley was angry at himself. He should have known that Lang would have men watching him twenty-four hours a day.

Seeming pleased, Whittier laughed. "While I was in Chicago, Smith, I hired two detectives—one to do research on the entire Hunt family, and you to come out here to apprehend the rustlers. I never like for my right hand to know—"

"I know," Bradley said.

"Now that I've discovered the skeleton in Miss Hunt's closet, I have a negotiating tool."

"Then Mister Lang, your researcher either did not do conclusive research on Miss Hunt, or you underestimated the woman. Eleanor Hunt will no more be blackmailed than she would stoop to blackmail. In case you haven't noticed, Eleanor Hunt is an emancipated woman. If there ever was a skeleton in her closet, she'd have dug it out and aired it herself. She doesn't allow herself to be bound by society. She would laugh in your face if you made her this offer."

"Oh, dear, I'm afraid I did underestimate her," Whittier said, mockery apparent in his voice. He began to straighten the stacks of bills. "But I don't think I've underestimated her father."

Bradley tensed. At a definite disadvantage, he did not like this game that he and Whittier were playing. "What has Alex got to do with this, Lang?"

"Did you know that Harry Prescott and Alex Hunt are lovers?"

"I don't believe every rumor I hear," Bradley returned.

"I don't either, but this—whether it's rumor or not—will work to my advantage." Whittier slid into his chair and reached for a cigar. Biting off and spitting out the tip, he held it over the chimney and lit it. He leaned back in his chair to roll the cigar between his fingers. "I don't think Alex Hunt would like his daughter to hear about this."

Bradley walked over to the window to watch dawn streak the sky with light. "You're going to gamble that Alex will pay to keep Eleanor from learning all this?"

Crossing his hands behind his head, Whittier leaned back in the chair. "I am. As I said, whether it's the truth or not, it'll cause Hunt's little girl many an hour of consternation."

Bradley clenched his hands into fists and walked to stand in front of Whittier's desk. "You're a bastard, Whittier."

"And you're in love with the little woman," Whittier said. "Now, if Alex Hunt loves his daughter enough, he'll pull her from the case or he'll help her see facts a little differently than she's seeing them right now. The matter is out of my hands. It's up to you and Papa Hunt to protect the little woman."

Balancing the tips of his fingers on the desk, Bradley leaned even closer to Whittier. "You're scared, Lang. You think Eleanor has a chance of getting Masterson out of this." Looking into the fearful eyes, Bradley began to smile. "You believe Jeffrey's story about the note."

Whittier rose, the gaunt face even with Bradley's. "I always erase the odds, Smith, and this time is no different. I promise you, I'll bring Alexander Hunt to his knees. With your help it will be easier and more profitable for you, but it'll get done with or without you."

"How do you know you can trust me with this information?" Bradley asked.

Whittier laughed smugly. "You're enamored with Miss Hunt, and you certainly don't want her to learn that you've been hired by Whittier Lang to work against her father. That, my boy, would ruin your game. And why should you tell her the truth when you can marry into the Hunt fortune?"

"You think I want her fortune?" Bradley asked.

"All of us are hunting fortunes one way or another. You're no different."

"Eleanor," Harry said and knocked again, "I know you're up. Please let me talk to you before I take the Gilmores to town."

"It's unlocked. Come on in." Eleanor laid her brush on the dresser and stared straight ahead, playing with the ruffle of her dressing gown. When the door opened and Harry walked into the room, Eleanor did not turn around. Rather she watched the older woman through the mirror. Having been up since sunrise, Harry was already dressed. Her auburn braid was wound into a coil on the crown of her head, and she wore her shirt, divided skirt, and boots.

"I wanted to know how you were feeling."

"About what?" Eleanor asked perversely, folding her hands over her breasts and hugging herself.

291

"About your father and me."

Eleanor ignored the pleading in Harry's tone. "Does it really matter what I think?"

Harry sighed. "It doesn't matter to me, but it does to you and to your father."

The woman's honesty jarred Eleanor into a reaction. She whirled around to glare at Harry. "And what's that supposed to mean?"

"I didn't have time to tell you last night before you rushed out of the room, and even if I had had time, I'm not sure last night was the right time to tell you, but your father has proposed marriage to me."

"He can't," Eleanor gasped incredulously.

"He has. We were going to have been married on his next trip out. He was going to bring you to meet me."

Bitter laughter accompanied Eleanor's words. "And pretend that the two of you had met after Mama died, and everything was fine?"

"I suppose we would have liked for it to be that way, but I've learned during my forty-three years that although life generally turns out as we want, the road for getting there is quite often different from that which we would have chosen. It was idealistic and rather naive of your father and me to believe we could have fooled you."

"Deceived me, you mean," Eleanor said. "The two of you were going to deceive me. Just as Papa deceived Mama all her life."

"I know you're going to have a difficult time believing this, Eleanor, but your father did not purposely set out to deceive you or your mother. He merely fell in love with me—"

"*Love*," Eleanor scoffed. "How can you call what you and Papa share *love*? It looks more like lust to me."

Harry's face hardened. "I don't care what you call it, Eleanor, but I do care how you affect your father. I love

292

him, and I won't see him hurt by a spoiled child, hell-bent on destruction. He's suffered enough during his life. Can't he have some respite in his old age?"

Harry turned and walked brusquely out of the room. Eleanor rushed to the door and caught her at the landing. "You can't marry Papa!" she cried.

Without turning, Harriet said, "If your father still wants to marry me, when he learns that you know about us, I shall. Nothing shall stop me. This is my chance for happiness, and I'm going to take it." She smiled kindly at Eleanor. "One of these days you'll fall in love and will understand what I'm talking about."

Again Eleanor wrapped her arms around herself and squeezed tightly. She had already fallen in love and had wrestled with her emotions all night. She wanted to accept Bradley's proposal, but not for the same reasons as he. She could not endure a marriage of convenience.

"I'm taking the Gilmores into town today," she heard Harry say. "I probably won't be back until tonight. When you've had time to think over what I've said, we'll talk again."

Harry quickly descended the steps and was soon on the porch calling orders to the hired help and to the Gilmores. Shaking all over with anger, Eleanor headed for the kitchen for a strong cup of coffee. She was angry at herself for having been so weak-willed where Bradley was concerned and angry with Harriet for having wrapped her father around her little finger. Eleanor would never have believed her father could be so blinded, so manipulated by a woman like her.

"What are you upset about?" Gaspar asked.

"Why?" Eleanor looked at him in surprise.

"The way you're banging that coffeepot around. Bet it's plumb bent out of shape. Glad you ain't that careless with my cup. It'd be broke into smithereens."

293

Eleanor grinned sheepishly and returned the pot to the back burner. "I'm sorry. I was deep in thought."

"Knew that. Just wondered how bad them thoughts was."

Eleanor sipped the coffee and walked to the window. "Bad enough," she answered finally.

"It's amazing," the old man said, "how when you look back on a situation months or years after it happened, just how insignificant it really was. In fact, most time you can laugh about it."

Eleanor actually laughed. "If Bradley's not spitting out adages to me, it's you."

Gaspar grinned. "That's better, missy. Rather see a smile on your face than a frown. How about some breakfast?"

"I'm not really hungry," she began.

"Well, you better get while the getting's good," he answered. "As soon as I get this kitchen cleaned up, I'm taking the wagon and heading into town for supplies. You'll be on your own until dinner."

"All right," Eleanor said. Through the window she saw the bunkhouse door open, and Jeffrey walked out. "And cook some for Jeffrey also. He's on his way—"

She stopped speaking in the middle of the sentence. Jeffrey headed for the barn, not for the house. Setting her cup on the counter, she rushed out of the house and across the back lawn. "Jeffrey!" she called.

He stopped, turned around, and waited for her. Grinning he said, "I thought I'd get away without your seeing me."

"Good thing I was looking out the window," she said breathlessly. "Where are you going?"

"To take care of some business," he answered.

"Jeffrey—" her face screwed up in displeasure "—you promised you would tell me about the note!"

294

"And I will," he answered, "but not right now. I—want to talk with someone first."

"Jeffrey—" she threw up her hands in the air "—it's not right. You're expecting me to defend you against Radford Vaughan, and your only hope of getting out of this mess is that note. I don't even know if I believe in it anymore or not. You're helping his case, not mine."

Jeffrey moved closer. "I know I promised that I would tell you about the note, and I am. But I have something I must do first."

"My God, Jeffrey! Nothing can be more important than this. You've been accused of murder, and this note will—" Her voice trailed into silence. Then she sighed. "Oh, go on. I don't know that it matters that much anyway. The note will only prove that you were informed about the rustling. It won't help you in the murder conviction."

Jeffrey grinned. "Thank God, they can only try me for one crime at a time."

"And it's murder first," Eleanor said. "Jeffrey, you are going to straighten all this out for me before I meet with Radford tonight, aren't you?"

"I promise that I'll straighten it out before the trial. I don't know if I can do it before you meet with Vaughan or not."

Disappointed, Eleanor shrugged. "You're not going by yourself, are you?"

He nodded. "I have to, Eleanor. Please understand. This is something I must do for myself."

"All right, but please be careful, Jeffrey."

He leaned over and placed a quick kiss on her forehead. "I will, little friend. Now make sure no one follows me."

"What am I supposed to do?" Eleanor asked dryly. "Scream? Shoot into the air three times? Or shoot the person following you?"

"Shoot whoever is following me," Jeffrey answered without second thought.

"Jeffrey!" she chided. "I don't even like words like that said in jest."

"Believe me, Eleanor," he returned solemnly, "I wasn't jesting. Anyone who follows me is after my life. I'd rather you took his first."

A sick feeling in her stomach, Eleanor watched Jeffrey ride away. When he was out of sight, she slowly retraced her steps to the kitchen and ate her breakfast. She was still sitting at the table when Gaspar left for town. Deciding to have one last cup of coffee before she went to the study, she walked to the stove. As she picked up the pot, Bradley entered. She turned and eyed him. He wore the same clothes he had had on the night before.

She smiled apologetically. "You forgot to get clean clothes out of your closet when you left last night."

He nodded. "A person can't think of everything. May I have a cup of coffee?"

"How about some breakfast?" she asked. "Gaspar had to go into town for supplies, but if you're hungry, I'll cook you some eggs and bacon and biscuits."

"Thanks. That sounds good."

When she set the cup in front of him, he imprisoned both it and her hand. "Did you do your thinking last night?"

She stared at his hand for a long time before she gently withdrew her hand, and returning to the stove, she lifted the burner and stuffed in several pieces of wood. Then she picked up her coffee and took several swallows. "Yes, I've been thinking."

He pushed back in the chair. "And?"

"I'm glad that we had last night together, Bradley, but I don't want a marriage of convenience."

The chair grated against the floor as he got up and

moved to where she stood. "I think you misunderstand the concept of a marriage of convenience. It's a marriage based on convenience—on barter. You have something that I want, and through marriage we can attain it. That's not what I'm talking about, Eleanor. I care about you; you care about me."

"I care about Jeffrey," Eleanor said, "but I don't want to marry him. I don't want to spend the rest of my life with him. The kind of marriage I want, Bradley, needs to be built on a foundation much stronger than caring."

"Caring is the first major step in loving," he said and moved closer, his hands sliding between her arms to clasp in front at her waist, his breath brushing against her neck. "And besides, last night should prove that we share a great deal more than caring."

"I meant what I said last night, Bradley. I must be the center of my husband's universe." She lowered her head and gazed at the strong, callused hands that held her. Jeffrey's word returned once again to haunt her; she had to put her fears to rest. "Bradley, if I marry without my father's blessing, I stand to lose my inheritance."

Bradley spun her around so quickly her head jerked back, and her coil came unpinned, her hair spilling over her shoulders. Anger burned brilliant in his eyes. "I didn't propose because I wanted to marry a fortune. I want to marry you, Eleanor Hunt, because of what and who you are, not because of your father. I want money, but I'll build by own empire. I don't have to marry to get it. Do you understand?"

"Yes," she whispered and melted into his arms, "but I had to hear you say it. I had to know, Bradley. Can you understand?"

He nodded, and his embrace tightened as her arms banded around him. Then when she felt the full length of his hard body molded to hers, she lost all control. Her hands slid between his arms and up his chest to twine in thick dark hair. She angled his face toward hers.

Her lips parted, allowing his tongue—hot, wet, and boldly delicious—to seek hers. This initial mating of tongues was delightful. Hers, plunging audaciously; his retiring and demure, until his arms tightened and he shifted her so that he directed a counterthrust into the sensual haven of her mouth.

Bradley's deep moan of primeval pleasure began in the depths of his chest. The vibrations still reverberated through Eleanor's body as his lips left her to forge a path of fire across her cheeks, the tip of her ear, and down her temples to the tip of her chin. He sighed her name once, then more demandingly as his large hand molded the curve of her breast.

"Eleanor."

Her body throbbed with desire. She wanted to melt into his strong, hard body.

But a noise in the distance jarred Eleanor from the heady magic of the moment. Her palms flattened against his chest, she pressed herself away. Licking her passion-swollen lips, she smiled tremulously. Her hands lifted, and she rubbed his unshaven jaws, tracing the hard line from ear to chin, her fingers scratching against his beard. His neck was thick, his shoulders wide, the muscles like small, smooth ridges immediately under his tanned skin.

"Not in the kitchen, Mister Smith."

"I'll take it wherever I can get it," he whispered. She felt the heat flushing her cheeks as he laughed softly. "Does this mean, Miss Hunt, that you accept my proposal of marriage?"

Eleanor pulled out of his arms altogether and gazed solemnly into those beautiful dark green eyes. "I have one more task to perform before I give you my answer."

The eyes narrowed, dark sooty eyelashes fanning

against his bronzed cheeks. The sensuous mouth thinned. "May I ask what that is?"

"I'm going into town tonight to meet with Radford Vaughan."

"The hell you are!" His voice was gruff and unyielding.

"The hell I am," she echoed quietly. "I intend to lay to rest once and for all a ghost from my past."

"Just remember he's the ghost. I'm the real thing." His hands moved to her face, and he lifted it, his lips coming down on hers, hard and demanding.

Chapter 16

"I wish you'd reconsider," Bradley said when he stopped the buckboard in front of Blissful Hotel.

"No, it's something I must do," Eleanor told him. Only by meeting Radford Vaughan face to face could she kill the demon that had chased her for the past few years. Once she exorcised him from her mind and body, she would be free to love—she turned to look at Bradley—whomever she chose.

"You mean something you want to do." He leaped out of the buckboard. When he reached her side, his hands clamped on her waist—bands of pure fire that burned to her soul—and he swung her out.

She reached up to straighten her hat. "Yes," she returned evenly, although her heart was racing and left her breathless. She wondered if Bradley's touch would always set her afire with longing. With all her heart she hoped so. "I do want to see Radford again. Surely you can understand that, Bradley?"

He never moved his hands, and his face, reflected fully in the light that filtered through the open door, was brooding and morose. "I do, but it doesn't mean that I like it. Let me come with you?"

She smiled and shook her head. Her gloved hand

momentarily cupped his cheek. "Thank you for the concern," she said, "but this is something I want to take care of myself."

"Eleanor, I know you can take care of yourself, but I want to."

"I know," she murmured, loving Bradley more at this moment than she had ever thought possible.

He caught her hands in his and squeezed them tightly, as if he feared to let her leave him. "It's you I care about—all of you. It's not only passion. While that is wonderful, I care about everything that is Eleanor Hunt."

"And I care about you, too," she murmured. "Please don't worry."

"I'll be waiting for you," he promised. "No matter how long it takes."

Bradley's promise lingering in her ears, Eleanor moved through the lobby, the yellow taffeta swishing gently as she walked. When she reached the desk, she tapped the bell, and the manager scurried out of the back room.

"Yes, ma'am," he said, "and what can I do for you today, ma'am?"

"I'm Miss Eleanor Hunt." She smiled. "Please tell Mister Vaughan that I'm here."

The man straightened some papers on his desk and replied without looking up, "Mister Vaughan asked me to tell you to go on up to his room, Miss Hunt. That would be Number Seven."

Knowing how the locals would interpret such an action on her part, Eleanor was angry at Radford. How dare he leave such a message with the desk clerk? Then she was angry at herself. How dare she react like this— like a simpering female. This was a business meeting, not a social call. Men met with each other in their hotel rooms. She could at least walk upstairs and get Radford. But after her long discussion with Bradley on the way to town, she had a new understanding of emancipation. It was not merely a phrase that excused any and every action on her part and released her from taking the responsibility for her actions.

She smiled at the grinning clerk and said softly, "Send a messenger to Mister Vaughan's room, and let him know that I'll be waiting for him in the dining room. I'll wait no longer than thirty minutes."

"Yes, ma'am." His grin left his face, and he bobbed his head energetically and eased from behind the desk to walk toward the spiral staircase.

"Thank you."

Eleanor turned to sweep across the lobby into the large dining room that was already filling with patrons. When the maitre d' approached, she said, "A table for two in a quiet place, please."

"Under what name was the reservation made, ma'am?" he asked.

"Radford Vaughan," she answered.

After checking his guest list, he shook his head. "I'm sorry, but I don't have a table reserved for Mister Vaughan. Perhaps there is some mistake."

"Perhaps," she said but knew differently. "Do you have an extra table for two that we could have?"

"Of course. Follow me, please."

In a short time, Eleanor was seated at a small table in the far corner of the room. "May I have the wine list, please? Mister Vaughan will be joining me soon, and I would like to order now."

"Yes, ma'am," the man said, leaving and reappearing shortly. As soon as she had studied the wine list and made her selection, Eleanor sat back and relaxed. As she looked around, she had to chuckle to herself. This really was an extra table. She and Radford would literally be hidden from sight by the huge potted plants. She unclasped her hands and realized that beneath her gloves her palms were perspiring. In fact, she was shaking. She wanted to turn and run back into the safety of Bradley's arms. She wondered if she had only been fooling herself when she said she wanted finally to lay the ghosts of her past to rest.

"Eleanor." She heard Radford's husky voice and looked up. There he was, taller and even more handsome than she remembered. He gazed down at her with adoring tawny gold eyes that still sparkled with that enigmatic quality she had found so provocative. His golden brown hair was brushed back from his face, an errant shock falling across his forehead. His lips—those sensual lips—were curled into what she had once thought was an endearing smile. Now she realized that it was no smile at all. It never reached his eyes; it was not a reflection of happiness. It was merely the upward movement of his lips, a hollow gesture at most.

"Eleanor," he murmured, "it's been a long time."

"Quite," she returned, pleased that she sounded so calm and assured. He seemed to be consuming her with his eyes. "I believe you said dinner was to be at seven o'clock."

His smile widened; he lowered thick brown lashes seductively. "I did."

"But you forgot to make a reservation?"

He sat down across from her and picked up her hands in his. "I didn't forget. I hope you'll forgive me, but I intentionally did not make a reservation."

Surprised at his confession, Eleanor did not immediately draw her hands away from his. "Are you saying that our dinner engagement is canceled, Radford?"

"No, I merely wanted to change the place."

The pressure of his hands tightened to remind Eleanor that he still held hers. She withdrew them from his clasp. "I'm afraid I don't understand."

"I wanted us to have some privacy tonight, so we could

talk about old times and perhaps about the case without being interrupted. I thought we would dine in my rooms. I've already ordered dinner to be served."

"I don't think that would be appropriate." She picked up the menu and opened it, only her eyes visible over the top. "What would the inhabitants of Blissful think of an unescorted young woman going to a man's apartments?"

Radford's lips slowly curled into a smile; his golden eyes glowed. Leaning closer, he lowered his voice to say, "But when was Eleanor Hunt concerned about what people thought?"

Eleanor laughed quietly and lowered the menu. As if she were joining a conspiracy, she leaned forward also, her forehead almost touching Radford's. She whispered, "Eleanor Hunt the woman doesn't, counsellor. Eleanor Hunt the attorney does, and she would do nothing to ruin her chances of winning her client's case."

Displeasure darkened his eyes. "Damn this case, Eleanor! What about you and me?"

Eleanor arched her brow. "What about you and me, Radford?"

"You can't sit here and pretend that we've never meant anything to each other, that it's—" he looked around as if searching for a word "—it's fate bringing us together again."

Bradley had said she and he were together because of fate; now Radford was telling her the same thing. "You're right," she replied. "Fate did bring us together. You see, I've been living under your shadow for many years."

"Eleanor, I'm sorry for the way I treated you," he apologized. "I was young and impressionable. When Corrine came along with all the credentials my family were looking for, I gave in."

"That didn't bother me as much as the way you treated me when you came to Chicago, Radford. You were married, yet you never let me know. You led me on and would have made love to me, had I allowed you to."

"Can you blame a man for giving in to passion when he's with the woman he loves?"

"I blame any person who allows an emotion to dominate his thinking. One should be influenced by one's emotions, heed them, surely—but should not be controlled by any one of them."

"Did you hear me, Eleanor. I love you. I've regretted the day I sent you away from me. I've despised myself for my weakness all these years. I've lived for the day that you would forgive me. Corinne is dead. I'm a free man. We—"

"No, Radford."

"Why not? You love . . . loved me?"

"I thought I loved you, but I loved only what I thought you were. I loved your strength and intelligence; I admired your ability to see every facet of an issue and to be so open-minded, especially where suffrage was concerned. It wasn't until recently, Radford, that I began to see that you possessed none of these attributes."

Angrily, Radford rose from his chair. "You sit here and point a finger of accusation at me." He seemed to snarl the words that echoed loudly through the dining room. "You—a woman who was willing to—"

"—to leave her home in Chicago to come to the wilds of the Kansas frontier to defend a man against charges of rustling when an entire town had already condemned him." From behind Eleanor came Bradley's deep, familiar voice. His green eyes pinned Radford to the wall. Then, as if Radford were of no more significance than an insect, Bradley turned his head and looked at Eleanor. "When you're ready to go, let me know."

She smiled. "Bradley Smith, may I introduce Radford Vaughan, an old acquaintance of mine and a fellow attorney."

306

Radford's gaze swept contemptuously over Bradley's western trousers and shirt to the guns that were strapped to each thigh. "And who are you, Smith?"

"Smith," Bradley answered, his voice deceptively soft. "Bradley Smith."

Radford barely controlled his anger. "How do you fit into Eleanor's life?"

Looking down at Eleanor, Bradley winked and grinned. Every inch of her body burned. She was not so sure how she fit into Bradley's life, but she vividly recalled how well she fit into his body, and he into hers. Only too well!

His head lifted, and his gaze shifted to Vaughan. "I'm manager of the Hunt Cattle Station. You may say I'm Miss Hunt's bodyguard."

Radford glanced suspiciously from Eleanor to Bradley and back to Eleanor again. "Do you accompany her everywhere she goes?"

"I try, but the woman has quite a mind of her own, you know. I have a difficult time keeping up with her."

"You don't have to stay with her tonight," Radford said and reached into his pocket to extract a large roll of bills. As he counted and dropped them to the table, he said, "She'll be with me, and I'll escort her home personally."

"Is this what you want?" Bradley looked down at Eleanor. She could see the pain in his eyes.

"I want you to give me a few more minutes alone with Radford," she said.

"Eleanor—" Bradley said.

"Please."

Time faded into eternity as the green eyes stared into her soul. Finally he sighed and said, "All right. I'll be waiting outside. Thirty minutes . . . no longer."

Love swelling in her heart, she nodded and watched him walk out of the dining room. She knew that Bradley felt honor-bound to marry her because he had been the first man to make love to her, and a man naturally reck-oned a woman's innocence by her virginity. A tiny mem-brane—totally insignificant—blocked out any other vir-tues or innocence she might have.

He was also protective of her because she was his employer's daughter, and he was jealous of Radford Vaughan. Eleanor knew that Bradley was not inordinately jealous by nature, but because Vaughan was the first man of consequence in her life, he felt threatened by him.

While his protectiveness and obvious concern touched her deeply, she still yearned for love—the one ingredient that had been missing from her parents' marriage—the lack of which had caused her father to turn to another woman. Bradley promised to care for her, but she yearned for love.

"Eleanor!"

She looked into Radford's face. "That's the third time I called your name," he said. "Where were you?"

"I was thinking."

"Eleanor, give me a second chance."

Shaking her head, she said, "We never had a first one, Radford. You and I were never meant for each other. You don't admire any of the principles I embrace and I don't admire you."

"You're being premature." His countenance was ugly; his voice a low growl. "You always were rather melodramatic and childish."

"So you thought," she returned. Rising, she picked up her reticule. "Now, Radford, I'll bid you good-night. I'll see you in court tomorrow."

"I don't think it's in your best interests to leave, Eleanor."

"More than if I stayed," she countered.

"You'll rue the day you ever faced me in a court of law, Eleanor Hunt."

"Whether I win or lose, it'll be the greatest day of

308

my life, Radford. I've faced a ghost from my past, and I've won. Good night."

Smiling, she swept out of the dining room, her head held high, the yellow taffeta gown gently swishing about her feet. Even it seemed to be congratulating her on her emotional independence from Radford.

When she walked out the front door, Bradley pushed away from the porch column and turned. The light flared through the open doors to spill outside, illuminating his face.

"Let's go home, Mister Smith."

The bronzed features creased into a wide smile.

The match scratched over a rough surface, spattered to life, and flared brightly in the cabin. The tip touched to the candle gave way to a brighter flame as the wick caught on fire. Light chased darkness from the room and played over the crude, homemade furniture. Altogether the small room was friendly and inviting.

"Thank you for bringing me." Eleanor moved further into the cabin.

"Rather comfortable for a line shack, don't you think?" Lifting the candleholder, Bradley carried it across the room and set it on the kitchen counter. Then he crooked his hands into the metal handles and opened the doors to the large safe that stood nearby. "How did you know about it?"

She smiled. "This is where Jeffrey and Sarah spent their evening together. You could call it a lovers' hideaway."

"I'll have to admit," Bradley said dryly, "I'd never thought of it that way."

"Do you now?"

Without dropping his hands from the door handles, Bradley stopped his inspection of the larder and turned his head toward her. Across the softly lit room their eyes caught. They gazed into each other's souls; they smiled.

"Yes," he finally answered, "I do."

Reality as Eleanor knew it quietly slipped away, taking with it time. Momentarily she felt cut loose from her body, a feeling that was heightened by the sheer power of love that she and Bradley exchanged in one glance.

"Wherever you are," he said, "it's lovely and warm and golden. In such a short time, my darling, you've become the center of my universe."

Eleanor laughed, a joyous release of the happiness she felt deep within her heart. He released the doors and held out his arms; gladly she raced into his embrace. Tightly they held each other. She pressed her face against his chest; he laid his cheek on the top of her head.

While she wanted, in fact needed, the passion she and Bradley shared, Eleanor needed this comforting and reassurance as much. To know that he was here for her and that she was the very core of his life filled her with immeasurable pleasure. She had known love before, but none so deep as this.

After a moment she heard his deep, rich laughter and pulled back her head to look into his face, his cheeks shadowed with beard stubble. "If I don't feed you, I fear there will be nothing left to love, and I have plans."

Gently moving out of his embrace, Eleanor smiled in return. "Then, my lord, feed me. I'm quite eager to hear about those plans of yours."

"And you shall," he promised, reluctantly returning to his pilfering of the cabinet.

"Do you need any help?"

"No, as you'll soon discover, our china and cutlery is not of choice quality, and neither is the cuisine. Be thankful I bought us a basket lunch from the hotel. Harry stocks the shack with nonperishable foods."

Harry! The word brought Eleanor back to reality with a

jolt. Moving around the small room and looking at the sparse furnishings, Eleanor wondered if her father and Harry had ever spent the night here. A noise to the right caught her attention, and she turned to see Bradley squat in front of the cabinet and shuffle through some canned goods.

The material of his trousers was pulled tight against his buttocks and thighs, and she gazed unashamedly. He was hers to love, and yes, she loved him. Her gaze swept to the bed, and she shivered with anticipation. Before the night was over, she and Bradley would be there, making love.

Abruptly another thought shot through her mind, quickly subduing her happiness and anticipation. Bradley had admitted that he didn't think of the shack as a lovers' hideaway, but that would not have kept him from bringing another woman here. She closed her eyes tightly, as if the action would erase the troubled thoughts from her mind. She did not want to imagine him with another woman, here or anywhere else.

"Have you been here frequently?" she found herself asking.

Bradley rose with two of each, plates, forks, and cups in one hand, a bottle of wine in the other. Setting them on the counter, his gaze locked with hers. He understood her question and the reasoning behind it. "Only to check on it," he replied. "I've never had a desire to come here. Tonight is different . . . you and I are creating our own world, making our own happiness."

"Have—you ever created this magic here with another woman?" she asked.

"No."

Her heart pounded rapidly as joy surged through her. "This is our world alone?"

"Ours alone," he promised and smiled slowly. His hand curled around the bottle. "Shall we celebrate the creation of our world?"

Excited and glad to be alive, glad to be with Bradley, she laughed aloud. He uncorked and poured the wine. They each sipped from their own cup, then they twined their arms together and sipped from the other's, deliberately placing their lips where each had pressed his.

"Now for dinner, my sweet."

"I'm famished." She took the cup from his hands and set both cups on the table. "But not for food, and don't worry, love, I'm not going to fade away for lack of it. I shall if I don't have your love . . . and your loving."

"That you shall have . . . I promise." Bradley slipped his arms around her, and she leaned against his chest to give herself up to the comfort of his strength, a habit she could very easily acquire.

"I'm hungry for lots of sweet kisses," she murmured.

Thoughts of food all but forgotten, he unbuttoned the top of her dress and brushed her collar aside to kiss her neck. "Lots of sweet kisses."

She turned her face so that her mouth met his in a quick, light caress.

"But no silk, or flowers, or straw." His hands fastened in her hair and in a matter of seconds, her hat flew across the room. "You look really cute in these things," he said, "but right now is not the time or the place. This veil keeps getting caught on my fingers or in my mouth, and I'd much rather munch on you." His lips kissed along the tender hollow of her neck and jaw before they captured hers, soft first as a gentle morning breeze, then more deeply. His tongue brushed against her outer lips, against the inner; then her mouth parted wider to welcome the fullness. His tongue worked its magic with delicate but thorough exploration.

Gone were the line shack and the outside world. Eleanor could not resist Bradley. She could not deny what was his to take. Condemnation and judgment flew out the window to be replaced with the hot surge of

312

desire. Beneath her stroking fingers she felt the flexing of his taut muscles and thrilled that she aroused such explosive strength. Bradley's lips moved to her cheek and to the pounding pulse point at the base of her throat.

"With or without Newland's finery," he murmured, "you're beautiful, Eleanor Hunt."

"And so are you." As he had taken off her hat, Eleanor reached up and shoved his Stetson off. She heard the soft thud when it landed on the floor, but it was soon forgotten. "Even with Haggarty's scar running across your abdomen, you're beautiful, Bradley Smith."

Her hands stroked his neck and shoulders, then her arms wrapped about his waist, and she clung in sweet surrender. She threw back her head when he began to unbutton the front of her dress. When his head lowered, and his mouth touched the flesh revealed above the top of her chemise, she trembled in his embrace.

"Your beauty is enough to drive a man insane."

"Not insane," she breathed raggedly, "but to the height of passion."

"The height of passion." Bradley's hands cupped her face, and he moved his lips from hers to kiss her eyes, her cheeks, and at last the corners of her mouth. Her hands were on his chest, feeling beneath the soft shirt material the flexed muscles and the lean hardness of his body. Her fingers crept upward and locked around his neck. He pulled her closer, his hands massaging their way back to her buttocks.

Having been awakened to passion, she safely tucked her inhibitions away; she would not be denied. She lived only for the moment, and this moment belonged to her and Bradley. She molded her body to his, gasping when he nibbled at her lower lip. His open mouth clamped onto hers, hotly, demandingly, and she responded in kind.

With a desperation born of need, Bradley quickly divested Eleanor of her clothing and lowered her gently

313

on the bed. Then he began to undress himself. As she lay on the bed watching him, she thought him a golden Adonis slowly revealed in the flickering candlelight.

The shadows veiled the intense passion that gleamed in the fevered depths of his green eyes, but Eleanor felt the intensity of his emotions, and they ignited anew in her the passion they had shared the night before.

He unbuttoned his shirt and shrugged out of it, letting it drop to his feet. Then he sat down on the bench and pulled off his boots and socks. Standing, he moved his hands across his flat, taut stomach as he unfastened his belt and unbuttoned his trousers. They slid down his legs to bunch around his feet.

Muscles rippled from his chest to his feet, and Eleanor's eyes touched every feature discernible on his face, his chest, the thin, hard line of stomach. His gaze moved to the fullness of her swollen breasts, down the curves from midriff to hips. His eyes lowered to the beautiful triangle, and his manhood stiffened.

As he watched her, Eleanor reached up and began to take the pins out of her hair and to drop them one by one on the floor. She rose from the bed, her hair tumbling about her shoulders. Her body, gleaming proudly in the soft light, throbbed her needs and desires. Gazing at Bradley, she realized that she had never loved Radford; she had never felt for him what she was now feeling for Bradley. Radford may have awakened her passions, but he could never have satisfied them.

"Tonight is ours," she whispered, and one arm went around his neck. She pressed her body close to his, feeling the warm moistness of his skin. Her face raised and angled, her lips gently touching his as her other hand slowly moved down, circling his nipple, arousing it to a hard point, moving down the line of crisp hair to his navel. She reveled in her power as a seductress when she felt his hard, masculine body tremble from her ministrations of love.

Her fingers touched the thick mat of black hair that pillowed his manhood, and she tantalized him with her touch, so close, yet so far away.

He moaned low in his throat, and his hands banded around Eleanor, locking her, pinning her against his strength. Yet her fingers would not be stilled. When the pressure of his mouth pushed her head back, when his lips opened hers, and his tongue slipped into the sweet domain of her mouth, Eleanor's hand curved around his masculinity, the soft tips of her fingers caressing the area of greatest sensitivity.

His soft moans turned into a groan of pleasure. When her face lowered, and she circled his nipple with her mouth, he slid to his knees, pulling her down with him. Eleanor lifted her face, her hair brushing against his hot skin, and she began to fondle his other nipple with her tongue. The fingers of one hand splayed through the thick hair of his head, the other one gently touched his most intimate part.

As Bradley began to breath more raggedly, Eleanor's head lowered, her hair and her lips brushing down his torso, her tongue flicking designs on the muscle-taut stomach. "Oh, God, Eleanor," he rasped thickly, "I can't stand any more of this. Give me—give me a chance if you—"

Eleanor sank fully onto the floor with him. "Last night you gave to me. Tonight I'll give to you." She lowered her head to plant multitudes of kisses across his stomach, to trail her long fingernails up and down his thighs. Then she straddled him and slowly lowered herself on him.

"Eleanor," he breathed almost incoherently. "You don't know what you're doing to me. I don't know how much of this I can stand."

He was encased fully within her warm femininity. When she leaned over him, balancing herself on the palms of her hands, she ran the soles of her feet down his legs, stretching her length with him.

Bradley captured one of her nipples in his mouth, and as he began to tug gently, he caught her buttocks with both hands, settling her on him as he began to rear and to thrust. Crazed with desire to please him and to be pleased, Eleanor began to work with him, their bodies moving in matched rhythm.

Finally Eleanor murmured, "Kiss me, Bradley. Kiss me, please."

Bradley released her breast, and he caught her face in both hands, bringing her lips down on his, gasping and arching as her tongue darted into his mouth. But then in the duel of love, of aggression, his tongue pushed into her mouth. Filled with her man, Eleanor groaned her pleasure, moving more frenetically, racing the summit of her joy, carrying Bradley with her.

When they reached the top, Eleanor was gasping for breath, but did not pull her mouth from his. Rather she cupped his buttocks with her hands as he cupped hers and they made the last arch and thrust together, their climax so nearly together that it could have been simultaneous.

Spent, Eleanor collapsed on top of Bradley, breathing heavily, drawing in deep gulps of air, hoping to replace the passion in her system with the long-needed oxygen. She closed her eyes and reveled in the sweet aftermath, enjoying Bradley's fingers as they pushed perspiration-dampened tendrils of hair from her face, as they traced the outline of her ears.

"What are we going to do about this?" Bradley deftly shifted her weight to the side and stood; holding out his hands he pulled her to a standing position and into his arms. "We can't go on hiding what we feel for one another, meeting in out-of-the-way places, hoping that no one finds out, praying that you don't get pregnant."

"I know," Eleanor sighed and reached down to pick up her undergarments. As she slipped into her chemise, she said, "What would married life be like for us, Bradley? You've told me nothing about yourself or your plans for the future. You know so much about me, and I know so little about you."

The room grew silent as both of them dressed, and Eleanor wondered if he intended to answer her. He had his back turned to her, and she could not see his face. Still she felt him withdrawing. He slipped into his socks, but not his boots. Quietly he walked to the table and began to unpack the basket, setting out the food.

"Bradley, I deserve to know something about you."

"You're right," he answered, but still did not answer. Finally he said, "The first day you met me, you made some startling but accurate discoveries. I do love the west, Eleanor, and I want to spend the rest of my life out here."

"As a cattle station manager?" she asked, aware that the atmosphere crackled with a strange intensity.

Bradley held a loaf of bread in his hands for a minute before he said, "No, I'm going to buy my own property, thousands of acres. I want to farm and ranch. I want to build a large house, one that will hold a big family comfortably."

"Beautiful dreams, Bradley," Eleanor said quietly and drew near the table, "but all of this is going to cost money. How are you going to get the money to build this empire out here?"

Bradley set down the bread. Again his answer seemed to be dragged from him against his will. "I've been saving my money for years. I have enough to buy the land."

"You're just waiting now for the right woman to come along?"

"No."

Eleanor's heart skipped a beat.

317

"She's already here. I just don't know if she's willing to accept what little I have to offer."

"She is," Eleanor whispered, touched by that vulnerability she witnessed in him. Forgotten was her curiosity about his past; her only concern was the future—hers and his together. "In fact, she'll help you get what you want. I have my mother's inheritance. We can use that."

Bradley moved around the table and caught her hands in his. Somberly he gazed into her face.

She smiled tremulously. "I'm seriously considering your proposal, Mister Smith, but I'm not sure how good a wife I'll be to a rancher. You see, I've never taken much of an interest in the art of homemaking."

"We'll learn together," Bradley promised and embraced her tightly.

She pressed her cheek against his chest and found great comfort in the steady beat of his heart. "We'll work hard, Bradley. Our ranch will belong to us; we'll build it from scratch without anyone's help. Out here, Bradley, women are freer, and I can continue to practice law."

"Yes, you can." After long, sweet moments in which they clung to each other, Bradley said, "I want to tell you all about myself, Eleanor, but I can't right now. You must trust me."

A part of her cried out that Bradley was being unfair. She had opened herself completely to him, and he was not willing to do this for her. This same part of her pushed her to demand a confession from him now.

Her heart persuaded her otherwise. She had witnessed and shared that sweet moment of vulnerability with him. Now was not the time for him to tell her more. With a wisdom that comes from loving, she would be patient with him. In due course he would tell her. She knew he would; that was Bradley's way.

"I'll wait," she said when she had gotten control of her disappointment. The moment as fragile as china was shattered and lay about her in tiny slivers. The magical spell was broken. Pulling out of his embrace, she gazed into his eyes. "But not long."

"Thank you."

She moved to pour more wine into the cups. "Right now I must concentrate on winning this case."

"Has Jeffrey told you anything more about the note?"

She shook her head. "He promised to tell me all about it before we go into the court room."

"He's pushing his luck."

"I know." Sitting down at the table, Eleanor began to spread butter on a slice of bread. She was not hungry anymore, but this gave her something to occupy her hands. "And that's his only defense against the rustling. He has none against the murder. I must convince the jurors of his innocence, Bradley."

When she realized the liberal amount of butter she had spread, she dropped the knife and laid the bread on her plate. Leaning forward, she said, "They must understand that Jeffrey was in no way connected with the rustling. He merely went out to confirm a message he had received."

"But why was the message delivered to Jeffrey, not to the sheriff or the mayor?"

"Because this person trusted Jeffrey, not the sheriff or the mayor."

Evidently not interested in his food either, Bradley leaned back in the chair and sipped on his wine. "This is getting more complicated by the second, Eleanor. Now you're implicating by inference the sheriff and the mayor—or both."

"Bradley, I don't know who was responsible for the rustling, but someone wanted Jeffrey at the scene. He was planted there for a specific purpose—to be blamed for the rustling and the murder of David Lang."

"You think Jeffrey is protecting Sarah?"

"I don't know. One minute I do; the next I don't. Perhaps she overheard her father or the sheriff talking. If they were involved, she couldn't tell them. The only person she could trust was Jeffrey."

Bradley reached up and rubbed his eyes. "I don't know, Eleanor. I simply don't know anymore. I don't know the mayor that well, but I'd trust Carl with my life."

"But you do believe in Jeffrey's note, don't you?"

"Yes," he grudgingly admitted, "I believe in it."

"And so do Whittier Lang and Radford Vaughan. Whether I can do anything with it or not, at least it will cause them great concern."

"Are you frightened about tomorrow?" Bradley asked.

"Not frightened, only concerned."

"If Jeffrey doesn't tell you the truth, you don't have to defend him," Bradley said.

Eleanor smiled sadly. "Yes, I have to defend him, if not for Jeffrey, for myself."

"How can Eleanor consider defending him?" Alex exclaimed more than asked as he prowled the large upstairs bedroom that he and Harry shared when he was at the station. "Discounting the fact that her life is in danger, Jeffrey Masterson is a bastard."

Harry dropped the cigarette she was rolling onto the night table and walked to where he stood. Smiling at him, she said, "Even if she knew what Jeffrey was up to, she would defend him. She's your daughter, Alex, and much like her father."

She reached up to brush her fingers through his hair and delighted when she felt his arms slide around her body. He lowered his head and rested his face in the curve of her shoulder and neck.

"I never thought this day would come, Harry," he agonized. "She was my baby from the minute she came

320

into this world. I've never thought of her as being adopted, and I never knew she thought—"

"It's all right, love," Harry whispered, rubbing her hands up and down his back. "We're not going to let Jeffrey do this to us."

Alex tensed in her arms. "When I think of that sniveling little bastard, I could—"

"No," Harry soothed, "don't get riled up. I've wallowed in enough anger, hatred, and bitterness for the two of us. Now we have to consider what we're going to do, how we're going to handle this so that we take the initiative out of Jeffrey's hands."

Alex lifted and pulled his head back to stare into Harry's face. Slowly he stepped back, his hands sliding beneath her arms to fall to his side. His gaze went to Abigail's diary lying on the dresser.

"Yes, you should give it to Eleanor," Harry said, reading his thoughts, "but not first. Give it to her only after you have told her the truth."

"Truth!" Alex exclaimed, the stooped shoulders squared, the slender physique once again exuding strength and authority. "What is truth, Harry? It's merely the way a person perceives something and varies from person to person. In order to extort money from me, Jeffrey plans to blackmail me with the history of my daughter's birth as he thinks it is." His hand waved through the air. "And this, this Lyle Pearson, thinks Eleanor is his daughter. And I think she's mine."

Understanding her love's anguish, Harry smiled gently. "That's why, my darling, you hold the trump card. She is your daughter and should hear the story of her birth from no one but you."

Alex sighed, the sound a wilting of his resolve. "I can't do that, baby. I can't stand to see her love turn into hatred for me."

"You're wrong, Alex. If you don't tell her, you'll see

her love turn into hatred. If you tell her, she'll be shocked, angry, and hurt, but she'll respect you. She'll have her integrity intact and will never be threatened by this again. She'll love you more deeply than she ever has . . . and she does love you."

He reached up to clasp the back of his neck. "When she was growing up, Abigail and I talked about telling her the truth. Abigail wanted to, but I refused to let her." He shrugged. "I guess Abigail was the better parent, or maybe the stronger of the two of us. I always wanted to wait for the right minute to come along, and it never did. That's why she wrote that diary, but I couldn't even honor her deathbed request. I couldn't give it to Eleanor."

Harry moved to where he stood, pressed herself against the length of his back, and slipped her arms around his waist. "Recrimination isn't going to solve the problem, Alex. The past is done; you can't go back and change that. You can do something about the present and the future, and ultimately you will honor Abigail's deathbed request. You will give Eleanor the diary. Right now, you must tell Eleanor who her mother really is."

He turned, his gray eyes stark with anguish. "I've hurt all the women in my life, haven't I? Eleanor, you, and Abigail."

"Not as much as you think, darling." A tiny smile touched her lips. "You're forgetting your daughter is a woman now. A woman who is experiencing love for herself. She's going to be evaluating the entire situation differently than if she were not in love."

Alex's expression lifted in surprise. "Who?"

"Bradley."

"Has she said anything about it?"

Harry shook her head. "She doesn't have to. It's in her eyes, her face, the very way she moves and speaks. He took her into town tonight to see Radford Vaughan."

"I need to meet this Bradley Smith."

"You will," Harry said and caught his hand. "Tonight, when he brings her home. Now let's go downstairs and see if we can rustle you up something to eat before they get home."

As they walked across the room arm in arm, the lamplight flickered on Abigail's diary, but Harry no longer feared it. She was apprehensive about Eleanor's reaction to her father's confessions, but knew that she and Alex were doing the right thing; she also had confidence in Eleanor and in her deep love and respect for her father.

Chapter 17

When Bradley and Eleanor returned to the house, lights were blazing in the parlor windows. "Go on in," Bradley said. "I'll be in as soon as I take care of the horses and wagon."

Nodding, Eleanor climbed down and hurried up the sidewalk. When she stepped onto the porch, she heard voices, raised in anger, coming from the parlor. Harry and her father. Her father was here. She paused and drew in a deep breath. Although she was no longer angry and condemning, she had not forgiven Alexander Hunt. Certainly she was not ready to face him. Yet she must.

She quietly opened the front door and stopped in front of the mirror to straighten her hat and the collar of her dress. But quick touches would not totally eradicate evidence of her lovemaking with Bradley. The yellow hat with its black net and silk flowers did nothing to hide the disarray of her hair. Strands escaped her chignon and whisked around her face. Her dress was wrinkled from lying bunched up on the cabin floor. As best she could, she hand-brushed the wrinkles and straightened her back.

Time had whipped her forward and demanded she face Alexander Hunt. She would. She was not his daughter for nothing.

Her head held high, Eleanor opened the front door and slammed it so that her entrance was duly noted. She swept down the hall and into the parlor. "Hello," she said, "I'm home."

"Thank God!" His arms extended, Alex moved toward her, but when Eleanor sidestepped him, his arms dropped to his side. "I've been worried ever since I learned that you went into town to see Vaughan."

"I told him," Harry said quietly.

"You ought to know that I can take care of myself, Papa," Eleanor said coolly.

"But you don't have to," he said, rubbing his silvered temples with his fingertips. "I'm your father, Eleanor. I want to take care of you. Harry was right—you shouldn't be traipsing around like this. Think of your reputation."

"Like you did, Papa?"

Alex recoiled visibly, a scowl of displeasure on his face. "Harry and I were most careful. No one knows—"

"And because it's hidden, it's all right?" Eleanor asked.

"No," Alex reluctantly admitted, "it's not. But we didn't flaunt it for all the world to see, Eleanor."

Eleanor sighed. "Papa, please let me live my own life."

"I know what's best—"

"You think you know what's best," Eleanor corrected.

Alex stared at Eleanor for a full minute before he threw up his hands in exasperation. "You don't have to worry about defending Jeffrey any more."

"That was thoughtful of you," Eleanor said quietly, "but I'm not worried about it. No matter who you brought, I'm defending Jeffrey, Papa."

"Not any more," Alex said, his brow furrowed, his voice unusually loud and domineering. He began to pace the room nervously. "You must get out of this, Eleanor.

You're in over your head."

"This is my case, Papa, and I'm going to handle it."

Harry walked to the liquor cabinet and opened the door. After she poured two glasses of whiskey, she lifted one and sipped. "Tell her the truth, Alex. She deserves it."

"For God's sake, Harry," Alex exclaimed, "let me handle this."

"You owe her the truth, Alex." Harry carried the second glass of whiskey to him. "Can't you see? She's not a child to be protected any longer; she's a woman, and she deserves to know. She deserves your truth and honesty."

Alex looked imploringly at Harry; Eleanor looked from one to the other. "I don't think I can stand it if she—"

"She won't," Harry assured him with a soft smile. "She's your daughter, Alex, and she loves you."

Alex quaffed his glass of whiskey and prowled the room like a cat searching for prey. His lean, muscular body belied his fifty-one years and modeled to perfection his tailored suit. The silver at his temples added to his handsomeness.

"What about you, Harry?" he asked softly. "I don't want to do anything that would hurt you."

"I'll take my chances," she returned with that same gentle smile that Eleanor had never seen before.

Listening to the strange conversation, Eleanor continued to look from one to the other and wondered about her father's confession. Surely he could not add much more than Harry had already told her.

Alex sat his glass on the nearby table and caught Eleanor's hands in his to guide her to the divan, where they sat down. As he began to talk, his voice was low and tentative. "Your mother and I shared a marriage of convenience. I wanted her money, and she wanted an important name and a family. While we were honest with

327

each other, we were never honest with the world or with you."

"You and Mama never loved each other?" Eleanor whispered. "Not even in the beginning?"

"At first, we pretended to care for one another, but after you were born, the pretense stopped. You were all she wanted, and I was happy because I could return unhampered to my life. Both of us were determined to maintain our end of the bargain."

Eleanor turned to look at Harry, who gripped the whiskey glass tightly.

"I never realized what a price I would pay for your mother's money," Alex continued in a heavy voice. Eleanor's gaze returned to him. "When I met Harry, I fell in love with her immediately, but I could never offer her marriage. The only part of my life I could offer her was the hidden side. Because she loved me, she was willing to accept this."

Because she loved Bradley, Eleanor began to realize how much her father must love Harry. But her realization of this did nothing to ease the pain. Seeing her father as an ordinary man with vices like everyone else was a new and disturbing experience for her. Still she squeezed Alex's hands reassuringly. "Papa, I'll admit I was angry and hurt when I learned that you and Harry had been— were—" Even yet she could not force herself to say the words, but her gaze softened as she looked first at Harry, then at her father. "But I'm seeing things differently now. I can . . . can accept your feelings for one another, but please don't push me for more now."

Rising, she smiled sadly at them. "If you'll excuse me, I think I'll go to my room. I need to go over my notes before I go to sleep. Tomorrow is the big day, you know."

Alex's brown eyes darkened, and his brow furrowed. He tugged on her hands. "Please sit down, Eleanor, I have more to tell you."

She looked at him curiously.

"I love you, Eleanor, more than words can ever tell. You are my daughter, the child of my choosing."

Eleanor flashed him a broad smile. "Harry told you what I said about your being disappointed that I was a girl."

He nodded and smiled gently. "But I could not have been disappointed, my darling girl, because I knew the minute you were born that you were my child, my daughter."

"But deep down, Papa," Eleanor insisted, "you wished Mama had given birth to a boy, didn't you? An heir for your name and the company?"

Releasing her hands, Alex stood up and walked around the room for a few seconds before he came to stand in front of the fireplace and stretch his arm along the mantle. "Eleanor, Abigail did not give birth to you."

Bradley walked out of the kitchen into the hallway in time to hear Alex. Immediately he looked at Eleanor. Her jaw went slack, and all color drained from her face. Her fingers gripped the armrest of the divan. He wanted to rush to her side, to hold her, but he did not. As much as he wanted to protect her, he knew this was a battle she must fight for herself. While he was eternally grateful to Alex for telling Eleanor the truth about her birth, he wondered why the hell he had waited until now. At least, Bradley no longer feared that Whittier Lang could use it to blackmail Eleanor.

Finally in a weak, agonized voice Eleanor said, "What do you mean, Papa?"

Alex swallowed and spoke, his voice rather thick. "Biologically you are not Abigail's or my child."

"Not your child." The words were a hollow echo. A few seconds passed, then she leaped to her feet and yelled, "For God's sake, who am I, then?"

Hurting for her, Bradley barely held himself in check. He knew her integrity was at stake, but he felt her pain. Again he was consumed with the desire to love her grief and sorrow away. By sheer willpower he remained where he was. Instead her father ran to her. When he tried to take her into his arms, she refused to be held. She looked accusingly at him, then at Harry.

"Tell me, Papa, who am I? Who are my parents?"

Harry rose and walked to the mahogany secretary, where she opened the drawer and pulled out a small box. Walking toward Eleanor, she said, "I don't know who your father was, but I knew your mother. She worked for me many years ago. Here, take this. It belonged to her, and she would want you to have it."

Her eyes filling with tears, Eleanor took the box, but her attention was centered on her father. "Why, Papa? Why did you let me think I was your child?"

"You are my child, Eleanor," Alex said in a pained voice. "It doesn't matter that you're not of my loins; you're of my heart. Abigail and I chose you because we wanted *you*."

Harry smiled. "Your father had no choice but to keep you, Eleanor. He helped deliver you."

Her gaze bounced between Harry and Alex. "You—you knew my real mother?"

"I really knew her; he didn't," Harry answered gently. "He happened to be visiting with me when she fell down the stairs and went into premature labor. By the time the doctor arrived, the baby was born and your father was already in love with it. In fact, he named you Eleanor after his mother."

Tears trailed down Eleanor's cheeks. "What happened

to my mother?"

Harry drew in a deep breath and gazed at Eleanor with compassionate eyes. "She died shortly after you were born. She died knowing that you were going to be adopted and cared for. Alex assured her of that."

"What about my father?" Eleanor asked. "Why didn't he keep me?"

"We don't know who your father was," Harry said.

Eleanor's eyes widened, and she gripped the small box tightly. "I don't understand. Surely my mother would know—"

"I ran a brothel, Eleanor," Harry confessed quietly. "Your mother was one of my ladies. If she knew who your father was, she never told me. At the time of your birth, she was unwed."

"Oh, my God!" Eleanor's hand came up to her face, and she stumbled back to collapse on the divan.

This time Bradley did not wait. Regardless of what Alex or Harry might think, regardless of the fact that both of them ran to Eleanor, he rushed into the room and reached her before either of them. Scooping her into his arms, he held her tightly against his chest and rocked back and forth as she cried her heart out.

"Oh, Bradley," she sobbed, wrapping her arms about him and burrowing her face against his chest, "did you hear?"

"I heard." He brushed his cheek back and forth over the crown of her head.

"What am I going to do?" she wailed. "I don't know who I am."

"Of course you do," he replied, choosing to answer the second question. His conscience smote him; she did not know who he was, either. She had given him the perfect opportunity to tell her, but he had not. His job required secrecy, and although he loved Eleanor, he was not sure

331

he could trust her with his identity at the moment. But he was not altogether sure who he was, either.

As he had unhitched the buggy, he had made a promise to himself: he would not make love to her again until he told her who he was and what he was doing at the cattle station. He loved and wanted to marry her, but she had a right to know all about him before she made her decision.

"Who am I?" she sniveled.

Quieting the turbulent thoughts that riddled his mind, he said, "You're Eleanor Hunt, daughter of Alex Hunt."

She pulled her head away from his chest and looked into his eyes. Her face was so grief-stricken, he thought his heart would break in two. Sobs racking her body, she gulped, "No, I'm not. My mother . . . was . . . a . . . a whore, Bradley, and I don't . . . even know who my . . . my . . . father was—is."

"Eleanor!" Alex cried. "I am your father."

He started to move toward Eleanor, but Harry reached out to catch his arm and stop him. Ignoring them, Bradley rose, and cradling Eleanor against his body, he walked out of the parlor.

"Your mother was Abigail Hunt," he said softly. "Your father is Alexander Hunt. That's all that matters, my darling."

He carried her up the stairs and into her bedroom. Kicking the door shut, he laid her on the bed and stretched out beside her. During his life he had cared about more than one woman, really cared, but what he felt for them diminished completely when compared to his feelings for Eleanor.

Now he wanted nothing more than to hold and to comfort her. For a long time, his hands moved gently up and down her back reassuringly until her tears were spent and she lay quietly beside him.

Accustomed to the darkness of the room now, he brushed the tangled hair from her cheeks, then lowered his head and brushed gentle kisses over her forehead, across her cheeks, and along her lips. She sniffed, and he caught her to him and wished to God he could bear her grief himself.

She met his embrace with one of her own. Her arms wrapped about his shoulders, and her hands came together at the nape of his neck, her fingers spreading through his thick, silken hair. She moved so that her body fit itself into the angles of his lean frame. Her lips sought his, and the comforting turned into desperate wanting.

In the rush of desire, he allowed himself to forget his purpose in bringing her to the room. He conveniently forgot his promise to himself. Although her desire for him was physical, he could and would fulfill that need.

Passion matching passion, he deepened the kiss as she opened her mouth to him. She quivered in his arms, and his body again throbbed with an urgency that only Eleanor could arouse in him. A wild beat with a frenetic rhythm of its own coursed through his body. Everywhere he seemed to tingle with pleasure, and had never felt more alive.

And still the ardor of her kiss increased, and before he quite knew what had happened, her tongue was moving inside his mouth, working in moist, probing demands. Breathing in deeply, his hands played against her back and buttocks, pulling her against his chest and hips, letting her know how real and urgent was his need for her.

It was a need she evidently shared. When his lips moved from hers and he pressed her onto the bed, her hand lightly touched his chest. Through the material of his shirt, each finger felt as if it were a brand of fire. She began with steady deliberation to unfasten the buttons of his shirt, then to push the cotton aside.

Her fingers stroked the tiny whorls of hair on his chest, and he tightened his stomach muscles as desire burned through his body. Bending her head, she pressed her lips against his chest, her tongue moving seductively over his nipple.

"Eleanor," he whispered.

"Don't try to stop me," she whispered.

"Your father—Harry," he muttered thickly.

"I don't care," she answered, her lips seeking his. "You're what I need right now."

They pulled away from each other just long enough to divest themselves of their clothes; then they came together again. Bradley rained hot kisses along her face and throat, his tongue dancing across her skin to settle hotly on the sensitized tips of her breasts. His hands stroked and caressed her lovingly. As he sought the dark, moist valley between her thighs, she wrapped him in her arms and legs.

Closing out reality, Bradley gave totally of himself to her.

After Eleanor had gone to sleep, Bradley eased out of bed, covered her with the sheet, then moved across the room to dress. Returning to where she lay, he brushed tendrils of hair from her cheek and kissed her on the forehead. He straightened and looked at her for several minutes. She inhaled deeply, squirmed, and curled up again.

Quietly he crossed the room and opened the door. He fully expected to be met by a wrathful father, but surprisingly was not. The upstairs was dark, the only light a sliver in the downstairs corridor that came from

334

the lone oil lamp burning on the kitchen table. Not ready for bed himself, Bradley slipped out of the house onto the back porch. He had not been sitting there long before the screen door opened and Alex joined him.

"How is she?" Without looking at Bradley, the older man walked to the edge of the porch. Sliding his hands into his pockets, he stared skyward.

"She's asleep," Bradley answered.

"Are you in love with her?" His voice was even, but Bradley heard the undercurrent—part pain, part anger.

"I've asked her to marry me," he said tentatively, surprised that Alex was not railing at him. The man certainly had a right to be angry; had he been in Alexander Hunt's boots, he would've been.

"I didn't ask that." Alex turned around, his face barely visible in the pale shaft of light that filtered through the screen door. "I want to know if you love her."

"Yes," Bradley said.

"Don't hurt her," Alex said, his voice thick. "I couldn't stand that. If she were the daughter of my loins, I couldn't love her more."

How ironic! Bradley thought. Alex was worried about his hurting Eleanor, while he was worried about her hurting him. After a thoughtful pause, he said, "If you loved her so much, Hunt, why in the hell did you choose tonight to make your confession? The trial is tomorrow, and Jeffrey's not even here to help her sort through the evidence."

Alex rubbed his forehead. "I had no choice but to tell her now. I should have years ago, but I was frightened. I didn't want to lose her. And now—"

"Give her time," Bradley said, deep in his heart agreeing that Alex was right in telling Eleanor the truth. "She's in shock now, but she'll be all right once she thinks her way through it. Let's hope she can do that in

335

time for the trial tomorrow."

"She's not my daughter for—" His voice broke as he cut himself short. He swallowed and turned, eventually to ask, "When are you getting married?"

"We haven't set a date," Bradley answered.

"I'm glad she's chosen someone like you. You're everything I could have wanted in a husband for her." Composed once again, he turned to Bradley. "You'll do fine in the meat-packing business. Harry tells me—"

Bradley leaned forward, and the legs of the chair thumped heavily to the floor. He rose. "Mister Hunt, I'm marrying your daughter, not your financial empire. I want no part of the Hunt meat-packing industry."

"You can't mean that!" Alex exclaimed.

"I do. Eleanor and I are going to buy us a ranch and live out here."

"Absolutely not!" Alex thundered.

"I don't think that's your decision."

"You can't ask Eleanor to subject herself to the harshness of frontier life."

This was certainly one of Bradley's concerns. He was afraid that she'd agreed to marry him while she was riding high on dreams and romance. He wondered if she would regret her impulsiveness, perhaps change her mind, when she awakened in the morning. If not then, would she change her mind when she learned who he was and what he was doing out here? Her father was correct: she was not accustomed to the harsh realities of frontier life.

Over the silent arguments of reason, he heard himself say, "I can ask. It's up to her to decide."

"I'll do everything in my power to persuade her otherwise," Alex promised.

"I expect you to. That's why I told you."

"We'll talk about this tomorrow, when you've had time to think about it," Alex said and raked his hand

336

through his hair. "I'm going to bed now. How about you?"

"I'll wait longer," Bradley said.

As the kitchen clock chimed the hour, Alex went into the house, but Bradley remained on the porch. Sitting down once again, he leaned against the wall and balanced the chair on its back legs.

All his life he had thought about the inevitability of settling down and marrying, but he had never imagined falling as deeply in love as he had. He had known Eleanor for only a few weeks, but already she was an integral part of his life—a part he could never do without.

Although he honestly wanted her to think of the consequences of marrying him and living on the frontier, he knew that if she refused, he would be sorely tempted to return to New York or Chicago or anyplace else with her. That was how much he loved and wanted her, even though he did not like city life and hadn't ever really fit in.

He no more belonged in New York or Chicago than did the buffalo or the Indian that freely roamed the plains. This was his home, and it always would be. He hoped it could be so for Eleanor. If it was not, he could understand and accept her decision. It would not stop the hurting altogether, but it would ease the pain somewhat.

Half an hour later, he heard a rider approach. Time passed, then he heard the back gate open and close. Without moving, he could see Jeffrey clearly outlined in the moonlight as he walked across the yard.

"I wondered if you were coming home tonight." He shoved away from the wall, the legs of the chair thumping to the floor. Rising, he walked to the edge of the porch to stare into Jeffrey's face, fully illuminated in the wedge of light that filtered through the screen door from the kitchen.

Jeffrey paused at the bottom step. His brow was furrowed, and his eyes narrowed. "You sure take a lot upon yourself, don't you? My whereabouts are none of your business."

"When it concerns this ranch and Eleanor Hunt, it becomes my business."

Jeffrey laughed softly and quickly mounted the stairs to get out of the light. Whisking off his hat, he ran his hands through his hair. For all the man's bravado, Bradley sensed a certain desperation about him. "So it's that way, is it?"

Ignoring the innuendo, Bradley said, "You were going to tell Eleanor about the note before the trial, and if you haven't forgotten, the trial is set for nine o'clock in the morning."

"No," Jeffrey drawled insolently, "I haven't forgotten. I've had things to do today, and I may not have many more days in which to do them."

"Anything as important as working on your murder defense?"

Jeffrey flipped his hat onto one of the cowhide chairs that lined the porch. "The way I figure it," he said, "no matter how good my attorney is, the people of this town already have me pegged as David Lang's killer. Even if I had evidence to prove otherwise, they wouldn't believe me. Furthermore, they'd hang me for trying to steal Old Man Lang's cattle. One way or the other, I'm convicted."

"The note would be a good start toward proving your innocence," Bradley said. "Why don't you level with me about it?"

"You don't believe me about the note, do you?"

"No. But Eleanor does."

"Well—" Jeffrey sighed, as if it no longer mattered whether anyone believed him or not; he walked to the door and crooked his fingers around the handle. "There

338

was one."

"But not the note you've been talking about."

"No."

Instead of pressing him about it, Bradley said rather matter-of-factly, "How long had you and David been rustling cattle?"

Dropping his hand from the door, Jeffrey whirled around. "I told you—"

"Don't raise your voice," Bradley ordered. "Everyone in the house is asleep but you and me. And don't lie to me anymore. If we're going to save your hide, your only defense is the truth—the absolute truth."

"I could run," Jeffrey said.

"You *could*," Bradley agreed easily. "But you're too smart for that . . . Lang would never rest until he found you."

Jeffrey walked to the edge of the porch to stand beside Bradley. "Where's Eleanor?"

'She's asleep," Bradley replied. "I told her I would wait up for you, and if you didn't come home, I'd go looking for you."

Jeffrey's hand circled the column, and he stared straight ahead but said nothing.

"She's almost worried herself sick over you, and you're doing nothing to help her."

"Is the old man in yet?" Jeffrey asked. When Bradley nodded, he said, "Good. I need to talk with him."

"Right now you're going to talk to me."

"Yeah," Jeffrey drawled, "I guess I am. Hunt can wait a while longer." Looking across the darkened horizon, he said, "I met David not long after I arrived. Although he was quite a few years older than me, he was my only friend. We met weekly at the saloon and commiserated on having to live out here. He was tied to his father's coattails, just as I was to Alex's."

He paused, then continued, "Both of us resented this and wanted to be wealthy in our own right—and sooner than either old man promised. As a game, we devised a plan for stealing a few cattle from here and there. Then David became obsessed with the idea. He wanted us to start rustling cattle so he could make his own money and start his own life. When I realized he was serious about it, I backed away and quit going into town on Friday nights to meet him."

"Did you encourage David to rustle cattle?"

Jeffrey shook his head. "Never. Several weeks after this he rode over and asked me to go into town with him for drinks and a game of cards. We did, and he told me he had decided to stay on the right side of the law. His old man was going to give him his inheritance on his next birthday, and he could hang on until then. By selling a few cattle and horses here and there, he could make his drinking and gambling money. I thought that was the end of it."

"And with this drunken confession you continued to buy cattle from him?"

Jeffrey wiped his hands down the sides of his trousers. "Yes."

"You were never at all suspicious?"

"No," Jeffrey exclaimed in a harsh whisper. "I didn't know why a rich man would mess up an inheritance that was only months away. I didn't think he'd be so stupid."

"But eventually you did figure it out?"

"Yeah," Jeffrey drawled, "even I figured it out. Newspaper articles reported the rustling around the time that I bought some cattle from David."

"What did you do?"

"I stopped buying cattle from him. I hadn't seen him for several weeks when Harry sent me into town with the grub wagon to buy supplies. I met David, and he invited

340

me into the saloon to have a drink. He told me that I would buy his cattle and that I was as mixed up in this rustling as he was. He said I could never take my suspicions to the sheriff or mayor because they were friends of his father and would not believe my claims. I was so angry, I jumped up, leaned across the table, and belted him one."

The screen door squeaked open, and Eleanor walked onto the porch. Her hair hung in waves about her shoulders, and her dressing gown, buttoned all the way up, billowed around her legs. To Bradley she'd never looked more lovely.

"A fistfight with David Lang in a public place! You never told me about this, Jeffrey." Before he could say anything, she continued. "I wonder how much more you've kept from me and how many lies you've told."

"Eleanor—" Jeffrey began, but she quieted him with a wave of her hand.

"No woman never played a part in this," she said, her voice hard. "I'd already figured out that much. And no one was trying to frame you."

"There was a note," Jeffrey insisted, "and someone *was* trying to frame me."

"I wish I could believe you," Eleanor said, "but I don't."

"How much have you heard?" Bradley asked.

Eleanor crossed her arms over her chest. "Enough to know you were right. He's been lying to me." It seemed as if everyone who mattered to her had been lying to her all her life.

"I wasn't part of it, Eleanor," Jeffrey explained. "I knew about it, but I didn't steal any cattle."

She sighed. "How did you know David was going to be stealing cattle from his father that night?"

"The last time I talked with David, he was extremely

341

jumpy. Because I feared him implicating me, I begged him to get out of rustling. I knew sooner or later people were going to suspect something. If I had noticed the pattern just by looking at our books, so would others. But he wouldn't listen to me . . . he was more determined than ever to get me involved. The night of the rustling at the Rocking W, someone tossed a rock through the window with a note attached."

"Who wrote it?" Eleanor asked.

"David Lang. He said it was urgent that we meet. He had learned something about the rustling that I should know. His life was in danger, and I was the only one who could help him. We had to meet immediately, before they struck again. He asked me to meet him at the Rocking W, giving the specific place and time."

"How do you know it was David's handwriting?" she questioned.

"Look, Eleanor!" He was clearly exasperated. "I've been doing the books for Hunt Cattle Station for nearly a year now, and David Lang had to sign every time I purchased cattle from him. My drawers are crammed full of papers with samples of his handwriting."

"Do you still have the note?"

"I have it hidden in a strongbox."

"I want it for the trial tomorrow, Jeffrey."

"And it'll hang me for sure, Eleanor. People are more likely to believe David was apprehending me and my gang of rustlers than the other way around. They'll remember the fight we had in the saloon and believe that I was out to kill him."

"I'll try not to use it," Eleanor said, "but I must see it. I must know exactly where you stand in this puzzle; otherwise, I cannot give you a defense."

"You've got to trust Eleanor," Bradley said. "She's your only chance. She knows what she's doing."

342

Jeffrey moved, turning his back to them, and gazed across the lawn. He sighed deeply and brushed his hand through his hair.

"Archer is here, Jeffrey," Eleanor said quietly. "Papa brought him. He wants me to give up the case. I will, if that's your desire."

Jeffrey was silent for a long while; then he said, "No, Smith's right. This is your chance—as well as mine. You know what you're doing."

"Are you sure?" she whispered.

"I'm sure."

"Then get me that note and some samples of David's handwriting." Her voice was more vibrant and confident than it had been in days. "We have a case to win tomorrow."

Smiling, Jeffrey opened the door and walked through the kitchen into the office. He had hardly settled the chimney on the lamp when he heard the door open and turned, expecting to see Eleanor or Bradley.

"Hello, Jeffrey," Alex said. "I hoped you were the one I heard moving about in here."

"Alex!" Jeffrey said, moving around the desk toward his employer. "I'm glad you're here."

Alex looked down at the extended hand for a second before he grasped it. He still found it hard to believe that the boy he'd befriended and in a sense adopted as his own son would even think of blackmailing him. "I'm glad to be here," he finally said, his gray eyes moving curiously over Jeffrey's face. "You're looking good."

Dropping his hand and moving back to the desk, Jeffrey nodded and smiled. "I'm feeling better now than I have in weeks," he admitted. "Eleanor thinks we have a good chance of winning."

"Did she tell you that I brought Archer with me?"

"Yes," Jeffrey answered as he pulled open one of the

drawers and began rummaging through it. "She even offered to step aside to let him defend me, but I told her no, that this was her chance to prove herself an attorney, and I wanted to give it to her."

"I'm glad you did that," Alex said. In order to protect Harry, he had to be careful in his handling of the conversation. "This hasn't been a real good evening for Eleanor."

Jeffrey stopped his search and looked across the desk at Alex. The lamplight glowed on the bottom part of his face, accenting the heavy beard stubble.

"I—I had to tell Eleanor that she wasn't . . . my daughter by birth."

Jeffrey half rose from the chair and flopped down again. "You told her that?" he murmured.

"I should have told her a long time ago," Alex admitted, "but I was a coward, Jeffrey. I thought it would cause her to love me less."

"How—" Jeffrey cleared his throat "—how did she take the news?"

"Better than I had expected. You don't seem to be too surprised with the news," Alex said.

"Oh, I am!" Jeffrey exclaimed. "I'm—I'm flabbergasted, Alex. I don't know what to say."

"Really, there's nothing for you to say," Alex replied and walked to the door, his hand closing over the knob. "I just want to admonish you to cooperate with Eleanor if you expect her to represent you."

"I am, and, by the way, sir, I'm glad you told Eleanor the truth."

"I am, too," Alex replied. "Good night, Jeffrey. I'll see you in the morning."

When Bradley stopped the buggy in front of Blissful

State Saloon, the crowd was large enough that it overflowed the room. Casting disapproving and hostile glances, those who stood on the porch watched Eleanor, Jeffrey, and Archer Cormack disembark. Then, seemingly by silent command, they divided to make a path through which the three of them could walk into the saloon.

"Miss Hunt," Barber Craven waved to her from the front of the room. "I'd like for you to meet Judge Neeley. He and I have been friends for years."

"Will you come with me, Archer?" she asked.

The tall, lean man at her side shook his head. "No," he said softly, "this is your case. I'll let you handle it. I'll sit down at the table and get our papers in order and instruct Jeffrey on proper behavior in court."

Nodding, Eleanor turned away from her employer and took several steps toward the distinguished gentleman in his early sixties. His white hair was thinning on top; his bushy sideburns blended into a thick white beard. His smile was friendly, and his deep blue eyes twinkled.

In one quick but thorough glance, the judge assessed Eleanor. She was quite pleased with her choice of clothing. Gone were all frills and furbelows and bright colors. Deliberately she dressed so as not to call attention to her person, her being female would be enough of a strike against her. She could stand no more. Her straw bonnet, small and obviously plain, covered all of her hair except the neat coil at the base of her neck. She wore a blue suit with a white collar, her only accessory a gold watch hanging about her neck on a white velveteen ribbon.

"Hello, Miss Hunt," Ted Neeley said. "Needless to say, I've heard a great deal about you. I only hope for Sarah's young man's sake you're as good as she seems to think you are."

"I do too, Your Honor."

"I want you to know, young lady, that although I'm a close friend of Barber and his family, I will not let that friendship in any way influence my ruling on this case. I'm a hardline judge, and I believe in the letter of the law. I instruct my juries to look for hard evidence."

"I would ask for no more and except no less, sir." Eleanor returned his smile and his handshake. Moving back to her table, she said, "And, Judge Neeley, may I present the senior partner in the firm, Archer Cormack."

"Mister Cormack," Judge Neeley said as they shook hands, "I've heard about you. It's my distinct honor to meet you, sir."

"And mine to meet you, Your Honor."

Eleanor laid out her materials: writing paper, pens, inkwell, blotter, and her notes, her precious notes—all of them carefully organized and indexed. The door opened, and she looked up to see her father and Harry enter; Bradley followed. They moved down to the front, Alex and Harry sitting in the first row of chairs behind Eleanor and Jeffrey. Bradley walked to the table where Eleanor stood.

"You look quite intimidating, Miss Hunt."

She smiled. "I'm trembling on the inside."

He reached out and caught her hand to give it a quick, reassuring squeeze. "That's the way it ought to be. That trembling on the inside keeps you on your toes. When you lose it, you lose your edge on your enemy. It's going to be all right, sweetheart." When she smiled at him, he lowered his voice even more to say, "I wish we were in a place where I could take you into my arms and kiss you senseless."

Eleanor smiled. "I would do Jeffrey very little good if I were senseless. This sounds like a conspiracy to me, Mister Smith. I'm beginning to wonder if you're working for Whittier Lang, and whether he told you to do this to me so I couldn't provide Jeffrey with a defense."

Bradley's eyes darkened momentarily. "No, my darling, my thoughts are purely my own. They are totally selfish, and a product of undeniable desire for the object in question."

"You're so good for me, Bradley," she murmured and laid her hand over his lower arm. "In my topsy-turvy world, you're the only consistent person I know. The only one who hasn't lied or deceived me in some way."

Bradley laid his hand over hers and pressed. He looked as if he wanted to say something, but the door opened, and Eleanor looked up to see Radford Vaughan enter the room. To his right walked Whittier Lang, and behind him were two of his henchmen. Haggarty would not be coming in until later, since he was a witness for the prosecution. Radford tipped his hat to her and smiled; Whittier glared; the hired gunmen leered. Eleanor's face went expressionless; she had never disliked anyone as much as she disliked these gunslingers who worked for Lang.

"Your Honor—" Radford Vaughan's deep, resonant voice echoed through the saloon-turned-courtroom "—I'd like to call my first witness, Saul Haggarty."

Haggarty, sworn in as a witness, sat in the chair beside the judge's desk. He glanced over at Eleanor and grinned rather suggestively. Despising him and all he stood for, Eleanor refused to be embarrassed or intimidated. Beneath her relentless gaze, he finally broke eye contact and squirmed nervously in the chair.

With guidance from Vaughan, he began his testimony. "Gideon Davenport—he was then manager of the Rocking W—told me he was suspicious of this cattle rustling. According to him, it began about the time Masterson showed up at Hunt Cattle Station."

347

"I object, Your Honor," Eleanor said. "Mister Haggarty's evidence is hearsay."

Ted Neeley adjusted his spectacles, then said, "Objection sustained."

Vaughan smiled thinly and walked to his table, where he picked up several sheets of paper and brought them before the judge. "I'd like to have these presented in evidence, Your Honor."

"What are they?" Taking them, the judge began to sort through them.

"Newspaper clippings and official reports that prove the rustling began soon after Masterson's arrival at the Hunt Cattle Station."

"Miss Hunt, would you care to see these?"

Eleanor rose and approached the bench. Taking the papers the judge offered her, she quickly scanned them. "I have no objection."

When she returned to her chair, she sat down and forced herself to listen calmly to the remainder of Haggarty's testimony, every word of it damning to Jeffrey. He positively identified Jeffrey as David Lang's killer.

Finally it was Eleanor's turn to question the witness. Rising from her table, she said, "You expect the court to believe that at midnight and with all the raucous goings-on that you could spot and identify Jeffrey Masterson as David Lang's murderer?"

Haggarty's eyes shifted nervously around the room. He crossed and uncrossed his legs several times. "Yes ma'am, I shore do. Like I said, the moon was shining bright, and anybody who sees halfway good could spot that white horse Masterson rode. All of us boys can see purty good, ma'am, and none of us was riding a white stallion that night." Looking at Vaughan, he snickered and leaned forward. "Course, you could always point out

348

that maybe somebody wanted us to think it was Masterson bad enough to ride a white horse. But, then, ma'am, we all know it was Masterson, 'cause he's already admitted to being there."

Laughter twittered through the saloon. Restraining her anger, Eleanor said quietly, "Thank you, when I want your opinion I'll ask for it; otherwise, restrict your answers to the questions that I ask."

A satisfied smirk on his face, he leaned back in his chair and folded his arms over his chest. "Yes, ma'am."

Thinly veiling her anger, Eleanor said. "No further questions."

As she returned to her chair, Vaughan stood. "Your Honor, I would like to call Maude Livingston to the witness stand."

Surprised, Eleanor gazed around the courtroom, which had suddenly come alive. People craned their necks in order to see better. Dressed sedately in a black taffeta gown, the saloon owner walked to the chair, laid her hand on the Bible, and allowed herself to be sworn in. She gave Eleanor a defiant glare, as if to say, "I'll get even with you for getting Early shot." Then she tilted her chin arrogantly and looked at Vaughan. Eleanor listened as Radford questioned her about the fight in the Two Bits Saloon between Jeffrey and David.

"They were talking too low for me to hear at first," she said, her eyes settling on Jeffrey. "But after a while, they begin to talk louder. I heard David tell him to stay away from *her*."

"From whom?" Radford asked.

"I wasn't sure," Maude answered. "Jeffrey jumped up and began throwing punches at David, yelling he would see *her* if he wanted to, and that nobody was going to stop him. 'Nobody takes my woman away from me,' David said, and Jeffrey just laughed. 'Watch and see,' he said."

"Who was David's girlfriend at this time, Miss Livingston?"

Maude lifted a hand to tuck a curl beneath her hat. "Julia," she answered. "Julia Stanwood."

A deafening hush fell over the courtroom, and people turned to look at Julia, who sat stiffly and straight, her veiled face toward the front of the building. Eleanor's hands were clammy with perspiration and were shaking so badly she could hardly hold the pen in her fingers. She could only wonder if Jeffrey had lied to her again.

"No further questions," Vaughan announced rather arrogantly.

"Miss Hunt?" Judge Neeley said.

Pushing herself up on trembling legs, Eleanor walked to where Maude sat. "Miss Livingston, did either David or Jeffrey ever mention the woman by name?"

"Well, no," Maude drawled, "but everybody knows—"

"Was the woman's name ever mentioned?" Eleanor demanded.

"No," Maude repeated, her arrogance apparent, "but we all know that David had been seeing Julia."

Knowing she had scored a point, Eleanor smiled. "So you don't know for certain that they were fighting over Julia?"

Maude glared at her for a full second before she said, "No."

"No further questions."

Her steps lighter, her lips curled into a contented smile, Eleanor returned to her seat and had no sooner sat down than Vaughan said, "Your Honor, I call Julia Stanwood to the stand."

Stiffly Julia rose, and still looking straight ahead, she walked to the front of the room, her voice loud and clear as she was sworn in. Never lifting the veil from her face, she sat down.

"Miss Stanwood—" Vaughan began.

"Mrs." Julia interrupted.

Vaughan snorted contemptuously. "*Mrs.* Stanwood, exactly how friendly were you and David Lang?"

Eleanor leaped to her feet. "Your Honor, I object. This line of questioning has no relevance to the case we're trying."

"Mister Vaughan," the judge said, "I tend to agree with the attorney for defense."

"It does have some bearing on this case, Your Honor," Radford assured the judge smoothly. "If you'll bear with me for a few minutes, I think I'll be able to prove that to your satisfaction."

Tom Neeley leaned back in his chair and waved his hand. "Objection overruled. Proceed with your questioning, Mister Vaughan."

Venting her frustration in a sigh, Eleanor sat down.

"Now, *Mrs.* Stanwood, will you please tell us exactly how friendly you were with David Lang?"

Julia smiled coolly and said, "You tell me, Mister Vaughan. You seem to know so much about him and me."

Laughter rippled through the courtroom.

"Your Honor—" Vaughan turned to the judge.

The judge rapped the gavel on the table. "Answer the question, Mrs. Stanwood."

"We were quite friendly," Julia answered, her even voice carrying clearly through the room.

Radford slipped his hands into his jacket pocket and strutted arrogantly around the room, coming to stop in front of the jurors. "May the court infer from your statement that you and David were lovers?"

"It's your prerogative to infer whatever you wish," Julia returned.

Vaughan rubbed his palms down his waistcoat, and

Eleanor laughed softly.

"Were you more than friendly with Jeffrey Masterson?" Vaughan asked.

Julia raised her hands and lifted her veil to stare at Jeffrey. Smiling, she said, "Hardly. I have a penchant for men, not boys. And there's no need for you to question me further, because you have no proof of your allegations. And that is exactly what they are—allegations."

Julia lowered the veil and leaned back in the chair. Again laughter rippled through the room, and Jeffrey squirmed in the chair. Eleanor breathed a sigh of relief.

"Is it not ironic that you and Jeffrey were out of town on the same weekend?"

Julia smiled. "I can't see the irony in the situation, but I'm sure you can."

"Were you in Dodge City on the last weekend in May?"

Julia hesitated only momentarily before she answered, "Yes, I was."

"Registered as a guest at the Dodge House?"

"Yes."

"Were you there with Jeffrey Masterson?"

"No," Julia returned, never losing her composure, "I had no idea he was there."

Vaughan smiled mockingly. "Let me get this straight, Mrs. Stanwood. In a town as small as Dodge, and with both of you staying in the same hotel, you're saying that you had no idea Jeffrey Masterson was there, that the two of you never saw each other?"

"I didn't know Jeffrey was there," Julia maintained quietly.

"I find that hard to believe," he said.

"But it is the truth, Mister Vaughan."

352

Vaughan walked to where the jurors sat, and looking at them with a smile, he said, "You're asking us to believe you, Mrs. Stanwood, when by your own admission your reputation now lends itself to question and doubt."

For the first time since she'd taken the stand, Julia's composure was broken. "I'm telling the truth."

"So you say." Vaughan smiled smugly and turned to Eleanor. "I have no further questions. Counsel may cross-examine, if she wishes."

"Miss Hunt?" Judge Neeley asked.

Eleanor could not have stood had she wanted to. Her legs were too weak to hold her up. "No questions, Your Honor."

"Any more witnesses, Mister Vaughan?"

"No, sir." His entire personage and voice oozed confidence. "The prosecution rests its case."

As Radford walked back to his chair, Eleanor glanced at the jurors, all men, the majority of whom were sitting back with their legs crossed, their arms folded, their lips curled into smug smiles. She felt all her courage and confidence slipping away. It appeared that they were not even going to listen to her evidence.

Tom Neeley's gavel hit the table with a resounding thud. "Court will recess for lunch. We'll reconvene at two o'clock. We'll be ready at that time to proceed with your case, Miss Hunt."

Pushing through the crowd, Sarah ran up to Jeffrey and flung herself into his arms. The dark veil of her hat did little to hide her anxiety. "Jeffrey, it sounds so bad, your fight with David. And that white stallion," Sarah sobbed. "You had to have White Prince."

Jeffrey's hands clamped around her upper arms, and he set her away. Reaching into his back pocket, he extracted his handkerchief, then lifted the veil to wipe away her tears. "Don't worry, sweetheart. Eleanor will get me out of this."

She sniffed. "I don't know if she can or not, Jeffrey. It looks bad . . . you and Julia being in Dodge City on the same weekend."

"A matter you forgot to tell me about," Eleanor said sarcastically, the statement implying far more than she uttered.

Jeffrey shook his head. "I had no idea that we were there at the same time, Eleanor. Harry sent me to check out some cattle. I was hardly at the hotel, certainly not long enough to see Julia."

Eleanor's attention was drawn from the conversation when she felt Bradley's hand cup her elbow. "Let's go get something to eat," he said. "You've had a rough morning."

"And I'm in for an even rougher afternoon." She closed her portfolio and capped her inkwell. "Have you noticed the way the jury closes me out when I speak, Bradley? They've already pronounced the verdict."

"It looks like you're going to have to put Jeffrey on the stand."

"He's doomed either way." She sighed. "People around here will hang him for one or the other or both. Maude's testimony, followed by Julia's, gives Jeffrey motive enough for killing David."

They walked a short distance before Bradley stopped and said thoughtfully, "If other people bought the cattle and didn't realize they were stolen, why should Jeffrey be any different?"

Eleanor glanced down the alley at the corral behind Bundy's store. "Of course," she said, smiling slowly. "Do you mind if we skip the meal?"

"I should be getting used to it by now." In a low voice he said, "However, I prefer your canceling meals for me, rather than for other reasons."

Her thoughts going back to the line shack, Eleanor's face suffused with color, and she laughed softly. "You have yourself to blame for this one, Mister Smith."

He laughed with her. "So I do. Shall we go?"

"We shall. The prosecution has rested its case but not the defense."

Chapter 18

"Your Honor," Eleanor announced, hiding her anticipation behind a veil of efficient coolness, "I call Anson Bundy to the stand."

A murmur went up from the crowd, and shuffling could be heard as they turned to look at the store owner, a short, heavyset man in the back row, who rose and walked to the front of the building. After he was sworn in, he sat down, nervously fiddling with the buttons on his faded coat. His round face was set in a frown.

"Mister Bundy—" Eleanor moved to stand in front of him "—I understand that you're a businessman here in Blissful?"

"Yes, ma'am." He squared his shoulders proudly and smiled. Lifting his hand, he brushed his palm against his temple. "Right successful, too."

"And what kind of business do you have?"

"I own the new general store. Sell a little bit of everything, but mostly hardware."

"And you also sell cattle and horses for settlers who are going farther west?"

"Yes, ma'am. I keep a small herd in the corral behind the store."

Eleanor turned and strolled in front of the jurors, her

blue eyes making direct contact with each of them, one by one. Several squirmed in their chairs. "Did you do much business with the Langs, Mister Bundy?"

"Not much. But every once in a while David would come in and give me a list of groceries he wanted."

"Groceries for the ranch?" she asked.

"Not really . . . just small items he wanted to take on trips. Said one time that he didn't want his pa to know he was leaving town, and if he stopped by Jessup's place, they would say something to Whittier."

"That's not true," David's father shouted, leaping to his feet.

Neeley rapped the gavel sharply on the table. "Be quiet, Whittier, or I'll send you out of the courtroom."

"Your Honor," Radford said, "that's hearsay. I'd like you to instruct the jurors that they are not to pay any attention to it."

"The jury is so instructed," the judge said.

Smiling broadly at having made her point, Eleanor continued, "Mister Bundy, do you have any proof that David did indeed buy supplies at your store?"

"Yes, ma'am," he said and reached into his pocket to pull out a crumpled slip of paper.

Eleanor took it and handed it first to the judge, then to Radford. "I'd like to present this as evidence," she said, and after both the judge and Radford nodded, she returned it to the store owner. "Will you read this for me?"

In a low monotone Bundy began to read the list, ending with "Ten sticks of licorice."

"Licorice," Eleanor said.

Bundy grinned. "Yes, ma'am. David Lang had a sweet tooth. He always bought licorice from me. Many's the time that Jessup ran out and had to send down to my store to get some when David was in town."

Adrenaline was pumping through Eleanor's veins,

giving her the added strength she needed. "This is a grocery list that David gave to you?"

Bundy nodded. "Not only gave it to me, but I watched him write it."

"He wrote this list?" she reiterated for emphasis.

"Yes, ma'am."

"Thank you, Mister Bundy," she said. "Is it true that during the past year you have purchased cattle from David Lang on several occasions?"

Bundy's eyes darted back and forth between Whittier Lang and Eleanor, and he licked his lips. "Yes, ma'am."

Out of the corner of her eye, Eleanor saw Whittier's hands clench over the back of their chair in front of him. "Did you ever have occasion to check your purchase dates with dates of rustling in and around the area?"

"Why, no, ma'am." Bundy leaned forward. "David was Whittier's son. I didn't figure he'd do something like that."

"Like what, Mister Bundy?" Eleanor held her breath and watched the man closely. She could not afford one little slip, not one.

Bundy reached up and rubbed his head. "Like—well, ma'am, like rustling cattle."

"Thank you, Mister Bundy," Eleanor said softly and smiled. "Did you bring the list of dates on which you purchased cattle from David as I requested this morning, Mister Bundy?"

His forehead was beaded with perspiration, and he ran his palms down his coat. Again he gave Whittier a nervous glance. "Yes, ma'am, I reckon I did."

"May I see them, please?"

His short, stubby fingers fought the pocket but finally extracted a wrinkled sheet of paper, which he handed to her. As she unfolded it, she walked back to her desk and picked up another sheet of paper. Returning to the witness, she handed him her note and her pen. "I'll ask

Judge Neeley to read your list, Mister Bundy. For every date that correlates to one on my list, please check it off."

As Tom Neeley read the list, Bundy sat there and marked. When the judge was finished, the store owner reached into his pocket, pulled out his handkerchief, and mopped his face.

"Were there any dates on your list that were missing from mine, Mister Bundy?"

"No, ma'am."

"Yet you never thought of connecting the rustling with the cattle you were purchasing from David Lang?"

"No, ma'am," he said. "I really didn't."

"No further questions." Quite proud of the way her case was progressing, Eleanor turned to the prosecution and smiled broadly. "Your witness, Mister Vaughan."

She returned to her table. She had not proved Jeffrey's innocence nor David's guilt, but she had proved there was a doubt. For the first time today she felt as if she was in control. If only the remainder of the trial went as well.

Twisting slightly in her chair, she looked over her shoulder to see Bradley sitting in the back row. Their gazes caught and locked, and he slowly smiled—a special smile that meant so much to her and bolstered her spirits. Knowing that Bradley believed in her gave her added confidence.

"Do you wish to cross-examine, Mister Vaughan?" Judge Neeley asked.

"Yes, I do." He stood, never moving from behind his table. "Mister Bundy, is David's name anywhere on this list?"

"No sir, but—"

"So you cannot be absolutely sure that David wrote it, can you?"

"Oh, yes sir," Anson Bundy said, squaring his shoulders. "It's David's handwriting, all right. Turn the paper over, and you'll see a part of his father's letterhead from their stationery."

A strange smile playing his mouth, Radford walked forward and picked up the paper. "Still, Mister Bundy, this does not prove that David wrote the note, only that the note was written on a torn piece of Whittier Lang's stationery." He whirled around and returned to his table. "No further questions."

Anson Bundy rose and moved slowly back to his seat, his eyes on Whittier Lang's hardened face.

"I had to tell the truth, Whittier," he said in a rough whisper. "There was nothing else I could do."

Eleanor smiled at the judge. "Now, Your Honor, I would like to call Whittier Lang to the witness stand."

The room was quiet, everyone staring at her as if she were insane. Eleanor had the sudden impulse to laugh, but restrained herself. "Your Honor?"

"Ah . . . yes," he said, clearing his throat. "Whittier."

Slowly, like a very old man, Whittier stood and walked to the front of the room, his expression confused as he laid his hand on the Bible to be sworn in.

"Mister Lang," Eleanor said after he was seated, "do you do business with Bundy's General Store?"

"Not much," he answered cautiously, his eyes squinting, as if he was trying to figure out her line of questioning.

She handed him the grocery list. "Is this David's handwriting?" she asked.

After he had glanced at the paper, he said, "Can't tell."

"Read the other side," Eleanor instructed. The paper crackled as the callused fingers turned it over. When he did not say anything, Eleanor prompted him again. "Please read it for us, Mister Lang."

"It's my stationery," he snapped.

"Read the note."

"It could be anybody's—" he began.

"But it isn't," Eleanor said. "Read it for us, Mister Lang."

"Get feed for Papa's prize bulls."

"Your Honor—" Radford rose "—Miss Hunt is harassing the witness. He's no handwriting expert and can't know if that's his son's handwriting or not. And surely that message could have been written by anyone."

Eleanor looked at Tom Neeley. "I'm not trying to get an expert opinion, Your Honor, but a father would know his own son's handwriting, and that's all I'm asking for."

Tom nodded his head. "Is that David's handwriting, Whittier?"

"Could be," Whittier mumbled.

"Aren't you the only rancher in this area, Mister Lang, who breeds cattle and has prize bulls?"

Whittier did not answer, but he compressed his lips into a thin line, and his face grew red.

Eleanor said, "No further questions."

"Mister Vaughan," the judge said, "do you wish to cross-examine?"

"No," he said, and Whittier stepped down.

"Then I'd like to call Jeffrey Masterson," Eleanor said loudly and clearly.

The only sounds in the room were the grating of the chair as Jeffrey moved away from the table and the clip of his boots on the wooden floor. After he was sworn in, he began to answer Eleanor's questions, quietly repeating almost word for word the story he had told her and Bradley the night before. At first he stared at Eleanor. Then his gaze shifted to the jury.

"I was not intimate with Julia Stanwood and was not jealous of her and David. I did not rustle any cattle, and I didn't kill David Lang," he concluded, hanging his head. Then he raised it and looked at the jury imploringly. "Fact of the matter, I really don't know how to shoot a revolver. I wear one because everyone else out here wears them."

Eleanor returned to her desk and picked up a small, dirty sheet of paper. "Your Honor, I would like to present this as evidence."

"What is it?"

"The note Jeffrey received on the night that David was killed."

The judge took the paper and looked at it. He nodded, and Vaughan rose to approach the bench and examine the note. He frowned and raked his hand through his hair as he returned to his seat.

"So be it," Neeley said, and handed it back to her.

She carried it to Jeffrey. "Is this the note you received the night David Lang was killed?"

"Yes."

"Please read it to the court."

When Jeffrey finished, a low murmur passed through the crowd. "Can you prove this note was written by David?"

Jeffrey nodded. "My records are full of papers with David's handwriting on them."

"Your Honor—" Radford Vaughan stood up, looking like a veritable giant to Eleanor; his countenance was a sculpture in fury "—anyone could forge the man's signature. There's no way we can say conclusively that David Lang wrote that note."

"That's true, Mister Vaughan," the judge said.

"I can prove this is David's handwriting, Your Honor," Eleanor said.

"How?" the judge asked, adjusting his spectacles.

"By comparing it to other samples of his handwriting. It's the same handwriting as the shopping list that Mister Bundy gave to me, and the same as the note that's written on the back of the list. This proves, Your Honor, that my client has been telling the truth."

Vaughan leaped to his feet, almost knocking his chair over in his haste. "Objection! Counsel knows better than to make argument to the jury."

Eleanor said demurely, "My statement is withdrawn,

363

Your Honor." Before she looked at Radford, her glance passed over the spectators, finally settling on her father and Harry, both of them beaming, then on Bradley, who sat next to them. He grinned and tipped his hat. Eleanor returned the grin as she said to Radford, "I assume you have questions for the witness, Mister Vaughan."

Knowing she had scored a victory, and pleased that Bradley and her father had recognized it, Eleanor returned to her seat. No amount of verbal withdrawing would erase her words from the minds of the jurors. Perhaps they had started out in the palm of Radford's hand, but she knew that she had swayed them with Bundy's testimony. Still she could not rest easy; she had to turn Jeffrey over for cross-examination.

"Mister Masterson—" Radford caught his lapels in both hands and strutted up and down the line of jurors "—you've concocted quite a story. I say you stopped purchasing the cattle because it was a part of your plan to cast blame on David Lang."

"No." Jeffrey shook his head vigorously.

Eleanor pushed to her feet. "Your Honor, I object."

The judge waved her down. "Overruled, Miss Hunt. Proceed, Mister Vaughan."

Vaughan's long index finger pointed directly into Jeffrey's face. "I submit that David Lang was not a part of your cattle-rustling ring. You were setting him up to take the blame when you saw that you were going to get caught. You testified earlier that you rode into town on the day of June 19 and met David Lang here at the Two Bits Saloon."

"Yes."

Now Vaughan's index finger pointed to the floor. "Right down the street, Mister Masterson, you and David Lang sat in a saloon, had a drink, and talked. Is it not also true that David Lang had figured out you were rustling the cattle and confronted you about it?"

"I object, Your—"

"No, that's not true." His face contorted with fear, Jeffrey rose to his feet and shouted, taking no heed of Eleanor. "We met, had a drink, and talked, but he did not confront me about the rustling. David was the one who was rustling, not me."

The sheriff walked up to Jeffrey and firmly shoved him back into the chair. Jeffrey dropped his head and cradled it in his hands. Vaughan smiled slyly.

"Ah, yes, how convenient that David Lang is dead and unable to defend himself. Did you and David Lang fight that night, Mister Masterson?"

"Yes."

"And did you, in fact, threaten to kill him?"

"No!" Jeffrey shouted, "I did not!"

"But I have witnesses who testify that you did."

"They're lying if they do, just like Early Dobson."

"Is Maude Livingston lying when she says you and Lang fought over Julia Stanwood?"

"Yes."

"You did not tell David to stay away from Julia Stanwood?"

"No," Jeffrey answered in a rather subdued voice.

Vaughan's eyes glittered. His voice rose, and he laid his index fingers loosely over his mouth. "You concocted an elaborate scheme, Masterson, quite rich in drama, I might add. The note—which you allege David wrote—and the mysterious ride to the Rocking W to apprehend David as he robbed himself. I repeat, as he *robbed himself.*"

Jeffrey cast a frantic look at Eleanor and shook his head wildly. Reeling from this new line of questioning, Eleanor was confused. The chair grated on the floor as she leaped to her feet and cried, "Your Honor, I object!"

But Vaughan would not stop talking. "Once we reduce the facts to their proper proportions, your story sounds rather stupid, does it not, Mister Masterson? I contend that you were jealous of David Lang."

"Your Honor—" Eleanor leaped to her feet "—I object."

"Overruled," the judge replied.

Eleanor slid down into her chair. Judge Neeley was allowing Radford to badger Jeffrey, and there was nothing she could do to help her client.

Smiling, Vaughan continued, "Jealousy is the reason why you killed David Lang, but you wanted it to appear to be something else, didn't you? What were you doing, protecting the lady?"

"Shut up! You're telling nothing but lies!" Jeffrey lunged at Vaughan, but Carl rushed forward and caught him.

"Sit down, you fool," he gritted.

"You're lying!" Jeffrey shouted again.

"You wanted Julia Stanwood, didn't you, Mister Masterson, and you determined to take her away from David. But he was equally determined that you wouldn't have her."

"You Honor—" Eleanor's voice was much louder this time as her fist hit the table "—I object to Mister Vaughan's treatment of my client. He is not questioning the defendant; he's telling the story as he himself wishes it to be."

The judge removed his spectacles and wiped them with his handkerchief. Holding them up, he squinted to see if they were properly cleaned. "You're right, Miss Hunt. Question the defendant, Mister Vaughan. Don't make up stories as you go along."

"No further questions, Your Honor." As Vaughan walked back to his table, he looked at Eleanor and smiled contentedly. Then his eyes moved through the crowd, his gaze settling on Julia. Without a word, Vaughan emphasized his point.

"Do you have any further questions for your witness, Miss Hunt?"

"Yes," she said, "a couple for redirect."

She walked to where Jeffrey sat. "Have you ever been 'more than friendly' with Julia Stanwood?"

"No—absolutely not. I don't even know the woman, except by reputation. If it's true she and David were—well—" He shrugged and looked embarrassed. "I didn't know it."

"You and David Lang did not fight over Julia?"

"No."

"You had no reason to kill him over Julia?"

"No."

"Jeffrey Wayne Masterson, did you kill David Lang?" She asked her last question and hoped that Jeffrey would look at the jury as she had instructed him to.

"No." His voice was firm, and he slowly turned his gaze from her to the jurors. "I did not."

Eleanor inhaled deeply and said, "The defense rests, Your Honor."

Only now that the jury was out and the crowd mingled in front of the building did Eleanor really take notice of her surroundings. It was odd, she thought as she stood behind her table, empty since Carl had moved Jeffrey back to the jail—earlier the saloon had appeared like a courtroom, equal to any she had seen in Chicago; now it was a frontier saloon, the judge standing at the door, the bartender behind the counter, serving liquor.

"Here," Bradley said and handed her a glass of cool lemonade. "I thought you might need this."

After she had taken a long swallow, she said, "I think I need something stronger. The waiting is getting to me."

"No matter what the verdict," Bradley told her, "you did a marvelous job. Jeffrey couldn't have had a better defense."

"Thank you," she murmured, her heart heavy. "I just don't know how to read the jury."

"You had their undivided attention," he assured her. "Their being out this long means they're not coming to an easy conclusion."

Both of them looked over at Radford Vaughan, who paced restlessly back and forth in front of his table.

"You have him worried," Bradley said. "That is a good sign."

Another hour passed, and by this time Eleanor and Bradley were sitting in the back of the room beside her father and Harry. All of them were fretting over the verdict.

Then a yell filled the air: "The jury is coming back! They've reached a decision!"

By the time the twelve men filed into the room and took their places, the saloon had been turned into a courtroom once again, Judge Neeley sitting in front, Eleanor and Radford in their proper places. As soon as Carl brought Jeffrey in, Judge Neeley called the court to order.

"Has the jury reached a verdict?"

One of the men, tall and grizzled, rose. "Yes, sir, Your Honor, we have."

His gaze circled the building, skimming over Jeffrey, Eleanor, and Radford, coming to rest on Whittier. Eleanor could see the compassion in his eyes, and her heart sank. She gripped her pen so hard, she heard it snap. Laying it on the table, she dropped her hands into her lap and wiped her sweaty palms on her skirt.

Jeffrey lowered one of his hands and caught hers in a tight grip. She turned her head and looked into his whitened face. She smiled, but knew she was doing little to alleviate his fear and doubt.

"Bring it to me."

Spurs jingled through the tense silence as the man walked to the judge and handed him the slip of paper. By the time he returned to his place, Tom had his spectacles on his face. He opened the note, read it, and refolded it. Eleanor nudged Jeffrey and they rose, along with Radford.

"The jury has found Jeffrey Wayne Masterson—" his glasses slid down his nose and he pushed them up again "—not guilty."

"Thank God," Jeffrey breathed, his voice teary. His grip on Eleanor's hand tightened even more. Eleanor felt tears prick her lids, but they were not from pain; they were from sheer joy. She had won. Against all odds, she had won.

Judge Neeley looked at the foreman. "Is this the true verdict of the jury?"

"Yes, sir," the man drawled, "it is."

Wearing only a chemise and slip over her knee-length drawers, Eleanor sat in the slipper chair and wiggled her toes in her black lisle stockings as she reached for her high-button shoes. When she heard the knock, she looked toward the door.

"Eleanor, it's me," Alex said. "May I come in?"

"Let me put my dressing gown on," she called out, dropping the shoe as she reached for the white cambric robe. When she had it fastened down the front, she walked to the door and opened it to allow her father to step into the room.

As always, she thought he was impeccably dressed, his black suit a beautiful contrast with his silver hair. "I wanted to tell you how proud I was of you today in court."

"Thank you, Papa," she said, pleasure warmly racing through her body. She closed the door to lean back against it.

"I'm—" he hesitated, then lifted a hand and brushed it through his hair "—I couldn't have been any prouder of you, Eleanor, if you had been my son, and the fact of the matter is, I've never wanted you to be a son. I love you because you're you, because you're my daughter."

"Oh, Papa," Eleanor said, and rushed into his extended arms.

"I'm sorry I didn't tell you sooner that you were adopted. I was always waiting for the right time to come, but it never did. And I was afraid."

"Afraid?" Eleanor pulled out of her father's arms and looked up at him quizzically. She could not believe that Alexander Hunt had ever feared anything. "You afraid, Papa?"

He nodded. "You see, if a child is born with certain parents, she's stuck with them, but you were not. You didn't have to love me, and at times I thought perhaps you didn't love me as much as I loved you. You seemed to disapprove of me. At least, you never seemed to understand me."

"I think perhaps, Papa, we were both too busy proving ourselves to each other, don't you?"

"I think so." He reached into his pocket and pulled out a small book. "This is your mother's. She always wanted me to tell you the truth, and when I wouldn't, she recorded it in the pages of her diary. When she knew she was dying, she made me promise I'd give it to you." He drew in a deep gulp of air, then said, "But even then I couldn't do it."

Eleanor took the book and held it in her hands. "It's all right, Papa. Harry once told me that life generally turns out as we expect it too, but the road to getting to our expectations is generally different from that which we imagined."

"She's a wise woman," Alex said quietly. "That's one

of the qualities I love in her."

"About Harry, Papa—"

"I'm not going to apologize for loving her, Eleanor," Alex said before she could finish her sentence.

"I'm not going to ask that of you, Papa, and I should be disappointed if you did."

Alex looked at her in surprise.

"Bradley once accused me of being judgmental," she said, the memory of Maude flashing across her mind, "and I was. I think during the past months out here, I've grown up somewhat and learned that each person must be responsible for his or her life and live it as they see fit."

Her gown rustled as she walked to the dresser and straightened her brush and comb on the silver tray. "I'm sorry that you and Mama didn't have a better marriage. I still don't quite understand it all, but neither can I stop loving either one of you because of it." She looked up into the mirror at her father's reflection. "I wish you and Harry happiness in whatever you choose to do with your lives."

Alex exhaled deeply. "I came to tell you that I want to marry Harry . . . in the next two weeks. I want to take her back to Chicago with me as Mrs. Alexander Hunt. Harry would like for you to be her maid-of-honor."

Eleanor lowered her head so that her father could not see her face. She was struggling desperately not to let him see the pain that she felt. She liked Harry and did indeed want her father to be happy with her, but still she felt a little sad that Harry would be taking her mother's place in his life and in their home.

"Eleanor?" He sounded concerned.

She turned and smiled at him. "I would love to be her maid-of-honor, Papa."

They stood for a moment, staring at each other, neither quite knowing what to say next. Finally Alex said,

"If you were my biological daughter, I couldn't love you more, Eleanor, or be any prouder."

"And I wouldn't have any other man in the world for my father," she said, her eyes bright with tears. "Now you'd better go, so I can get dressed for the barbecue."

Alex walked to the door, then turned back to face her. "Eleanor, Bradley told me last night that you were planning on getting married."

She nodded.

"Do you love him?"

"Yes," she confessed, "I love him very much."

"You know he's going to want to live out here after you're married?"

"Yes."

He took a step toward her. "Eleanor, you can't. You don't know what life out here is like, day in and day out. You're not accustomed to this."

"Papa," Eleanor said firmly, "we just agreed to stop judging each other and to let each choose his own life. Believe me, I know what I'm doing. I would rather be married to Bradley and live out here than not to have him at all."

"Would you promise to think about what I've said?" he asked. "Please don't rush into anything."

"I won't." She grinned at him. "Now scoot, so I can get dressed."

Filled with townspeople, the lawn of Hunt Cattle Station was ablaze with lights and festivity. A three-man band, composed of accordion, violin, and harmonica, played from the porch; young and old danced in the yard. Hand in hand, Eleanor and Bradley stood on the porch.

"If I haven't told you, darling," Bradley said, "you were marvelous today."

"You've told me," Eleanor confessed with a tender

smile, "but tell me again. I love to hear it."

He caught her hand in a warm clasp. "Everyday I love you more."

"I love you." She laughed softly and breathlessly, and then said teasingly, "Bradley, I want you to make an honest woman of me as soon as possible. Let's announce our engagement tonight."

Bradley shook his head, and a shiver of apprehension ran down Eleanor's spine. In the pale light cast by the overhead lamp, she searched his face.

"I'm sure about myself, but I'm not sure about you," he said slowly, as if he carefully sought each word. "Your life has been one of luxury. Even now, you've only seen the best side of ranching. You don't know what's going to be required of you. You've only seen one side of me, the best side. You don't even know who I am."

Eleanor laid her hand over his mouth. "I've thought about that, and I don't care, Bradley. I really don't."

"I do. Later on, when you learn—and you will—I couldn't stand to see your love turn to hatred. I couldn't bear for you to leave me in a few years because of your discovery of the real me or the harshness of this kind of life."

"All you've said about my life is true," Eleanor answered, "and I don't know what's going to be required of me in marriage and in living out here. But I love you, Bradley, and I want to marry you; I want to live by your side. You must believe me. Even more, you must believe *in* me."

Staring into her face, Bradley opened his mouth to speak, but Deputy Tulford walked up to say, "You done good today, Miss Hunt . . . plumb good." Balancing a plate of heaped food in one hand, he jabbed his fork through the air with the other. "Telling them how well Masterson has behaved since he's been out of jail in your custody . . . yes, ma'am, he shore could have run, but he

373

didn't. He stayed to face his accusers and won."

"Keep talking, Tully. I like to hear good things about myself." Jeffrey and Sarah, both of them all smiles, walked out of the darkness to where the deputy stood. Eleanor thought they were a beautiful couple; Jeffrey's golden good looks were a perfect foil for Sarah's dark beauty. Sarah angled her head and gazed adoringly into Jeffrey's eyes.

"I can hardly wait for next week," she said softly. "We have so much living to do, Jeffrey."

Jeffrey caught Sarah's hands in his and squeezed gently. "I'm going to make up to you for all this suffering, sweetheart. I promise, life with me is going to be beautiful. In fact, I wanted to tell you that I've bought the Gilmores' place."

"Oh, Jeffrey!" Sarah exclaimed. "You didn't!"

"The Gilmores'," Bradley murmured.

Jeffrey nodded. "Ira and Letty are going back east."

"Don't you think it would be wise for you and Sarah to settle somewhere else?" Bradley asked.

Jeffrey laughed. "You think I'm frightened of Whittier Lang and his threats?"

"If you're not, you ought to be," Bradley said.

"When I first met the man," Eleanor said, "I thought his threats were idle, Jeffrey, but not now." In her mind, Eleanor heard Whittier Lang as he stood up in the courtroom after the jury had returned with the not-guilty verdict. He had pointed a shaking finger at Jeffrey and had promised to kill him. Even now, hours later, the ominous tones echoed in Eleanor's mind, filling her with fear for Jeffrey's safety.

"Give him time. He'll get over it," Jeffrey dismissed lightly and turned to Sarah. "Do you realize they have some of the most valuable land in the area? Why, Julia Stanwood, Whittier Lang, and Alex Hunt have been after Ira for years to sell it to them."

And another reason for Whittier Lang to kill Jeffrey, Eleanor thought.

"Yet he sold it to you," Sarah murmured. "Why, Jeffrey?"

"Because we're a young couple, and we won't become a part of these huge ranches. We'll keep his ranch separate, as he wanted it to be." Abruptly he said, "I know we don't have a house yet, sweetheart, but—"

"Don't worry, darling. I'm happy," Sarah assured him.

"Bradley . . . Eleanor . . . come join us." Alex Hunt's voice sang above the music and the laughter and the buzz of conversation. Looking around, Eleanor saw him sitting beneath one of the trees on the front lawn with Harry, Judge Neeley, Archer Cormack, and Julia Stanwood. A lantern gently burned above their heads. She glanced up at Bradley, and he nodded.

"We'll finish our conversation later. Right now, let's visit with your guests."

Stepping off the porch, Eleanor and Bradley meandered through the crowd toward her father. Her happiness, however, had been diminished. Bradley was an enigma, and she wondered if she would ever understand him. One moment he wanted to marry her; the next he withdrew. While she understood his reservations as he had explained them to her, she was irritated that he had no confidence in her ability to make decisions.

When she and Bradley approached, Alex rose to let Eleanor have his chair. When he spoke, his voice vibrated with pride. "Well, Eleanor, I've said it a hundred times already, but I've got to say it one more time, girl, you did an excellent job defending Jeffrey."

"I'm right proud to have you be a member of my firm," Archer said, then asked, "Where're you going, Alex?"

"To find some extra chairs."

"I'll do that," Bradley said.

375

"Come with me," Alex offered. "We'll find as many as we can. The crowd seems to be growing."

"Yes, sir—" the judge rose "—Cormack ought to be proud to be working with you, young lady. You did a fine job in that courtroom. I think justice was served today."

"Well, if justice were not served, Ted, at least womanhood was. Congratulations, Eleanor," Julia Stanwood said. Smiling warmly, she lifted her glass and winked. "Whiskey. Certainly not a lady's drink, and if she was going to drink it, certainly not in public."

Eleanor had never liked Julia more. "If you want whiskey, then drink whiskey. Let the world be damned."

"You're very much like me," Julia said. "I noticed it the first time we met."

A breeze rustled through the tree leaves overhead and touched Eleanor's heated skin. In the lantern light she noticed the glint of gold on Julia's shoulder. When she leaned forward to see better, Julia noticed.

Her hand went to the pin, her fingers caressing its delicate beauty. "My favorite brooch, given to me by the only man I'll ever have and probably will ever love," she said sadly.

"I wish I could see it better," Eleanor said. "It seems quiet lovely."

"More sentimental than lovely," Julia answered.

The jewelry forgotten, Eleanor settled back and listened with scant interest to the conversation going on around her. Her father and Bradley had not returned, but she had not expected them to. She assumed her father wanted to talk with Bradley, and going after a chair was his excuse to do so.

Abruptly she tensed: what if her father convinced Bradley that she could not adjust to life on the frontier? Fright rose up within her. While she was perturbed with Bradley's reasoning, she fully understood his misgivings. He was accustomed to the rigors of this kind of life; she was not. Because her father loved her, Eleanor also knew he would do everything within his power to persuade her to return to Chicago. Without hearing the argument, she knew what it would be. Wealthy and used to a life of luxury, how could Bradley expect her to fit into his kind of life? Alex would reinforce all of Bradley's reservations about her.

However, she thought, gently fighting back the demons of fear, if Bradley did not trust her ability to make decisions, if he did not believe in her, they had no foundation for a marriage. Deep down, she knew Bradley believed in her; everything would be all right. Her father might be talking to Bradley now, but she would have the last word. He had promised they would finish their conversation later. Then she would talk to him and convince him of her love.

Having reassured herself, she relaxed and let her mind wander, relishing her glorious moment of victory today. She could still see Radford's crestfallen face. He had been so sure of himself, or so sure of her, that he had not researched his case. Surely not even Radford would have been so naïve as to think he could sway her influence with sexual favors. Then again, maybe he did!

"You're smiling rather smugly, Eleanor," Julia leaned over to say quietly. "What are you thinking about?"

"The conceited absurdity of some men."

"The conceited absurdity of *all* men." Looking down at her glass, Julia tilted it so that the amber liquid swirled around, almost curling over the rim, but not quite. Her gaze wandered over the crowd. "I've met very few men who are not."

"I'm sorry about today," Eleanor said.

"Don't be," Julia said, her voice low enough that no one else could hear her. "I've learned that if you make a decision, you'd better be ready to face the consequences. I'll admit, in this instance, I'd hoped I wouldn't have to

377

do so in such a public way, but—" She shrugged, then added several seconds later, "I was lonely, terribly lonely after Lou died."

Julia reached up to touch the brooch. "He was nearly twenty years older than me, but I loved him. Most important, he loved me. He seemed to know what I was thinking before I ever said a word. He allowed me to be my own person. If I wanted to drink whiskey, he told me to drink whiskey. If I wanted to smoke cigars, he told me to smoke cigars."

Eleanor could not restrain her laughter. "And do you?"

"What? smoke cigars?" Julia hiked a beautiful brow and shook her head. "No, that was Lou's way of telling me to be myself. I miss him."

"How long has he been—"

Julia lifted the glass and quaffed the remainder of the drink. She lowered her head and stared into her lap. "Dead. That's the word, Eleanor. He's been dead for two years, and despite my having been friendly with . . . David, there will never be anyone to take Lou's place." Julia stared into the empty glass for a long time. Finally she said, "Shall we walk a ways?"

Knowing that Julia wanted to talk privately, Eleanor nodded. The women said their good-byes to the group and moved away from the crowd. Soon the noise died away. "There have been other men," Julia finally said and peered anxiously into Eleanor's face. "Does this surprise you?"

"I suppose it surprises me that we're discussing it so candidly," she admitted. "I've—never had a discussion like this with anyone before. Perhaps you've been drinking too much."

"I'm drunk," Julia admitted, "and liable to get more drunk, if one can. But I know exactly what I'm saying." After they had walked a little farther, she said, "You don't have to accompany me, if you don't want to."

Eleanor sensed Julia's loneliness and her sadness. "I do."

"I'll never find another man like Lou. I keep looking, but never find him."

"How did he die?"

"He had gone into town for a council meeting. Some drovers, drunk and half-crazed from many days on the trail, started shooting up Main Street. Lou happened to be one of the casualties." She reached up and snapped a small twig from the nearby tree. Playing with the leaves, she said, "I guess David's funeral and Jeffrey's trial brought it all home to me. Even though the man killed Lou, I don't know that his death righted the wrong."

Eleanor eased her arm around Julia and hugged her. "Words seem so ineffectual at a time like this. I wish there were something I could say or do."

In the mottled moonlight that touched Julia's face, Eleanor could see tears coursing down her cheeks. "Being with me and being my friend is all that matters."

When Julia's tears were spent, she pushed out of Eleanor's arms. "I must look a sight," she said, "my eyes swollen and my nose red."

"Let's go back to the house," Eleanor suggested. "You can wash your face and lie down to rest awhile."

"That sounds good," Julia said and allowed herself to be guided to the house.

Not long afterward, Eleanor tucked Julia into her bed. Returning to the dresser by the door, she blew out the lamp and stared at the sleeping woman for a few minutes. The window was open, the shade up; moonlight streamed into the room, gilding it silver; the gentle evening breeze billowed the curtain.

"Good night, Julia," Eleanor murmured. "Sweet dreams."

Chapter 19

"No, Jeffrey, you're not driving Sarah into town this late at night," Alex said, his tone of voice brooking no argument. "The men are too inebriated to escort you and Sarah, and sentiment is running too high. I'm afraid of what might happen to you."

"I think you're exaggerating the whole thing," Jeffrey scoffed.

"Nope . . . he's right," the sheriff said. His hat pulled low on his head, he stood on the sidewalk and lightly tapped the toe of his boot against the bottom step of the porch. "We have enough problems on our hands without tempting Whittier or his men. Let's give him time to cool down."

"Do you mind loaning us a buckboard, Harry?" Barber asked. "I'll bring it back tomorrow."

"I could, but it would be easier for everyone concerned if Sarah stayed the night with us. I'll be coming into town in the morning, and she can ride in with me. That way you don't have to worry about returning the buckboard tomorrow."

"Please, Papa," Sarah said. "I want to talk with Eleanor about my wedding dress. She's going to help me design it."

"Speaking of weddings—" A friendly grin curving his lips, the sheriff tipped his hat farther back on his forehead and looked at Harry and Alex. "I'm glad the two of you are finally tying the knot."

Alex dropped an arm around Harry's shoulder and pulled her closer. "Me, too. That was one announcement I enjoyed making tonight."

"Yes, yes," Barber said absently, his attention on Sarah, who sat beside Jeffrey in the porch swing. "I was pleased also." Then he mumbled, "I don't know why I didn't bring the buckboard this afternoon. I just wasn't thinking straight. I didn't think about having to bring Sarah home tonight."

"Well," Carl said as he walked toward the hitching post, "if you plan to ride along with me, Barber, make up your mind. I'm ready to get home and get some shut-eye. Tomorrow's gonna get here real quick-like."

The mayor nervously plucked at his cheek, his brow furrowed in thought. Finally he said, "All right. You'll see that she gets home tomorrow, Harry?"

"We'll take care of her," Eleanor promised.

After the mayor and the sheriff had ridden off, Harry turned to the men. "I guess you know what this means? Julia's asleep in Eleanor's room, so we have only two left. The three of you will sleep in the bunkhouse."

"We have nothing to say about this?" Alex teased.

Although she smiled, Harry folded her arms over her bosom and shook her head. "Nothing more than good night. You'll find extra linen in the closet in the washroom."

"Can Sarah walk me home?" Jeffrey teased.

"No," Harry answered to a background of laughter.

Pulling Eleanor away from the others, Bradley said softly so that he could not be overheard, "I really don't mind letting you sleep in my bed, but I do resent not being able to sleep in it with you."

382

Eleanor grinned. "You can. Since I'll be on the first floor, who's to know that you slipped back into the house?"

In the moonlight Bradley flashed her a quick smile. "Wait up for me."

"I will."

Grumbling good-naturedly, the men gathered linen from the closet in the washroom and headed for the bunkhouse, their laughter and talking growing fainter the farther from the house they went. The three women went upstairs, Eleanor to get her nightclothes, Harry and Sarah to retire.

Eleanor eased open the door and stood until her eyes grew accustomed to the darkness. Then she tiptoed to the large chest to get her gown and robe. Julia rolled over in the bed and pulled the sheet closer beneath her chin; then her breathing quieted and became more regular. As silently as she'd come, Eleanor left and slipped down the stairs to Bradley's room, where she dressed for bed.

Remembering his promise to return to her, she left a lamp burning on the night table. However, as the minutes slowly passed, she began to wonder if he was going to come. Unable to sit still, she stood and paced the room, moving to the window every so often to look down upon the silvered lawn. She heard the living room clock sound the hour, soon followed by the soft fall of footsteps in the corridor. When she heard a soft knock, she rushed over to open the door. Still dressed, Bradley stood there.

"I had almost given you up." Moving into the room and closing the door, she rushed into his embrace.

He laughed softly. "I had to wait until the others went to sleep."

Eleanor grinned. "Did you think they were going to do the same?"

Bradley also grinned. "Jeffrey, probably . . . he was still fully dressed when I left, but not your father. He was

383

snoring quite loudly."

"Or pretending to. But no matter which, you'll never be able to sleep out there. I suggest you stay here—in your own room and in your own bed."

Quite gently he set her away from him. His smile seemed rather sad. "I would like that."

"What's wrong, Bradley?" Eleanor asked, a sinking feeling in her stomach.

"I've been thinking about what you said earlier, and you're right . . . not only must I believe you, I must believe *in* you."

By the expression on his face and the way in which he paused, Eleanor knew there was more he wanted to say. She sat down on the bed.

"The same applies to you." In the center of the room he turned to look directly at her. "I'm not really a cowboy, Eleanor, and certainly not the drifter you first thought. I'm a highly successful businessman in New York."

She knew from the first minute she saw him that he was different; so she was not surprised. "This is nothing to be ashamed of, Bradley, certainly nothing to keep hidden."

"I have my own detective agency and was hired to come to Blissful to find the cattle rustlers."

Now she was surprised. "Did my father hire you?"

"Whittier Lang."

Eleanor took a step backward, her eyes never leaving his face. "All this time you've been at Hunt Cattle Station, you've really been working for Lang?"

Bradley nodded. "I didn't want anyone to know who I was or what I was doing out here. Otherwise, my purpose would have been defeated."

A knot forming in her throat, her breathing constricted, Eleanor folded her arms over her chest. "Were you—using me to get information?"

384

"Never," he answered, his eyes darkening with pain. He reached for her, but she moved away from him. "You and I were working to the same end, to find the rustler. You wanted to prove Jeffrey's innocence—"

"And *you* wanted to prove his guilt," she accused.

"No, I simply wanted to find the guilty party. Who he was didn't matter to me. I had no personal interest in the case until I began caring about you." She said nothing, but only gazed at him. "I meant every word I said, Eleanor. I love you, and I want to marry you. I want us to buy a ranch and live out here."

Hurting inside, hurting so badly she did not think she could endure the pain, she walked over to the window and stared into the moonlit yard. "Why didn't you tell me this sooner?"

"At first I saw no reason to tell you," he said. "And later, I found I couldn't. You kept talking about my honesty and integrity. I put off telling you until I had to. I was afraid that when you learned, you'd be disgusted with me."

She moved away from him and said faintly, "I wouldn't have been pleased that you were working for the man who openly hates my father, but I would have understood. Whittier has made no secret that he thought Jeffrey was the rustler."

Knowing that revenge was Lang's primary motivation and that he had already been deprived of the ammunition to hurt Eleanor about the details of her adoption, Bradley figured that he would love nothing better than telling Eleanor all the facts about his contract with the agency. "He thought your father was the man behind it."

Eleanor twirled around, the tail of her gown billowing around her ankles. "You thought it was my father?"

"No, Whittier Lang did. He hired me to find out. I hadn't been at the cattle station before I figured it couldn't be either your father or Harry, and I did think it

385

was Jeffrey."

"During your investigation, did you learn about Papa and Harry?" Eleanor asked.

Bradley nodded.

"Are you going to continue to work for Whittier to find the rustlers?" Her back to him now, she stood in front of his dresser, idly playing with the hairbrushes that lay on either side of the hand mirror.

"No, we've parted ways, and I have a feeling that the rustling around these parts has ended. If David was the rustler, he's dead, and his gang won't take the chance of being caught for a long time. If it was Jeffrey, he's smart enough to stop."

She spun around to demand incredulously, "You still think Jeffrey is involved with the rustling?"

"Yes, but I'm not sure how."

"You think I'm responsible for the exoneration of a guilty man?"

"No, I don't think Jeffrey was guilty of murder."

In the distance Eleanor heard the lonesome echo of a train whistle. It seemed so long ago that she had boarded the train in Chicago to begin her journey to Blissful, Kansas. She had known that day that she had a date with destiny and that she was making an irrevocable decision, but she had never contemplated such dramatic changes in her life.

Even if she were to return to Chicago tomorrow, her life would never be the same again. Somehow Chicago was a dim memory in comparison to life as she was experiencing it now, and she could not imagine ever returning for any length of time. She was a child of this frontier, and as such she wanted to stay and tame the land. And she wanted to be with Bradley.

At the same time, she was hurt that he had deceived her. While his deceit had been deliberate, she did not feel that he had necessarily misused her, as Radford had. She smarted from the idea that he had been hired to investigate her father, but she could understand that not everyone knew and trusted him as she did.

"Eleanor, say something . . . anything."

She focused on him. "When we're married and ranching, are you still going to be investigating every little suspicion you have?"

Bradley smiled slowly and held out his arms. "I may. Does that bother you?"

Eleanor moved into his embrace. "As long as there are no more secrets between us, Mister Smith."

"There's only one left. My name—"

"Of course, you've been going by an alias?" Eleanor grinned.

"You might say that. My full name is Bradley Smith . . . Newland."

"Bradley . . . Smith . . . Newland," she murmured.

"As in Newland's Fashion Salon in New York. Now you can know in truth that I'm not a fortune hunter." A tentative smile fluttered at the corners of his lips, but Eleanor did not return the gesture.

She pushed out of his arms completely to back up two steps. "I don't know quite how to take this. I know Bradley Smith, the detective who posed as the cowboy drifter who wants to own his own ranch. I'm not sure I know Bradley Smith Newland of Newland's Fashion Salon."

"For a long time I thought there was a difference," he said, "but since I've met you, I've learned that there isn't. The name doesn't really matter, Eleanor. It's the man inside that counts. That's what I love about you and what I want you to love about me."

Shaking her head in confusion, she said, "Oh, Bradley, why does life have to be so complicated?"

"We wouldn't enjoy it if it weren't," he said rather sadly.

387

Overwhelmed, Eleanor could not think straight. Never had she been so confused and frustrated. Her decision to marry Bradley had seemed the right thing to do, but now she was not sure.

He walked to where she stood and clasped her upper arms. Leaning down, he pressed a light kiss to her forehead. "Would you like for me to go?"

"Yes," she murmured.

"Eleanor—" his fingers touched her chin, and he lifted her face so that they were looking at one another "—I love you."

Her thoughts churning in her head, Eleanor said nothing; she simply stared at him. He dropped his hand and backed to the door.

"Please remember, sweetheart, I love you."

She did not plead with him to stay with her for the night. She never doubted for a moment that he loved her and wanted to marry her. Of her love for him she was sure. But she was confused and hurt. Everyone who meant anything to her seemed to have deceived her for one reason or another.

She had known when she left Chicago that her life would change. She had always known that coming to Blissful was her destiny, but she had not reckoned on so many jolting changes in her life in such a short time. Her life had become so complicated since she'd arrived in Blissful.

Walking to the window, she leaned against the casement. She heard soft laughter and saw two silhouettes, a man and a woman, standing at the edge of the orchard: Jeffrey and Sarah. Standing on tiptoe, Sarah looped her arms around Jeffrey's neck and brought his face close to hers. He said something, and she laughed. He pulled out of her embrace and caught her hands, and together they disappeared into the shelter of the trees.

Eleanor smiled. If life was not simple for her, it was for

Jeffrey and Sarah. A chill ran down her spine as she recalled Whittier Lang's threat when Jeffrey had walked out a free man. She only hoped her father could talk Jeffrey into moving elsewhere. He would never be safe so long as Whittier was alive and held him responsible for David's death.

Turning from the window, she moved back to her bed to unbutton her dressing gown. Lonely was her heart . . . as well as her bed.

In one swift movement Eleanor bolted up in bed. Still not fully awake, she looked around and wondered what had roused her. Then she heard another piercing scream and knew. Leaping out of bed, she grabbed her dressing gown and slipped it on as she ran out of Bradley's room. Upstairs doors opened and voices buzzed, and footsteps thumped on the stairs. She did not wait for anyone. She sped down the corridor, past the kitchen, and out onto the porch. As she hurried down the steps into the yard, Julia came out of the orchard, her face ashen.

"Jeffrey," she screamed and clutched at her throat. "He's—he's—"

"He's dead." Alex, closely following Julia, caught her as she collapsed. "Someone get a ladder, so we can cut Jeffrey down."

Not worrying with the buttons on her gown, Eleanor raced through the orchard to find Bradley standing beneath one of the trees. Hanging from one of the higher branches was Jeffrey, his head twisted at an odd angle, his body swaying slightly as the branch gave beneath his weight.

Unable to believe what she was seeing, Eleanor stood transfixed for a moment and stared. Sticking out of Jeffrey's trouser pockets was a sheet of paper that Bradley reached for.

"Justice is served now," he read, then folded the note and stuffed it into his vest pocket.

Eleanor was vaguely aware of the flurry of activity around her. She was not aware that Sarah stood behind her until she heard her scream.

"Jeffrey!"

Before Eleanor knew what was happening, Sarah pushed past her to grab Jeffrey by the legs and to press her face against his ankles. Rushing after her, Eleanor clasped Sarah by the shoulders and tried to pull her away, but Sarah would not turn loose.

"No," she sobbed. "This can't be happening. He's free. We're going to be married. Oh, Jeffrey, you can't be dead. You can't go off and leave me alone like this."

Bradley moved Eleanor out of the way, and catching Sarah firmly by the shoulders, he tugged. She fought, but he held on firmly. "Sarah, Jeffrey's dead," he said. "There's nothing you can do. Go into the house with Eleanor. We need to cut him down."

Tears pouring down her cheeks, Sarah shook her head wildly and said between deep, gulping sobs, "No, I'm not leaving him. He can't be dead . . . he *can't* be."

Alex appeared with a ladder. "I've taken Julia inside and left her with Harry," he said to no one in particular, "and I've sent Frisco into town for the sheriff."

Bradley nodded curtly. "Good. Let's get Sarah into the house."

"No," Sarah shrieked. Tearing loose from Bradley, she threw her arms around Jeffrey's legs once again. "I'm not going to leave him."

"Here, I'll help," Gaspar said, shuffling through the trees, his apron flapping around his legs. His gnarled hands deftly unclenched hers, and he dragged her toward the house. "I've got a pot of fresh coffee on the stove, missy. That'll do you some good."

390

"With a shot of whiskey," Bradley muttered and watched as Alex balanced the ladder against the branch.

"Yes, sir."

Between Gaspar and Eleanor, Sarah was soon sitting in the parlor with Julia, both of them drinking a cup of hot coffee laced with brandy, wrapped in the shroud of death that hung over the house. After Bradley and Alex laid the body in the upstairs bedroom that Jeffrey had occupied during his residence at the cattle station, they came downstairs to the parlor to await the arrival of the sheriff.

Julia leaned forward and set her cup on the coffee table. Twisting the tear-sodden handkerchief in her hands, she mumbled, "I always take a walk first thing in the morning. I was walking toward the orchard when I—when I saw him."

"You didn't actually go among the trees themselves?" Bradley asked.

Julia shook her head. "No. I saw him before I reached them."

Bradley turned his head, his eyes flicking over everyone who sat in the room and finally coming to rest on Alex, who sat beside Harry. "I guess you and I were the last ones to see him alive."

Wiping the tears from her swollen eyes, Sarah said, "No, I did. He—he asked me to meet him at the orchard and I did. We—we talked for a while before we went to bed. Oh, God," she wailed, "if only I hadn't let him persuade me to return to the bedroom, he would be alive today."

Or you might be dead, Eleanor thought, a shudder running through her body. She downed her coffee.

"Did you see him return to the bunkhouse?" Bradley asked.

"No," Sarah whispered. "He walked me to my room."

"Did any of you hear them?" Bradley looked from

Harry, to Sarah, to Julia. All three shook their heads.

"Whittier Lang." Sarah's voice was wooden, and she stared blankly into space. "He did it. He hated Jeffrey and promised to kill him. We all heard him say it."

After a moment of thoughtful silence, Alex said, "That's possible, Bradley. His men could have been watching for the right opportunity to present itself when Jeffrey was walking back to the bunkhouse by himself after seeing Sarah."

"Surely we'd have heard something," Harry said.

"Evidently we didn't," Sarah sobbed. "Jeffrey's dead."

"Evidently not," Julia said and rose. "Harry, would you have one of your men bring my buggy around? I— need to get home."

"Of course, and if you don't mind, I'll have one of my men drive you," Harry said. When Julia nodded, Harry quietly slipped out of the room.

Hours later, Bradley, Carl, and Alex stood on the front veranda and watched Barber Carven's buggy disappear down the dusty road as he drove his grieving daughter home. Upstairs, Eleanor and Harry prepared Jeffrey's body for burial.

His hat pulled low over his face, Carl looked at Bradley. "Did you notice the lump on the back of his head?"

Bradley nodded.

"I guess we know why nobody heard anything. Jeffrey was unconscious when he was hanged." Deep in thought, Carl tugged at his lower lip.

"But why hang him?" Alex asked.

"It's a quiet way to kill someone," Carl answered.

"And it looks like it's a fulfillment of justice. Had Jeffrey been convicted of murder, he'd have been hanged," Bradley said.

He contemplated telling Carl and Alex that he was a private investigator, but did not. There were too many

392

missing pieces to this puzzle . . . somehow, all of these were tied to the rustling, and Jeffrey seemed to be at the very core. The more Bradley learned, the more certain he was of this.

Finally the sheriff said, "Well, I guess I'd better get going, folks. Looks like I need to talk with Whittier."

Chapter 20

"What brings you to the Stanwood?" Julia's eyes were swollen and red and dull, her voice expressionless. Not even the rich green of her day gown made her look anything but exhausted.

"This." Bradley reached into his shirt pocket and withdrew a gold brooch, which he held out in the palm of his hand. He turned it over so that she could read the inscription: *to Julia with love*.

Julia stared at it for several seconds before she slowly lifted her face, her expression never undergoing a change.

"It's yours, isn't it?" he asked.

She countered with a question of her own. "Where did you find it?"

"In the orchard, where you lost it. You were looking for it this morning when you found Jeffrey, weren't you?"

Her hand lifted, and her long, slender fingers, slightly shaking, curled around the base of her neck. "I—I must have lost it there last night when Eleanor and I went walking."

"You and Eleanor walked in the front yard, not the back."

"What are you implying?" Her voice was calm.

"I think you met Jeffrey in the orchard last night."

Julia's hand slowly dropped down the bodice of her dress to brush over the taffeta ruffles and frills. She walked across the room to stand in front of an elegant table. Picking up the cut-glass decanter, she poured herself a drink, the gentle splash of whiskey echoing loudly through the quiet room.

"Would you care for one?" When Bradley shook his head, she lifted the glass and quaffed the liquor in a single swallow.

"Do you want to tell me about it, Julia?"

"I didn't kill him." Her back to him, she set the glass down and ran her finger around the rim. After a lengthy pause, she turned around, her skirt rustling around her ankles. The eyes that had been dull and listless were now defiant. "I loved him."

"What happened?"

Julia laughed bitterly, with no humor softening her face or her eyes. "Jeffrey and I were lovers. He claimed to love me, and he wanted to marry me. Then he met Sarah and fell in love with her. Rather, he fell in love with her innocence. Once this happened he stopped seeing me."

"Did you meet him in the orchard last night?"

Julia nodded her head. "I wasn't nearly as drunk as Eleanor thought I was. When Jeffrey walked Sarah to her room, I was awake. I cracked the door and waited until he was alone to slip into the hall and join him. Not wanting a scene, he agreed to go with me to the orchard so we could talk in private. I begged him to come back to me. He laughed in my face, then turned and walked to the bunkhouse. In my anger I tore the brooch from my dress and threw it after him. This morning I regretted my stupidity and went to look for my brooch. That's when I found him."

Sobs began to rack Julia's slender body, and Bradley

396

returned the jewelry to his shirt pocket and crossed to where she stood to take her into his arms. Wrapping her arms around him, Julia pressed her face against his chest.

"I loved him, Bradley. You don't know how I felt when I saw him hanging there. Oh, God, I felt as if I died, too. Only I didn't."

Bradley held her until her crying subsided, then he guided her to the sofa. Sitting down beside her, he stuffed the handkerchief into her hands. "You saw and heard no one?"

Julia shook her head and whispered, "No one."

"Did Jeffrey kill David?"

Julia's head flew up, and she stared at him in shock. "No."

"Jeffrey was rustling cattle, wasn't he?"

Two large tears slipped down Julia's cheeks. Finally she nodded. "Jeffrey didn't rustle the cattle himself. He stumbled onto the truth about David when he noticed that the cattle he'd been purchasing for Hunt Cattle Station always coincided with local theft reports. One night he told me about his suspicions. I wanted him to go to the sheriff with this, but he didn't want to. Smarter than David, he figured he would benefit from the criminal activities without becoming directly involved."

"Did you know David was stealing cattle before Jeffrey told you?"

"No." She twisted the handkerchief in her hands. "Jeffrey started blackmailing David."

"So that was it," Bradley drawled. "David wasn't rustling cattle from his father, he was planning to kill Jeffrey to get him out of the way. That's the reason for the note."

Bradley rose and moved to the center of the room. "Jeffrey told Eleanor that a woman had written the note, then later changed his story. Did you write it for David, Julia?"

Julia shook her head, her eyes wide and dilated with fear. "No, I had nothing to do with this, Bradley. I swear it. I loved Jeffrey and wouldn't have set him up to be murdered . . . no matter how angry I am with him. As long as he was alive, I had a chance of getting him back. Now that he's dead—" She ended her sentence with a shrug. "I suppose you're going to tell the sheriff?"

Bradley had dealt with people long enough to believe Julia was telling him some of the truth—but not the whole truth. "Not necessarily," he answered and was glad to see a flicker of interest in her eyes.

"Why not?"

"I don't have a personal stake in this, and I'm going to be moving on."

She gazed at him suspiciously. "I thought you were in love with Eleanor."

He moved to the table and poured himself a drink. "She did, too."

"You're not?"

Without answering her question, he said, "Let's say I found it beneficial to cultivate her friendship and trust. I needed it to get the information I wanted."

"And what was that?" Julia was clearly interested now.

"Whittier Lang hired me to investigate the rustling in these parts. He figured Hunt was behind it."

"A gunslinger?" Julia asked.

"A less sophisticated person would call me that," he said, "but a more sophisticated one would call me a detective."

"Well, detective, now that you know it was David, I suppose your job is finished?"

"It is with Lang and Hunt," Bradley said and lifted the glass to his lips to down the fiery liquid.

Julia twisted the handkerchief nervously in her hands. "Will you investigate Jeffrey's death?"

398

"No, I don't think so," he said, "although I know why he was murdered."

Julia went still.

"Jeffrey was in the blackmailing business."

"David, you mean?" Julia's voice was shriller than usual.

"Him, among others." Bradley set the glass on the table and strode across the room. "Well, I guess it's time that I moved on. The longer a person stays in one place, the greater the chances that his past will catch up with him."

"Why do you think there are others?" Julia asked.

Bradley smiled. Julia had swallowed the bait. "When Harry was going through his personal belongings, she found a journal with daily entries."

"Jeffrey was careless enough to leave such a book lying where anyone could find it?" She stood and walked to the cabinet, her back to him.

"He wasn't worried about its being found because he coded the entries."

Julia laughed, the sound one of relief. "Then you're only guessing. You don't really know what's in his journal."

"Yes," Bradley said softly, pushing his hunch all the way, "I know. My specialty in the army was decoding messages. Jeffrey used a fairly simple one that could be broken within minutes."

"If you know, why haven't you told anyone?" she asked, the nervous tremor back in her voice.

"I figure it's information I can use to my best advantage," he answered.

"To pick up where Jeffrey left off?" Julia said.

"Perhaps," he answered. "Well, I guess I'll be leaving now. Need to get back to the station to get my things."

"I'll see you out," Julia said. As they stepped onto the veranda, they saw a rider in the distance.

Bradley said, "Expecting someone?"

"No." She walked to the edge of the porch and lifted a hand to her forehead to block out the glare of the sun.

"Someone you know, or shall I stay here?"

Julia did not answer immediately; rather she watched the rider approach. When he was close enough for her to make out, she waved and smiled at the visitor. "Thank you, but I know him. He's an old family friend. I met him through my husband."

"Hello, Julia." The man dismounted and tied his horse to the hitching post. As he climbed the steps, he took off his hat and briskly ran his fingers through his white hair. His blue gray eyes carefully assessed Bradley. "I do hope this isn't an inconvenient time for me to visit."

"Not at all," Julia answered.

"I was just leaving," Bradley said.

"No need to go on my account," the man said.

"No, it's on mine," Bradley answered.

Julia said, "Lyle, I'd like for you to meet Bradley Smith, manager of the Hunt Cattle Station."

"Lyle Pearce," the man said and shook hands with Bradley. "Glad to meet you. Maybe we'll see each other again."

"That's doubtful." Bradley swung himself into the saddle. "Since I'm no longer working for the station, I'll be moving on."

Two long weeks dragged by, not even the coming wedding taking Eleanor's mind off Bradley. Still not wanting to spoil her father's and Harry's happiness, she had not allowed them to see her grief. But this morning, when she had awakened and seen her new dress, the one she would wear this afternoon as maid-of-honor when Harry became Mrs. Alexander Hunt, Eleanor had no longer been able to hide her feelings. She could only wonder if she would ever wear a wedding dress herself and become Mrs. Bradley Smith.

Lonelier than she had ever imagined possible, and needing to get away, she donned her riding clothes and hurried to the barn, where she had her horse saddled, then headed for the line shack.

Opening the door, she walked in, but it was not the same. Taking off the Stetson Harry had bought for her, she laid it on the table, then slipped her hands into the pockets of her trousers—specially made and fitted by Sarah. She stood for a moment looking around. She had made the trip today in search of something, but as her eyes roamed the room, she knew she could recapture none of the magic she and Bradley had shared here so many weeks ago. All evidence of their visit had long been erased: the wine bottle thrown away, the glasses and tin dishes washed and replaced in the cabinet, the food basket returned to the Blissful House Hotel, the linen on the bed changed and the bed freshly made.

Having grown accustomed to wearing boots and western garb when she went riding, she crossed the room easily, and trailed her fingers over the rough blanket that served as a bedspread. The memories of that night were vivid enough to be real, yet they were not. Bradley was gone and had been for two weeks. Lying down on the bed and crossing her legs at the ankles, she closed her eyes and thought about the night he had left, of their passionate good-bye and of her promise not to reveal his identity yet.

"I have to do it for two reasons," he'd told her. "My first reason is rather selfish: I want to find the person who's behind this rustling. He's a dangerous man who brilliantly hides behind many pawns and evidently has no conscience. The second is to protect your father by clearing his name. As long as Whittier thinks your father is responsible for the rustling, his life is

401

in danger."

"You really think Whittier would kill my father?" Eleanor asked.

Bradley had paused, then said, "We can't take the chance that he won't."

"Where will you be?"

"It's better that you don't know, darling," he had whispered, and they had clung tightly together. "The less you know, the safer you are, and I'm not sure with whom or what I'm getting myself involved."

Although the following days were full and eventful with her father's marriage to Harry, time passed slowly for Eleanor. She had never thought it possible that one person could become such an integral part of her life. In a matter of days Bradley had completely insinuated himself into her life, and now he was gone. How she missed him! Tears slid from between her tightly shut lids down the sides of her face. She dug her fingers into the mattress and crushed the blanket in her fist.

Even now, as she lay on the bed in the line shack, Eleanor was racked with the same clammy chills of fear she felt the night Bradley left. What if something happened to him and she never saw him again?

Unable to bear her tumultuous thoughts, she sat up. When she lost Radford Vaughan, she thought her heart was broken, but she learned that he'd never touched her heart, had not even come near to it. Only her pride had been involved with him.

It was different with Bradley: he had reached into the inner recesses of her soul to touch her with his love and caring. While her love for him included the passion they shared, it was far more. Bradley was her friend as well as her love; he was an intellectual soul mate. They had shared so much together: their joys, their sorrows, their hopes and dreams.

The words reverberated in her mind, and she

wondered if they would see the fruition of their hopes and dreams. More tears coursed down her face. With a sob she turned to bury her face in the pillow and cried until she had no tears left. Finally she rose and crossed the cabin to peer into the small shaving mirror that hung on the wall.

Her eyes were red and swollen and her hair mussed from lying in bed. This would not do, she told herself, and moved to the pail of water that sat on the counter. Filling the basin, she washed her face with the clear water and gently patted her eyes. She must not let her father and Harry see signs of her grief, not on their wedding day.

She emptied the basin and returned it to the cabinet. Then she moved to the bed to straighten the covers. Her hands slid one last time over the blanket, and she felt something bulky. Curiously she ran her hand beneath the blanket and grasped the object. When she withdrew her hand, she opened it to gaze at the gold brooch on her palm . . . Julia's gold brooch.

Eleanor stared at it for what seemed like an eternity before she closed her fist tightly around it, the point of the pin digging into her tender flesh. She could only wonder how Julia's brooch had come to be in the line shack—and on the bed in particular. Julia would have no cause to be here unless . . . unless someone had brought her. Unbidden thoughts of Bradley's business trips to the Stanwood came to mind.

No! Eleanor shouted to herself. Bradley would not do that . . . he loved her, and he had asked her to trust him. Her own words returned to check the jealous anger that raged through her. She had asked him to believe and to believe in her. Now, without his asking at this moment, without his being here to ask about the brooch, she must believe and believe in him.

Dropping the brooch into her trouser pocket, she walked out of the cabin and moved to her horse, tethered nearby. She must hurry home and get dressed for the wedding. Also she needed to pack her suitcases. Since Harry and Alex were not taking their honeymoon now and were newlyweds, Eleanor felt they should have the house to themselves. She accepted Sarah's invitation to stay in town with her.

"You seem withdrawn," Sarah said and looked across the veranda at Eleanor, who sat in the swing. "Am I boring you?"

Eleanor stopped playing with the brooch in her pocket and withdrew her hand. Unwilling to share her thoughts with Sarah, she said, "Are you happy about going to New York?"

"Not as happy as I would have been if Jeffrey had been going with me." Sarah rose from the rocking chair and moved to the edge of the porch to wrap her arm around the large column. "Before I met him, it was my dream to be a part of Newland's Fashion Salon. Now . . . I'm not sure."

Eleanor rose to put her arm about Sarah's shoulder. "Now that Jeffrey has touched your life, it will never be the same, but time will heal the hurt."

Sarah lifted her head and smiled, her eyes brimming with tears. "It's nice of your Aunt Edna to let me move in with her."

"Don't underestimate Aunt Edna." Eleanor grinned. "She's been wanting to return to the family home in New York for years. Now that Papa and Harry are married and will be returning to Chicago, it's Aunt Edna's chance. But she didn't want to live alone. You were the opportunity she was waiting for. You don't know the plans she's been making since she learned that you'd be staying with her."

"You love her very much, don't you?" Sarah asked.

"Very," Eleanor answered. "She's opinionated and bossy, but she's one of the most loving people in the world. You'll love her, too."

"I'm sure I will."

"Sarah—" Clementine called from the hallway "—if you're going to be at Darlene Lambert's house by two o'clock, you better get a move on."

"Are you sure you won't come?" Sarah asked. "I know it sounds boring to you, but a quilting bee can be fun."

Her hand sliding into her pocket once again to touch the brooch, Eleanor shook her head. "Not today. You run along—and don't worry about me. I'll entertain myself today. You'll be going right past the livery stable, won't you?" When Sarah nodded, she said, "If you don't mind, will you have Frank saddle my horse and bring it to me? I'll give you the money."

"You're going riding?"

"I thought I would," Eleanor answered.

"If you'll wait, I'll go with you," Sarah said. "I don't want you to get lost."

"I'll be all right," Eleanor assured her. "I won't go far."

After Sarah left, Eleanor went up to her bedroom and changed clothes. She kept telling herself she was merely going for a ride, but deep down she knew differently. Loneliness and curiosity were getting the best of her. She wanted to visit with Julia.

Tucking her shirt into her trousers, she walked over to the window and saw Frank Ebersteen hitching her horse to the post. She returned to the dresser and picked up the brooch from where she had lain it when she undressed. Holding it in her palm, she gazed at it, then slid it into her trouser pocket.

An hour later she stopped the roan on a rise behind a grove of trees, and pulling the Stetson lower on her forehead to shield her eyes from the glare, she gazed at the Stanwood. Dismounting and walking onto the porch was Saul Haggarty. Julia walked into the yard to greet him, a welcoming smile on her lips. They talked awhile, their voices too low for Eleanor to hear, but their periodic laughter floated up to her.

Something was wrong, Eleanor thought—Saul Haggarty should not be at the Stanwood. But, she conceded, perhaps her judgment stemmed from her hatred of the man. Surely there was nothing unusual about Whittier's ranch hand visiting the Stanwood, and there was no law that said Julia could not be civil to Haggarty. Then she heard Julia's husky laughter and knew the conversation had gone beyond the bounds of civility; it was downright friendly. If Saul Haggarty had been an ordinary cowboy, Eleanor would have found nothing unusual about it, but he was not—he was a gunslinger.

She slid her hand into her pocket to touch the brooch. Since she'd found it, she'd been filled with questions and wanted answers. This had been her reason for riding out here today. She did not plan to reveal anything Bradley had told her, but she had a suspicion that Bradley was in trouble and needed help. Julia was the key to his whereabouts.

Not taking a chance, but also determined to find out exactly what the two of them were discussing, Eleanor dismounted and tethered the roan to the nearest branch. She slipped through the trees and brush until she was beneath one of the parlor windows but heard no conversation. On the other side of the house a wagon rumbled past. Eleanor edged closer to the front.

"I don't like it," Julia said, her booted feet moving briskly across the veranda. "It's not like Lyle to behave this irrationally."

"Don't rightly matter whether you like it or not," Haggarty answered. "This is the way it's gonna be."

"You're sure Lyle told you to plant those stolen cattle at the station?"

"Yep," he drawled. "He wants me to leave 'em at Hunt's place. Once they're discovered—and Mister Pearce has already figured out the way they're gonna be discovered—he figures Lang will take care of the rest."

"He will," Julia said. "He's beyond reason and won't wait for justice. Before they have an investigation, he'll kill Alex himself."

Eleanor drew in a sharp breath and flattened herself against the house. She would have believed this of Haggarty, but not of Julia. She must get help. The moment she moved, a hand clamped down on her shoulder and the barrel of a gun pressed painfully into her back.

"We don't like snoopers around here, lady," a thin voice whined. "Come to the front with me."

Eleanor recognized the voice. He was the one who rode with Haggarty, the one called Neb. He shoved her forward and called out as they rounded the house, "Hey, Boss, look who I found hiding back here."

Julia spun around, her face draining of all color. "Eleanor," she murmured, "what are you doing here?"

"It don't matter," Haggarty said, his eyes raking lustfully over her body. "She's here and we gotta take care of her."

Ignoring Haggarty, Julia asked, "How long have you been here?"

"Too long." The graveled tone of the gunslinger sent chills of fear down Eleanor's spine. "We can't take a chance."

Julia's eyes darkened, and she said softly, "I wish you hadn't come, Eleanor. I would rather you hadn't gotten involved."

"I wish I weren't involved," Eleanor answered dryly, sinking her hands into her pockets.

"I'll take care of her," Haggarty said and brushed past Julia.

Julia's hand darted out and curled around his arm. "No," she said and pulled him back, "we'll take her with us."

"Mister Pearce ain't gonna like that."

"I'm giving the orders," Julia said coolly. "She's to go with us."

Haggarty eventually shrugged, and his gaze swung from Julia to Eleanor, his bloodshot eyes running blatantly up and down her body. "Neb, tie her up and put her into the buckboard."

"Gotta go get some rope," the little man grumbled and shoved her down on the bottom step. "Sit here until I get back."

"Go get her horse," Julia ordered. "We can't have anyone finding it."

"All right," Neb answered, then mumbled under his breath.

"Have you loaded the ammunition Lyle asked for, Neb?"

"On the other side," he called and cast her a scowl as he disappeared out of sight.

Julia walked around the wagon, stopping in front of several large wooden crates. Her hand went to her hips and she shouted, "Haggarty, have Neb straighten these up. The way they're stacked now, they'll fall off at the first big bump we hit."

"We'll take care of it," Haggarty promised absently. "You worry too much."

"I'm not worried," Julia replied. "I'm thoughtful and cautious . . . traits you and Neb could use."

Haggarty pulled his sweat-soiled hat lower on his face and glared at her. His hand hovered over the handle of his revolver. "We get along fine."

"That's what I don't like," she said. "I want more out

408

of life than just getting along." Julia reached up and shoved on one of the crates. It was balanced precariously, and rather than moving into line, it toppled toward Julia. Screaming, she lifted both hands and braced the crate to keep it from falling on her. "Don't stand there like a dolt," she snapped to Haggarty. "Get over here and help me."

When he went to Julia's rescue, he left Eleanor unguarded. Although they were close by and would see her, Eleanor knew that slight as it might be, she had to take this opportunity to escape. The sheriff must be informed. If Julia and Haggarty succeeded in planting those stolen cattle at the cattle station, Whittier Lang would not wait for justice. In order to save her father's life, Eleanor had to warn someone.

Drawing a deep breath, she lunged forward and ran toward the hill where she had tethered her horse. Julia called her name; Haggarty cursed and grunted. Wood scraped against wood. Then she heard the heavy, lumbering footsteps of Haggarty behind her. For the second time in her life he chased her. She closed her eyes and ran faster, but she felt him catching up with her.

His hand caught her shoulder, and he yanked her around so roughly she fell to the ground, bringing him with her. The fall, combined with his weight, knocked the wind out of her. Stunned, she lay there, her face in the dirt.

"Get off of her," Julia shouted as she rushed up. "My God! You could have killed her."

"Here, Boss—" Neb came running, a rope in one hand.

"It's about time you got here," Julia said. "Thanks to you, she could have escaped. Now get over to the wagon and make sure those crates are loaded right and cinched tightly."

"Yes, ma'am," he mumbled, his eyes not quite

meeting hers.

Julia shook her head in disgust and walked back to the house. Yanking the rope from Neb, who shuffled to the wagon and muttered under his breath, Haggarty tied Eleanor up. After he gagged her, he carried her to the wagon and deposited her in the bed. His hands brushed over her thighs, and he grinned at her. Unable to protect herself, Eleanor shot him daggers of pure hatred.

"Haggarty," Julia called from the veranda as she put her hat on, "let's get moving."

Slowly the miles clicked off as morning turned into afternoon. Eleanor worried about her father and wished there were some way she could warn him. Even her escape would not guarantee this. To a person who knew the route they were traveling, the journey home would take hours. For her, a stranger, it would taken even longer—possibly too long to save her father's life.

Even time seemed to be her enemy.

Chapter 21

Standing in an upstairs room miles from the cattle station, her hands bound behind her back at the wrists, her eyes blindfolded, Eleanor heard a door shut. Footsteps, muffled by a carpet, came closer, and fearing that it was either Haggarty or Neb, Eleanor tensed.

"Now that we're here—" Julia said and Eleanor relaxed "—there's no longer any need for this."

When the handkerchief fell from Eleanor's forehead, she blinked rapidly against the first rays of afternoon light that spilled generously into the massive room from the half-drawn pull shades—the window itself covered with heavy wrought-iron bars. As she got her bearings, slowly looking around, Julia circled behind and untied the cloth that bound Eleanor's mouth. Next came the ropes on her wrists.

Eleanor flexed her shoulders and rubbed her wrists. Then she gently touched the corners of her mouth where the cotton material had cut into her flesh and winced. By this time Julia stood in front of Eleanor once again and closely scrutinized her face.

"Your mouth is bruised slightly from the gag, but it's nothing serious."

"What are you going to do with me?"

Stripping off her hat and gloves, Julia shrugged and lifted a hand to brush through the flattened curls that framed her face. "That depends on Lyle."

"He's the man you mentioned at the Stanwood," Eleanor said, "the one who is framing my father. Who is he?"

"Lyle Pearce," Julia answered and laughed. "Do you know any more than you did before?"

"Let me go, Julia," Eleanor said, picking up the thread of argument she had begun on the journey here, the agrument that had resulted in her being gagged again until they reached their destination. "Whatever you may be, no matter how you're involved in this operation, you're not a murderer."

"I'm not going to kill anyone," Julia answered.

"You're going to be responsible for my father's death," Eleanor pointed out.

During her long, arduous journey to this place—wherever it was—Eleanor had done a great deal of thinking and worrying. Several weeks ago she had come to the realization that regardless of the true facts of her birth, Alexander Hunt was her father. She loved him deeply and forgave him for not having told her sooner. Now that she had confronted her own fears, she could understand his fear of losing her love; she had gone through similar emotions all her life, not realizing that love was hers for the taking. She had to save her father. They had so many years to catch up on, so many years of loving to share.

"Surely you don't want his death on your hands," she said.

Julia shrugged. "Planting those stolen cattle at the station is so blatant that his innocence of rustling will be proved."

"You know as well as I do that Whittier Lang is not thinking rationally. The minute he learns of those cattle,

412

he'll be after my father."

Julia smiled and flung her hands out. "That, Eleanor dear, is your father's problem. I shouldn't worry . . . he's a smart man and can take care of himself."

"Julia, it's not too late for you to get out of this," Eleanor began.

"Please don't try to convert me," Julia said, her voice hard, adamant. "I'm too deep in this to think of getting out. Futhermore, Eleanor, I don't wish to. In any occupation one may choose to pursue, there are unhappy choices to be made. Everyday people make them; I'm no different. That's life."

Realizing that further discussion would get her nowhere, Eleanor asked quietly, "How did you get involved in this, Julia?"

Her gloves and hat still in hand, Julia walked to the dresser and stared at her reflection in the mirror. Lifting a hand, she fiddled with the strands of hair that brushed against her cheeks. "I was a dance hall girl when Lyle Pearce first met me. My father and mother had died in a fever epidemic, leaving me and my younger brother. I had to take care of him."

When Julia paused, Eleanor asked, "Where's your brother?"

"He was killed several years ago," she answered. Then her voice changed, and nostalgia, sentiment—whatever had softened its quality—disappeared. She straightened her back, and now staring at Eleanor's reaction in the mirror, she continued. "Recognizing my talent and intelligence, Lyle took me away from that kind of life. He educated me and taught me to act like a lady."

"The other night was all an act," Eleanor said.

"Not all of it," Julia admitted. "I meant what I said, but I wasn't talking about Lou Stanwood. I was talking about Jeffrey." Julia turned so that she confronted Eleanor. "You see, I loved him, and he said he loved me.

413

Until he met Sarah."

Eleanor should have been surprised, but for some reason she was not. She had always known there was a side to Julia Stanwood that no one fathomed. "Did you kill him?"

"I said I loved him."

"Jealousy is one of the strongest motivators in the world," Eleanor said.

Julia laughed. "How little you know me, Eleanor. I never allow my emotions to rule me. I certainly would not have killed Jeffrey. I would have waited for him. His infatuation with Sarah would not have lasted."

"Who killed Jeffrey, then?"

"Lang," Julia announced as if she were tired of the subject and walked to the door. "I'll send you some salve up that will ease the rope burns."

"Julia—"

Opening the door, she stopped and turned to look at Eleanor.

"What's going to happen to me?"

For the first time since they had arrived at their destination, Julia gave evidence of concern. Her eyes shadowed, and a tiny frown puckered her brow. "I don't know," she finally said. "Lyle will make that decision."

"Will he kill me?"

Another long, ponderous pause: "There are worse fates than death."

"You would allow this—this *fate worse than death* to happen to me?"

"Blame no one but yourself. You allowed it to happen when you decided to snoop around my ranch. By the way, I shouldn't think of escaping." Her eyes deliberately settled on the barred window. "Lyle also took the precaution of posting a guard outside your door. They have orders to shoot to kill."

Smiling, Julia stepped into the hallway and locked the

door to leave Eleanor in a deafening silence.

In a few minutes a friendly, chatty maid brought a tray of food, which she left on the reading table in front of the window. When the young woman withdrew, Eleanor was surprised at how much the simple conversation had lifted her spirits. Sitting down at the table, she ate heartily. To do differently went against all she believed in. If she were going to escape—and escape she would—she needed her strength and presence of mind.

The maid made several trips to Eleanor's room— first to prepare her bath, then to bring some clothes that Julia had provided. Eleanor gladly bathed and slipped into the clean, soft undergarments. The shoes—satin evening slippers to match the gown—were a little larger than that she ordinarily wore, but not so large that she could not keep them on comfortably. After she had combed her hair into a neat, coiled chignon on the crown of her head, she moved to the bed and picked up the blue silk gown with its lace ruffles and furbelows. The latest fashion from New York, possibly Paris, Eleanor thought.

She was standing at the window, gazing into the front yard, when she heard the key slide into the lock. She turned as the door opened and Julia entered. She, too, had bathed and changed into an evening dress.

"You look lovely . . . as usual," the older woman announced.

"So do you." Eleanor appreciated the mauve satin creation Julia wore, the ecru lace and silk flowers lending an ethereal quality to her beauty. The same silk flowers were pinned into her hair, which she swept back into an elaborate chignon of curls. Several strands of pearls encircled her neck, and pearl droplets hung from her ears. "I almost envy you your seamstress."

"Sarah," Julia announced, at the same time opening a jewelry box from which she withdrew a sapphire necklace and earrings. "She's quite a talented lady. She made this gown for me also. I had to listen to her chatter about the new Butterick patterns she had ordered. Here. These go with that dress."

"No, thank you."

"You will wear them," Julia said in a voice that tolerated no disobedience.

Tired and not willing to argue with her captor because she wanted to occupy her mind with more useful thoughts, such as escape, Eleanor sighed and reached for the necklace and earrings. Walking to the mirror, her disinterest apparent, she quickly put the jewelry on.

"Do I meet with your approval?" she asked.

Julia moved closer to Eleanor and reached out to touch the necklace. "Sapphires are so lovely," she mused. "Truly, they should be your stone, Eleanor. All fire and ice. Paradoxical, to be sure, but true nonetheless."

Her hand lowered, and she began to straighten the ruffles that decorated the front of the dress. Irritated, feeling as if she were a prize animal about to be auctioned off, Eleanor stepped back and brushed a hand against her bodice.

Julia grinned. "Somehow the dress never looked right on me. Now I know why . . . that's definitely your color, not mine."

"What am I all dressed up for?" Eleanor asked.

"You're going to be meeting Lyle later. Then all of us shall have dinner together."

"What in the hell do you mean by bringing her here?" Lyle stopped his pacing long enough to shout to Haggarty, who stood nervously in front of the cold, dark fireplace.

Lyle was curious about his daughter and wanted to see her, but not under these circumstances. Neither did he wish for anyone to know that Eleanor was his daughter.

416

Suddenly his plans seemed to be going awry, and that troubled him. He had worked too long and painstakingly to build himself a financial empire and a veneer of respectability. He would be able to retire to the life of a country gentleman. He envisioned himself to be active in the political life of Kansas one day and would allow nothing to stand in his way.

"She was snooping around the Stanwood and overheard us talking, Mister Pearce. I thought—"

"I've told you time and again that I don't pay you to think, Haggarty." Lyle stopped his pacing and glared across the room at the gunslinger. "I pay you to follow orders. I cannot understand Julia's doing this."

"As Haggarty said, we had no other option, Lyle." Julia's voice came from the door, and Lyle turned. Looking quite refreshed and lovely, as usual, she entered the study. The soft, musky pink was an excellent color for her. He marveled that the older Julia became, the more beautiful, the more vibrant. "Eleanor overheard him telling me that you had set her father up to be killed by Lang." She stared directly at Lyle, as if willing him to deny the story.

"Tell her it's true, boss. She don't believe me."

Reluctantly Lyle's gaze fastened on Julia's. "I ordered him to do it."

"Why?" Julia moved to stand in front of an elaborately carved table, where she poured herself a whiskey.

"Haggarty," Lyle said, "see about the unloading of the wagon."

Hostility shadowed the gunslinger's eyes, and his face hardened. He stood for a moment longer, staring at Lyle, but finally he said, "Sure, Mister Pearce." He turned and marched out of the room.

"Setting such a sloppy trap to ensnare Hunt's death isn't like you," Julia said as soon as the door slammed

417

behind Haggarty. She sat in one of the large wing chairs in front of the fireplace, one hand casually draped over the end of the armrest, the other holding her drink. "Not only is it sloppy work, it reeks of emotional involvement."

Deliberately turning his back on Julia, Lyle walked over to the cabinet and poured himself a drink. "Appearances can be deceiving," he replied, his calm tone belying the tension he felt inside.

Julia took several sips of her drink. "Lyle, no matter what our differences in the past, we've never lied to one another. Let's not start now. You and I both know you want Hunt out of the way quickly, and you don't care how you do it. I want to know why."

"If it concerned you, my dear," Lyle replied, careful not to reveal his personal involvement; it would never do for her to learn that he was in love with Harriet and wanted her for himself, "I would tell you, but it doesn't."

Julia threw the glass to the floor, the amber liquid quickly seeping into the Persian rug, and leaped to her feet. "The hell it doesn't concern me. You don't think I married and lived with Lou Stanwood all these years because I loved him, do you? No, I did it because you convinced me this was the way we could set up our business. No one would ever guess that the stolen cattle were being kept on a local ranch by the grieving widow Mrs. Julia Stanwood."

"All would have continued to go well," Lyle pointed out, "if Masterson hadn't shown up and learned that David Lang and Haggarty were rustling cattle, and if you hadn't become emotionally involved with him."

Julia's countenance fell, and she folded her arms over her chest and hugged herself. "I loved him, Lyle," she finally said. "He was the first man I ever really loved. But I did not let that interfere with our business."

"No, you didn't," Lyle answered, his voice softening. He set his empty glass on the nearby table and walked to stand behind her. His large hands gently clasped her shoulders. "He was no good for you, Julia."

"I know," she murmured, "but to have him killed . . ."

"That's the only way it could be," Lyle answered. "He knew too much about us, and it had to be done quickly. You knew what the rules were when you allowed yourself to fall in love with him."

Julia turned to look up into his face. "Lyle, let's get out of this. You and I have what we set out for. We're rich beyond our dreams, we can move where no one knows us and establish new lives with new identities."

"You have what you want in Blissful?" Lyle said more than asked. "The ranch and your respected widowhood."

"Yes," she answered eagerly, "I'm satisfied with that."

He slowly stepped away, rubbing his chin thoughtfully. "We'd have to get rid of Haggarty and Neb. They're the last ones who can link us to the cattle rustling in that area."

"That would be easy enough," Julia replied. "You've always told me to cut my losses without a backward glance."

Lyle moved to stand behind his desk. "But then, my dear, we have another problem. What about Eleanor Hunt?"

"I don't see her as a problem," Julia returned. "We can get rid of her with them."

For the first time in his life, Lyle regretted the direction his life had taken nearly thirty years ago. He had never allowed himself to become emotionally involved with anyone and had never had any qualms about his decisions. That had changed now . . . he wanted Harriet, now more than ever. Strangely enough, he also found himself wanting his daughter.

419

"You think no one will trace her death to you?" he asked, still unwilling for Julia to know who Eleanor really was, to know what she meant and possibly could mean to him.

"I think not," Julia answered. "I brought her horse with us, and the only ones who knew she arrived at the ranch were Neb and Haggarty. That knowledge will remain a secret with their deaths. No one can prove she was at the Stanwood."

"So, we have three more people to dispose of before we can become the respectable, law-abiding citizens we want to be," he drawled sarcastically.

"In the grand scheme of things," Julia said, a glitter in the depth of her eyes, "it's not so many, Lyle, and simple enough to accomplish. We could set it up to look like Haggarty and Neb kidnaped Eleanor. Her death would be at their hands, and I would be responsible for killing them and bringing her body home."

"Not only would you be the respectable Widow Stanwood, you would be a local heroine." He had always known Julia was ambitious to a fault. Now she was proving to be even more cold-blooded than even he was.

Julia smiled. "That's right. A role I would enjoy playing."

"Exactly what role is Bradley Smith going to play in this?"

"I think it's time we tested his mettle," Julia answered. "Let him kill Haggarty and Neb . . . and Eleanor."

"And Eleanor?" he managed to keep his voice casual.

"And Eleanor."

Curious about his invitation to join Lyle and Julia in the drawing room for drinks before dinner, Bradley descended the spiral staircase, his bronzed hand brushing

420

lightly down the highly polished mahogany banister, and walked into the parlor. Like Lyle, who was wearing a black suit, Bradley was formally attired.

"Bradley, I'm glad you could make it." Lyle stood in front of the fireplace, his arm extended along the marble mantel. He looked up at Bradley and smiled. "Punctual, as usual . . . a trait I most admire in a person."

The rustling of material alerted Bradley to another presence in the room. He looked toward the medallion-backed sofa, fully expecting to see Julia.

Eleanor! Never had she looked more beautiful. Her eyes were wide and lustrous, gloriously enhanced by the blue silk gown and the sapphire jewelry she wore. But they were also filled with question, and to him who knew her so well, with no small measure of fear. One of her hands rested casually on the floral damask upholstery.

"We have company for dinner tonight, Bradley. Miss Eleanor Hunt."

Although he was startled and wondering what she was doing here, Bradley simply nodded and turned to say, "Hello, Miss Eleanor Hunt. To what do we owe the pleasure of your company?"

"She was snooping around the house when we found her." Julia swept into the room.

Bradley poured himself a drink, sat down opposite Eleanor, and listened while Julia related the details of their journey. When she was through, he said, "What are we going to do with her?"

"Not we," Julia answered smoothly. "You, Bradley."

Bradley's entire body tensed. He had known that Pearce was suspicious of him and had suspected that a test of loyalty would be forthcoming, but he had never expected this.

"Lyle and I figured that it was time for you to make a total commitment."

Crossing his left leg over the right one, Bradley let his

gaze, outwardly cool and assessing, pass over Lyle, then Julia, finally letting it settle on Eleanor. He lifted the glass to his mouth and held it against his bottom lip while he gazed at her. Then he drank, swallowed, and lowered the glass.

"What does this total commitment entail?" He never broke visual contact with Eleanor.

"Death."

Eleanor sucked in her breath and dug her fingers into the lush damask upholstery.

Standing at a large, imposing rosewood desk at the far end of the room, Julia casually rolled a cigarette. "Haggarty and Neb kidnaped her," she said. "Naturally they had their way with her, and after she had outlived her usefulness, they killed her."

"Haggarty and Neb will enjoy their assignment," Bradley said sarcastically, "but I see no total commitment in it for me." He uncrossed his legs and placed the glass on the nearby marble-topped table. Surreptitiously he glanced at Eleanor, who sat quietly, outwardly poised and calm.

Her right arm horizontal against her stomach, her palm cradling her elbow, Julia held the cigarette inches from her face. A strange smile curved her lips. "Once Haggarty and Neb do this horrible deed, you will ride upon them. They'll fire at you and you'll have to kill both of them. Naturally, you'll take Eleanor's body home for burial."

"If you should be fortunate enough to live through this, you can bury her alongside her father." Eleanor picked up on the story. When Bradley looked at her quizzically, she said, "Mister Pearce had Haggarty plant stolen cattle at the station. By the time it's discovered that Papa didn't steal them, Whittier Lang will have shot him."

"Are you sure this is the way you want this handled?"

Bradley directed his question to Lyle.

Lyle inhaled deeply and said, "I would have preferred it to be different, but certain choices lead to certain consequences. This is one of those unfortunate situations."

"Are you having difficulty in accepting the assignment?" Julia asked, his face hidden by a thin, gray veil of smoke.

Bradley rose. "None. How do you propose to carry this execution out, or are you leaving the details of the plan up to me?"

"I worked out the details," Lyle answered. "During the weeks that you have been with us, you've proven your ability, but I believe this needed special planning. In view of her station in life, Miss Hunt deserves every consideration."

Lyle glanced over at Eleanor, who gave him a contemptuous smile. She was indeed one of the most beautiful women he had ever beheld, strong and intelligent. Through the entire conversation—and it had been a grueling experience for her—he had been studying her as she sat quietly composed. Nothing in her expression or posture gave away any inner tension or anxiety.

He was proud of her; truly she was his daughter . . . and Lyle wanted to tell her so. She was nothing like Alexander Hunt; she was like him. He had told Harriet that he only wanted to see her, and he had been granted his wish. Now he wanted her to know that he was her father. The confession hovered at his mouth, gnawed at his soul, but as he looked at her, so young and indomitable, he could not bring himself to do so. For all his faults, Lyle did not wish to see her spirit broken by him or anyone else. He only wished it was in his power to save her.

He also knew she was in love with Bradley Smith. Every time her eyes touched him, she told him so. She might not know what he was doing here, but she trusted him.

It was such a shame that her life had to be sacrificed! She was young and had so much to offer humanity, but he could not allow her to live. She knew too much and was basically honest. A quality he usually admired . . . but not this time. It was definitely a vice, not a virtue. No matter whether he was her father or not, she would tell the truth about him and Julia.

"Miss Hunt—"

Eleanor looked at Lyle questioningly.

"I must applaud your ability to appear unaffected by the conversation going on around you."

"No need to applaud me, *Mister Pearce*," Eleanor said, "I've been trained to do so. I'm quite accustomed to being talked about as if I'm not present."

He winced at the sarcasm in her voice. She was so young to be so bitter. But he could understand. Her strength of character daunted weaker men, and they tried to reduce her to their level by ignoring her. They had failed. Despite them, she had played the game of life by their rules and had risen to the top. She was as tall as any of them, and taller than many.

"My curiosity is quite piqued, my dear. I'm wondering why you were snooping around the Stanwood."

"If I hadn't seen Haggarty," Eleanor returned evenly, "I wouldn't have been."

"Excellent answer. That would be a dead giveaway," he said, nodding his head. Then he thought of his pun and laughed at himself. "And dead he shall be. It's time to do away with Haggarty; he has definitely outlived his usefulness. But what was the reason you went to the Stanwood at all?"

424

Eleanor looked at Bradley—Lyle followed her gaze—who stood in front of the window next to the oval reading table. Light shone brightly from the large double globes. Her attention was centered on Bradley, Lyle's on her. She reached into her pocket and withdrew the brooch.

Extending her hand, she opened it to reveal the brooch in the center of her palm. "This."

Lyle observed the gaze Eleanor shared with Bradley. Not a word was uttered, yet they had spoken volumes. With a glance he was reassuring her, begging her to trust him. Lyle sighed. As much as he liked Bradley, he was not a man to be trusted.

"Where did you get that?" Julia demanded in a shrill voice that broke Lyle's train of thought. She rushed forward. Galvanized into action, Lyle reached Eleanor first and took it from her. Julia stepped back.

"At the line shack at the station."

Lyle looked at it, turned it over, and read the inscription aloud. "Ah, Julia, how frequently have I told you that there is no fault quite so dangerous as jealousy? Had you not left this, Miss Hunt would not have been at your ranch. You, Julia, made a mistake, and a big one. Because of you we shall have three deaths on our hands. Now tell me, what were you doing in the line shack at the cattle station?"

"I—I wasn't—" Disconcerted for the first time that evening, Julia looked wildly at Bradley.

"What she was doing there is her business," Bradley said and returned to the chair opposite Eleanor.

Lyle stared at him, shook his head, and chuckled softly. "I think I begin to understand how things are between the two of you." Now he looked at Eleanor. Her eyes had narrowed; she was not so impervious to the conversation as she would like for him to believe.

Her head lifted and she caught him unawares. "What will happen, Mister Pearce, if rather than Haggarty and

Neb having *their way* with me, I have my way with them?"

Lyle studied her a minute before he said, "I wouldn't like that, my dear, not at all. You've already killed one of my best men."

Eleanor's countenance darkened in thought, then brightened. "The man who killed Early Dobson! You had him shot?"

"I did."

"But why?"

"I am the one, my dear, who framed Masterson."

"You!"

Lyle laughed at her surprise. "The same." Quite proud of himself, he looked at Julia and added, "Indirectly I even nudged Whittier Lang into hiring the attorney of my choice. In the very beginning when Whittier went back East to hire an attorney, I had Julia recommend Radford Vaughan—an attorney I have used on occasion."

Eleanor gasped her surprise.

"That's right," Lyle admitted. "But I do confess to one error in judgment. I had not reckoned on Jeffrey's having such an astute attorney himself. Alas, my dear, you were the death of the poor boy."

Her eyes were large and round; they accused; they questioned.

"Don't waste your sympathy on Masterson," Lyle said softly and found that he hated Alexander Hunt passionately. He hated the man who had fathered his daughter, and no matter that his blood ran through Eleanor's veins, she was the daughter of Alexander Hunt. "Masterson's not worth it."

Julia, hugging her arms about herself and walking to the window, turned her back to the others in the room.

"What do you know about Jeffrey?" Eleanor asked.

Chapter 22

"What do I know about Jeffrey?" Lyle repeated, and slowly began to talk.

Eleanor listened in stunned silence, all the pieces of the puzzle finely fitting together. Through his amorous liaison with Julia, he had stumbled onto the truth that David Lang, Haggarty, and Julia were rustling cattle. Now Eleanor could sympathize with Whittier Lang, who had honestly but mistakenly blamed Jeffrey for rustling the cattle and for David's death, who had thought her father was the one behind the rustling. From the beginning Lyle Pearce had been the culprit, the man behind the scenes who pulled the strings that made everyone else jump. He was like a spider spinning his web larger and larger, his victims the flies caught in his snare: Julia; Haggarty and Neb; Early Dobson; even the unsuspecting Whittier Lang, who hired Radford Vaughan—Lyle's personal attorney. Yet in the end, all of them had been victimized by Jeffrey.

"Blackmail," she murmured. "I can't imagine Jeffrey doing something like this."

"None of us is above doing something like this," Lyle said, "if the price is right. I had to prove to him that it was not. Had Jeffrey not had an excellent attorney—"

427

"Thank you, Mister Pearce," she said.

"—he would have been hanged for David's murder, and I should not be having the problems I'm having now."

"Why didn't you want Jeffrey to work with you?" she asked.

Lyle smiled and admitted, "I thought of that, but quickly realized that Jeffrey Masterson was not the kind of man to work with someone, rather one who works best for himself."

The bedroom was dark, the pull-shade raised halfway so that pale moonlight shone into the room and reflected its silvery glow on the Oriental rug, the brilliant colors now nothing more than haunting black-and-gray shadows. Eleanor, wearing a dressing gown provided by Julia, assumed that everyone had retired. She had heard no noise in the house for several hours.

She had to find a way out of the house; she had to get back to Blissful in time to save her father . . . if it were not already too late. She needed a revolver. At the moment it all seemed impossible.

She heard a soft knock and stopped pacing, but did not answer. It sounded again.

"Eleanor," she heard Julia call softly; still she did not move. "It's me."

The lock clicked, the knob turned, the door opened, and Julia stepped inside the room. She was dressed in her riding clothes, her guns strapped to her waist.

"You have to get out of here."

"Why should you think that," Eleanor asked, "when you're the one who brought me here?"

"You know why. Lyle is going to let Haggarty and Neb kill you," Julia said. Silhouetted in the moonlight, she

428

walked to the bed and tossed some clothes on it. "You were right earlier when you said I wasn't a murderer. I'm not. I can't let that happen."

Eleanor wanted to believe Julia's good intent, but in the past few hours too much had happened to change her opinion of the woman.

As if Julia read Eleanor's mind, she said, "Please trust me."

"Where are you taking me?"

"First, to the corral. I have a horse saddled and waiting. Then to the cattle station."

Eleanor laughed, the sound devoid of any mirth. "You expect me to believe you, after all I heard this evening?"

"Lyle and I had an argument after you came upstairs. I want out of this. I'm tired of this kind of life. But we don't have time to waste talking about this now. Here." Julia pointed to the clothes on the bed as she moved toward the door. "I've brought you one of my riding skirts and a shirt. If you want to go, be dressed when I come back to get you in about ten minutes. This is the only chance you're going to get. Lyle is going to let Haggarty and Neb leave with you early in the morning."

Hardly had the door closed and the lock clicked into place before Eleanor had made her decision. This could be the only chance she would have of getting out of this room. She glanced at the barred window and thought of the guard posted outside the door. After she lit the lamp, she quickly shed the nightclothes and put on the clean trousers and shirt. Next were her socks and boots.

Dressed, she walked around the room, looking through all the drawers, searching for some kind of weapon to take with her. All she found was an ivory-handled, silver letter opener. It was not much, but it would have to do until she found something better. She did not want to trust Julia, yet she had to. This would be her only chance

429

to get out of this room, a chance she must take.

When Julia returned, Eleanor was waiting, her heart beating fast, blood running to her head. Tucked away in the pocket of her trousers was the letter opener. The two women crept through the darkened hallway and down the stairs. They were on the veranda when a chill of apprehension ran up Eleanor's spine and some sixth sense warned her that all was not as it seemed. She suspected that Julia was planning a double cross.

"The horses are over there," Julia whispered and pointed to the right of the house. "Follow me."

Glad that she was accustomed to the dark, Eleanor obeyed. At the moment it was in her best interests. They scooted across the veranda and sidewalk. As they turned the corner and crept alongside the house, Eleanor searched through the dark for something. Her hand slipped into her pocket, her fingers closing over the ivory handle. Eleanor was unaware that Julia was behind her until she felt a knifepoint pressed into her middle back.

"I'm sorry to have to do this, but do it I must," Julia said. "Don't move and don't utter a sound or you're dead."

"Why didn't you wait until morning?" Eleanor asked. "Why all this secrecy?"

"I told you that Lyle and I argued after you went upstairs to bed," Julia answered, keeping her voice low. "He had a change of mind. You see, he wanted to let you live."

Her mind seeking all kinds of reasons why Lyle would change his mind and liking none of them, Eleanor did not repress her curiosity. She had nothing to lose. "Why?"

Julia laughed shortly and pushed the blade against Eleanor's back so that she began to walk toward the corral. "Not what you're thinking. In fact, it was downright chivalrous and disgusting. In case you don't know, Lyle Pearce and Harry have known each other about thirty years. Harry ran a brothel, and Lyle was an outlaw; they lived together, and she became pregnant by him."

Despite the pressure of the weapon on her back, Eleanor stopped walking. "What are you telling me?"

"Strange as it seems, Lyle Pearce is your father, and Harry is your mother," Julia said, a smug delight in her voice. "Lyle had to leave her, and she gave you up for adoption to the Hunts." Now Julia laughed. "How does it feel to know that Alexander Hunt is not your father? That you're the daughter of a whore and an outlaw?"

"My father had already told me that I was adopted," Eleanor answered quietly. "But Lyle has the story wrong. Harry is not my mother, and he is not my father."

"He thinks he is, but it makes no difference to me. He's been to Blissful and talked about you to Harry. I guess both of us can deduce why he wants your father dead. He wants Harry."

"He won't get her," Eleanor said, amazed at her defense of the woman she had condemned so roundly only a few short weeks ago. "Harry Pres—Hunt is a better woman than he is a man. She may have been a whore, but she's not a murderer, and she tells the truth. If she is my mother, she'd have told me so. If Harry was my mother, she'd never have let me go for adoption. That's the kind of woman she is."

"Already protective of your stepmother or mother, whichever the case may be," Julia mocked and jabbed the blade against Eleanor's rib cage.

"My stepmother," Eleanor answered steadily, clinging to the belief that Abigail would not have lied in her diary.

"What will Lyle do when he finds out that you've killed me against his orders?"

"He won't do anything. You see—" she paused, then

431

said, "I had to kill Lyle. He was so adamant about our not killing you. No one will know that he's dead until tomorrow when he doesn't come down for breakfast. I have him tucked away in bed and covered up; he looks as if he's asleep."

Eleanor could not believe that she had once liked this woman, had felt that the two of them were friends. Julia Stanwood was a stranger, a cold-blooded murderer, worse than Lyle Pearce.

"You killed him!"

"Very quietly, with my knife, so that the household didn't awaken." She laughed, the sound maniacal. "I'm getting rid of all evidence that will tie me to this place and to a life of crime. I shall execute your death and that of Haggarty and Neb exactly as I planned them."

"What about Bradley?" Eleanor asked.

"I would like to spare him," Julia said, "and maybe I can. It all depends on how he reacts when he finds your body tomorrow after Haggarty and Neb are finished with you."

"He's not going to suspect that you had anything to do with this?"

"No, I went by his room before I went to bed and we—well, we . . . Afterward, we had a drink, several of them, and I told him that I wanted out of this, that Lyle and I had argued about killing you. Bradley and I devised a plan whereby we would save you. I made sure he's in his bed, sleeping like a baby. He won't wake up until very late tomorrow. By that time, my dear, you will be nothing more than a memory." Her fingers clamped on Eleanor's upper arm, and she pressed the blade into her stomach more firmly. "Now turn around and walk quietly to the corral."

Eleanor did so, her mind awhirl with thoughts. According to Julia's inference, Bradley could not come to rescue her. Was he in the throes of deep sleep merely because he was sedated with lovemaking or had she sedated him with something more potent? Eleanor realized that she was the only one who could effect her escape, and at the moment this seemed virtually impossible. Then she wondered what she had to lose. If she did not escape, she would be killed.

She spun around quickly, catching Julia unawares. Her hand struck Julia's wrist, the knife thudding to the ground. Julia grunted and twisted around, but before she could run or call for help, Eleanor's hand closed about the material of her shirt and yanked her back. Surprised, Julia staggered backward to land against Eleanor, who clamped an arm under her chin, putting pressure against her throat and larynx, and pulled her tightly against her body. She maneuvered them behind a clump of bushes, then pressed the letter opener into Julia's back.

"I have your knife," she said, tightening her hold on Julia, glad when she heard her gasping for breath, "and I'll use it if I have to. You're not going to turn me over to Haggarty and Neb."

"Don't kill me," Julia pleaded, "I'll help you."

"No, thank you," Eleanor said. "I'll plan my own escape."

Eleanor heard a noise and looked around, unconsciously letting her grip slacken on Julia. The other woman quickly took advantage and threw her body forward to release herself completely from Eleanor. Snarling low in her throat like an animal, her arms began to rotate like a windmill as she flailed at Eleanor. Dodging the blows, Eleanor staggered back and dropped the letter opener. As quickly she regained her footing and lunged forward, her arms circling Julia's waist, her weight knocking her down.

"You're not going to turn me over to Haggarty,"

Eleanor grunted as they rolled on the hard ground.

"Just how do you think you're going to stop me?" Julia returned. She tangled her hand in Eleanor's hair and tugged; the coil came loose, and hair streamed down her back.

They clawed and scratched; they pulled hair and tumbled; they returned blow for blow. Finally Eleanor flung her body over Julia's and doubled her hand into a fist. One hard blow to the chin, a soft moan from Julia, and she lapsed into unconsciousness. Her breasts heaving, Eleanor sat astraddle Julia, drawing painful gasps of air into her lungs.

Quickly she unbuttoned Julia's shirt and ripped it into strips that she used to gag and tie her. Once this was done, Eleanor removed her gun belt and strapped it around her own waist. She returned the letter opener to her pocket, then carefully moved straight ahead to the backyard and hoped she was going to the corral.

Eleanor slipped through a rear gate, behind an outbuilding of some sort. Then, in the shadowy distance, leaning against the corral fence, Eleanor saw two silhouetted figures, one of them squat, like Haggarty, the other tall and slim, like Neb. As she inched closer, careful to remain concealed in the darkness, she heard them talking, their voices so low she could not discern what they were saying. Hidden behind a bush, wondering how she would get past the two of them to get a horse, she contemplated the next step in her escape.

Eleanor had no idea how long she crouched behind the bush and watched Haggarty and Neb. Frequently they turned to look toward the house; they would gesture and talk. Finally Haggarty walked away and Neb, his back to the fence, watched his departure. Evidently they were getting worried and Haggarty had gone to check on Julia. When Neb turned around, Eleanor decided this was the moment for which she had been waiting. Slipping her hand into her pocket, she pulled out the letter opener and straightened up to move from behind the bush and walk toward the man.

In the dark it would be impossible for him to tell her from Julia. He might be suspicious, but he would wait until she was close enough for him to see before he did anything. Eleanor was also sure that if Julia had refused to use a gun, she had given them orders not to fire either, so as not to wake anyone. But she also remembered that Haggarty handled a knife with great skill.

"That you, Julia?" Neb called in a gruff whisper.

"Yes," Eleanor whispered back. "Where's Haggarty?"

"We thought something happened. He went back to the house to check on you. What took you so long?"

"Lyle," she said, keeping her answers as succinct as possible.

"Where's the Hunt woman?"

"The bushes. She started fighting with me, and I had to knock her out."

"Good," Neb said. "That'll make it easier for me and Haggarty. Where's that place you said you wanted us to leave the body?"

"Uh—Haggarty knows."

"No, he don't, but he does know you're not Julia." Though distant, Haggarty's voice came from the velvety shadows.

"Hunt!" Neb exclaimed, still careful to keep his voice down.

"Don't let her get loose," Haggarty ordered.

Neb rushed forward to grab her at the same time that Eleanor lost her footing and fell against him, the extended letter opener sliding into his body. She gasped—truly she had not meant to harm him—nor had he been expecting a weapon. Shocked, she turned the

435

ivory handle loose and backed away. Neb moaned, doubled over, and clamped his hands to his wound. Eleanor began to run. She did not know where; she simply ran. She heard the lumbering steps behind her and knew that Haggarty was following close behind.

"Help me, Haggarty," Neb called in a pain-ridden voice. "She's stuck me with a knife. She's killed me. This damned bitch done and killed me."

Her breath short and getting ever shorter, her chest hurting, Eleanor continued to run. She could hear Haggarty behind her . . . the thick clumping steps, the crunch of dead leaves and twigs beneath his boots, the swishing of branches as he ran past the bushes. Finally Eleanor saw a small stand of trees and dodged between them, into the center of a clump of bushes. The branches slapped against her skin; the rough edges dug into her flesh; they stung and burned, but she did not murmur a word. In fact, she was frightened to such a degree that she was not conscious of her pain. With one hand she brushed the foliage away from her eyes, with the other she slid the revolver from the holster and cocked the hammer. She would be prepared for him this time.

Slowly her breathing regulated itself, and she watched and waited for Haggarty. It seemed like hours that she knelt there, her legs and arms beginning to cramp. Tension grew as she strained to hear every little noise, as her head turned to find the source. He was out there somewhere, and he was waiting for her.

She could not allow herself to panic. That's what he was counting on. She inhaled and exhaled slowly; she counted to twenty. She wiped her left hand down her thigh, then her right. Using her shirttail, she wiped the perspiration from the handle of her gun. Then she heard the tiny snap of a twig, and she knew Haggarty was here.

Perspiration beading up on her forehead and upper lip,

she crouched forward. She waited for him. For a short, squat man, he moved quietly and quickly. His gun was drawn—evidently he did not intend to follow orders—and he looked around.

"I know you're out here," he said in a tone that was not quite a whisper. "Come on out. I promise I won't hurt you. I'm going to find you anyway."

Something—a small animal, an insect, a snake, Eleanor did not know what—scampered through the brush, and she lost her balance to tumble out of the clump of bushes into the clearing, but never let go of her weapon. Haggarty immediately ran to where she lay. By the time he reached her, she had scrambled to her feet and aimed her gun.

"Don't come a step nearer," she warned. "I'll shoot you."

Haggarty laughed and slowly advanced. "I'm the gunfighter, Miss Eleanor Hunt, not you. You may wound me, but you won't kill me. You're not a killer."

"I've killed before," she said, not at all proud of the fact, "and I'll do so again, if I must."

"The first time was reflexive," the man told her. "And the man you shot wasn't thinking about you shooting him. He was only interested in killing Dobson. You're gonna hafta face me, knowing that I'm coming after you, Miss Eleanor Hunt. If I have this figured right, you're scared to death right now."

"That may be true, but it won't stop me from killing you if I have to," Eleanor said, her hand trembling. Haggarty was right: her killing the man in the Two Bits Saloon had been a reaction; she had not had time to think about it. This time she had had plenty of time to think about it, and she had wanted to do it for a long time. Every time she thought about him violating her person she wanted to kill him, slowly, painfully.

437

"I promise you'll never touch my body again. Never."

"Then you'd better shoot."

"She doesn't have to." Bradley stepped up behind Haggarty and shoved the barrel of his revolver into his back. "I will if you give me the least reason. Now drop your gun."

Eleanor had never been so glad to see someone in all her life. Limply her hand dropped to her side. It seemed as if all her insides melted and flowed down her legs to pool at her feet.

"Where's Neb?" Bradley asked.

"By the fence. He's wounded." She slid the revolver into the holster and neared them. Quickly she told Bradley what had happened.

"We still have to be careful," Bradley said and pulled his handkerchief from his pocket. "Here, gag him so he's not tempted to call out."

When Eleanor was through, Bradley nudged Haggarty forward, and they retraced their steps to the corral. They saw Neb lying in a crumpled heap on the ground. Her gun drawn, Eleanor cautiously advanced with Bradley right behind her. Bending down, she reached out and touched the man. When he groaned, she knew he was not dead.

"Sit down," Bradley ordered Haggarty, then said to Eleanor, "Get the rope off his horse."

As soon as the two men were tied up, Eleanor fell into Bradley's arms. Now that the fight was over, reaction set in, and she shook from the top of her head to the bottom of her feet.

"Are you all right?" he asked.

"Yes," she murmured between chattering teeth. "Just hold me tight."

"How about my holding you for the rest of our lives?"

"I'll settle for that."

* * *

438

"I guess we did look like a couple of foolish old men, didn't we?" Alex said as Harry dabbed the corner of his mouth with the damp washcloth.

She smiled gently and stopped her ministrations to place a gentle kiss on his lips, careful not to touch the cut at the corner. "You ought to know that I'll never think of you as old, darling, but foolish, yes. You and Whittier were quite a sight. Still I'm glad the two of you fought it out, Alex. Now maybe both of you can put your grudges aside and can at least be tolerant of each other."

"I never had a grudge," Alex confessed. "I had no idea the man thought I was behind the rustling. But when you stop to think about it, I can see why he jumped to that conclusion. I wish Bradley's message about the stolen cattle Haggarty planted on the station had arrived a little sooner. Maybe Whittier wouldn't have jumped on me, and we could have saved wear and tear on both of us."

"If I remember correctly," Harry said, "you seemed to be enjoying it quite a bit, Mister Hunt."

Alex tipped his head and grinned. "I was known for fighting in my university days."

"We're a little past those days," Harry teased.

"Thank God. If we should have occasion to fight again, love, I'm a goner. He's a tough old man, and I don't know that I could whip him the second time."

"There won't be a second time. I think the two of you settled the score this time. Now we can plan our futures: you and me and Eleanor and Bradley."

Both of them laughed, and Alex reached out to circle her waist with his arms and to draw her closer to the bed where he sat. Pressing his cheek against her midriff, he said, "I don't know that I deserve you, Harry, but I'm sure happy that you're my wife."

The washcloth slid from her hands, and Harry caught his face to lift it up. "People don't have to deserve one another to be in love, Alex. We simply love one another;

439

our strengths compliment each others and help us overcome our weaknesses."

His arms tightened about her, and Alex tumbled back on the bed, bringing her with him. His lips closed over hers in a long, drugging kiss.

When finally he lifted his face from hers, Harry said, "I hope your sister approves of me, Alex."

Alex grinned, the gesture more endearing to her because of his bruised and swollen lip. "Don't you think it's a little too late to be concerned about Edna's opinion of you? Certainly I'm not."

"I'm not as concerned about Edna's as I was about Eleanor's but I do want your family to like me. It'll make the adjustment to life in Chicago a little easier."

Propped up on an elbow, Alex peered down at her. "You're having second thoughts about coming with me?"

Harry shook her head. "No, we've been separated too much during our lifetime, my darling. I want to be with you no matter where you are."

"It's going to be different," Alex admitted, "but you'll like it, Harry. My friends can't help but like you, and we'll come back here . . . frequently, I promise."

Harry chuckled quietly. "I wonder how Bradley is going to take it when he learns that you've deeded the cattle station over to Eleanor?"

"It'll be quite a while before he and Eleanor realize there's a world outside the two of them, but when the honeymoon's over, he'll just have to accept it. Makes sense to me, since the two of them are so determined to stay out here."

"You can't tell me that you're not happy about their decision to live out here?"

"Well," Alex drawled, "to be truthful, I am. I'm glad to have someone dependable to handle this end of the business. And Eleanor's not too far away for us to come

440

visit, or for her to come visit with us . . . when she presents us with grandchildren."

"Until then, love," Harry said, scooting across the mattress, "I'd better get up and see about lunch. Carl said they should be arriving home sometime this afternoon. I have an idea they're going to be tired and hungry."

"No hungrier than I am," Alex murmured as he dragged her closer to him. "Let Gaspar handle the kitchen, and you handle the man of the house."

"Gladly, my husband." Her words became the essence of their kiss.

Epilogue

Sitting on the upholstered wall bench, Eleanor Hunt Newland watched her husband play billiards. When he abruptly turned to look at her and to smile, all his love in his face for her to see, she smiled back.

"Well—" a deep voice boomed teasingly "—it looks like I win through default . . . again." Tall, like his son, though white-haired now, Josiah Newland laid his cue stick down, looked at his daughter-in-law, and winked. "If I ever win a game fair and square, Eleanor, it'll be when you're not observing us."

Eleanor grinned. "I'll leave, if you wish."

"Never." The big man smiled glowingly at his son and clapped him on the back. "Billiards aren't nearly as important as having my son back, as understanding and accepting why he left, not nearly as important as his bringing home a lovely daughter like you."

Basking in Josiah's warmth and love, Eleanor smiled, and pleasure warmed her cheeks. Bradley walked to her, held out his hand, and caught hers to pull her gently to her feet. Then he encircled her waist with his arm.

"I think we'll go for a walk, Papa," Bradley announced and guided Eleanor to the French doors that led to the back garden of the Newland country estate, miles away

443

from the heart of New York City.

"Eleanor, remember that Sarah is going to come over this afternoon to fit you for your new dresses," Hilda Newland said from the doorway. A sweet smile lit up her face and glowed in her green eyes, the only physical characteristic Bradley inherited from his petite mother.

Now Eleanor felt sure her cheeks were a rosy hue. Bradley's hand tightened around her waist, and he swept her through the opened doors. "I'll remember," she called over her shoulder.

"And don't forget dinner tonight with your family," Josiah added. "And your Aunt Edna and Sarah."

When they were out of hearing distance from the house and hidden behind neatly trimmed hedges and bushes, Bradley took her into his arms and held her tightly, his face lowering to hers. After a long, satisfying kiss, he raised his mouth from hers.

Inebriated with happiness, Eleanor laughed and brushed her cheek up and down the firm, solid chest of her beloved. "As if I could forget Sarah was coming," she breathed.

Bradley's hand rested on her stomach. "It's rounded a little."

"A great deal," Eleanor told him.

"And will get a great deal rounder."

"Will it bother you?" Eleanor asked.

Bradley smiled and shook his head, his cheek rubbing against the crown of her head. "The thought of your carrying our baby is one of the most wonderful I've ever had," he said. "You've been so very good for me, Eleanor."

"I feel the same way," she murmured. "Your parents are wonderful, Bradley. They couldn't treat me better if I was their own daughter."

"You *are* their daughter." He laughed. "In fact, I think they're more enamored with you than me."

444

"I was worried when we decided to tell them about my . . . real parents. I thought maybe it would make a difference to them."

"No, my darling," he whispered and held her even tighter, "they love you for what you are, just as I do."

"Although I'm happy here, I can hardly wait for us to return to Kansas," she said. "I never thought this possible, but I'm homesick for Blissful."

Bradley pulled back from her and looked into her face. "I'm glad you are, sweetheart, because I can think of nowhere I would rather be than at our ranch.

"You're not going to miss Newland's?" she teased.

He grinned and planted a quick kiss on the tip of her nose. "I'm glad I came home and made peace with my family," he confessed, "but right now running Newland's isn't for me. And Papa accepts that I must make my own life, where as before he didn't. Maybe later."

Eleanor laughed. "Probably later. Your father is as conniving as mine."

"Imagine deeding the cattle station over to you so I'd have to manage it. Makes sense, too, since it's adjacent to our land and does have a habitable house."

Eleanor settled back into the circle of his arms, resting her head against his chest. She loved to listen to the steady rhythm of his heartbeat. "Ira and Letty were happy for us. And while Julia wasn't happy for us, at least she sold us the Stanwood. I think maybe this is what Lou would have wanted." She was silent for a while, then said, "It's difficult to think of Julia being dead."

"She couldn't bear the idea of going to prison," Bradley consoled. "She felt that suicide was the answer."

"Although she would have killed me, somehow I can't hate her." Eleanor recalled the night Julia had told her that Lyle was her father, Harry her mother. Even then Eleanor had refused to believe the story, and later when

445

she retold it to her stepmother, Harry assured her that though she would have loved for Eleanor to be her daughter, she was not. She did get pregnant by Lyle and give birth to a daughter who died in infancy. "I can almost understand why Julia did what she did."

"No more talk of Julia," Bradley whispered, his lips slowly moving down her neck. "Right now I want to enjoy you, my darling wife."

Eleanor looped her arms about his neck. "Then I suggest we go to the cottage. You could enjoy me so much better if we were upstairs lying on that large four-poster mahogany bed."

"That's one order I wouldn't dare disobey."

Their laughter mingled together as he swept her into his arms and carried her down the narrow trail through the blaze of springtime forest to the frame house nestled in a grove of trees.